A Deepening Nuclear Divide

by

Terence A. Robinson

PublishAmerica
Baltimore

First printing

ISBN: 1-4241-9565-9
PUBLISHED BY PUBLISHAMERICA, LLLP
www.publishamerica.com
Baltimore

Printed in the United States of America

To Lingo

With Best Wishes,

[illegible signature]

Feb 14/2008

2007, North Korea, little has changed, an independent kingdom for a thousand years. No bigger than the state of Mississippi, yet it borders three other countries. South Korea forms half of the peninsula while the northern border separates Russia to the northeast and China to the north. Roughly speaking the northern border is about 1435 kilometers, of which Russia's portion is a mere nineteen kilometers and heavily guarded/patrolled, compared to the China boundary.

After the Russo—Japanese war Korea was occupied by the Japanese, shortly thereafter, some five years later, Japan annexed the whole peninsula. Subsequent to World War Two Korea was divided into North and South. The northern half was under Soviet-sponsored communist domination. Post Korean War (1950-53) in order to conquer US backed republic in the south, North Korea under President Kim Il Sung, adopted a policy of diplomatic and economic self reliance to offset excessive Soviet or Communist Chinese influence. In essence it molded political, economic and military policies around the core ideological objective of eventual unification of Korea under Pyongyang's control. The current leader Kim Jong Il took control from his father upon his death in 1994, no one contested, and authority was final.

Many years of mismanagement and resource misallocation, the North since 1995 has relied enormously on the goodwill and charity of the western nations, in order to feed the twenty-three million-plus starving population. In contrast the army of one million is not hungry and remains a force to be reckoned with. Several years ago with the proliferation of nuclear arms, and North Korea's aggressive research into chemical and biological weapons alerted the west and the international community. What was the agenda was not certain, but since 2002 when it was confirmed that North Korea was pursuing a nuclear weapons program based on the enriched uranium in violation of a 1994 agreement with the USA to freeze and eventually dismantle its existing plutonium-based program, North Korea expelled the expert monitors from the International Atomic Energy Agency. Shortly thereafter North Korea openly declared that they were withdrawing from the international Proliferation Treaty. By 2003, North Korean scientists had successfully completed the reprocessing of spent nuclear fuel rods. Weapons grade plutonium was now readily available for the construction of nuclear warheads. Proof of the pudding was witnessed by satellite with the detonation of a nuclear test in 2006. The west was not amused and concern was growing in China, Japan, Russia, Canada and of course South Korea. In 2007 there was a warming of relationships and a commitment on behalf of North Korea to halt their nuclear research into weapons of mass destruction, but few thought that the posture was genuine; the west remained cautiously guarded.

North Korea's countryside may be considered as more attractive than the South, with mountains, hills and valleys the vegetation is lush and dense. Tourists would most likely embrace the country as a destination must, but given the nature of government and the uncertainty of war between neighboring countries yet another form of revenue is minimized. From his vantage point Kane Austin, alias James J. Jeffries, could see intermittent shadows of the undergrowth. The sky was moonless and thunder clouds showered the forest below. Claps of thunder right now were a blessing, lightning momentarily illuminating the canopy of forest above, yet little light penetrating the darkness below.

Suspended from a wild boar snare he was some fifteen feet off the ground. Suited in a black neoprene wet suit, his face blackened, his black hair tight to his scalp, he flexed his muscles to elevate his torso; if you could see him, he would appear as a large tree fungus about to fall to the ground.

Kane Austin

Kane Austin, born 1979, adopted son of an eminent London judge who was married to Lomei, an Asian immigrant to the UK. Adoption was an easy task for the judge, his reputation was platinum and he moved in the highest of social circles. Kane was abandoned at the foot of St. Paul's cathedral, no doubt by a stressed young mother. The story was on the front page of the Telegraph. Kane's upbringing was a pleasant one, in fact, extremely happy for the family of three. At age seven his life took a twist when his mother uprooted him from the fog of London to the pearl of the Pacific, Hong Kong. For the next three years he would embrace the Asian British culture. Attending the public schools, Kane excelled in all subjects, especially including the sciences.

Hong Kong was a place they had to be, his adopted mother's attendance was necessary to care for her failing mother and father, both of who were dying of cancer. In the case of her father it was lung cancer, and the mother, bone cancer. Grand Papa and Mama both adored their only grandson; only Kane's mother knew that her parents' wealth, approximately twenty-five million Hong Kong dollars, was entirely willed to Kane.

The mother was first to pass away, departing within the first year of their arrival in Hong Kong. The father stubbornly held out for an additional two years. Judge Austin made the journey from London to Hong Kong whenever possible, and for certain visited during the summer recess. The schooling in Hong Kong was exceptional, every parent expected one hundred and ten percent from their children, and this was the norm. For Kane the time spent in Hong Kong at school and with mum and dad was just a great experience. Judge Austin was keen to explore the country side and loved the Aberdeen port, Victoria Peak and the white beaches that sparkled like a French Chardonnay. The judge was an avid lover of Chinese cuisine and fondly introduced Kane to many exquisite meals; the ingredients of many were best left unquestioned. The judge idolized Kane and tutored him amongst other topics, in the art of self defence and, pure and applied physics, the judge's second passion surpassed only by law. During his tutoring time Judge Austin was referred to by his son as Judge Jeffries, after the Somerset judge of the Tudor times in England; also known as the hanging judge. He was merciless in his method of teaching and perfection was expected. Perfection was not an issue for Kane, he had a natural ability to learn, absorb and retain. By the time he was ten years of age he was fluent in four languages and later at age twenty he was fluent in seven languages.

After the grandfather slipped into the new beyond they returned to the UK where Kane continued his education, attending Cambridge University. At the age of thirteen, he was the youngest ever student to be admitted. At seventeen years of age Kane had earned his Bsc and Msc in physics, at which time he had had enough of schooling. To the chagrin of the judge he fought off the continuous requests to continue on for a PhD. Not only was he now seventeen but he was six feet two inches tall weighing in at a sleek 215 pounds. He was an impressive Homosapien, a hunk of a man. He was not in any way interested in body building; he was naturally very strong, lean and mean with a keen love of rugby.

In a sadistic way he could wage war with the rival team players, and complaints about his aggressive play was constant. Other players if wise would stay well clear of Austin.

In every University match, two or more players would be devoured by Kane and escorted off, or indeed carried off the field of play.

The coach however would hear nothing negative about his star forward, Kane's touchdowns were regular and on occasion he could be seen clamoring to the line with two bodies attached to his six foot two frame.

He was often referred to as the lean mean killing machine by the other team mates, a fact not unobserved by the judge and certain of the judge's colleagues who worked at the Downing Street foreign office. The coach was devastated when his star player decided to leave the campus and engage a different theatre, the University of Life.

Kane did not want for anything in his life, he was certainly not spoiled, yet the judge made it perfectly clear that it was time for him to advance his career. At seventeen Kane decided to satisfy his fascination with the North Sea oil rigs. He had watched for years the gas platforms offshore the east coast flaring off the yellow orange flame that never ceased to die. The North Sea production was in decline, yet certain Canadian and Danish companies remained exploring the previously un-economical fields. Again to the blatant disdain of the judge Kane took off for the port of Aberdeen with a handful of named companies identified in his notebook. He would figure out everything once in Scotland.

Although Kane was to inherit a small fortune, he did not know the fact, this secret was the latest of two, the first being that of his adoption. The judge believed emphatically that knowledge of adoption could only create an uncertainty in a young growing mind, and perhaps he was right. The will was very clear in that Kane was to know nothing until age 21.This no doubt was a cultural matter, again a mix of Asian and colonial tradition.

Nonetheless Kane had a healthy bank account totaling a little more than five thousand pounds. His wallet was stuffed with five hundred pounds, a mother's gesture; hence furnished with a cell phone, reading material which included quantum mechanics, advanced nuclear physics, lap top, a large bar of chocolate and a carryall of mainly working gear; he was good to go, Heathrow to Aberdeen.

Heathrow

The judge and Lomei agreed to take their son to Terminal One at Heathrow, some twenty miles to the west of the heart of London's city where they lived in Mayfair. Even on a Sunday, the journey was bumper to bumper yet the comfort of the judge's toy was always a pleasure, a sleek silver colored Bentley Continental GT Mulliner, less than six months old, one could still smell the richness of the tan/ochre leather. The 6.5 litre engine was running, but no one could tell, proof was confirmed only by viewing the tachometer, albeit in the traffic it barely reached 1,200 rpm.

The judge looked stoic, his broad shoulders and body filling the sumptuous drivers' seat. His short cropped grey hair made him look very distinguished, although his hair was cropped short due to the nuisance need to wear the insidious knotted wigs still mandatory in the British courts, long tradition once again prevailing. When cloaked in his courtroom garb, the judge looked awesome, somewhat frightening, a majestic figure of a man, a person Kane thought could be capable of flying like Superman, but of course this was not the case, but Kane always mused at the thought. Kane believed that his dad was indeed his biological father. They had similar characteristics; both were large men although the judge was sporting a slightly larger waste line than his slim, still growing son.

Just observing him driving one of his prized possessions gave Kane a great deal of comfort; he admired his father and loved him enormously. His other prized possession included a stable of fine horses, a mix of Arabian stallions and North American quarter horses.

Kane shared this passion and rode with his father at every opportunity; there was no doubt in Kane's mind that he was sired by this fine gentleman, a man of good breading, culture and wealth, the latter of which came from a sizeable interest in a zinc mining business which was recently sold for an undisclosed sum…this was the third family secret.

Of late the judge had been working long hours presiding over a case of national importance intrigue and great sadness. A year earlier a terrorist cell had successfully dealt a blow to the British public, and other western countries which included Germany, France, Spain, Italy, Canada and USA, a blow that resonated around the world. Although not a world trade center event by dollar quantum, the enormity of the event was the death and casualty toll.

More than 8,700 people had been killed in multiple explosions all of which took place within minutes of the other.

The worse carnage was located at London's Wembley stadium where two soccer teams were playing in the quarter finals of the EUFA cup. Although not publicized too often the death toll was 4,210 and 2,400 injuries in the stadium alone. The perpetrators were sympathizers of Al Qaeda and members of a north London Muslim radical group known as The Black Watch Warriors. These radical fundamentalist were just part of a wider network funded allegedly by Iranian militants. In London, these radical warriors totaled four in number, each outfitted with what was considered to be over fifty pounds of trinitrotoluene explosives. They were suicide bombers, their true identity never confirmed as nothing of their remains provided any form of forensic clue. Two of the four targeted Wembley Stadium, and one other rode the under ground, the circle line train to Tower Hill; the fourth suicide bomber walked the theatre district. Concurrently in Frankfurt, Paris, Rome, Madrid, New York and Toronto a similar story was unfolding, but none matched the ultimate carnage inflicted within the stadium grounds of Wembley stadium. The New York and Rome attack faired very well as the explosive packages carried by terrorists detonated, it was believed, prematurely, the terrorists being the only recorded fatalities, with minor injuries inflicted upon the unsuspecting public, and modest property damage.

Subsequent to the event, resolve to inflict a greater blow to the axis of evil became paramount, headed of course by the USA. Regardless of the resolve of the governments, the general public in the targeted countries were fearful of the inevitable follow up; it just never seemed to stop. Everyone feared a dirty bomb, a chemical attack or a tainted water supply; the list of threats was never ending. Many people relocated, working in places believed to be less of a target, but of course the majority had no choice but to stay and continue life as best they could. Normality quickly returned in most cities, but the talk in London stayed very much alive with people second guessing the next possible scenario.

The Bentley purred along towards the city limits, Heathrow was less than five miles away. The radio was tuned into a Chinese station; it rarely was tuned to anything else. The newscaster commenced discussing the upcoming sentencing of the group, namely the Black Watch Warriors, the very case that the judge was presiding. The judge casually pressed the off control; he had no need to listen to the guesswork of the radio host. While scratching his skull as if he was wearing the daily horsehair wig which was infuriatingly irritating, Lomei gave him a glance indicating approval, her smile in concert with her eyes confirming her reassurance that everything would be fine; he would do the right thing.

Kane's mother and father were pillars of the community, they were honorable in every way; they were always positive and encouraged all people to do right.

Lomei was just remarkable and Kane easily understood why his father would be so attracted to her. Her smile was infectious, her eyes ebony brown with a never fading twinkle. Like his, her hair was black in color.

She wore her hair long, although in recent years, she always had it arranged in a neat roll at the back, he could not recall the proper term for the style but it looked good and made her appear very refined. Kane observed her closely from his vantage point some two feet behind her. She was almost devoured by the thick leathered upholstery and he concluded that she was graceful beyond measure.

Taking a deep breath he was somewhat saddened by this

upcoming departure. He knew that he had to make his move at some time but something was not right. He rationalized the obvious and put his feelings down to anxiety and butterflies of a new chapter in his life. Little did he know that in six months time he would be back in London, facing first hand the reality of terrorism.

Ten minutes more and they would reach Heathrow. Kane talked with his parents about his plans, the fact was that he had no plan other than to venture into a field that he thought may be of interest to him. He would in essence work for a year and re-evaluate his direction.

Music to his fathers' ears was the statement that he had not ruled out engaging the PhD program upon his return; after all he was still only seventeen years old, whereas most PhD students are upwards of twenty three.

The judge wore that familiar smile, well perhaps it was a grin; he obviously believed that his son had after all been listening to him. The judge smiled knowing how much he loved his son, he was a proud father and once again the gentleness of Lomei radiated in her face acknowledgement of the fact.

Arriving at Heathrow was always a great disappointment to Kane. Here they were at one of the world's busiest airports and yet it remains a dismal mess of architecture, construction and dirt. Heathrow should be demolished, raised to the ground and reconstructed; perhaps in time a terrorist strike could do the demolition….he mused over the thought briefly but then scoffed at his wicked mind.

Stopping outside the terminal he bid his farewell to his parents. Uncharacteristically he took up his mother in his arms and squeezed her, almost too hard for the porcelain like five foot seven inch tall graceful lady she was. He kissed her on both cheeks and gently whispered in her ear that he loved her very much. She in turn talked in Chinese and reciprocated, but her face said more, he knew that she was magic. Almost like recharging his very soul she imparted love and strength through her eyes, her gentle smile containing her inner love which wanted to ooze out of her and shower him. His father watched, all knowing what his son was feeling, the judge had gored himself on the same love; it sustained him everyday in the confines of the British courts. Kane turned to his dad and hugged him, repeating the same words that he had spoken to his mother. This time the hug was all powerful but his dad could take the bear hug, although he was taken aback by the power his son's arms. He too told his son that he loved him and also that he was extremely proud of him. His parting words were, as expected, *always do what is right, always do the right thing.* Kane watched the Bentley cruise away, they exchanged waves and looks of love and they were gone.

Kane wondered whether that car would ever be truly opened up, then turned to enter the multi-cultural, hovel of an airport, Heathrow.

The airport security was intense; Kane had to remove his jacket, belt, and shoes. He was questioned as to the nature of his travel, and given the fact that he was traveling on a wing and a prayer with respect to finding work they hassled him further. Ironically the security guard was small in stature, an East Indian Londoner. Kane could have squished him in a moment yet he had to respect the little man and the job that he was employed to do. Eventually he made his way through the coral of shoeless people and made his way to the departure gate. The flight to Aberdeen was uneventful and short. Within two hours of saying farewell to his parents he was on route by Taxi to the Dyce Holiday Inn.

Aberdeen

This would be his base for the next couple of days. The hotel was tired and the accommodations in need of an overhaul, but then again the same could be said for most of the local hotels. The room was outfitted with the normal, bathroom, queen size bed, mini-bar, television and a small desk, adequate enough for a cup of coffee and a laptop. Internet facilities were available albeit at extra cost.

During check in the dark haired receptionist had thrown in the Internet package, she was one of many young women prepared to throw herself at the hunk, the UK version of Michael Angelo. Kane was polite and chose to engage in dialogue of a more personal nature at a later time, first things first was the order of the day.

British hotels had the most impracticable of shower units, in fact bathrooms in general throughout the country failed to be efficient and definitely did not cater to the taller crowd. This particular shower facility met the same poor standard. As an integral part of the bath, the shower head provided a stream of water that had little or no pressure; the temperature fluctuated simultaneously to other patrons' usage of the bathroom facilities.

Taking a shower instead of being a pleasant experience became a test of skill by avoiding a scolding or freezing cascade of water. Nonetheless it was time to challenge the plumbing; he took a shower within minutes of entering his room. With knees bent he arranged his body beneath the shower head, naturally the fixture was at a height which catered to midgets. In an effort to soak his body he had to focus his efforts on replacing the tap which fell off when rotated. Although a nuisance the experience was amusing. Taking a bath, he thought would be even more uncomfortable as he could definitely not fit into the bath tub itself, or at least if he could, he would most likely be unable to get out. Not to be negative he inwardly laughed at the situation, concluded his freshening up and dressed for the evening. Prior to leaving his room he had powered up his laptop and emailed his parents to state that all was well and that the journey was a safe one. It was appreciated at the other end, acknowledged by an almost immediate response. As per usual the email ended with, *always do what is right.*

Well, right or wrong, he was going to explore the jewels of Scotland one of them being the stunning receptionist at the front desk. It was not only his good looks but his charm that melted the hearts and limbs of just about every female he encountered. Elspeth McTavish was no exception. She was off work in twenty minutes so he decided to sit by the large ornate granite fireplace in the lobby and observe. Her skin was as white as milk and smooth like silk. He knew that hey had chemistry but where this would lead he was not certain but for sure he would like to sample the beautiful package.

Twenty minutes passed by quickly and, grabbing a taxi, they were off.

Her Scottish accent was not of the local variety but more so Edinburgh, it was simply delightful, so much so that Kane encouraged conversation to be more one sided so that he could delight further. She was truly charming. She had agreed to dinner and of course he requested that she choose the restaurant. Before reaching the Quail's Head pub/dinner restaurant he had established that she was twenty two years of age and a graduate of geology; she too was sourcing a job in the offshore and worked part time in the hotel in order to pay off her student loans. She lived, like he did, with her parents who lived some eighty miles south of Aberdeen. Accents seemed to vary all over Scotland as they did in England, but the Edinburgh brogue was the smoothest of them all. Almost mesmerized by her voice she advised him of her lodgings. Right now she had a small room in the hotel, small being the operative word. Apparently it accommodated a single bed and a sink and toilet, all of which was nestled in one space; charming he thought, and secretly vowed not to verify the fact.

Although under the legal drinking age Kane was not questioned. Already at six pm he had shaved for the second time that day. By ten pm he will have his second five pm shadow. His dark beard shadow added years to his seventeen years of age, he certainly looked at least late twenties; anyway she was polite enough not to question him, she had already been told that he graduated with an Msc, which, she had assumed, placed him at least 24 years old or more.

Besides she did not care, he was at this time a gift from heaven, as was the delightful dinner. The dinner was quail, with duchess potatoes, cauliflower with cheese dressing and French beans, topped with a light sauce which favored a cognac aroma and taste. They chose not to drink wine but to stick with their pre dinner orders. In Kane's case he savored Bourbon on the rocks, Elspeth was partaking in Crantinis. They both sipped their drinks carefully and indulged in four glasses each. Conversation was light but informative, especially for Kane. He had no idea that a prerequisite to go offshore included survival training, a five day course which included fire, first aid, and hydrogen sulphide training, culminating with the helicopter dunker; an emergency escape requirement for downed helicopters. Elspeth had already done the course. First thing in the morning he would phone the Robert Gordon Institute and inquire. He hoped that this faux pas would not delay him too much.

The restaurant was just one mile away from the hotel and given the fullness of the moon and a mild evening they decided to walk off their meal. Elspeth casually reached for his hand; and they strolled hand in hand at a very modest gait back to their temporary abodes. Elspeth sported an alcohol induced glow; it made her look a little mischievous and even more irresistible. They reached the entrance of the hotel after twenty minutes or so, and at the request of Elspeth she would enter the hotel alone, it was the right thing to do.

She asked for his room key, and departed. Kane would wait outside of the hotel for ten minutes prior to entering the lobby. When he did so, he engaged in a little banter with the night receptionist, an East Indian lady from Leeds. She was very pleasant, in her case she spoke with a Yorkshire accent which was rather grating to the ear compared to the smooth Edinburgh accent delivered by Elspeth.

With perhaps fifteen minutes having elapsed he entered his room. The next few hours was magical, ecstasy for both partners. He found her partly clothed in black lace bra and panties, the type advertised on the London underground tunnel walls by Victoria's Secret. The models looked good on the tunnel walls, but the real thing was a different matter. The clothing partially covered her milky white skin, she had no blemishes. With one knee elevated both athletic looking thighs were exposed. Her breasts filled every space within the confines of the bra, the design of the bra enhancing every curve. She was without a doubt exquisite, a women with beauty, a keen mind and a voice that could melt any man. They said nothing, he approached the bed and disrobed, within minutes she was witnessing the Michael Angelo, a full blooded male blessed or perhaps cursed with a penis that could take any women's breath away. His shoe size was thirteen and yes his love member was in proportion. She was somewhat apprehensive but he was gentle and she satisfied her curiosity by fondling him. Fore play was unrushed and perhaps after one hour of passionate kissing, exploring and gentle fondling Kane removed her lace under things and seductively entered her. He knew that he had to be extremely careful for he knew only too well that he was magnificently endowed, perhaps medically speaking classified as deformed. He had been the focus of many other males when in the change rooms /showers whether it was at the rugby matches or after a fox hunt; others would look in awe or shock and constant ridicule would result. He was often embarrassed but of late he was less concerned, it is what it is and as he would find out over and over again the ladies adored the fact. Elspeth was not his first sexual encounter but he had not had many, mainly because of his self-consciousness.

His father had once stated that he would need a blood transfusion prior to making out, if not he would surely black out, this was a statement made at a horse meeting where the conversation had been initiated after one of the quarter horses had been aroused by something, hopefully a mare.

Kane did not know how his father knew but apparently his mother had commented on his manhood during his early years of growth. Any way he could do nothing about it, but use it.

Elspeth eyes rolled way back into her head and with every half inch of insertion a groan would follow, pain and pleasure. Her lungs would fill and with each new groan the lungs wanted more air; fully expanded yet no room for the next groan she had her first orgasm; they had not even started their gyrations. He was only half way inside her when the river of passion commenced. She could not believe what was happening, the orgasm just kept flowing. She was speechless and unable to even voice a word or a moan. She was spaced out with pleasure and yet there was more to come. Minutes seemed like hours, multiple orgasms did not occur; it was a never ceasing, never ending ebb and flow. After ten careful minutes he was deep inside, Elspeth was being drained of all her juices, she was wet, no soaking and with his movements the cascade of juices just kept flowing. Kane took pleasure in what he was controlling; his lovemaking was truly an art form. Elspeth transformed into a body of silky gel, her brain unable to function.

The continuous orgasm had left her immobile unable to respond in the normal act of making love. It did not matter; Kane took his pleasure but paced himself admirably, he prolonged his orgasm for as long as possible. They both knew that Elspeth was "protected", so they could relax in each others arms and enjoy this most intimate of experiences. After perhaps an hour of rest and pure contented silence, the insatiable Kane began again. The exhausted Elspeth speechless and incapable of responding laid in awe after an orgasm lasting an exquisite fifty minutes or so, she was drained in every sense of the word.

Kane, with the strength and stamina of an Olympic Tri-athlete did not need more than four hours of sleep per night. Some may see this as a negative yet he looked at this positively and used it as his opportunity to seek more knowledge and understanding of the world around him. Speechless from the lovemaking they both knew a slight respite was necessary if they wanted to continue and indulge their insatiable appetites for each other.

The alarm rang at 5:00 a.m., Elspeth awoke thinking what a ridiculous time, but thought that she should make her way back to her own room. Kane of course took advantage of Elspeth just one more time, and of course Elspeth accommodated her man. With this and after their tremendous night of lovemaking—her legs were like jello, making it difficult to walk. Somehow she managed to claw her way back to the bathroom. Inching her way to the bathroom she was able to climb into the tub. She scuffled her way forward to reach the taps. Thank goodness there was an abundance of soothing hot water. She languished there for some time drifting back over the experience of the last few hours. Surprised, she felt her legs shake as a phantom wave of pleasure seized her body one more time. Like the others, a flood, one continuous orgasm. Similar to the many she experienced the night before, she ended up breathless and weak. The phantom finally stopped and she could breathe normal. She thought to herself, this is incredible, was this real or a dream. She opened her eyes and catching her breath—there he was watching her with adoring eyes. He smiled his mischievous grin, and she knew it was no dream. She asked for his hand to help her out of the bath. It was just as well since her lower limbs remained elsewhere. Without any effort he scooped her up and took her to the bed. He propped her up gently with the pillows provided and then proceeded to make the morning coffee.

Perhaps caffeine would help find her legs. While waiting for the coffee to brew, Kane took advantage of the bath and was pleasantly surprised, as the water pressure had increased significantly—the pulsing streams of water providing a gentle massage to his young muscular body. Smelling the freshly brewed coffee, he finished his shower, and quickly toweled his wet body dry. He donned a bathrobe and went to pour their coffee.

The coffee worked well for Elspeth and she soon found that her legs were beginning to respond. At last, having found her voice, she advised Kane, in that sensuous Scottish accent, the evening had been amazing and that she had just returned from "Cloud 59", and had not quite landed. Elspeth had a second coffee before she could finally dress and exit the room.

Not forgetting his task for the day Kane started to make his phone calls. At 7:00 a.m. he called the training institute, he was anxious to see if he could get registered at the last minute. He knew it was early, but luckily he got through to someone. He established that there was a vacancy but he had to be there within the hour, complete with ID, credit card, work clothing, including a swim suit. Rushing like a mad man,

he made it there with five minutes to spare.

By mid morning Kane was engrossed in his training and thoroughly enjoying it. He had no time whatsoever to mentally revisit the events that unfolded the night before.

On the other hand by mid morning Elspeth had to vacate the reception for almost an hour. Sitting at the front desk, she found that she couldn't concentrate and before she knew it and somewhat to her delight another phantom wave took over.

Management feeling she was taking ill, permitted her to take the morning off. With her mind elsewhere, she thought more coffee would help and bring her back to earth.

The next few days passed by very quickly, Kane and Elspeth's paths did not cross. This was a deliberate action for Elspeth as she knew that she wanted more of the Michael Angelo. She feared the reaction, after their first evening together and right now she needed her job, and couldn't risk taking more time off work. Kane on the other hand was relishing the training and he easily managed all the tasks given to him. The fire-fighting was a breeze as was the confined space entry task. The under water escape was his favorite, the exercise required composure and a stable state of mind.

He managed the exercises with no problem, yet for some found the dunker a terrifying ordeal. By Friday the course was over and the weekend was free. During the lunch periods, Kane had arranged for interviews with several companies over a period of four days. Two Canadian companies—Nexen and Talisman were set up for Monday. Tuesday he would meet with British Gas and Hess Oil, Wednesday Dan Oil, and Shell were scheduled in, Maersk Oil and Gas and Schlumberger filled out his schedule on Thursday.

Upon return to the hotel and to his pleasant surprise, he found a note under his door. It was a mischievous note which simply said, *I have the weekend off, I will be your patient for the weekend if you promise to be my doctor, reply cubbyhole room 101.* He responded with a short note of his own. *Renting car for weekend. Going to Balmoral and the Moors. Pick up at 7:00 p.m., Budget Rent-a-Car...signed, The Doctor.*

7:00 p.m. came quickly, and on time, Elspeth equipped with a small overnight bag sourced the rental unit, it was easy as the car rental ID number was still suspended from the rear view mirror, besides nearly all of the rental cars appeared to be white Ford Escorts. Of course, another clue was the huge hunk of man completely filling the driver's seat. He smiled at her and said welcome aboard, EMS unit 101, physician in charge Dr. Kane Austin.

For a brief moment he thought of his father and the PhD program; with a sense of duty he committed to himself that he would complete the course, majoring in Nuclear Physics, after all it was the right thing to do. They sped away toward the A road that headed west to Balmoral, they would find a hotel later.

The weekend was off to a great start, and as a precaution Elspeth packed in her purse a couple sachets of extra strong Columbian coffee.

They drove west to Balmoral and the Cairngorm mountains. In one hour they had left Avimore in pursuit of another pub restaurant, in fact a traditional Inn with low ceilings and low oak rafters, large fireplace where one could sit within the confines of the hearth, if moved to do so. Not too far down the road they stumbled upon The Inn. Venturing inside the three hundred year old building the vote was a resounding yes. It was perfect, but for Elspeth a real challenge. She could not fail to notice the warped twisted flooring of their room, it matched the ceiling. She already found walking difficult to negotiate. It looked as if the building was suffering from acute arthritis, with no remedy for a cure. Elspeth mused over the thought of walking in the morning after what she knew would be yet another parallel to epilepsy.

They dined a typical pub supper, a mixed grill with the works. Grilled Ham, two sunny-side up eggs, black pudding (Scottish style), fries, sweet peas, button mushrooms, a type of Peas pudding (mush) and Coleman's mustard on the side. The meal was huge and swilled down with room temperature local ale. Not the healthiest of meals yet, tasteful and extremely satisfying. They finished off the meal with Crème Brulee for desert. Up until now Elspeth had no return visits of the phantom wave. A weeks respite seemed to have done the trick, but all about to change now.

The dessert was exquisite, both of them engaged in sensual and provocative gestures while deliberately and slowly using their lips and tongue to play with the creamy textured brulee. The teasing was so intense, and was exacerbated by Kane's smoldering stare. His tender deep brown eyes locked her own and she couldn't look away. They melted her into a deep pool of desire where she didn't want to be rescued. His tongue rolling over each morsel, his grin so naughty she felt the onset of yet another phantom wave of ecstasy. She felt her knees quiver and her pulse started to race. Her heart became bellows, sucking in and pumping out volumes of blood—her panties suddenly saturated—there it was another orgasm had started—the phantom was back. Before it became too embarrassing she found the strength and composure to discretely excused herself and retreated to her room.

Barely able to walk (once again), with the crooked floor of the old pub camouflaging her predicament, she exited and was gone.

Kane completed his dessert and reached over to polish off Elspeth's last portion. The dessert itself was ecstasy to him, with the last morsel sliding over his tongue and deep down into his stomach. He finished the meal with a glass of port, with a silent toast to his father who never finished dining without the traditional London Port. The port was of average quality, but he enjoyed it all the same. Once finished, he charged the bill to his room and sauntered back, negotiating the arthritic floor and the twisted stairs that led to their room.

He found Elspeth lounging luxuriously on top of the bedcovers—she was wearing a white lace bra and panty set that took Kane's breath away. Even though Elspeth had already experienced Kane this encounter surpassed the first. She had fondled him seductively and confirmed every inch was for real, Kane took his time. Before an inch of penetration Elspeth was off to never land, closing her eyes—the beginning was here, the surprise would be when this moment would end. Kane was a passionate lover and three rounds exhausted his partner, she was putty, with zero strength, overwhelmed by her lover, his insatiable appetite never waning.

Elspeth could not raise her arms or legs, her head was heavy as if drugged, her hands lost with no control. Unable to speak, she slipped back into her never land to rest.

The next morning they privileged themselves the luxury of sleeping in, at least that was the case for Elspeth. Kane had been awake for hours, drinking Columbian dark roast while reading quantum mechanics. He instinctively knew that Elspeth would lack energy to walk if he did not let her soak up the zzzzzzzzzz.

By noon they were showered and dressed for the moors, they would hike ten miles or so to the summit, some 3,300 feet above sea level. The air was fresh and the wind was keen but they soldiered on.

Kane couldn't help but notice and admire Elspeth's athletic limbs and how it was so obvious she enjoyed the vigorous trek. She never complained even though Kane was increasing his stride. She kept up knowing he was trying to make this a competition. From somewhere Elspeth had a resurgence of strength and started to stretch herself by walking briskly ahead of her Michael Angelo. The response was that same seductive grin that had caused the quick exit from the supper table the night before. It did not work on her now; the wind was gusting and cold. Her nose constantly running and her face was apple red. They covered the ten miles in three hours and sat briefly at the summit. Kane unbuckled his ruck sack and retrieved the thermos of apple juice laced with whisky.

The hot fluid flowed through their bodies revitalizing limbs and spirit. They admired the view and they talked of returning to the same spot in ten years time to the very day, Kane liked the idea and wondered if she would show up. He told her that he would follow through with his PhD, and that he favored a term in the USA just to avoid the hum drum surroundings of the UK universities.

Elspeth genuinely supported his idea and encouraged him to involve his father in the choice of the US facility. He appreciated the suggestion. With the thermos empty it was time to retrace their steps back down the slopes. Going back took less than two hours; the speed was exhilarating as was the cold.

It was early evening when they entered the pub and headed for the inviting hearth. The fire was crackling, the three foot long logs glowing red hot. Occasionally a spark would explode and shoot out onto the flagstone floor in front of the fire. With blood and limbs slightly overheated it was only twenty minutes when they retreated to a corner booth, another half frozen couple immediately seizing their hearth seats. There was no need to freshen up; they had just had almost six hours of all the freshening they could take.

It was Saturday night and nowhere to go. Kane suggested that they feast on a steak, apparently the house specialty. They ordered the meal, prime Angus steak, both to be cooked medium rare. The meal came with baked potatoes which were already in the ashes of the fire, albeit wrapped in shining foil. Mushrooms and French beans would be prepared in the back kitchen. He asked of Eslpeth whether she would like a bottle of wine with the meal, she did so and was encouraged to choose one of the twelve varieties that were available. She chose a Chilean merlot which they later agreed complimented the meal very well.

The meal was very good, the meat being lean and cooked just right. The jacket potatoes having been cooked in the fire grate ashes tasted delicious. The butter soaked into the potato and the skins which resulted in a taste that just had to be repeated—perhaps in ten years time. With nothing to do but drink at the bar they decided to retreat to their love nest.

Heading up the crooked stairs to bed, Elspeth took in a huge breath and opened the door to their room, well, and the rest was a repeat of history.

Early on the Sunday morning Kane had just completed his fourth coffee when Elspeth emerged from never land. Her thighs sticky after hours of lovemaking.

It was almost 11:00 a.m. Kane talked to her softly and responded to her question with respect to what he had been doing. He replied that he had read more and just a while ago, emailed the judge, requesting his input into the US university idea. She was pleased at the action taken and rewarded him with a very delicate kiss.

Although the day before was strenuous to every limb, by one strenuous feat or another, neither had aching bones. They were ready for the next challenge. Where would they go today, there's at least seven hours to go before they would return to their bed. After a brief debate they decided to drive no further than thirty-three miles west for a ploughman's lunch....they had to hurry. They left the safe haven of the Inn to venture west at about 1:00 p.m. The road catered to two way traffic only, but with careful driving negotiating all of the curves the road had to offer, they took less than one hour to reach their destination. This time they stopped at the Swan and Finch. The drive was pleasant and once again Elspeth was encouraged to do most of the talking, Kane just adored listening to her. She talked about the work offshore; she had done a summer term before when in her last semester. She liked it but stated that she was really there for the money and time off. She could work a rotation of twenty-one days on/off and still make sufficient funds to buy an apartment, car and assist her aging parents. Kane gave no impression to Elspeth that his parents were well-healed. He had told her only that his father was a judge in the London courts; she knew nothing of his Mayfair address, or of his fathers' wealth in breeding horses. There was no relevance, and Elspeth never dove into that side of his life. She was certainly not ready to know that he was some five years her junior. Upon entering the pub they saw a bizarre group of aging men, Elspeth was the only female in the bar. Looks came from everywhere. Kane thought that this was only natural after all she was stunningly beautiful. Her short black hair made her milky white face radiate, and after the last two nights she was glowing even more, evidently Kane was a good "doctor."

All of the men were dressed in shabby short jackets, kilts and dark knee length socks and dirty work shoes. They looked like sheep farmers, reminding Kane of the endless number of jokes he had heard with respect to sheep and Scottish farmers. They were speaking to each other in Gaelic, hence he had no idea what they were bantering. Elspeth gestured to the table close to the fire. Sitting down she told him that they had commented on the two newlyweds, meaning the two of them. You speak the language Kane declared. Elspeth responded with yes, and French also. For fun Kane responded in French to her and she was evidently shocked. This Michael Angelo was casually speaking in the language of great lovers, how much more could she take? Responding in French, she said to him that she loved the French language and she would appreciate him speaking in French for the evening, just so that she could hone in her language skills.

She crossed her legs tightly in the hope that the phantom stayed away, at least for the time being. Kane went up to the bar and placed his order for two ploughman lunches, he waited for the local brew to be poured from one of the three porcelain arms. The lunch was served and they munched over the rolls and a variety of cheeses, pickled onions, Branston pickle and thinly sliced ham. Talking throughout in French they discovered even more about each other. Kane had agreed that he would speak in French on the understanding that she made the effort to speak to him later in Gaelic, to which she had agreed. They stayed at the pub for almost two hours, Kane having downed four pints of the local bitter to Elspeth's two. Kane could obviously hold his ale, she thought, yet for safety sake suggested that they had had enough and reminded him that he was driving.

Already over the legal limit yet as sober as his father, they departed and headed back to the Inn. The weekend was almost over but it had been a wonderful time, for Kane he was keenly aware of his contentedness and of course Elspeth was floating for the best part on cloud nine, having descended three times now from cloud 69.

Returning to the Inn they decided to rest up, staying in their room they sat cross-legged on the bed facing each other—speaking fluidly in French—the language of love. By nine pm they were between the sheets, behaving as if they were indeed French newlyweds. Elspeth had no expectation of what would take place to better the prior nights, but this "Frenchman" pulled out all of the romantic stops, causing her to peak at cloud 89, descending to cloud 9 and ascending again, as if on a giant roller coaster. With such intense passion she didn't know until the following morning that she had bitten her lower lip—it was swollen and tender—not unlike other areas of her love worn body. By six in the morning they were up and out of the Inn, Elspeth was pleasantly weak with significant areas of memorable tenderness. She walked gingerly to the nearby parked car.

The drive back to Dyce was quick, there being hardly any traffic at that early hour. Kane started the conversation and casually guided Elspeth to take it over. He smiled to himself; he had maneuvered their conversation on purpose. He wanted to enjoy the softness of her accent, and was delighted at the thoughtfulness and overall intelligence of her conversation. Kane concluded that she was truly beautiful inside and out. He found himself noticing she was somewhat like his mum.

Upon arrival at the hotel, and to avoid inquisitive eyes, he dropped her off at the far end of the parking lot. They agreed to meet in the week and would pinpoint the time and place with a telephone call. She disappeared into the hotel, she was now fully aware that she was falling for this voyeur of a man, and she knew that not only did she yearn for his body—but she wanted the man himself.

Kane parked the car and waited a few minutes prior to going in through the side entrance, heading for the breakfast lounge where he would take in the breakfast buffet. This traditional Scottish morning feast was terrific. Kane was famished.

He ate a breakfast equivalent to that of three people, whilst paying for only one. His hunger was accompanied by an equal thirst—drinking two full pots of tea to reach satisfaction. Kane finished the morning meal, checked his notes to confirm his interview schedule, signed the tab to his room and departed. He headed to his room, cleaned his teeth, changed into his business clothes and headed over to interview address number one. This format was the same for the first few companies. Thursday, he was due to be interviewed by Maersk Oil and Gas and Schlumberger. So far all the companies recommended that he should engage on the career path as a drilling engineer and or a mud engineer. Maersk was much the same, however Maersk strongly suggested that he should use the first three month period in a familiarization program as a roughneck. It was ten am on Thursday and Kane had, in essence, made up his mind.

Kane had his heart set on Maersk, and subject to a clear medical and drug screening Maersk was his! The Maersk building included a Medical Clinic with supporting Laboratories. He was dispatched forthwith for an immediate medical. Providing he passed the blood screening, he would be offshore by Friday, pretty efficient he thought. The medical center was modern and sterile. He handed over his papers to the attendant and took a seat. Even though there were no other people in the waiting area he was left for twenty minutes to read fashion magazines or the new issue of Town and Country, he chose the latter. It was 11:30 a.m. when he was ushered into the examination room, the nurse advised him to strip off and to put on the sterile blue hospital gown.

He stifled a groan—he had always hated these gowns that tied in the back—left you open and a little vulnerable he always thought. He waited for another ten minutes, after which the doctor strolled in.

To his surprise it was a female doctor. She was about thirty years of age and to make matters more complicated—she was a knockout. She looked like a Swedish movie star with full lips, strong facial bone structure, long blonde hair and Tanzanite-colored eyes. She stared at this young man and asked for confirmation on his date of birth. He advised "yes" that it was not a mistake—he would be just eighteen years old next week. She was stunned at this huge man sitting before her—she was sure he looked her age; little did she know that she would be further awestruck as she proceeded with the examination.

She went through a barrage of medical related questions which included the medical history of his parents. To his knowledge his parents had never been sick, but he had also to inform the doctor that his grandparents had both passed away due to cancer. Accommodating the doctor he performed various basic tasks, touching his toes, his nose, and reading with 20/20 vision the smallest letters some twenty feet away. The examination was proceeding fine and he thought that the doctor was very thorough, and then it was time for him to lose the gown. He did so with modest embarrassment which was further exacerbated by her staring at his relaxed penis. She choked on her words when advising him that she would want to explore his genital area and would need him to cough. He sported that grin of his which caused her to blush crimson red. She fondled his groin for several minutes and asked him to cough at least six times. He in turn was attempting to focus on the Town and Country magazine that he had recently put down. It was uncomfortable for Kane, but at last she stopped and requested him to turn around. The doctor was experiencing a little discomfort in that her underwear was literally soaking wet. She politely asked him to lean over the edge of the bed while she put on surgical gloves; she took several sighs to maintain her composure prior to performing a prostate examination. Fortunately for Kane, she used a gel to make the experience a little less uncomfortable, more importantly her fingers were long and slim. With little concern for his comfort she thrust her finger into his anus and started to swirl her finger in a clockwise direction. It was quite the turn off and any concern for his lower limbs responding was dismissed instantaneously.

The rectal exam was over almost as quickly as it started—it took maybe fifteen seconds. Kane's backside had now lost its virginity, upon turning, he once again managed to smile that wicked smile and she in turn mirrored the same. Still naked he was asked to sit down and rest his arm on the side support arm. She would sample his blood and they would be done. She took three samples of blood and tried not to stare at his groin, but it was difficult for her as he was indeed a medical anomaly. Finally it was all over and she advised him that he could dress.

The Doctor turned briefly, jotting down a brief note she turned to him and said it was good to meet him and placed the note in his shirt pocket and vacated the room. He continued to dress and once ready to go he read the note. "I am off at three p.m., address: 23 Caledonian Street, near the Bank of Scotland, would you like a nibble?"

Kane's curiosity and youth allowed him to immediately dismiss the fact that he had yet one more interview to go. He decided on a whim he would call and cancel—after all, his ass had been violated and he deserved a little "distraction."

He assumed that the note did not imply a late lunch, so he strolled down the road to the closest pub where he would devour a pie and a pint.

At 3:15 p.m. he was ringing the townhouse door bell. Almost immediately she was there, having herself arrived just moments before. She gestured him in and closed the door. Kane did not have any time to survey the one bedroom town home; the doctor was climbing his torso hanging on to his broader than broad shoulders, legs wrapped around his waist. Her proposed "nibble" was more like a "three course meal" and he was the "main course." The Doctor became almost possessed. Kane accommodated her desire and managed to negotiate the passageway leading to the one and only bedroom. Her mouth was sensuous, hot and moist. Her desire deafening. They fell onto the bed where they ripped at each others clothes. This was setting up to be quite the experience he mused and allowed the horny vixen to have her way. She rolled him over so that she could mount him, but first of all she teased him. She was mesmerized by his length and breadth. Fondling him—licking and teasing his manhood with her tantalizing tongue. Ah, hah, he thought—this is what she meant when she said a "nibble." Finally, having stimulated him almost to a frenzy with her slow deliberate movements she moved ever so much closer to the "meeting" point. She eventually placed his enlarged member at the entrance of pleasure land, and unexpectedly thrust her body downwards. She moaned in the combination of pain and accompanying ecstasy, she felt certain this compared to no other lover in her varied sexual escapades. Her groans grew loader and heavier with her mounting desire. She rode him as if she was on a bar room mechanical bull, bucking, writhing, howling. Kane wondered whether any one else could hear this performance but then decided he didn't care—this woman was wild. He had no idea whether the doctor had experienced the Phantom as the performance started in high gear and never missed a beat. He came to the conclusion that this must be a symptom of Nymphomania. After ninety minutes of non stop galloping the spurs came to rest. She had said nothing through out the encounter, but for sure she was done, she had run ten miles and she had won the Grand National, having cleared all of the jumps.

Kane showered while she lay there like Sleeping Beauty in her ninety-nine-year sleep. The shower was a marvel. Unlike most showers he had experienced, this one was actually installed at a height of six feet, six inches, enabling him to stand fully upright. In addition the water was intense with pressure and the ultimate marvel—the water temperature was hot. The Doctor awoke later that evening only to realize that they had never exchanged a word; Kane had showered, dressed and was now gone.

Returning to his hotel he picked up his messages at the desk, Elspeth was one of two receptionists, and she took it upon herself to serve this guest. The message had been hand written by Elspeth so she had prior knowledge of its content. The human resource manager from Maersk had instructed him to proceed to Copenhagen for Sunday and to be available at the head office for Monday morning. Telephone number and hotel address will be emailed to him on Friday Morning. He assumed at that point that he must be medically fit and drug free.

Elspeth knew that her champion was about to leave, so she whispered, *How about dinner tomorrow night, Chinese, perhaps?*

Her very mannerism was so similar to his mother that it was uncanny. He looked into her eyes and simply replied, "Wouldn't miss it for the world."

Back in his room he fired up his laptop to find the email already there, complete with flight details for Sunday, so much for being offshore by Friday he thought. There was also an email from the Judge; it addressed the possibility of a compressed PhD course that could be fast tracked over a six month period. The Judge provided contact e-mail addresses, telephone numbers and a host of other details. No doubt his long term secretary had been hard at working sourcing all this information. The email was a thesis in itself.

The judge signed off as per usual but included that he was so fortunate to have such a loving and hard-working son and that he knew in his heart that he *would always do the right thing*. Reflecting on his most recent guilty pleasure and the silence which accompanied it with "The Doctor", Kane wondered what his father would have done given the same circumstance. Of course he could not answer, or at least decided not too.

Saving the email to a Maersk folder, he deleted the message. Later that day he would make contact with the appropriate authorities in addition to one of his old professors. He mused over the thought that the Judge may be calling in some favors.

Again his hunger was clawing at his gut; he thought that he would order in a pizza and just confine himself to his room and take pleasure in his books. This was the order of the evening, and he was grateful that there were no interruptions.

His e-mail to his old professor was acknowledged within one hour of being sent, he discovered that many of his course requirements could be sourced vie the internet, how ever he did need to contemplate a seventy five thousand word thesis, his topic was buried deep in his brain yet to surface. The pizza arrived encased in a large square shaped insulated leather carrier. The pimpled delivery boy must have been newly seventeen and newly licensed to drive, he looked as if he needed to feast himself on many pizzas to put some flesh on his bones. He found his mind wondering to thoughts of his most recent conquest. Musing over what she must be doing right now, secretly wishing she would call. He shook his head and brought himself back to reality, realizing the doctor—whatever her name is would not be calling any time soon.

He devoured the pizza in less time than it took the delivery boy to bring it—that time spent with the Doctor had created an appetite like he hadn't had in awhile. He had to admit that it was filling and a tasty treat. He called home to his Mum and the Judge—as always it was a delight to speak with his Mum—she was always so happy to hear from him—he never wanted to disappoint her—he would try to do what was right—for her. After hanging up from his parents, he lay back on the bed and swiftly drifted off to sleep—capturing himself a good solid four hours.

By three am he was back at the books, and by 6:00 a.m. he had found all of the registration forms required for his PhD. He took great pleasure in emailing the Judge, knowing how pleased he would be that Kane was well on his way to the starting the next level of his education—it was the right thing to do. The dream of studying in the USA—was slowly fading away. The thesis question had been resolved—Nuclear Division between Nations, a scary and controversial subject he thought! Friday morning was slow, but the afternoon was pleasant. He decided to drive up to Inverness to the site of the Battle of Culloden. There was nothing much to see at the site other than to appreciate the terrain of the bog, and to read the information murals which described and pictorially portrayed the Battle with Bonnie Prince Charlie. He read the text with interest: The Battle of Culloden (April 16, 1746), was the final clash between the Jacobites and the Hanoverians in the 1745 Jacobite Rising. It was the last battle to be fought on mainland Britain, and brought the Jacobite cause—to restore the House of Stuart to the throne of Great Britain—to a decisive defeat from which it never recovered.

The Jacobites—most of them Highland Scots—supported the claim of Charles Edward Stuart (aka "Bonnie Prince Charlie" or "The Young Pretender") to the throne; the British army, under the Duke of Cumberland, younger son of the Hanoverian sovereign, King George II, supported his father's cause.

The aftermath of the battle was brutal and earned the victorious general the name "Butcher" of Cumberland. Charles Edward Stuart eventually left Britain and went to Rome, never to attempt to take the throne again. Civil penalties were also severe. New laws dismantled the Highlanders' feudal clan system, and even highland dress was outlawed.

He compared himself to the Duke of Cumberland and concluded that the pink faced butcher could not compare to the lean mean killing machine of rugby.

From there he traveled on to the firth of Cromarty, only to sight several oil rigs at anchor, no doubt undergoing refit or waiting for another charter—perhaps both. Overhead RAF jets graced the skies sneaking up on him flying at an altitude of less than one thousand feet; three of them roared by declaring their ownership of the skies. He relished the thought of commanding one of those machines, and wondered whether a career in the RAF was for him?

With the night drawing near in he decided to drive back to the hotel and meet with Elspeth for a western Chinese dinner.

He took a shower and modestly cursed at the tepid water and the lack of pressure. After the short ordeal he straddled the tub and grabbed the bath robe, when for the second time that day, someone else had crept up on him. Elspeth stood in the doorway of the bathroom with that sensuous smile and looked him up and down taking it all in as if standing in the corridors of the Louvre. She saucily elevated her face

soliciting a response by way of a kiss, which he willingly obliged. Flirtatiously she confirmed the dinner at seven pm at the Shan Tung restaurant in the heart of the city. With a naughty look again at his body she turned and vacated the room, while on her way back to the reception desk she was already sensing weakening knees and a little dampness between her thighs.

Inwardly laughing at her advances, Kane realized she had come and gone just as fast as those fighter jets. He knew that he liked this lady very much, his fractional increase in heart rate and a swelling in his loins substantiating the fact.

They met in the car park just before seven pm and drove the rental towards the city. She gave the directions and in twenty minute they were entering the restaurant car park. Elspeth was dressed in a knee length, lined, grey mohair dress. The dress complimented her figure and the opened neck permitted her silver cross and chain to rest on her breast bone. Her shapely athletic limbs were hidden beneath shear black nylons. She wore black patent high healed shoes that elevated her to within three or four inches of his six foot two frame; she barely had to look up to him.

Her neat little ears were the home of two half carat diamonds which sparkled with intensity. Reservations having been secured by Elspeth earlier in the day—they entered the restaurant and were greeted by the host and accompanied to their table without delay. Elspeth asked of him whether he liked the idea of Chinese food, candidly he responded, "But of course I am half Chinese myself." She took this statement as light hearted humor—and then was shocked when he proceeded to order their entire meal in Cantonese—she hadn't a clue what he just ordered. The waitress scurried off somewhat amused at the situation that had just unfolded. Naturally

Elspeth asked more questions, with emphasis on where did he learn to speak the language? And so began Kane's story of his Education in the Languages. He briefly explained that his mother was indeed Chinese and that she talked to him at all times in Chinese, even though her own command of English was exceptional. He continued with more details, sharing with her the three years he spent in Hong Kong and that to make matters even better he was blessed with very strong language learning skills. His story continued—four consecutive summers as an exchange student in Zurich, Switzerland, and thus by age fifteen he was fluent in German, French, Austrian, and Cantonese and of course English. In university his second major was in the languages and was quite competent with Russian as well. Kane advised the one language he had wanted to learn but, as yet had not, was Gaelic—Elspeth's mother tongue. She smiled and committed to teaching him in due course.

The meal arrived—the waitress busy serving several plates. There was traditional steamed rice, mixed vegetables, a beef dish with noodles and green onions, a fish dish with a Tilapia encrusted with capers and onions, and finally a vegetable called Dow mew with garlic cloves. The main meal was simply delicious culminating with a walnut based cream dessert. Knowing that their time together was limited Elspeth asked if he would be free the next day? Kane asked what had she in mind to which she saucily responded that she had booked a room for the night in the five star hotel—The Glen Eagles and thought that they could pretend they were on their honeymoon. She quickly grinned at him—making sure he realized she was not pressuring him—but also mentioned they might not see each other for ten years. Shouldn't they seize the moment? Kane simply said that she had seized him a few days ago, but the idea was indeed a perfect one. And thus, with that general agreement they left the restaurant and drove west to The Glen Eagles. The hotel was not too far a drive and soon they were in the midst of the upper echelon of society or at least many people were under that illusion. The hotel's ambiance was lovely—typical of the era in which it was built. It was outfitted with exquisite antique furniture dating back some four hundred years or more. They both were keen for a nightcap or two, so headed into the bar. It was a masterpiece of design—no doubt maintained by the exorbitant profit earned from the sale of the spirits. Kane almost choked on the price of his bourbon on the rocks and Elspeth's Crantinis. The Scottish bar man who could barely understand anyone cast an evil eye on Kane when he ordered his Bourbon. After all it was almost a sacrilege to their senses, an offence to the Scottish traditional malts to sip on bourbon.

Like most hotels this one boasted a larger than life fire place, the logs were over five feet long and crackled away, the radiant heat warming everyone within a six foot radius, and almost immediately the heat transfer was lost to the continual damp air. They spent the next three hours talking and laughing, both totally absorbed in each other—oblivious to those around them. Well past midnight they retired to their spectacular Five Star room. It was a masterpiece, and well deserving of the highest rating. This room also had a fireplace—with a well-attended fire, crackling away. It was evident that someone was kept very busy tending to the fire. The grate was freshly stacked with logs and the fire was well established, a most wonderful delight on the cool damp evening.

A king-sized bed was draped in a red silk cover, embroidered with white and crimson roses. This special evening together was second to none in Elspeth's or Kane's minds—the details too intense to focus on—suffice to say it was a night to remember. The following morning they laid curled up in each others arms each of them willing the time to crawl. However it was inevitable they had to fall from the clouds and prepare to check out of the hotel.

This day would be their last together and like Elspeth had stated they did not know what the future held in store for either of them—let alone if they would meet again and when. But, for the moment life had delivered the very best of everything for both of them and for that experience they were both grateful. Noon was check out and they made sure they were prompt. To stay any longer would require a bank loan and a line of credit. Elspeth had paid for the evening and it was a cost he knew she could barely afford. From the hotel they returned to Aberdeen and spent the afternoon walking the Granite City, the weather was accommodating, although as always, it was damp. Elspeth had to work at six pm so this was indeed their last opportunity to enjoy each others company. Kane was well aware of Elspeth's feelings for him, although she had not pressed the issue. He felt a connection to her and wanted to leave her with something to remember him by. He took her into the only jewelry store in Aberdeen that sold the Cartier line. Kane left Elspeth perusing the display cabinets. Kane knew insurance companies of stores like this would not allow the store to display stones of greater weight than one and a half carats. Having already sized Elspeth's finger Kane and the store manager, disappeared into the rear private office to peruse the remainder of their collection. He felt this was an extraordinary circumstance and he wanted to leave her with this gesture of love. He bought her a solitaire diamond, clear and as bright as the star Sirius, weighing in at two and a half carats, with no inclusions. This ring would certainly meet most women's heart's desire. In a store such as this one, that carries such quality pieces—price was not mentioned. Kane had a credit card with a very large limit, one which he never dreamed he would need. The limit was almost exhausted even after he negotiated a thirty percent discount with the willing manager. Kane left the store with the ring in his pocket, whilst Elspeth was unaware that he had actually made a purchase. Kane simply stated that everything was beyond his reach. Elspeth had no issue with this and continued to feed her batteries simply by holding his hand.

They embarked on their own mini pub crawl and ended up in the Loch Ness Inn. The Inn was quiet with few patrons, obviously a little too early for most to be drinking. They decided to order a baked potato, and for some unknown reason they chose to drink Guinness. The dark beer with the white frothy head came immediately but it took fifteen minutes or so for the potatoes. Nonetheless the wait was worthwhile. To bring closure to their last supper they ordered coffee, and sat together sipping the delicious brew. Kane opened his heart, showered her with loving terms of endearment. Praising her person—all the while indicating that he truly loved her—but deliberately choosing not to say the sacred three words that Elspeth so desired to hear him say. He chose to say that he would return one day and that he wanted her to know that their brief encounter was forever burned into his heart, his mind and most importantly his soul. He told her of the constellation of Orion and that the brightest star in the universe was Sirius, a star just to the bottom right of the largest constellation. He told her that whenever he would see Sirius from now forward, he would think of this moment. At this point he handed her the silver ring case. To say Elspeth was surprised was an understatement. She watched in awe as he opened it, she sat there in silence. She was stunned and mesmerized by its beauty and most of all by the sentiment. Her Michael Angelo, her love was indeed a god. The ring was enormous and brilliant. Even in the dark shadows of the inn she could see the intensity of the stone. She imagined that his diamond was illuminating the bar, but to the contrary it was her glowing face. Her eyes welled up with tears and her voice was lost to her soul. Speechless she placed it on her right hand, not making any false assumptions. He in turn cupped her hands in his and assured her that he would return one day and that they would get to know each other even more. Before she found her voice Kane softly spoke to her in french—advising her that this gift to her was as precious to him as he hoped it would be for her, and that he would not entertain even the suggestion that she would not accept the ring. She honored his request and simply returned his sentiment and stated that their moments spent together were indeed precious to her and that she felt their feelings and thoughts were in tune with each other.

Finishing their coffee they returned to the hotel. What a brilliant day he thought, as did she.

The night was long and Kane read and absorbed, he rarely became fatigued with learning, in fact the reading was almost a must in order to tire his mind, if not, sleep would not come. He telephoned his mother and had over an hour's conversation, something that was not a regular event. He told her of Elspeth and how they enjoyed each other; his mum was forever attentive and genuinely interested. The judge was at the city club so his call was a welcomed distraction. The Judge was still busy with the Black Watch Warrior case, but she advised Kane that it would be completed very soon. Kane informed her that he hoped to have a couple of week's vacation in about two month's time, this of course delighted his mother. Kane talked a mile a minute in fluent Cantonese; he was obviously intoxicated and smitten, by this young Gaelic speaking woman. Kane enjoyed the openness of the dialogue with his mum, and the feeling was mutual. He could charm his mother but he had to be very careful with the judge. The Judge was hard to read and Kane often didn't know his mind set. He was certainly not predictable, with the one exception, the PhD matter. Completing the call just before the onset of Sunday he said his farewells and rolled onto his queen size bed. He was asleep before the clock hands met at midnight.

Kane checked out of the hotel with plenty of time to drive to the airport which was already in ear shot of the Dyce hotel. He returned the budget rent a car and then proceeded through to the security and departure lounge. Unlike the last encounter Kane sailed through without any additional hassle. By noon after flying in a Dash 8 propellor job, he was in Denmark and the interesting city of Copenhagen.

As per instructions he made his way to the designated hotel, it was called the Carlton but it was not affiliated with the Ritz group of hotels. It was very modest, dirty and in need of many repairs, or perhaps it should be put out of its misery and be demolished and a new hotel built in its place. He concluded that Maersk were obviously cheap where the hotels were concerned. He checked in to his room which was yet another surprise. The bed was a single with a hollowed center, having been in use for two lifetimes. The shower/bathroom was so bad it was almost funny. He knew that it would be difficult to wash as the shower again catered to in the likes of, Danish Dwarfs and certainly not a man of his height. The toilet was so close to shower and the hand basin, he doubted whether he could even perform anything meaningful there. He laughed softly to himself and decided to flip the mattress over and then sit down and email his folks. Elspeth of course, continued to be constantly on his mind. Subsequent to organizing the few items that he had in his possession, he decided to walk the sea wall and to reconnoiter the following days meeting place, the head office of Denmark's largest company.

He had read on the internet that they were into oil and gas exploration and production, operators of a marine tanker, and container fleet of significant size, a grocery chain, shipbuilders, and the list went on. There was no question; this company was a force to be reckoned with.

Kane took a break in a small coffee shop which tempted him with a variety of pastries and cheeses. He spoke in German and most of the Danes understood him. Learning the Danish language would not be a huge challenge—and he would add yet another language to his list.

While he was relishing a Danish delight and drinking his coffee, he was shocked to see a familiar figure approach his table, it was the judge's closest friend Sir William P Myers, DSO, CBE, he was a very senior cheese in the British Foreign Office. He could be found most evenings at the city club, chewing on a cigar, and sometimes seated with the judge. Sir William pretended that he was surprised to see him, he always referred to him as "my boy" and, as if playacting, showed the expression which questioned, what the heck he was doing there. He pulled up a seat and readied himself to take in a little Sunday afternoon chit chat. He extended his hand and Kane shook it with a firm grip. Kane's grip was met with Sir William's strong grip. It was very apparent that this stately gentleman's grip was the result of his desire for tennis; he played tennis three times per week. The truth being that he was in fact an extremely good player and needless to say was a very fit man. His father once told Kane that the old boy, as Sir William was often referred by, could still serve a ball at 105 miles per hour, which was pretty damn good.

Kane addressed his father's friend as Sir and explained his business there—the upcoming adventure into the Exploration Field offshore. He asked the same of the diplomat, to which Sir William replied that he was here for a Monday morning meeting which would commence at the foolish hour of 8:00 a.m., hence the need to be there a day early. The response appeared to be satisfactory yet it was only half of the truth.

Sir Billy as he was referred to, had watched Kane grow up over the years and was astonished with his academic acumen, his physical attributes and his positive outlook on life. Sir Billy thought that he would make a great addition to his elite team, known only by the elite of elite, as the Alpha Omega Group. The Group comprised of about twenty six extraordinary people, people who had unusual talents and driven by an inner strength which defied the normal human. These chosen few were trained to standards well in excess of the US Seals, the SAS, the KGB Elite forces, CIA, and MI6. The significant difference being, the aforementioned agents fundamentally took no survivors. They were sadistic killers and anonymity was key to their longevity.

The chosen few were hand picked for assignments ranging in scope. These men did the UK government's dirty work, the list was ugly. Assassinations, destruction of property, counterterrorism tactical support, approved murders, they were the real killers, every nation had them but the UK crews were different, almost characterized as trained psychopaths. They were on the payroll of the government but the government would never admit this. The chosen few were always on their own, they were persona non gratis. They had no history; everything about these men was false. Each agent would have several identities with several supporting documents to suit each non de plume. Bank accounts would be setup in several locations under several non de plumes. Certain of these agents eventually forgot their individual roots accepting a new ID at the drop of a hat; to the normal person they were sadistic freaks with no human emotion, no hearts, no compassion, yet this is how they survived, after all someone had to do the government's dirty laundry. They would receive large deposits of funds channeled via many devious routes but all ending up in the banks of the Isle of Man, Jersey, Luxembourg, Bermuda, Cayman Islands, Iceland and the list was endless.

As long as an assignment was going well then the AO team agents had all of the backing and resources that they needed, but in the event that plans went askew, then they were figments of the imagination, they became automatic lepers, known only as whom? Sir Billy was looking to Kane to be groomed to take his place, but not for covert operations. The life expectancy of field operatives was less than five years, he needed someone to lead not to do the all too familiar distasteful tasks of the AO group. This encounter had been arranged by Sir Billy, he knew all of Kane's business including the recent large credit card transaction. The head of the AO Group had greater access to the resources of government, greater than MI6 and the black operations group, far more reaching than Special Branch, and in many ways greater than the PMO. Sir Billy was genuinely in Copenhagen for business but the trip was two fold, he particularly wanted to further assess this young man, hence the articulate questioning began.

Without pulling any punches he asked Kane whether he had a woman in his life, knowing only too well of his purchase of the Cartier diamond ring. Kane was frank about his response and simply stated that he had met a very lovely lady in Aberdeen that just may be the one. Kane advised his focus right now was his PhD, the focus would shift later to a career path, albeit he was uncertain of the career route. The diplomat asked with a steadfast stare, the woman in Aberdeen, would she be your fiancée? Kane was slightly startled by the question and responded no, however that he had said farewell with a very nice ring. He emphatically stated that the ring was neither a promise nor engagement ring; in fact he had no description for it other than a very special gift, which was the truth. Sir Billy was satisfied with his response and then started to grill him on the PhD program. Kane stated that his father had sourced a means for him to fast track the system and for him to enroll into the Nuclear Physics program. Sir Billy smiled and said that his father had discussed the matter with him recently at the club; but Sir Billy did not expand on the subject and the fact that he had arranged the entire matter with the university even down to the course content which was skewed to Foreign Office criteria, and more so to AO group requirements. Unknowingly Kane was already a candidate for the team. The barrage of questions continued at rapid fire. The questions were causing Kane to be somewhat confused, as some, he felt were none of Sir Billy's business. The judge had always stated that the safe strategy to adopt anywhere in the world was to simply avoid topics that include, religion, sex, and politics. Sir Billy had directly delved into all of these off limit subjects and more. The judge had also taught Kane to practice listening more so than talking, it was safer, and with this in mind he turned the tables and started to grill the diplomat, and of course the diplomat was very skilled in all of his responses, letting nothing meaningful slip through his lips; he was very good, he had survived to sport a head of silver hair; quite the achievement for an ex operative, now head of the Alpha Omega Group.

The diplomat appreciated the skill of this young man and decided to make his exit. He was satisfied that this Kane Austin could be groomed over the next ten years to become a candidate to lead the AO Group; he would continue to monitor his progress carefully. Prior to leaving the coffee shop Sir Billy said that he would be sure to mention the chance meeting to his father tomorrow night at the club, said their goodbyes and was gone.

Kane remained in the coffee shop for a little while longer, eating more assorted cheese, crackers and Danish wafers and left. He made his return along the sea wall to the Carlton, walking quickly, with the cold damp sea breeze mixed with beach sand, it felt as if his face was being sand blasted. He mused to himself—it would sure be nice if his destination was a Ritz Carlton and not it's poor cousin! The small hotel room was at least warm, he felt the need to test the commode and as he feared he was wedged into position with his shoulders crouched forward and three sides of his body crimped by the confining wall and sink unit of this so called bathroom—the bathroom fit only for Irish Lepricorns and West African Pigmy's. None the less he smiled at his surroundings, making the best of a-none so-great situation.

Kane fired up his laptop. To his pleasant surprise he had a mixture of emails, and most importantly one from Elspeth. She was just a delight and her text was long and most interesting. She too would be going offshore next month as a "rock hound" for Dan Oil. Apparently "rock hound" is what Geologists are referred to on a world wide basis in the offshore. For Kane it was the first time that he had heard the phrase, yet it seemed to fit the profession. He could imagine her voice and accent with each sentence, and he suddenly felt a loss, he was already missing her. Before reading his other emails he would respond with a lengthy email—stating that he was missing her—which was not his normal style—he was throwing caution to the wind. He gave her the details of his trip and the chance meeting with Sir William Myers. He even joked about the hotel bathroom commenting on its miniature size. Throughout his response he wished that she was there so they could enjoy the splendor of the old city together.

After completing the email and pressing send, he read the emails from his professor and his mother and responded accordingly. With the professor's he was intrigued by the out line of his courses, he would be sent by securemail certain tasks to study. He must maintain an eighty percent average mark in all topics and his thesis must be ready within five and a half months. He will receive a separate email on other internet related course materials. He was warned that there was a zero tolerance regarding late submitted assignments. He knew they meant business. This would not be an issue for Kane as he had already been studying relevent material to the course, due to his own personal interest in the subject of Nuclear Physics. He was indeed a very keen student. The Judge would be proud.

He responded next to his mother and sensed the same feeling of loss/separation as had felt when responding to Elspeth, he loved his mother dearly and mused at the thought that he just may be falling in love with Elspeth. Deleting several items of junk mail he shut down his laptop and picked up his book. He read until midnight and fell asleep fully clothed. By 4:30 a.m. he was awakened by the wind and the rattling of the window; once again he turned to his book.

The morning hours passed by and it was time to enter the closet bathroom and attempt a shower. Undressing he opened the tap water to allow the water to heat up, and to his surprise it did so within seconds. The temperature was good and the pressure perfect; he would get down on his knees and enjoy the occasion. By 7:00 a.m. he was down at the buffet breakfast which was a continental breakfast only.

The pastries were exquisite and the coffee superb, his morning was starting off just right. Fifteen minutes later he was off, headed toward the Head Office of Denmark's largest group of companies, he would be on time. Once again battling the wind, sea spray and sand, his face was partly sand blasted again and mildly frozen upon his arrival at the main door of the building. The interview was to take place on the fourth floor in room 444. For the Chinese this would be a bad omen, the number 4 represented death.

Kane was welcomed by a pleasant young lady with short blonde hair, dressed in a striking Jones New York pinstripe suit. She accessorized with a red tie and matching red silk handkerchief in her breast pocket. She simply stated in very good English that the managers were waiting for him in the adjoining board room. He was impressed to think that there would be more than one manager to interview him. Escorted into the room the hand shakes began. There were in fact three people sat on the other side of the table. The heavy set fellow was the production manager; the skinny gaunt looking gentleman was the exploration manager and the overweight lady with the thinning hair and "John Lennon" style eye glasses was the Human Resource representative. He mused to himself that this group of three reminded him of the Punch and Judy shows that provide millions of children entertainment on the beaches of Europe during the summer time.

The interview lasted a full ninety minutes. It was immediately apparent during the interview that Kane was overqualified for the regular engineering jobs that were presented to him, but suffice to say that he would continue to embark on the familiarization program. He felt there was time later to manipulate their focus towards a more defined career path within the organization—one that would be better suited to Kane. The interviewer's were impressed that he was engaging in the PhD program and offered the company's generous financial assistance to complete the course. Kane knew this company was not renowned for being a leader in the area of remuneration, benefits and compensation packages, so he was pleasantly surprised that the company offered him a reasonable deal to train and study. Kane was grateful for this, as he wanted to maintain as independent of a lifestyle from his parents as possible. The plan was set in motion—he would be proceeding offshore the following morning, he successfully hid his inner excitement from the management team.

He left the building only to feel the laser burning eyes of Miss Jones New York on his back; he turned casually waved and gave her his famous naughty grin.

Walking back to his hotel room he was wondering what he would do for the remaining part of the day. First off he thought he stopped at the coffee shop to savor yet another cup of coffee and mouth watering Danish. Just the day before Sir Billy had been there but this time on his arrival the shop was almost empty of customers. To Kane's surprise he found a British Newspaper freshly unopened. The front page news as in most countries identified the current status in various parts of the Middle East. The conflict never ceased and the solutions never found, a fact of life for two thousand years. Kane was impartial about the region, as long as it did not affect him he really did not care. Another headline referred to a British MI6 agent killed with the poison of the times, namely plutonium-210. The previous number one poisons, Dialdrin and Ricin, having taken a backstage to this incurable nuclear poison. Kane immediately thought of Sir Billy and wondered whether his visit in Copenhagen had anything to do with the newspaper article. Kane stayed in the shop a full hour and completed the crossword in quick order, after that it was time to get back to his meager lodgings. Once back in his room he powered up his laptop and reviewed his new emails. The judge had sent him a short note and the rest was junk mail, nothing as yet from Elspeth. Needing some stimulus he turned to his books and read and absorbed. Totally engaged in the subject matter of enriching plutonium he was suddenly distracted by a gentle tap at the door. He got up, stretched his arms and quickly made the short distance to the door knob. To his pleasant surprise the doorway became a picture frame for the luscious 5-foot-10-inch blonde, still in her Jones New York—minus the tie and a significant number of buttons opened revealing the most attractive breasts—that were rising and falling quite rapidly with her anticipation of surprising him. She addressed him as Kane and wondered if he was in need of being "entertained" for the evening? Kane's eyebrows rose with his surprise and his naughty smile indicated his consent. Her lovely mouth, those sensuous lips...were the last thoughts that went through Kane's mind before she planted her lips on his, with tongues searching each others mouths. Soon their hands joined in the exploration—passionately searching each others bodies. Her hands, moving slowly over his hard body; his hands grasping her taut ass and pulling her closer. Closing the door they continued exploring—for at least 3 hours. They found everything the other needed to reach the ultimate climax. This young Scandinavian blonde named Lille Anderson became the next woman to fall under his sexual spell. The way she created such a stir in his loins so quickly—it was debatable who was under whose spell. The room did not cater to two young lovers who were above average in size. After three hours of peaks and troughs of pleasure and pure ecstasy combined with sexual gymnastics Lille had not experienced before, she had to stop, regain her composure and strength only to suggest that they relocate to her apartment. Kane was understanding and very quick and eager to accommodate and so they ventured out.

Her apartment was but a thirty-minute walk away. She had a tasteful apartment, which she shared with Lola Peterson. Upon entry the picture was clear. Lola embraced her partner with a mouth to mouth kiss, a kiss that lasted, several seconds. Kane's age and inexperience caused him to be a little off guard. This situation proved to be a little uncomfortable for him, but he managed to not show his modest embarrassment. Lille stated that they should take a shower and gestured Kane towards the bathroom. The bathroom appeared to be larger than Kane's hotel room. Slowly Lille started to undress him and to his surprise and delight Lola started to undress in front of him. Her body was a fit for centerfold of Playboy. She was indeed a knockout a ten. Kane mused to himself, who was he kidding they were both knockouts—had he died and gone to heaven? With the shower providing a curtain of pulsating hot water they kissed and fondled each other. He was overwhelmed with the sexual exploits but he was not complaining. Of course a great deal of attention was favored to his manhood. Both of them wanted to take him in their mouths and one by one they had their fill. The shower was an experience of a lifetime—something Kane had not accomplished in his tender years. After almost an hour of incredible foreplay they toweled each other dry and made their way, hand in hand to the bedroom. The wall was covered with tasteful photographs of nude females, several of which were portraits of Lille and Lola. In his mind he had already classified them as L squared, mathematically speaking of course. They led his willing body to the king-sized bed—this 45-square-foot area would prove to be his exercise mat for the next four hours. Lille had already sampled this giant of a man, but Lola had her initiation to come. Lola ended up being a screamer and scream she did. Lola was explored by and at the mercy of both Kane and Lille simultaneously. Orgasms were plentiful and Kane satisfied them both without losing a beat. His stamina and unbelievable ability to keep his erection strong proved to be an extremely beneficial trait—where Lille and Lola were concerned. With the evening coming to a close Kane was still fully engaged with the two lesbians. He found his focus was waning as he needed something to fuel his engine. He was famished. Having missed lunch and as of now he had been fully engaged in what was now seven hours of rigorous passionate lovemaking with two gorgeous horny women—no wonder he was running on empty. The women did not complain when he withdrew from Lola's warm, wet cavern—they laid side by side stretching and delighting as the last tingle of orgasms moved through their bodies. The women started to speak in Danish and were commenting on the wild ride and just how good this stud was when Kane got up and made his way to the Kitchen/pantry—smiling to himself, as he had understood every word they uttered, just not quite capable to speak it fluently in the lovely sign-song banter they had. The two girls snuggled into each other while Kane devoured a Baguette laced with butter and Gouda Cheese. Unfortunately there was no Bourbon to be found, so he made do with the Heineken. This chased the food nicely. Naked in the living room he swallowed the last drops of lager and made his way to the bathroom, picking up pieces of his clothing en route. He thought that he would dress and make his exit, but only to find that the ladies wanted seconds. Seconds they had and then it was time for Kane to go. Before leaving, the two ladies had instructed him to call in again on his way through. This was a request that Kane would honor and found he got excited in anticipation—even though he had no idea when that would be. He finally left this unique love nest around six am to make his way back to the hotel. It had been a long time since Kane had missed a complete night's sleep. Even though four hours was all he usually needed, he knew he was going to miss this set of four.

Back in his hovel, Kane quickly packed his things and made a quick exist from the hotel. He had already ordered a taxi for the 7:00 a.m. departure to the heliport some twenty miles south. By eight am he was in the pre flight safety meeting suited up in a survival helicopter suit, watching the pre flight video that was standard practice each and every time the crews went offshore. Surveying the others he noted that he must have been the youngest although he was probably the only one who really knew. In no time at all Kane felt like he was back in grade school. Yes, there was the school bully. Hans Doerksen was a derrick man; he was huge, towering in at least six feet, six inches. He was in the region of 325 pounds and it looked as if he was all muscle. Kane had heard other crew members referred to him as the Dork rather than Hans, but it certainly wasn't said to his face. The survival suit had to have been tailor-made for this worker, and it fit him like a glove. Most of the other workers looked like bedraggled seals with pot bellies. Before they knew it they were marching off like trained seals to board the helicopter. A Super Puma, with blades rotating everyone crouched down on their approach broadside to the helicopter doorway. One by one they embarked and strapped themselves in. The trip offshore would take one hour five minutes. This was Kane's first experience flying in a helicopter hence it held a degree of interest to him. The flight was noisy and uncomfortable, Kane watched with interest the approach to this monstrous platform which was secured by eight 15 tonne Steven anchors which in turn were connected to over three thousand feet of K4, four-inch-diameter chain, which safely secured the unit in place.

They arrived safely on the Danish Flagged semi submersible named the Deep Sea Digger. With the rotors still turning the helicopter passengers disembarked in an orderly fashion following the directions given by the heli-deck crew. Within five minutes everyone was off and escorted to the arrival room. Kane being a new hire would have to undergo a briefing on the bridge and a tour of the safety equipment, being sure to note the muster stations around the rig. Kane thought that this was turning out to be interesting, and was anxious to commence this new chapter in his life.

London Fog

The fog which spewed into the London streets from the Thames Estuary was beginning to thin; the forecast was for the sun to burn off the fog by noon. Nonetheless it was cold and damp, perfect weather to enhance any form of arthritis, a common ailment in the Metropolitan London area.

Judge Austin casually thought that it would be a good day for a beheading and or a public hanging, in the confines of Tower; the accused eleven had been spared by a few hundred years of so called progress.

The black Mariah vans, six in total turned into the side entrance of the court building. For security reasons only two vans held the prisoners, ten men and one female.

There were no attempts made to ambush and free the prisoners on route, Sir Billy combined with Scotland Yard and special branch had meticulously changed the planned route everyday, and today was no exception; just five minutes before the scheduled departure from the holding cells in Brixton, the final route was relayed to the commander in chief of Scotland Yard.

The court steps were littered with a multinational group of journalist, TV cameramen and field crews. All onlookers were jockeying for a good vantage point. They did not come to enjoy the architecture of Sir Christopher Wren which was abundant to the area; to the contrary, many were out for cold blooded revenge. Emotions were running very high and the two hundred policemen assigned to the court that day would have their hands full. All of the police men would be armed, there would be twelve mounted police, riot squad teams were ready. Dozens more security cameras were erected to ensure that screening could be as efficient as possible. There would, no doubt be additional fanatical team members watching and possibly planning some sort of retaliation. It was going to be as hectic outside the court as it would be inside.

The judge had discretely arrived two hours extra early in his toy, just to avoid the kafuffle. Subsequent to a morning tea and a slice of toast and marmalade it was time.

The judge after several weeks of review finally left his chambers inhaling a deep breath, and made his way up to the bench. Even with his head somewhat tilted down he could see the people in their various colored attire, women with varying hairdos with assorted colors; and men dressed in traditional attire, single and double breasted suits, some still wearing the typical London mohair great coats. The barristers were there in their silk gowns and the traditional itchy wigs that he so fondly hated. Momentarily the scene unfolding reminded him of the Profumo affair, a political story of intrigue, spies and prostitutes; it all happened before when he first articled in the same building many moons ago.

All rise was heard and like school assembly everyone stood upright. The court clerk bellowed to the court, "The Honorable Judge Austin now presiding." The judge sat down and the court room was alive with mumbled noise as all parties took their seats. The terrorists were about to be sentenced, the lengthy court process was about to come to an end, the judge of all people, being greatly relieved that this matter was finally concluding, having consumed all of his effort over the past year. The judge commenced reading from his notes and detailed the horrific nature of the crimes committed. The acts of violence and murder somberly relayed by the judge in that particular court room voice created a deafening silence in the court. He looked over to the dock, the glass bowl which caged the eleven members of the Black Watch Warriors, there were five white faces and six colored, all but one were men. The very fact that they took on the name of an elite British fighting force annoyed the judge immensely; and although he was to remain impartial, deep down the judge had great disdain for the people in his dock. The jury of twelve listened to all of the charges, and there were many. Each time the foreman of the jury responded with Guilty as charged. Upon completion, the judge had the stage.

Judge Austin referred to the terrorist as a group of cowards, spineless men and women who could only be described as human parasites feeding off the fear that they imposed on their victims. The enormity of the events that unfolded some fifteen months earlier had no prior comparison; the Black Watch Warriors/Al Quiada had paralleled the World Trade Center and Pearl Harbor events in one cowardly act. The court would show no leniency to any of the villains standing in the dock. The sentence, the judge stated would be death by hanging but regrettably that fate was not permitted any more; the judge emphasized the fact that he would welcome reform in this instance, and wished that he had the power to modify the law right then and there. After the Judge had completed reading his notes the same sentence was handed down to all parties in the dock, the sentenced echoed throughout the court and via the televised media, like a tsunami wave the bulk of the British public were now informed. Life in Prison, life meaning until their natural life terminated by natural causes; there would be no chance of parole.

The terrorists/prisoners would be separated, remanded and held prisoner in a variety of high security prisons throughout the UK, they would not be permitted visitors for their term, they would not enjoy the privileges available to other inmates; it was for certain they would definitely not enjoy their stay in her majesties prison, they would in fact welcome death. The ruling took the judge over one hour to deliver and as each minute elapsed the judge was feeling lighter, an overwhelming weight being removed from his burdened shoulders. After the sentencing had been delivered the prisoners were taken from the fish bowl dock, several of them shouting Islamic slurs of profanity. They were escorted to a high security holding center. The judge would retire to his chambers, change out of his robes and make his way to the Savoy where he had previously agreed to meet and share an afternoon tipple with Sir Billy. The overwhelming burden of this matter was now, thankfully over for the judge. He would wait for the crowds to disperse and then enjoy the drive over to the north side of the Thames embankment.

Very few people knew what the Judge would permit after the ruling and what would transpire as the matter was highly classified.

The Judge, knowing Sir Billy so well and unbeknown to him, his views had been taken on board by the diplomat and became an influential factor in the clandestine outcome. From the holding center the prisoners would be chained and cuffed, hooded and taken to the city airport where they would be ferried off by RAF helicopter some fifteen miles South West of Dover where the aircraft carrier USS Eisenhower was steaming westbound, headed for the Caribbean island of Cuba. These men would remain hooded and bound for their entire journey with no comforts as afforded to the crew of the carrier. These human parasites would in due course be landed at Guantanomo Bay.

Guantanamo Bay is the oldest overseas US naval base and the only base in a country with which the US does not maintain diplomatic relations. Guantanamo Bay is a base where the primary objective is to protect the US Navy and Coast Guard ships when operating in the Caribbean, offering support, re-supply and other logistical tasks to aid their operational commitments. Besides being a look out center for drug trafficking and a major center for the Coast Guards continual challenge with respect to illegal immigrants to the USA, the base, post the 911 incident had become the center for detainees apprehended under the homeland security legislation. This jewel of an island in the Caribbean is where the Black Watch Warriors would be interrogated by the US seals. The goal, rarely not achieved by the seals, would be ultimate submission by the London 11, submitting to their captors divulging their secrets to their captors. The London 11 would reveal the secrets necessary to permit the capture of more extremists and permit the growth of inmate numbers in the confines of the camp on the eastern edge of Cuba, their last stop on earth, none would survive the year, and like bugs they would be squished.

A fact that pleased the judge immensely was that the British taxpayer would not pay an iota to the carrying cost of these vermin, with the sole exception of the cost for the awaiting RAF Sea King helicopters to transport this group he likened to a human cancer, from the city airport to the deck of the awaiting aircraft carrier.

Sir William Myers task was to create the allusion that the prisoners were transported and ended up in Brixton, Parkhurst and Dartmoor, all very nice accommodations offered at no cost, to HMP. The Black Mariah's would head off from the court building to various destinations and actually complete their journeys. Only one would make the short journey to the closest airport.

The following days the newspapers would report that there were only minor disturbances in the streets of London and only a hand full of arrests. The whereabouts of all the detainees would be echoed, Brixton, Parkhurst and Dartmoor; but in fact, as per the plan, this group that plagued the UK—the cowards that orchestrated carnage—these radical fanatics, would in fact be enjoying the brig aboard the US aircraft carrier.

Their interrogation, he knew would start upon their arrival, no quarter would be spared, their only cruise would be to the antipodes of the jewel in the Caribbean, in fact, it would be the cruise to hell.

Offshore

Kane had completed almost ten weeks of his orientation to the Offshore when his father sent him the email that his long trial was over and that his father and mother would be taking a short holiday in Andorra, a haven they both loved. Kane had already been back to London just once for two weeks. He had seen his professor and he had talked at length with Elspeth in Aberdeen. He had also visited the two Scandinavians on his return leg of his working tour. He had maintained what can only be described as a healthy, sporty relationship with them.

Working the rig floor as a roughneck was absolutely no challenge to Kane. There appeared to be no magic formulas on how to drill a well. In fact he was shocked at the low skill set truly required. Working shifts of twelve hours he spent much of his off time talking with the Geologists, mud engineers and the Marine Captain. In fact the Marine element offshore was modestly challenging. After reviewing the manuals on drilling a well he voraciously read the marine manuals which included topics on Rig stability, stress and strain forces acting on the vessel, ballast control; he actually enjoyed reading these four inch manuals. Clarity on any issue was remedied with a chat with the Captain or Offshore Installation manager as they were called. He spent many hours investigating the structure inside the eight main columns, and two pontoons which were knitted together by horizontal and vertically diagonal cross members which secured the 26,000 tonne monster. This eight legged rig had the carrying capacity of almost four thousand tonnes. The deck area was larger than a football field. Like an erect penis the derrick stood vertical and capable of pulling 1.35 million pounds, everything was heavy duty. He learnt that almost every operation depended on a combination of power sources ranging from electricity, compressed air or hydraulics; and or quite often it would be made up of a combination of these energy sources. The heart of the drilling platform was the engine room. Noisy and forever running there were four diesel generators which could generate some 12,000 kilowatts of power. The main propulsion units also sourced their power from the main engine room. Beneath the rig and diagonally opposite, hanging like mechanical hemorrhoids were two omni directional 360-degree azimuth thrusters, each capable of producing 4000 horse power. The rig could be turned 360 degrees in her own length. Without tow assistance the rig could be self propelled boasting a speed of six knots, sea state allowing.

The drilling department had the care and custody of the drilling fluids, the mud hoppers, and the barite, bentonite, hematite, cement tanks and various drilling consumables. The Mobile Offshore Drilling Platform was a little town of eighty-five people all of whom were isolated, in the middle of the sea, a seascape that was the same wherever the rig was positioned. All of the crews were there prostituting their lives for a reasonable pay check. Kane knew that this career would be short lived for him, but he would make the most of it for the time being.

In three months he knew he would be in possession of his PhD and that in and of itself should open up many new doors and much more interesting career paths.

Kane explored the rig on a daily basis. He read an abundance of Nuclear Physics in addition to the Rigs design and operational material. He had become particularly friendly with his driller, a Dane by birth yet he chose to live in Dramman, Norway. Kane had easily mastered Norwegian when talking with him, the Danish language was coming albeit somewhat more slowly. George the driller was a tall well built athletic man with muscles bulging in every quarter. He had a passion for archery and after each shift Kane and George would challenge each other with bow and arrow shooting at a makeshift bull's eye at the end of the one hundred-fifty-foot length of the upper box girder. They both became very good with no losses of arrows over the side, throughout their working schedule.

A strong bond was developed between them which was of paramount importance as Kane's life took yet another twist, this time for the worse.

Since Kane's arrival on the rig he had been on George's team which included amongst others Hans Doerksen alias the Dork. For some reason the assistant driller continually harassed the new roughneck, the roughneck with a brain, as Kane had begun to be known. During a tripping (tripping out of pipe) operation, retrieving the drill pipe from the ten thousand foot depth, the hydraulic machine apparatus known as the iron roughneck failed which meant that the crews had to resort to the old method of spinning chain. Like most roughnecks new to the industry this method of pipe handling was awkward and somewhat difficult to master. This was a great source of amusement to Hans. For a full four hours Hans had belittled Kane. Hans foolishly started to slag Kane's parents and more so his mother. Kane warned the giant that he had had enough and to back off, but the Dork continued. He slapped Kane around the head three, four and five times before Kane gave his final warning, a warning that was not heeded. Again the giant slapped Kane around the head knocking off the safety hat; the hat took off down the thirty-foot Vee Door. Hans made his final slap when Kane, like a prize fighter delivered a combination of punches that turned the giant into Mush. The final blow was aimed straight at the nose and landed full on target. Hans went down heavily and failed to return to his feet. His entire body twitched violently until his brain stopped emanating electrical signals, then all was still. Rig operations came to a halt and the rig nurse was called to render first aid. The rig floor was suddenly silent as the nurse inspected her patient. The drilling superintendent too was on the floor lording over the emergency. The nurse upon seeing her victim became pale almost sickly. Hans's nose was no longer on his face but rather punched completely inside the skull. Hans was cold dead, there was nothing she could do. Drilling operations ceased, the drilling superintendent groaned in disbelief and retreated to the rig office where he would make the call to the shore. Within ninety minutes the police were on board accompanied by a host of management, some representing the contractor and others the operator of the rig. Kane was escorted off the rig floor and interrogated in the rig office. The explanation was given and witness statements delivered. It was the statement of George that assisted Kane's case but regardless of the facts Kane was allowed to shower and change prior to be taken ashore under what appeared to be House Arrest.

Kane regrettably had no choice but to call his father in Andorra. Amazingly even in the Pyrenees the cell phone reached his dad. He talked at length explaining what had happened and the judge took on the role of judge and dad. At the end of the call his father reassured him that they would do what was right and for him not to worry, things will work out ok.

In Police Headquarters in Copenhagen, Kane was provided with an unlocked cell. There would be many more hours of questioning, meanwhile the body of Hans the Giant, lay inert with feet hanging over the end of the stainless steel table in the city morgue awaiting autopsy the following morning.

Kane probably had the worse night of his life, and for once could not slip into a four hour sleep. He inadvertently remembered the last reason for no sleep, but it was of no comfort to him. Having killed another human being did not sit too well with him, even though he had not intentionally extinguished his lights; even the Dork had a right to life. Kane would later be told that the skull of the giant was exceptionally strong there being no calcium deficiency as was originally thought. No one before had seen such damage to the skull with one blow delivered by a human fist.

The next morning Kane was visited by Sir Billy carrying a tray of tea and toast. Sir Billy cautiously stated that he had not expected to visit him under these circumstances. Kane was glad to see a familiar family face. Sir Billy explained that his father had called and requested his assistance. Under the circumstances, and given the fact that Sir Billy was not too busy, here he was.

With a degree of diplomatic sensitivity, he stated that his father was on his way and should arrive by early evening.

While chewing on toast and sharing tea with Sir Billy, Kane explained the regretful incident. Sir Billy had already been briefed by the highest of authority but permitted the young man to empty his thoughts; after all, it was important and therapeutic for the young man to speak his soul. Sir Billy knew that everything was going to be fine; it was just a formality that Kane was being held on a limited watch arrangement. Everyone had known what had happened, the statement of George the driller cemented Kane's freedom. Within the hour of Sir Billy's arrival Kane was released, later the death certificate would read death by misadventure. Kane and Sir Billy left the police department holding cells and prepared to exit the station, when the police commissioner approached them. It was self evident that the two elder gentlemen knew each other; they were talking on a first name basis. Sir Billy and the commissioner talked quietly in the Danish mother tongue, Kane was unable to discern what was being said and really did not care, as he was just relieved to be getting out of the building. The commissioner turned to Kane and simply said that he had some pretty impressive players going to bat for him, Kane nodded in agreement and expressed again his regret for any and all inconveniences caused. Sir Billy and Kane bid their farewells to the men and left the building. The North Sea air never felt so refreshing to Kane and he took in a deep luxurious breath. They walked to the Ford Taurus rental and driving sedately the diplomat took Kane to the British Consulate where they would have lunch and await the arrival of the judge.

The British consulate was typically European; the furniture was mainly French Napoleon with many pieces painted with faux gold leafing. Sir Billy walked the premises with full knowledge of every space, this old fox had many stories to tell thought Kane, but he instinctively knew that no one would ever be privileged to hear them. The ceilings appeared to be twenty-five feet high with crown moldings upon crown moldings. Painted white the moldings accented the wedge-wood blue walls. It was a soothing space; perfect for the person trying to put aside in his mind the fact that he had just ended someone's life.

Kane liked the Consular office, and realized that he was famished and needed to eat.

Sir Billy took Kane to the second floor where there was a sofa and two armchairs surrounding a glass coffee table. On the far wall adjacent to two long windows reaching floor to ceiling was a white marble Fireplace lit with the coals glowing red hot. It provided a little warmth to the room and definitely a warm ambiance. At the far side of the room there was a dining room table draped with a fine Italian lace table cloth. The table was set for twelve persons, the silverware and the china flatware provided the elegance which complimented two large vases of both red and white carnations, flowers. Sir Billy telephoned down to the kitchen and ordered the lunch of the day and suggested that the chef provide sufficient food for four persons, although they would be dining together. Before the food arrived Sir Billy talked a little about death and being the instrument thereof. He openly stated that he was responsible for dozens of deaths, being ex-military, as well in his present role with the foreign office, there were occasions when the sacrifice of another human being, became the right thing to do, for the common good. He was very careful with his words and was as abstract as any director of operations could be. Kane simply responded that he was only too well aware of his extraordinary strength but his fuse was lit when the Dork started to slag his parents; he regretted the event but there was nothing one could do to remedy the outcome. What was done was done. Death was final. Kane's mind wandered—remembering the interview process, perhaps an omen, the fourth floor and room 444.

The lunch arrived and it was truly a feast. The chef had prepared a filet mignon wrapped in back bacon. A deep silver dish contained milky mashed potatoes which breathed butter, the top of this creamy mix was peppered with some green condiment, and Kane had no idea what it was. Complimenting the large silver tray of potatoes were three eight-inch diameter silver bowls containing the vegetables—cauliflower topped with cheese, baby carrots and peas. On the side was a turin of rich brown gravy, and an even smaller silver pot filled with mustard. The usual baguette was already sliced and appeared to be freshly baked as it was scrumptiously warm and melted in your mouth, it was delicious. The butter and bread alone could have been a meal, it was simply divine. Sir Billy went to the side wall and pressed a well hidden button. Like magic a complete wet bar rotated out into the room, the bar was as well stocked as any British pub and all of the bottles were full, none of them that he could see had ullage. Reaching for a twenty year old Taylor's port, he returned to the table supporting the bottle and two glasses on what else than another silver tray. Like a well trained waiter he poured the drinks and they made a toast to better times and good food. With the toast made they began their meal. Between the two of them they were able to make a significant dent in the food that was set before them. Both of the large men's appetites were satisfied. The bottle of port vanished quickly and a second bottle was accessed from the bar. The port went well with the variety of cheese on the table. Dessert, or pudding as Sir Billy stated, was deliberately left off the menu as his passion in Denmark was the assorted cheeses. Kane concurred on this point and he willingly engaged in the task at hand to empty bottle number two and to polish off the cheese tray. They managed not only to devour the cheese but the two bunches of grapes which served to decorate the cheese platter. Like two contented lions they stood up from the table and retreated to the casual sitting area where a large sofa and armchair beckoned. Sir Billy took out a six inch Cuban cigar from his pocket and indulged himself. Kane was not offered, but then Sir Billy knew that Kane did not partake in this after dinner nuance. The aroma of the cigar was pleasing to Kane and he felt the stress of the past twenty four hours begin to evaporate, he was truly appreciative of this time with Sir Billy and inwardly thought that he liked the old fart. There was a knock on the door and the chef entered the room with two maid servants who attended to the table. The chef asked Sir Billy whether everything had been satisfactory. Sir Billy responded that it was as usual—exceptional. The chef's question was indeed rhetorical, given the enormity of the food consumed by both of these large men. Kane echoed the statement of Sir Billy, which just added to the chef's pleasure. Within minutes the two young maidservants had cleared the table, and once again it was prepared for twelve. The kitchen staff quietly vacated the room. Sir Billy was feeling the glow of the 40 proof port, whereas Kane was alert and anxious to exercise. With that thought in his mind the moment was interrupted by Sir Billy's cell phone. It was the judge calling, confirming that he would be there in six hours. Sir Billy spoke for a couple of minutes and then passed the cell phone to Kane. Kane was happy to hear his dad's voice and talked mainly of his vacation and continually apologized for the interruption.

The judge and his mum, of course were only too keen to come to the aid of their only son, after all, it was the right thing to do.

Concluding the call Kane requested the permission of Sir Billy to be permitted to go out for a walk. Sir Billy, said by all means go but make sure to be back on time to meet his parents. This would allow Sir Billy to let the alcohol quickly weigh down his eyelids and permit him to indulge in a rare afternoon snooze.

Kane made his way to the reception where he retrieved his coat and left the grandeur of the British consulate building and stretched his legs on the side walk and almost unconsciously made his way to the apartment of the two Scandinavians. After almost forty five minutes of brisk walking he was at the front door. Momentarily he hesitated before ringing the bell, he was a little hesitant to engage in love making, but then his hormones took over, he rang the bell three times. Lola answered the door and with a refreshing smile waived him in. She informed him that Lille was not in but she would be happy to "entertain." Lola was all knowing and took him in her arms. She told him to say nothing and escorted him into their large bedroom. She ever so discretely became Venus, The Goddess of love. She was enraptured by his body and took immense pleasure in his size. The lovemaking that followed consumed them both. Most importantly it consumed Kane's mind and he had soon forgotten his entire burden. They engaged in a marathon of duo-love-making carried on for over three hours, until Lille arrived. To Kane's surprise and delight a third heavenly body joined the foray in the king-sized bed. With glistening bodies, accentuated by certain muscle contours they put their bodies to the test once more. Now it was Lillie's turn to be satisfied by both Kane and Lola. Time flew and before he knew it was time to leave the love nest and make his way back to the Consular Office. The two ladies stayed in the king-sized bed, they kissed their toy boy farewell and returned to their own sexual play.

Kane walked back to the consular office at a blistering pace. He did not want to be late to meet his parents. The walk was exhilarating to him, making his mind keen and as sharp as a tack. He made it with five minutes to spare. Upon his arrival Sir Billy gave him a glance as if he knew exactly what he had been up to, and of course he did, it was his job to know, he knew everything about this to be protégée. Kane's face was still cold and red when the judge and his mother were escorted into the same dining room where he had shared lunch and several hours with Sir Billy. He was pleased to embrace his parents and to have them rally around him so. Sir Billy, like a robot made his way to the hidden wall button to perform the bar magic. Within minutes they were all supping their drinks, in this case Kane was sipping, like his father, Bourbon, his mother tippling an Australian sherry and the diplomat a Bombay gin and tonic. Unbeknown to Kane there was about to be a sequel to the luncheon which now seemed to be such a long time ago. Within half an hour they were sitting at the dining room table, sharing a Canadian red wine from the East banks of the Okanagan Valley. It was quite a robust wine which everyone appeared to enjoy. The luncheon was exceptional yet the dinner was beyond belief. Kane pondered the thought, how the heck do these diplomats maintain a sensible waistline? Of course many did not!

Dinner comprised of a combination of Pheasant, Quail, and Duck, accented with a variety of seven or more vegetables, miniature roast potatoes and a dish of pilaf rice. There were several sauces all of which tasted heavenly. All parties at the table sampled the cuisine with bated interest, and all appetites were well satisfied. On this occasion there was a desert, a type of tiramisu, but it did not share the same name, in fact the desert was an innovation of the chef and had yet to be christened. None the less it was light and delicate to the taste buds and the stomach. The tradition continued with the port another bottle to consume, at least this time there were three thirsts to quench, Kane's mother sticking with her sherry.

Throughout the evening there was no mention of the incident, it was left alone for other more suitable times. The judge and Kane's mother had discussed the matter at length during their drive from Andorra and up through the motorways of central France. They had decided that they would wait and leave the subject matter to their son. At the present time they would celebrate the occasion of being together and privately revel in the fact that the causation of the sad event was well established permitting their son to return with them to England. After the port and the after dinner drink it was time to leave the consular office and check into the hotel. The British Foreign Office had taken care of everything, and in fact the accommodations made available to the judge and his family was an old chateau which was situated some twenty miles away, privacy was required and this is what the judge was getting. Sir Billy was exceptional, he had preempted the fact that the judge would be over the tolerance levels for drinking and driving, hence the temporary loan of the consular chauffeur. The Bentley Continental was brought out front and all three of them easily sunk into the sumptuous rear leather seats, a place only known before by Kane. Handshakes and an embrace from Sir Billy to his mum and they were off. The judge was impressed by the fact that the car was filled with petrol and newly washed and detailed. With less than seven thousand miles on the clock the Bentley still appeared and smelt brand new. The judge enjoyed his brief experience in the back seat but very much preferred to be in the drivers seat. Little conversation took place in the car; it was as if everyone was evaluating the vehicle as if in a test drive. In less than one hour they arrived at the chateaux to be welcomed by a host of support staff. Their stay would last two days. Kane had a room with a real bathroom and shower. The old property was fitted with all of the convenience as compared to the Ritz Carlton. Once again Kane went on line to check emails. He was pleasantly surprised to see emails from the professor, Elspeth and his employer. He read Elspeth's first and was plagued by his conscience, once more knowing that his encounters with the two L's was not really appropriate. Elspeth had heard through the grapevine of a fatality on a North Sea rig in the Danish Sector and was anxious for him to reply. Her concern was genuine and her text far more emotional than emails received in the past. Kane was touched by her sincerity and quickly responded with a more than usual affectionate email.

After Elspeth, he responded to the professor, who had attached several more assignments to the email, all of which had to be completed within the next four weeks, he would then be ready for the finals. Kane acknowledged receipt and proceeded to read the company mail.

The company mail was brief and simply stated that he be available in ten days time to join another rig but this time offshore Aberdeen. Immediately his heart started to race at the thought of seeing Elspeth, he admitted then that he loved her and that this would be the women in his life. The remaining time spent with his parents was a relaxing time for all of them but the time soon past and they had to leave.

Two days later they had left the sanctuary of the chateau and proceeded south to the ferry channel crossing at Calais, they would be in Dover by 2:00 p.m. and in London, home by 4:00 p.m..

The crossing was uneventful although with a beam sea running the 20,000 tonne ferry rolled like a pig, Kane thought that the response of the vessel was indicative of a tender vessel, this simply meant that the righting moments were minimal, a common problem with these vessels. All of this he had read whilst on board the drilling rig. The white cliffs of Dover could be seen within fifteen minutes of sailing Calais, slowly they grew in size until they were about one hundred feet, and immediately next to the Dover docks. Kane

chatted with his father about the cliffs and how this eighteen mile stretch of water defied Hitler the occupation of the little island, an island guarded by a Bulldog, namely Sir Winston.

The drive to London was equally as tame as the crossing, yet a thousand times more comfortable, the Bentley seemed to recognize that they were home and driving on the left side of the highway, there being many signs posted to ensure that one remembers the rule. The Bentley Purred into the city and Mayfair.

Once home Kane retreated to his study which was part of his large bedroom. He immediately dove into his books, he wanted the PhD done and out of the way. Within a short while he would choose a career, quite possibly with input and the help of his dad. During his read his mother came into his room with a pot of tea and slices of Malt loaf bread. She stayed and talked for over one hour, not mentioning the rig incident, but more so a mum offering moral support to her son, always providing positive input into his life. More than once she emphasized that if you could not be positive then remain silent. Kane thought that his parents were so rare, in that they were always so very positive in every thing they did, but then they in turn thought the same of their son, hence the deep respect on both sides. With the tea pot emptied and the malt loaf simply vanishing off the plate, his mother left him to his books, the night was so young for Kane yet for the judge and her; they would be between the Egyptian cotton sheets and asleep very shortly.

Kane rested from his books after the passage of each hour, he had found his niche and knew exactly how he was best suited to read, learn and retain information. Each hour required a fifteen minute break. In this case he again checked his email. Elspeth had responded with an update of her situation.

For the first time she engage a white lie with Kane. With regret she said that she was leaving the rigs and was taking up a shore based assignment in Norway. This was in fact a half truth. Two months prior, when offshore as a rock hound she, with the crew underwent a spot check drug test. She had never taken drugs but upon her return to the shore at the heliport, she was approached by the company nurse who privately advised her that they had performed, as routine, pregnancy tests on all of the female workers. Her test was positive. She was not too surprised as she had been aware that she had missed her cycle not once but twice. She was also cognizant of the fact that her breasts were growing necessitating a larger bra size. As a matter of safety, and to reduce the liability to the company she was not permitted to work offshore, however they would permit a land based appointment for her, but it would be in Bergen Norway. Even though she had taken precautions, she was caught, the father was Kane a fact that she would not divulge to him. Kane felt a huge loss when he realized that she would not be there in Aberdeen when he returned offshore. He answered the email and poured out his heart and confessed that he loved her deeply and that he would want her in his life forever. This was the first admission to her of his love and Elspeth was deeply touched, but she reluctantly reversed the flood tide of emotion, the response was an ebb flow, with tears in her eyes, she addressed his career and that he must get established and that he did not need the weight of a women in his life at this juncture, she never mentioned his unborn child. Kane took this email as a modest rejection; a Dear John email, and for once he felt foolish. With great sadness he returned to his books and adopted a more aggressive learning style. The following days passed quickly, Kane had completed his thesis on nuclear division, the judge having read the paper twice over and marveled to his wife the content; his son was exceptionally gifted.

The professor was in touch with Kane daily by email and once during the week by phone. Kane would be able to complete his studies upon his next return home. Kane already knew that he would complete all assignments within two more weeks, the PhD was a given. Time spent with his parents was immensely enjoyable. The judge completed work each day at three pm and returned home extra early in order to enjoy the London night life. The incident with Hans had been artificially erased, it was obvious that his parents wanted Kane to be fully occupied and enjoy life with laughter. Kane and his mum did just that, they had many walks and opportunities to talk and joke; they really did have a common bond.

Most evenings they ate out and took in the London theatre district. They all enjoyed the Lion King, Phantom of the Opera, Dream Girls and the new production of Cats. The week was splendid but sadly it came to an end. Once again the trip to Heathrow terminal one was repeated and the farewells much the same although his mum shed tears and the hug from his dad was more powerful than before.

Back on the Dash 8 aircraft he was on route to Aberdeen, he had not contacted Elspeth since he spewed out his heart and was, as he perceived, rejected. Elspeth had emailed him back, but she remained somewhat removed from the romance, which in turn caused Kane to withdraw even more. With a heavy heart Kane made his way to the heliport the same day and once again embarked on a new journey to the Mighty Driller 6, which was a Semi Submersible Dynamically Positioned Unit. The trip offshore took ninety minutes, basically straight north of Aberdeen. By evening Kane was in his cabin reading his final chapter on plutonium enrichment, and to his surprise detonation methods of nuclear warheads.

No one knew of the new guys past incident in the Danish sector, but somehow Kane felt that the crews avoided him; nobody at all harassed him even jokingly.

Anyway this would be his last rig as he had made up his mind not to prostitute his life for the offshore environment; the pay was modest at best so it was an easy decision.

This newly built rig was much larger than the last; it had eight columns with eight thrusters which were housed in retractable pods. The unit stayed in position by the use of these thrusters which were linked with computers, GPS and transmitter/receivers/ responders on the sea floor. The engine room comprised of six large EMD engines, all of wnich drank diesel fuel at a phenomenal rate. Each producing five thousand kilowatts of power, sufficient electrical power to support a small Scottish village.

The unit could be self propelled at more than ten knots some thirty percent slower than most conventional oil tankers, but none the less a good speed for such a beast. Kane would enjoy the next few weeks exploring the inner soul of this steel monster, but he would come to miss his archery with George; he made a mental note to call George and have a chat with him; he needed to thank him for his friendship and support.

The phone call to George did take place but he was offshore, transferred to another rig, Kane never did link up with him to express his gratitude.

Black Friday

It had been almost three weeks since Kane had left for the rig and the rough seas off the coast of Scotland. Back in London the judge was presiding over a new multiple murder trial, a killer that was attempting to revive the deeds of Jack the Ripper. Londoners called the new psychopath, "The Butcher of Whitehall." Several prostitutes had been murdered in similar areas of the city and disemboweled in a manner almost identical to the work of the Ripper. In this case however, the killer was caught but like many murders, intrigue and mystery had captured the attention of the British public. The killer was caught in the act of mutilating a young street woman. Even more bizarre in this case was the fact that the killer would cook the heart and liver of his victims and prepare a meal for the person who discovered the body. The killer was a psychopathic police coroner who no doubt had been involved in many of the examinations of the victims prior to his capture. The list of victims had totaled five. The judge did not take any joy in his job when such perversion was involved; but then someone had to do the work of enforcing the law. It was during this trial when the judge decided to take a trip to Paris after the Friday session which would finish at noon. Kane's mother was going to meet the judge at the courthouse and they would immediately take off to Dover, a weekend at the George V Hotel on the Champs Eleysee would be a pleasant and romantic gesture on the part of the judge, after all, he needed to give the love of his life some quality time. Paris was the right city for lovers and this would be his second honeymoon at least that was his plan. The judge met his dream girl in the lobby of the court house, embraced her and then took her to the parkade elevator. They descended underground to the reserved designated car space, where the Bentley Continental stood waiting as if a silver chariot awaiting the gladiators arrival. They were both somewhat playful and excited; Paris not only being the city for lovers but of course home to fine restaurants and theatre. It was going to be a fun weekend. The drive to Dover would take a couple of hours, they would take Tower Bridge to the A2 and then onto the M2 Motorway. Traffic was as expected, the roads were totally congested, speed was down to a snails pace. It took a full thirty minutes to reach the Tower intersection before approaching the Tower Bridge. The judge thought to himself how people could mistake this unique bridge with London Bridge, for some reason tourists always got it wrong.

When traveling at some five miles per hour and at the midpoint on Tower Bridge the Bentley had a black Kawasaki 650 cc motorcycle draw alongside on his right. Motor cycles were always weaving their way through the tight squeeze of traffic. Then suddenly on the judge's left side another one, all three of them crawling along at dead slow speed. Both motorcycle riders were wearing black leathers, black helmets with black visors. The men were faceless. Regretfully, even if he knew what was about to happen, the judge had no where to go. The Bentley and its precious passengers were truly boxed in, ambushed. He saw the riders and their initial moves but it was too late, the execution was in progress. Almost simultaneously the riders reached into the jackets and removed from there body holsters black hand guns equipped with silencers. Four pops were heard by witnesses, two rounds penetrated each side of the Bentley windows, half inch bullets challenged both their skulls, and in the event that the first round was not fatal the second was. The Bentley gently rolled into the rear of the car in front as both riders accelerated off to the south embankment and into obscurity. Paris was not to be, the judge and his dream girl sat in a pool of blood which was freely running onto their respective plush leather seats. They were in the arrival lounge of heaven, a place far better than Paris.

Unknowing drivers started to honk their horns oblivious to what had just occurred; later in the evening the BBC early news would tell all that the Black Watch Warriors had acclaimed a victory and made the statement that they were seeking retribution, revenge and that there was more to come. Sir Billy heard of the incident within minutes of it happening; he immediately discussed the matter with senior foreign office staff and Scotland Yard. The surveillance video tapes were ordered from the Tower Bridge, Thistle Hotel, and the Tower of London, Threadneedle St., Lime ST., ST Mary's Axe, Lloyds St., Tower Hill tube station....and the list went on.

The police would do their forensic sweep and the car would be sent to the foreign office impound. The bodies of Judge Austin and his wife would be sent to the cold cellars of the city morgue.

Within thirty minutes of the event an RAF Sea King was dispatched from Montrose, the destination was to Kane's rig; Sir Billy wanted the young man in his office before the incident hit the North Sea radio waves. The appropriate calls were made to the employer and arrangements confirmed. Kane would be back at Montrose by 5:30 p.m. at which time he would simply change aircraft and fly south to the London City airport by Lear jet. By 6:30 p.m., Kane would be with Sir Billy. By 7:00 p.m., Kane would be a mental wreck, his life irreversibly changed forever.

Kane had just completed his "polishing" of his thesis, all of his assignments had been complete, he was ready for the examination when his tour offshore was complete. He heard the helicopter land but paid no attention to it, although not time for a crew change, it was quite common for helicopters to land carrying essential tools and or simply stopping to refuel. The Offshore Installation Manager accompanied by a very large black special operations agent went to Kane's cabin. Kane opened the door only to sense a problem. The black operative introduced himself as John, and simply stated to Kane that he was urgently required to come with him to London where he would be met by Sir William Myers. Kane asked what the reason was, but John replied with an, "I don't Know," and, of course, he did not. It took only moments for Kane to pack his gear and they were off to the flight deck of the rig. The helicopter had refueled and within minutes of boarding they were off, flying South West to Montrose. John escorted Kane, from the helicopter to the awaiting Lear Jet; they were in London for 6:30 p.m. on the dot. Sir Billy was at the airport to meet the jet; the jet cruised to a remote section of the airport and pulled up alongside the awaiting Austin Princess

Limousine, the wings of the jet actually covering the roof of the vehicle. Kane's gear was placed into the boot of the car; John sat in the front seat while Kane and Sir Billy sat in the rear. The glass partition separating the front seats and the rear was closed and the car rolled off to Downing Street and the Foreign Office.

Downing Street

Sir Billy felt stressed at this new task, he was close to Kane and he never dreamt that he would have to deliver such bad news about his parents, and his dear friends of so many years. Sir Billy chose to delay the news until Kane was in his office, and attempted to engage in small talk for the brief journey to Downing Street. Kane knew that something big was coming down but dismissed the thought of any disaster within his family; he really thought that it was something negative about the Hans affair. They arrived at the gates of Downing Street and the policeman on duty permitted access for the familiar figure, however, only after all occupants, ID was checked as per proper protocol.

Sir Billy took Kane to his office and poured him a crystal tumbler half full of bourbon and complimented the drink with several cubes of ice. Sir Billy had his usual gin and tonic. Sir Billy delivered the news. Kane sat alert and waited for the delivery of what he believed would be a twist in the Hans accidental death conclusion, but it was far worse. Sir Billy forced the words to his lips. "Earlier this afternoon a terrible terrorist act took place. A cowardly act planned and executed by the cell group known as the Black Watch Warriors. I am very sad to relay, Kane that your parents were the target; today, shortly after 3:00 p.m., a couple of terrorists ambushed the judges vehicle and both your parents were shot. I am deeply sorry Kane but they were both fatally wounded."

Kane went white; he placed his drink on the side and cupped his face. His stomach, rolled once, twice and three times. Tears flooded his eyes and he gulped for air as if drowning on his tears. Sir Billy gracefully handed him a handkerchief and sat next to him with one arm draped across Kane's broad shoulders. The room was silent except for Kane's muffled cry. Time passed by so very slowly but eventually Kane gained a degree of composure and asked for the details of the event. Sir Billy accommodated the response leaving out nothing. Kane listened with intensity gulping on his Bourbon, concurrently making his way to the wet bar to accommodate a generous refill. Kane was well aware of the terrorist cell group and he knew that his father was aware of the risks of his job, it was a given; but to execute his mother was vile/repulsive to him. Kane knew at this instant that he would revenge his parents, it was his new calling, and after all as his parents would say that *it is the right thing to do.*

Kane was extremely weak yet eating was out of the question, he was sad, angry, aggressively pissed off, an emotional heap of crap. His muscles were rigid he really wanted to pulverize another human being, preferably of Arab descent. Sir Billy was a blessing; he was his only family contact left, albeit a friend or at least that is what he had thought. Sir Billy on the other hand thought that it was an appropriate time to let him know that he was in fact his god father, although due to the constraints of his position it had been kept a secret. Kane needed this new bond and asked why all the secrecy? Sir Billy simply replied that the dirty work of the government required many unorthodox practices, keeping family and relative's private was paramount to their safety. Sir Billy now expanded on the necessary changes that must take place in order for Kane to be safe and to avoid a further extremist attack on his life. Kane began to appreciate the gravity of his situation and commented on the shit job that the diplomat managed. Sir Billy continued without faltering, he spoke with authority and every instruction was a fact that had to be dealt with exactly as he instructed. Kane listened with interest.

His home would be placed on the open real estate market and it would be sold within one month of the listing, at least the paper trail would endorse the latter. Kane was not to enter into the home except by the rear entrance until the sale had been properly processed. Of course the property would remain Kane's but he would be assigned a new name complete with the appropriate supporting documents dating back to his birth. The furniture would be removed and replaced subsequent to the sale. The charade would be perfect in every detail. Sadly the three support staff at the Mayfair home would be let go, all with reasonable severance packages. New staff would be hired accordingly and screened by Sir Billy's team. This was bizarre yet Kane understood the severity of the situation and obviously appreciated Sir Billy's thoroughness in the matter. The Bentley would be detailed and all of the glass exchanged with bulletproof Pilkington g.r.s rated glass. The tires would also be changed with a special Pirelli tires that catered to high speed driving, but more importantly the tires could not be punctured.

The engine would be tweaked to permit the passage of a few more horses. The registration would be altered to accommodate the new non de plume that was about to be bestowed upon him. Kane would be unable to attend the funeral of his parents, at least in the capacity of Kane; his new name would be assigned the following day. Right now Kane too was about to pass on with his parents. Kane never questioned his god father; everything remained somewhat as a fog although he instinctively knew that this was all too real. Sir Billy poured Kane another handsome refill of Bourbon and likewise indulged in a very large Gin and tonic for himself. Later in the evening Kane would be escorted to the Savoy where he would stay for two nights, then he would be assigned another hotel. This practice would be continued until Sir Billy sanctioned otherwise. Sir Billy stressed that his actual home was out of bounds until the sale had been completed. Sir Billy went on and on without interruption, stopping only for the need to replenish either his or Kane's drink. Finally the old fart stopped and asked whether he had any questions.

Kane did not ask, but made the statement that he would like to see his parents, to which the diplomat replied, "Of course," and made the factual statement, "In the morning. For the time being you will be escorted by John; he is a member of my team. Please don't ask of him too many questions, as he will not oblige you with answers." Kane finished his drink and should have been three sheets to the wind, but to the contrary he was sober and felt eager to kill any terrorists that came his way. He would pray for the opportunity.

Sir Billy picked up the telephone and requested his secretary to beckon John. John was there almost simultaneously and witnessed Kane shaking Sir Billy's hand which was then pulled into Sir Billy's side and a hug followed. "God Bless you, my boy," he said, and they, John and Kane, left the room.

The Savoy was at its regal best, everything was just splendid. John checked in at reception and Kane viewed the grandeur of the lobby. His dad had come here often and was a well known figure. There was no connecting Kane with the judge, he had not been invited into the inner circle of the Club, The Savoy or the Police Commissioners private smoke room, and after all he was only just of legal age to drink. John had arranged for a suite with two bedrooms, two bathrooms and a common living room. The unit was on the fourth floor, another bad omen but Kane pondered the number, only not to give a shit. John was a pleasant guy and upon entering the room offered Kane Bourbon. Kane accepted and they sat next to the artificial fire which glowed red with dancing flames. The flames actually looked quite real, warm air was fanned into the room; it was quite comfortable. Each room had a plasma television with a remote control. It was almost 10:00 p.m. and news time. Kane reached for the control and tuned into the ITN news. For the first time Kane witnessed the story visually, reliving what horror had been told to him some hours before. This time it was worse Kane saw the results of the police effort to secure the surveillance camera footage. The event unfolded in his living room. He could see the Bentley and the two faceless bikers. He could see both of his parent's upper bodies, unsuspecting and no doubt jubilant about their forthcoming romantic escapade in gay Paris. The thought pleased him that they were so much in love; he witnessed the execution and the cowardly retreat of the bikers, spineless people with shit for brains. Tears welled up again and he softly sobbed. John watched the tears and he put two and two together. He asked of Kane, was that your parents? to which Kane nodded. The six foot three black guy gently patted Kane on the back and spoke reverently and said that he was sorry. Kane drained the bourbon and helped himself to another and retreated to his room not saying a word more.

Kane sat in his room, his mind racing; he felt alone, he had lost the most important people in his life, he felt abandoned, an eighteen year old orphan. Feeling sorry for himself he attempted to drown his sorrows but his tolerance to alcohol was too great, even after killing a full bottle of Bourbon he was stone cold sober, he laughed to himself. "As sober as a judge." More tears welling up, his nose running he reached for the Kleenex. Unable to sleep he thought of Elspeth and reached for his laptop. He wrote the longest email that he had ever written to her. He mentioned the last few weeks of his life and the horrific act that he had seen on the evening news, his life seemed to be flushing down the toilet; he had at this very moment no purpose. He completed the email after an hour but failed to press send….he kept it as a draft…perhaps after all he would not send it to her. Finally he placed his laptop aside and lay on the sumptuous bed that only the Savoy could offer. Sleep eventually came and to his surprise he slept until 6:00 a.m. Kane awoke to the aroma of bacon and eggs, black pudding and mushrooms. John was fully dressed and already sat at the breakfast table scoffing down the tea and toast, obviously enjoying the morning grill. Kane still wearing the same clothes as he had the night before paid a short visit to the bathroom, washed his hands and face and unshaven joined John at the table. John commented that he looked just beautiful, evidently meaning the opposite. The food was well received and they both ate their fill. John had arranged for several new shirts for Kane, shorts and socks to be sent up from the men's store which was adjacent to the hotel. Hanging in the closest was a dark blue mohair suit which had arrived the night before, courtesy of Sir Billy….he seemed to know everything and of course he did. The two men were finished with the breakfast within twenty minutes of sitting; Kane was ready for the shower, a shave and clean clothes. The shower was the best tonic for Kane, he stayed consumed by hot water and soap lather for what appeared to John as far too long, but John was giving Kane lots of latitude, anyway, they did not have to be in the Foreign Office until nine am. Kane completed his shower just as John was knocking on the bathroom door to check on his status. Upon opening the door Kane stood there in the full monty; John looked at him and then smiled and said," Holy shit man, wow, do you have a license for that thing?"

Kane turned and flicked his towel at the intruder and shut the door on the black peeping tom. By eight am Kane looked like the Apollo of old. Dressed to the nines they both left the hotel and decided to walk to Downing Street. Women stared in awe at the two of them, one black handsome dude and the Apollo.

Any women that gawked too long would suffer the discomfort of wet underwear for the rest of the day; several had already met with this uncomfortable fate. The walk to the foreign office was the second tonic of the day, Kane and John were engaging in good banter on the way over, and both felt a bond between them growing. John had been with Sir Billy for four years, he had operational experience in the Middle East, Russia, Korea and Africa, but his conversation was limited as to what function he actually performed; but then Kane had a good idea. Kane honored the request of Sir Billy and kept his questions of John limited.

The two strapping cool dudes entered the gates of Downing Street and strolled the short distance to the main entrance. The Prime Minister was already up and about behind the door of number 10 on the sunny side of the street.

John and Kane made their way to the shaded side of Downing Street, the office of Sir Billy, who had been in for two hours already. John stayed outside and was offered tea by the receptionist who appeared to be somewhat uncomfortable; perhaps she too had looked for too long!

Sir Billy welcomed Kane into the room and gestured for him to join him with tea. There was no doubt that the tea in England tasted so much better than anywhere else on earth, Kane delighted in the offer and eventually had three cups.

Sir Billy asked of Kane whether he had thought about his future plans. Kane really had not but he offered up a few reflex thoughts. I wish to complete my PhD, my mother and father would appreciate that, to which the diplomat nodded as if approving. Kane said hat he could complete the program within the month. With respect to a career Kane stated that he would appreciate advice from Sir Billy.

The opening was perfect for Sir Billy and he dove right in. Well my boy you are aware that I hold a unique position within this department of government, it is a function that has many twists and turns and most of the time I deal with the crap of life; i.e. such as the Black Watch fanatics, some racist's people refer to them as sand niggers. Terrorism is a cancer and I am a surgeon, my team of doctors performs miracles every day but the job is distasteful to most normal human beings. Kane interrupted and stated that he would be most interested in becoming a field doctor. Sir Billy smiled but stated that he would prefer Kane to be groomed to one day take over his role, and that being a field operative was not in the cards. Kane emphatically stated that he needed to know the field work if he was to properly one day take over the reign of Sir Billy.

Sir Billy mused a little and then said that field operatives rarely top five years in the business, life being extremely dangerous and short lived. Kane responded that he wanted to feel useful and that he had everything to gain and nothing to lose. Sir Billy then said, let's leave this for another time, shall we say when you are a doctor perhaps you could be considered for surgery?

With the tea pot emptied Sir Billy escorted Kane to the door and schooled him on the three D's, this was the motto of Sir Billy's team, namely, Dignity, Discretion and Decorum. John was waiting outside of the office with the receptionist still squirming in her seat. John would be escorting Kane to the Scotland Yard city morgue. Scotland Yard was only minutes from Downing Street but with the traffic it took some fifteen minutes. Upon arrival the commissioner met the two with a strong handshake and a hug for Kane. They were offered yet another pot of tea prior to viewing Kane's parents.

The tea was good and strong, both men requiring a visit to the washroom before taking the elevator to the coolness of the morgue. Kane's parents lay side by side dressed as if going to a dance. The judge was ghostly pale with half of his cranium reconstructed for the viewing. The professionals that do this sort of reconstruction work are amazing but what a job Kane thought. He viewed his dad and bent over to kiss him farewell, and then whispered in his ear. Then he looked into the face of his mother and then once more tears flowed freely. The judge had taken the bullets full on the right side of his head causing the left side to be splintered with skull fragments/pieces the size of a fist exploding out from his left side. The artist had reconstructed him well, but not so for his mother. Kane now realized that his mother had turned to face the motorcycle rider and took two bullets full in the face. The back of her skull was blown apart and splattered onto the left shoulder of the judge. This beautiful woman with a face of a porcelain doll was now a reconstructed oil painting with age cracks everywhere. His tears flowed readily and literally poured onto the face of this person, a person that was his mum and yet was not. He bent over her to kiss farewell and struggled to find an open area of facial skin. Then he also whispered in her ear, for the second time he said, "I will do what is right and I love you."

John witnessed everything and found strength in this young man, he too knew what it was like to lose his parents, John had witnessed his parents being butchered in Zambia by militants. John as a boy had hidden under the only bed in the house and stayed there terrified for two full days soaking in the blood of his parents. The militants had mutilated his mother, both breasts had been severed; his fathers' eyes had been gouged out and his penis cut off and placed in his mouth. No one should ever see such an event and for John he saw it every day in his mind; one day he may share this with Kane.

When done, Kane needed air and retreated to the courtyard; John kept by his side and remained silent. Kane soaked up the sunshine and regenerated his soul with deep gulps of air, and with the satisfaction in his mind that he would do his part, right or wrong he would have his revenge. Kane suggested that he and John return to the hotel and get out of the suits. John would be his partner for the next thirty days whether he liked the fact or not.

The hotel was as usual decadent and full of suits and women in fine clothing. Kane and John went to their room only to find that the room had been ram shacked. John suddenly became a stalker of men. From beneath his suit jacket he retrieved his weapon, Kane had no idea of what type but he knew it was not a toy. Room by room the black predator sought his prey. Kane followed behind him. The place was a mess, papers everywhere and clothes strewn over the floor. The beds were turned over, sheets thrown aside, Kane wondered what the heck they were they looking for but the answer was simple it was him, and anything to do with him. Suddenly Kane caught a glimpse in the mirror of a man about to club him with a machete from behind. Kane eager for the confrontation spun around as if a male ballet dancer and blocked the blow with his left forearm, while concurrently grabbing the assailants arm placing him off balance, pulling him down Kane struck his right fist with full force into the temple of the man, a man clearly of Arab descent. John took off having seen a second assailant quickly run from the living room, through the door to the hotel hallway. John was gone only fifteen minutes before he knocked on the hotel room door. Kane peered through the peephole and let him in.

John approached the assailant and checked for a pulse. There was none, Kane had eliminated another piece of the cancer cell. John handed over the pistol to Kane and advised him that he has work to do. John disappeared and returned within the hour accompanied by four men in white coveralls and a wheeled basket full of laundry. The body was scooped up in minutes and wheeled off to an awaiting laundry van.

Two other men made ready the room so that it was as if nothing untoward had happened. Kane looked at John and said that he really did do Sir Billy's laundry after all. John showed no emotion and said that they had to move on. Kane showed no remorse and suddenly realized that the killing machine on the rugby field had transgressed to everyday life. He had killed two people within the same year. They left the room having packed their clothing, and whistled down a Hackney taxi.

Kane was furious in that the assailants had attempted to access his computer; he wondered whether they had any success. He asked of John of the implications given that one of the men had got away. John responded with a wicked grin and said who got away? Kane initially somewhat confused, suddenly got the message; the laundry was soiled with two items of shit. Without the need for clarification Kane instinctively knew that the two deaths would be covered up by the authorities after all this is what the Alpha Omega team did.

Kane's parents' funeral took place without Kane being present. The knowledge that the Black Watch Warriors knew that Kane was still alive meant that they had unfinished business. The entire event was caught on camera and every attendee would be profiled.

For the next month Kane and John would take safe haven in the outskirts of Cambridge. John initiated the follow up plan. Even Sir Billy would not know where they were staying, this was self preservation, and John was well aware that he was coming up for his five year term. Kane would challenge the PhD from the private residence only known to Kane and John. For the examination week the professor would personally invidulate and stay at the abode. Given the attempt on Kane's life the professor was accommodating. Leaving the grounds of the home was not permitted, for Kane it was like being offshore, but instead of being isolated by the sea he was now surrounded by green country side. They could see at least two fields of open pasture in all directions. Kane looked often to the skies imagining low flying Arab terrorists, hang gliding in with knives glistening, securely clamped between their teeth.

The month went by without any reoccurrence of the Savoy incident.

The plan of Sir Billy was finely executed, Kane's home had For Sale signs posted and after three weeks the Sold sign was adhered to the sign. Movers came and furniture in its entirety was removed. Sir Billy even had painters go into the home; the entire house was freshly painted. No colors were changed but the fresh paint and the white trim looked impressive. The hard wood floors that the judge had imported from Canada some fifteen years earlier were reconditioned and the result was magnificent. Nothing had been overlooked, even the window coverings had been sent out and dry cleaned. As an additional safety feature the home was fitted with the most modern of security devices. Cameras linked the home with the foreign office, both hard wired and by HF (high frequency) radio waves. Microphone bugging devices were everywhere.

Every room was covered including the bedrooms, there would be no privacy afforded.

The Bentley was repaired and the modifications made, the main difference in appearance was that the bodywork now sported a two tone color silver, and once again Sir Billy thought that it was an improvement and definitely changed the look from the original. Kane he thought would appreciate the auto and home makeover. Kane, still accompanied by John, returned to the house a day after the furniture had been returned under the guise of a different moving company. Sporting a well groomed beard he accessed the house from the rear. Inside the home he found Sir Billy drinking a freshly poured gin and tonic. The old fart had taken the initiative to stock the judge's bar, it apparently desperately needed it. The house still had the aroma of paint fumes, the home looked truly amazing. Kane approached Sir Billy and stretched out his hand, while John excused himself to wander the hallways of the Mayfair abode, and to meet the two newly appointed housekeeping staff.

Sir Billy kicked off the conversation. "You have been working hard my boy, and you will be pleased to know that you are now officially a doctor."

Kane knew that the results would be good and he also knew that the old fart had pressed the system for a fast review of the examination papers. "Your parents and particularly your father would be well pleased with the outcome." Kane poured himself Bourbon on the rocks and without hesitation requested a position within the surgical team, headed by Sir Billy.

Sir Billy stated that the past few months had basically cemented his place; however there was much training for him to do. Sir Billy expanded, he would be required to undergo six months advanced Marine training on the south coast of Devon, and then he would enjoy the riggers of flight training with the RAF, but on the north coast. From there he would go to Wiltshire to the biological warfare facility near Bath, and then onto Guantanomo Bay where he would undergo interrogation, weapons and a variety of explosive manufacturing training with the US Seals. Only then would he be ready to become a field operative an elite member of the Alpha Omega team. Kane asked about remuneration to which the diplomat smiled. Sir Billy replied, this is not a job Kane; do not forget that, you are no one to us, we do not know you what so ever, however your performance will be compensated for and handsomely. You will be given the task to provide five alias identities which will also correspond with five bank accounts; you will have all of the supporting documents for each identity. You will learn the files on each character and then you will destroy the files by burning them, is that understood? Each bank account will contain one million pounds and will be topped up on an as needed basis. Your true identity will be erased for a long period of time, and you will adopt the name of Michael Robinson residing at this address. All of your estate has been transferred to this domain, Kane are you aware of the estate? Kane had no clue as to what he had inherited and expressed the same to Sir Billy.

The estate is substantial, but in this case, as Michael Robinson we shall establish that this fortune was made in the internet gaming business. The Austin estate is valued at over one hundred and thirty million pounds. In your fathers study, in the safe you will find the details, but of course all reference to the judge and the shipping interest has been substituted with Mr. Robinson and his gaming interest. The small holding near Salisbury has been sold at a price well in excess of the market value, the property having been purchased by the crown. We shall appoint administration people to oversee the investments, and they will not lose value and will not earn less than 12.5% interest per annum

Kane had no issue with the management of his affairs, as he knew the only road to seek satisfactory restitution for his parents execution laid within the hands of Sir Billy. Money, or rather the quantum was not a surprise to him, but he was somewhat surprised as to see that so much had already been accomplished by the head surgeon.

Sir Billy broke stride and said, "Let's see the house; you will note that I have incorporated a few changes."

Kane was told everything, and he liked the changes or rather the makeover. When in the oversized garage he looked in awe at the Toy, it was indeed a great improvement. The registration too was intriguing as it was fitted with a vanity plate which read Prrrrr1. Kane appreciated the meaning as the Bentley truly did Purr along.

Sir Billy was always impressed by the skill set that Kane offered. We shall go over the nuances of the vehicles later but you will find that the manufactures specs have been significantly been altered. On the side of the garage was a Yellow Duccati, titanium-framed motor cycle. Kane was stirred by the race machine and observed the vanity plate which read FLDEM, interpreted meaning Fold Them; very original he mused.

Sir Billy encouraged the use of the motor cycle in preference to the Bentley; the reason did not have to be explained.

John called the house lookers into the dining room where two large Pizzas had just been delivered; tea was in the process of being made. As they ate their lunch Sir Billy received a call from the MOD (Ministry of Defence), it was confirmed that Kane would leave for Devon in four days time. Kane would need to hussle.

Sir Billy had one slice of Pizza and requested Kane to email him on one of his private addresses which he gave Kane. Kane had already been advised to ensure a test message first in order to provide a confirmed secure second transmission. His first task was to provide five names and five numbers suitable for banking access. After the pizza was finished and the tea drained Kane went to his fathers study to give the matter some thought. He adored the atmosphere within the room, he felt the presence of his father and suddenly remorse took over, he once again felt lost without his parents; he moaned softly to himself, "Jesus I miss them so." He forced himself to think, eventually he conjured up the prerequisite names and numbers, emailed Sir Billy a test message and then within minutes of receipt of the acknowledgement back, he emailed the text.

Ian Oscar Manley (Isle of Man account) Lloyds Bank, Douglas, logarithm one to five decimal places.

Bernard Switzer (Berne Switzerland) Swiss Bank, Berne logarithm two to five decimal places.

Newman York (New York New York) Chase Bank, New York logarithm three to five decimal places. Andrew Weinberg (Hamburg Germany) Deutzch Bank, Hamburg, logarithm four to five decimal places. Harold Kim (Hong Kong) H.S.B.C. bank, logarithm five to five decimal places.

The email went to Sir Billy who was intrigued at the simplicity yet the security of the accounts and locations, few people even thought of logarithms any more, Sir Billy thought that it would be interesting to see how many more names and bank accounts would be necessary during the reign of this newly recruited surgeon.

In short order the accounts would be set up and deposits made, signature cards would be requested from Kane and photographs taken for the various yet to be printed passports, four days was tight but his department could meet the deadline. Kane's first identity to be used other than Michael Robinson would be that of Ian Oscar Manley. Photographs were taken later that evening by a Foreign office photographer, the process was well underway.

For the next few days Kane and John went on daily trips out of the city driving the Bentley. Kane had not been allowed to drive the vehicle in the past so he found the experience new and simply a pleasure. The sleek automobile purred like a cat. They went hell for leather down the motorway to Plymouth, receiving two speeding tickets in the process. They had a late lunch on Plymouth Hoe at the New Meridian Hotel and booted it back to London. John drove back and covered the two hundred miles in just less than four hours. The Bentley was a charm, powerful, graceful, with horses to spare. Pulling into the rear garage was like stabling a race horse after a Newbury/Ascot race meeting. The few days they had shared together was enjoyed by both. John, having opened up, exchanged certain personal issues with Kane and visa versa.

When driving to see Cardiff Castle in South Wales, and Tintern Abbey in the Wye Valley, John had told the story of his parents' death and like Kane his eyes had swelled up causing a flood of tears to run down his cheeks. Kane fully understood and listened with interest and compassion, knowing only too well that John had harbored all of these emotions far too long. The last trip was to the Mersey and Liverpool. By the time the day trips were over they had become exceedingly good friends, each sharing a degree of admiration of each other. The Toy took it all in her stride and was well and truly tested. Speeding tickets totaled six before the race horse was stabled for a year respite. Sir Billy would handle the citations.

Prior to his four hours of sleep Michael Robinson wrote yet another email to Elspeth, he described a piece of literature, a story of two lovers who just could not be together at the time; it was frustrating but necessary. Michael found a depth of love that he just had to keep bottled and of course he never did press the send key.

The next morning Kane/Michael Robinson left instructions with the newly hired housekeeping staff and made his way to his room. The carryall was already on the newly made bed.

Devon

Kane packed his belongings and together with John exited the rear door. Within a short distance they had hailed a taxi and headed towards Lancaster Gate. The taxi weaved through the London traffic skillfully and ahead of time entered the south side of Paddington Station. After a solid handshake with John, Kane made his way to the platform. He would not see or hear of John for a long time, but now it was for him yet another new chapter in life. Kane boarded the awaiting train, made himself comfortable and began reading Matters of Force by Sir Isaac Newton. The train was headed south west heading for Plymouth where he would disembark and check into 42 Commando Unit for phase one of his training.

The train ride was slow, and no where near as fast as the journey accomplished in the Toy. He looked out of the train window when passing Newbury race track and his memory took him back to the many horse rides he had shared with his father, and the several horse track meetings close to this location. The smaller stations passed by, they stopped at Taunton and Exeter and then finally Plymouth.

Upon arrival at the station Ian Manley was greeted by two Military Police in white helmets. They zeroed in on Ian and asked for Passport identification. Ian obliged and once screened they were off in a military Hummer truck to the base camp. Training would start the following morning with a 5:00 a.m. start, just fine by Ian. The journey to the base was a good hour's drive, not a word was spoken on route, but when the silence was broken at the gate, Ian was referred to as "Sir." The vehicle was stopped at the gate of the camp by three heavily armed guards, all three were taller than six feet and with full gear they looked to be quite formidable. Ian was requested to get out of the Hummer and proceed into the main gate office. There he was almost stripped searched prior to the guards giving him the all clear for access. From the main gate the trainee was escorted by two more Marines to the commanding officers administration office. Ian was greeted cordially by the colonel, he too was a giant of a man; Ian's first impression was that he at least shared the height requirement if there was one. Ian would be referred to as Mr. Manley when on base, no one would inquire of the purpose of his training, and the people who were involved directly with the training had been informed that the government had hired a consultancy firm to evaluate the training standards at the camp, plain and simple. The C/O was a gentleman who politely offered the civilian a cup of tea prior to addressing the six month schedule. The discussion was to the point, the next day it would all happen.

Training

As expected the training kicked off at a relentless pace. Each morning would commence with a five mile run prior to breakfast. Martial arts training and killing techniques would follow. By eleven am each day they would embark on explosive devices, IED's arming and disarming, the latter would include military warheads including nuclear. The afternoon would comprise of coding and decoding techniques, mid afternoon was scheduled for weapons, including sticks, bow and arrow, knives, guns, swords axe etc, the list was exhaustive. The evening would close with another five mile run; all in all he would run excess of sixty-five miles per week. Each evening after supper the training continued. Interrogation and torture techniques, the latter would include painful torturing of Ian hence the need for rest after each evenings sadistic grilling. Rarely would Ian go to bed without a new bruise or cut being added, contributing to the daily pain. Weekends were slated for military maneuvers on the moors; they would be vigorous and grueling and always varied in scope. The Colonel told him flatly that there would be no friendships formed on the base, and dialogue at night between him and other trainees would be minimal, Ian could see early on that the colonel was right. He had stated that there would be ten trainees and most likely all would fail the grade, including Ian Manley, only six months would tell the story.

The running was a breeze and Ian enjoyed every mile his pace quickening each week, by the end of the six months he could not only run the four minute mile, but the eight minute two mile run also. The martial arts were not new to him and in fact the instructor was duly impressed by the trainee's abilities. During one morning session the instructor had foolishly insisted that Ian should not hold back his blows, whether feet or hands, full body contact was the instruction. Ian was reluctant to do so but after being the recipient of several kicks and punches he felt that he had no choice but to teach the instructor a lesson. Having been a punch bag for the instructor long enough, Ian blocked a flurry of moves by his opponent, one of which was a resounding kick to the tibia which resulted in a complete break. The instructor folded to the mat in agony and amazement; fortunately Ian did not follow through with the fatal skull blow. The instructor was removed to the base infirmary and the assistant instructor took over the class. Nothing was uttered, the floor mat exercises continued but not with full body contact. Full body contact would follow in due course with both instructor and trainee wearing the appropriate safety equipment. The previous instructor had broken protocol and would be reprimanded later.

It was less than a month when the colonel knew that this trainee was exceptional in every discipline. He rated A+ in everything and in fact often taught the teachers new tactics/disciplines.

Ian excelled in the archery, the fact that he loved the sport made the difference. In this case however the arrows were made of lightweight graphite shafts with laser beam accuracy afforded by the specially designed arrow head. The arrow head self guided to a target, once the distance and target confirmed by the lighted infra red beam and the velocity tension electronically calculated within the frame of the bow. The bow, up to one hundred fifty meters distance was silent and deadly accurate; within the body of the arrow shaft the designers had inserted miniature gyroscopes which could move the tail feathers upwards of one degree. Although the angular change was modest the effect meant that the chosen target once locked could in fact vary within a one meter radius and the arrow would successfully achieve its deadly mark. The cost of each arrow was estimated at four thousand pounds, however cost was not a factor, Ian would use this weapon in the future extensively and with great affection, he privately thanked George the driller for his shared passion. Weapon training was thorough and enjoyable for Ian but the greatest skill was his ability in the art of killing with his hands. The instructors had confirmed Ian's unusual strength, at least to a degree. Ian could bench press five hundred pounds and keep up a blistering pace of ups and downs. He could lift weights in a similar fashion with five hundred fifty pounds, these weights were of Olympian rating but Ian never challenged a weight that was purely a test, he was somewhat embarrassed.

In the "kill art" as the instructor called it, Ian could snap the neck of a human being as easy as snapping the neck of a chicken. Once again, when in the field he would come to like the silent kill, at least he would have to make contact with his prey rather than on a motor cycle equipped with pistol and silencer.

Weapons' training was exhilarating and Kane looked forward to each session. Kane took a liking to the pistol "Para Carry." It's a 45 ACP caliber semi-automatic pistol with a six-round magazine and with one in the chamber it provided seven rounds total. It was small enough to be concealed easily, good sights and trigger pull, very well made (made in Canada) and was a very popular weapon in the US/ CIA. Kane was taught well and was able to accurately fire six rounds using the "double tap", that is too quick but aimed shots with good control in two seconds. A reload would be about one and a half seconds and then the gun would be back in action. He liked the knockdown power of the 45 ACP as opposed to any of the lighter 9 millimeters or 40 SandW.

His choice in rifle for long range would be the Remington 700 bolt action in 308 Winchester with a 12 power scope mounted. This would be good for a kill at five hundred metres. For close in automatic, Kane preferred a Colt M4 which was the new type M-16. It had a twenty- or thirty-round magazine and fully automatic with semi automatic selector. The cartridge was a 5.56 millimeter NATO (civilian is 223 Remington). This would shoot a relatively small bullet at high speed. The U.S. and Canadian military liked to use this carbine. Kane would later learn that it was perfect in a confined space and for killing shots upwards of seventy-five metres; however, the weapon had its limitations if body armor was worn. Appealingly, this unit came as a small package with collapsible butt stock and an eleven-inch barrel with an Eotech holographic sight (similar to a fighter pilot's "heads up display" HUD).The sight being just a small orange dot enabling the operator to keep both eyes open, handy to have Kane thought in a close up gunfight.

Kane's love of weapons expanded when introduced to the well renowned shotgun model Bennelli Super 90 in 12-gauge. It had an extended magazine that would hold seven rounds. With a good shooter, this was perfect for those indoor targets. Using 00 (Double Ought) buckshot (9.33 caliber lead balls per shot shell) and a one ounce slug, which was good to seventy-five metres with good knockdown power.

The instructor commenting on the intimidation factor of the weapon, the sight of a shotgun often placed opponents somewhat off guard.

Life on the base was grueling, Ian even managed to sleep for five hours each night, and there was no need to read to induce sleep, all that he needed to control was his tolerance for pain…new and old. Ian listened to the radio to keep up with the world news. The Middle East was front and center every time. Iran continued with their threatening stance, to eradicate the Jews along with Hamas and Hezbollah.

The so called land of Israel was doomed. Iraq was a nightmare, with daily suicide bombers attacking the UN forces. Alfata was continuing to commit daily attacks on Israel. Al Qaeda remained very much alive in Afghanistan and Pakistan, bombings and killings occurring daily.

North Korea defied the western nations with their belligerent attitude to build nuclear warheads. Tension between North and South Korea again was heightened. In short nothing changed from the day before.

All of the North African countries were pushing hard for nuclear power, and Brazil was aggressively building three new power plants. Ian pondered the situation and felt assured that his thesis on deepening nuclear division was happening before his very eyes, but at an accelerated rate.

Training with the Marines came to an end after five months were completed; Ian had passed the grade while the other nine were dismal failures, at least to the five month mark. The early departure for Ian was due to the RAF squadron commander at Newquay requesting the availability of the new *special* trainee at an earlier start date due to a planned visit to Goose Bay in Labrador Canada for certain low level flight training.

No farewells were necessary, Ian had no true friends at the Marine base, everyone was guarded by the trainee who excelled in everything, they remained uncertain as to who he was and what was his true reason for him being there. Ian left the Marine base camp and traveled by Military Police hummer to the RAF training facility at Newquay on the north coast of Devon. Within one hour of his departure Sir Billy would have a written report on Ian's progress and of course it would be exceptional. Ian arrived at the RAF training facility after a slow two hour drive. The security was similar to the previous arrival at the Marine base five months earlier and like before he was welcomed by the squadron leader with the usual pot of tea. The squadron leader was a short man; he was balding and wore glasses that seemed to cover thirty percent of his face. He talked freely and informed him that he had flown in Afghanistan, Serbia, and before that the Falklands. Each time he addressed the arena of operations he pointed to his chest which sported a colored ribbon. The medal ribbons meant nothing to Ian other than they enhanced the look of the blue tunic uniform.

Ian was told that he would spend the first month learning to fly a light aircraft. The fourth week would cater to Helicopter flight training. The second month would be twin engine and jet engine craft. The third month would entail parachute jumping and mechanics. His fourth month would take him to Labrador in Canada, and the fifth and sixth month would be training offshore on a carrier. The meeting took the time taken to drain two pots of tea and then Ian was escorted to his private quarters. There were no other trainees with him, he was flying solo as it were…the training would be intense as it would be invigorating; it would start at 5:00 a.m. the following morning with a three mile run.

The run was three miles solely due to the fact hat the perimeter of the base was exactly three miles. It was basically a flat run and it would have been a breeze except for the fifty-pound knapsack that was part of the drill. Ian ran the lap faster than any other trainee had ever done before; the record would be constantly broken by him as the weeks went by. The other training that took place was magnificent and pure fun to Ian. He had found the activity that frightened him, thrilled him and consumed him. He loved flying, man controlling machine, a machine with enormous power, linked with massive killing power. Within the first two months Ian had control of the various aircrafts and not the other way around. He was intimate with the flying machines and handled them as if they were an extension of him. There was no doubt that he was in tune with the Wright brothers dream.

Similar to the off shore semi submersibles he read the manuals of each craft and searched the internet for deeper knowledge. He enjoyed the training so much that flying excelled over his love for nuclear physics. Ian even thrived on the parachute training and looked forward to every jump. The training consumed him and after what seemed to be at an amazing pace, before long he was off on his way to

St. Johns Newfoundland Canada by commercial jet. From there he would fly to Goose Bay; on the rocky shores of Labrador he would enjoy the thrill of low level flying, at almost Mach-1 and over the sea at almost Mach-2. Ian was in his element and it showed.

The Rock

Ian Manley flew by RAF SAR aircraft to Shannon Ireland; from there he boarded a regular 767 Boeing jet passenger aircraft bound for the Rock, the name adequately describing the landscape of Newfoundland, and in particular St Johns. Within twelve hours of leaving Devon he had landed at St Johns airport and transferred to the flight destined for Goose Bay Labrador. If Newfoundland was called the Rock then Labrador was a mere extension, the terrain supporting growth to boreal forest and rich green grass.

Upon arrival, he was once again met by Military Police and escorted to the remote air base location which was used by the British and US Air force, notwithstanding the Canadian Services.

Canadian security had once been described by a Canadian senator, as the soft underbelly of the USA; however, the security clearing practice adopted at the gate was exceptionally tight, Ian was taken into the change room and asked to strip. Everything was on camera, there was no place to hide and nothing to conceal. Ian was then given military garb which included long johns, tee shirt, blue coveralls, and a down filled parka which was quite necessary for the region. Escorted to the C/O office where he was offered coffee instead of the usual mug of tea. The C/O was a very young man having recently been sent from San Diego where he had been rated as Top Gun for three years in a row. There was little formality and the C/O delved immediately into the flight record of this new trainee asking questions that he really already new the answers to.

Ian was humble and frank and it came across that he had a passion for aviation. The young C/O immediately liked the new arrival and stated that he would start the same day with a familiarity flight in the F-18, in fact within the hour he would be back in the skies, but this time with the best of the best. After one cup of coffee they took off to the dog pound, the term used for the preparation flight room.

Ian was suited up once more but in the appropriate flight suit. The suit was so pressured his legs were almost unable to bend; with assistance from another serviceman he got rigged up and escorted to the awaiting F-18. The C/O was doing the honors and would put Ian's body through a few G's before landing and going to supper. Ian was ready to eat but was glad that he had not snacked on anything since the meal on the Trans Atlantic flight several hours before. He sat comfortable behind the C/O who piloted the aircraft.

Taxi-ing to the runway Ian braced himself for the upcoming event. The C/O did not hold back, he wondered whether the Brit could take the punishment that this powerful beast could put out.

Within seconds they were climbing at almost eighty degrees and pulling many G's, sufficient to cause a blackout or incontinence to the uninitiated. Ian prevailed, his shorts clean and his mind clear, although he some how knew that his eyes were bulging almost popping out of his sockets.

The pilot spoke to his passenger prior to performing numerous maneuvers which would promote puking to most, but again Ian's constitution held. After fifteen minutes or so he was in his element and enjoying the powerful machine immensely.

After thirty minutes the C/O gave him the controls and shock followed. To the pilots surprise the Brit started to repeat the maneuvers that he had just exposed him to, and the humble Brit excelled. The young C/O knew at that juncture that he had met a natural. After forty-five minutes of pure exhilaration and fun Ian's control was transferred to the front seat, the C/O would take them back for supper.

They landed safely and made their way to the parking pad. With engines off and chocks in place they both exited the aircraft. Once on terra firma the C/O cracked a smile and said "You enjoyed that didn't you, not bad for a Brit"; and rather like Douglas Bader he coined the phrase, "Jolly good show, ole boy." That would be the only compliment afford by the C/O.

Supper was a welcomed feast of lobster and steak with baked potatoes and cabbage. Ian devoured the meal and joined the remaining crews in the officer's mess where he shared a few jars with the others. It was the culmination of a very pleasant day, the next morning would start with breakfast at 5:30 a.m. and for a change, there was no running but rather straight to the class room.

For the next month the mornings were much the same, but the afternoons involved flying the F-18 at low levels, very low levels but Ian lapped it all up, within a week he was flying solo and was able to clock up more flight time than any of the others, an envied situation but in Ian's case it was the British tax payer footing the bill, the training instruction required forty percent more flying than the normal schedule.

From the birds eye view at eight hundred feet altitude, he could clearly see the fresh tracks of the Caribou.

The Labrador Caribou population had already started their annual migration to the high arctic, seeking and sensing the richness that the tundra provided on the Alaska and Yukon slopes. It was as if they too had had enough of this miserable climate, the sun being rarely visible, hidden behind the clouds. Ian was tempted to follow the track but then he had his flight instructions, which did not allow any deviations whatsoever; he was however still tempted to breech the rules, but he refrained from doing so.

On the third week of training the weather changed from cold to very cold, fresh snow covered the terrain. Apparently the climate could change every ten minutes or so, but when it was good, it was very good. It was on the base camp that Ian learned to cross country ski. He was already a good down hill skier but there were no ski slopes close to the base. Teaming up with two other pilots they would do, snow permitting, a ten mile ski run each evening. Cross country skiing was more of a slog than it was fun but the exercise was well worthwhile and kept the muscle tone in tune. Life was good but often during the peace of the skiing Ian would find himself thinking of his parents and their senseless killings. His recall of the Tower Bridge videos was only too real, the pictures in his mind were perfectly clear, they would never be erased. As a result during his daily slog, his focus too would be sharpened and his resolve deepened, he would make his life's purpose to assist in the eradication of terrorism; killing these radicals would become a passion; he wondered if the world would in fact ever be rid these fanatics?

The world was rapidly changing on many fronts. With Sadam Hussein's execution, the Middle East became a cauldron for all of the Arab nations to test the will and resolve of the west. Instead of withdrawing troops from the desert soil of Iraq, thousands more were dispatched from many UN countries, the USA of course having committed the bulk, with the UK a close second. Canada remained front and center focused on Afghanistan, fighting in the southern area of Khandahar. Even though the casualty rate was high in this theatre of operations the Canadian public had accepted their role, albeit there were the odd do-gooders and minorities that played the political football and objected to everything that made good sense. On another front the matter of global warming was becoming a real concern especially after the forecast that the Antarctica melt combined with the loss of ice from the land mass of Greenland was forecasted to raise the global sea level by some thirty to forty feet. Current melt rates were exceeding predictions. Former Vice President, Al Gore had made his life's work dedicated to enlightening the world on the need to save the earth. Ian had just recently watched his video presentation and applauded the work, yet questioned the accuracy of the science. Like many people Ian wondered when the politicians would really take the matter seriously. Insurance companies were already very sensitive to the issue and had already taken measures to reduce their exposure, especially after Hurricane Andrew and the more recent Hurricane Katrina which destroyed, allegedly two hundred billion dollars in property in the states of Louisiana and Mississippi. The next Hurricane Season was not too far off, the scientist being already alarmed at the increase in annual water temperatures; only time would tell, and after all it was not a long wait.

The wait for Ian to complete his training was rapidly diminishing. Before the month was completed he would be on his way to Miami and offshore to a NATO joint naval exercise. The USA and British forces were playing sea trials (war games) with their joint air top guns. Ian would soon be flying with the best of the best and for a change, he would be truly challenged.

Finally the last training day in Goose Bay came to an end, and on a rare sunny day, Ian was once again flown to the rock, but this time it was to a place called Gander, where the second largest airstrip on the baron terrain of Newfoundland served civil as well as military aircraft. From Gander he would fly by military service aircraft to Miami international airport. The journey would take almost five hours. Ian would enjoy the change in pace and absorbed himself in reading a paper on quantum mechanics, written by Peter Hawkins one of the most eminent scientists of the prior century.

The Carrier

Arriving in Florida Ian was met with a warm pleasant air mass under a bright blue cloudless sky, the transition was simply amazing. In the west quadrant of the sky the sun appeared naked with no clouds to clothe its yellow body, which thankfully, continuously radiated its warmth. Donning his sun glasses Ian was escorted to the awaiting twin rotor helicopter which would transport him to the awaiting offshore Aircraft Carrier, the British flagship HMS Sir Winston Churchill. The flight offshore would take a full ninety minutes. The trip was boring and noisy, helicopters not being the most comfortable and reliable means of flight travel. Upon approach Ian could see the silhouette of three carriers slowly getting larger until finally the British flagged carrier absorbed the miniature flying machine. The helicopter landed on the flight deck and was directed by the flight crew to edge over to the parking lot. Ian and the crew waited for the rotors to stop prior to exiting the craft. From the flight deck Ian was escorted by the deck midshipman to the Vice Admirals quarters. Once again tea would be the order of the day; in fact tea was awaiting Ian's arrival. Even the navy thrives on the Eastern delights of the tea trade, he mused. The Vice Admiral welcomed Ian with a solid and somewhat forceful hand shake and a "Welcome Aboard." The Vice Admiral was a large man with a pot belly, a bushy white beard and a crop of silver hair. Ian thought that this character, with a little extra padding around the waist, could easily be a Santa Clause. They drank tea and spoke on world events and in particular the growing concern with respect to the proliferation of nations requesting and or directly planning to engage on nuclear means to provide energy and in certain cases like the Middle East, desalinated water. Ian's thesis was coming alive with each television newscast on CNN, FOX, CBC, BBC, ITN, etcetera. The world's most significant concern remained North Korea and Iran. It was very clear that there was a clear division of countries with respect to nuclear power, namely those with and those without, and an ever growing list of countries applying for technology to create their own. The problem was constant to all nations in that the by product of nuclear power was plutonium, the prime ingredient necessary for the production of nuclear warheads.

The Vice Admiral voiced his opinion that the west would intervene very soon to halt the advances of nuclear technology to many nations; again the thesis was breathing life.

Ian's training was not discussed other than he would be attending the training quarters at 7:00 a.m. where his instructor would brief him. In the meantime he was free to roam the vessel with the company of sub left tenant Wilkins, a Wren Officer. As he mentioned the Wrens name there was a knock on the door and in she came. Mother Nature had not been too kind to this lady. She was about Five feet five inches tall and about the same around. Her face was dotted with warts and pimples, and her facial hair was very noticeable. Although she sported a pleasant smile with a brilliant set of pearly whites, none the less, in her naval uniform she looked like a Christmas plum pudding. Ian was introduced to her and Ian was gracious and extended his hand for the usual pleasantries. He was pleasantly surprised to hear her accent; she was a native of Inverness and spoke in a manner very similar to Elspeth. That was the only similarity, but his mind was alerted to the fact that he had not given the love of his life very much thought, but then again he immediately justified the oversight given the pace of his training.

Within minutes he was following this young officer to his cabin. Once at the cabin, and a brief look see at the quarters, there being not much to take in, she took him on a very thorough tour of the vessel which included the engine room, albeit the reactor room was off limits. Ian made a mental note to gain access when convenient. Throughout the tour they talked and they actually got along quite well. As with Elspeth he encouraged the Wren to talk and he would listen. There was no doubt that she was keen, professional and thorough. After the tour was completed Ian admitted to her that he had no idea that these vessels were so large, even after the three hour tour Ian remained somewhat lost. The Wren responded with the statement that the deck would look particularly small when coming into land at 140 knots or so air speed; it was a statement that he would appreciate in the very short term. The tour ended back at his cabin where she politely excused herself and wished him a pleasant stay. The Vice Admiral had left a note on his door for him to join him for dinner at 7:00 p.m., a steward would escort him to the mess room and the captain's table.

Ian read the note and realized he was hungry. Taking a second peek at his surroundings; he assessed that he was taller than the length of the room and the width was about the length of his outside leg measurements. These quarters were tight and yet he managed a smile, instead of outright laughter. His bed was a joke but he knew that this was considered four star accommodations for a carrier, others would be packed in quarters like Sardines in a tin; at least he had his own quarters albeit with no sea view, he quickly realized that he was in fact privileged. Ian sat down on his bunk, his eyes focused on the caged light fixture above, and pondered the fact that he was not claustrophobic, it was a real blessing. Ian took the time out to shave, as his beard was heavy.

Just minutes before seven pm the steward knocked on the cabin door, and then, as per instructions escorted him to the messroom.

The aroma of the evening meal wafted throughout the entire quarters, within minutes Ian was sat at the table sitting opposite the high ranking naval officers. Certain of the engineering staff sat adjacent to him including the nuke boys as they were commonly referred to. With the arrival of the Vice Admiral they all stood up from their chairs and waited for the senior officer to sit....the respectful action reminded Ian of the judge and the courtroom protocol. Shortly thereafter the messroom was like a beehive with chatter galore. Ian enjoyed the starch rich food and the banter with the nuke boys.

The nuke boys, not knowing the PhD credentials of their guest, were impressed at the knowledge of the newly arrived civilian, this respect earned Ian the right of passage to be escorted around the reactor room, at a later date of course. When catered to with mashed potatoes, gravy, cabbage and meatloaf, the desert followed with a traditional spotty dick pudding laced with custard. It was as if they had been sent back in a time machine to their school dinner days; it was an exact duplication of a period ten years prior for Ian.

Desert was followed by tea, pots of it!!! Once the tea was downed the officers vacated discretely to their individual quarters, many of them sharing upwards of six to a cabin. Before reaching the confined space, Ian could hear the lead group farting as their systems devoured the stodge. Ugh he thought, six men to a room and most of them farting at will; it was not a pleasant thought.

Before Ian reached his sardine can of a cabin he too could feel the bubbles gurgitating within his gut.

He found his cabin and lay on the bed with knees pointing to the deck-head. He would read a while and then attempt to sleep. The vessels motion was very slight with a gentle pitch and a very discreet roll. The motion was soothing and not at all discomforting. Ian read for two hours at which time his gut had done its thing, it was time to walk somewhat quickly to the crew washrooms. Ian made the fifty meters or so in the nick of time. Almost touching cloth he squeezed himself into the closet of a toilet, the whole experience took seconds and relief was instantaneous. WOW he thought that was too close for comfort, but he felt like a million bucks. On his way back to the sardine can, his path was crossed with the Wren, and surprisingly she gestured him to her tin can, and even more surprisingly Ian followed, after all it had been too long without a sexual encounter. He mused recklessly and thought, *Any port in a storm!* Throughout the remaining evening and well into the morning he accommodated her every wish. Even though she had less than attractive looks, she had the sexual appetite of a young bunny. He later knew that her dreams had been fulfilled many times over before leaving her cabin at 5:00 a.m. Ian's eyes was burning, having only slept for a couple of hours. Even with eyes bloodshot he saw the smile on the face of his recent companion grow from cheek to cheek like a Cheshire cat; he concluded that they had both done very well.

Ian needed to shower and freshen up before taking aboard the breakfast gruel. He freshened up in one of the many communal showers. The water was steaming hot. Ian indulged himself with an extra long stay under the shower head, not only washing but shaving also. By the time he was dressed he was ready for whatever the day had to offer. Dressed in blue naval fatigues (coveralls) he made his way to the mess. To his surprise he was recommended to start with the meal of the top guns, and it was not eggs with bacon and home fried potatoes but rather Scott's porridge oats. Apparently this gruel would stick to the insides during most of the aerobatic training maneuvers. Sensibly Ian adopted the suggestion and thoroughly enjoyed a good portion. The porridge was followed by tea although coffee was available. Ian downed his tea and left the mess, returning to the sardine can and awaited the steward to arrive and escort him to the main training room. By 7:00 a.m. Ian was in the learning mode once again, he would be instructed upon landing and take off and communications between tower and aircraft. There would be no lunch, at noon they (Ian and his instructor) would be catapulted off the deck of the carrier utilizing maximum thrust from the jet engines, flying due south for ten miles and banking left to complete 180-degree turn to a position ten miles north of the carrier and then commence a series of touchdowns/takeoffs only. By the time the fuel was too low for further practice Ian and instructor would complete some twenty touch and goes.

Ian was ready for the new experience and once suited up he and the instructor boarded their flying machine. What was to follow can only be described by Ian as terrifying yet totally thrilling. With engines roaring, producing thrust beyond imagining, yet the aircraft stayed anchored in position, secured solidly by the catapult deck wires, and then at the command of the flight deck and the deck signalman the aircraft was released. Like an arrow released from the bow the aircraft roared to the edge of the bow of the carrier. Ian's porridge stayed in place but his whole insides were pressed to his inner back and spine. The first experience was quite frightening especially with Ian sat in the rear as an observer. The remaining afternoon they flew in semi circles completing one touch down after the other. Of the twenty touchdowns Ian controlled five and was becoming quite comfortable with the procedure. Then it was time to land for the evening. If taking off was frightening the landing and stop was worse. With the instructor at the controls they banked for the last time and made their approach from the north. The wind was accommodating at some fifteen knots from the south. Just like all of the other touchdowns the procedure was the same except that on this occasion they would re unite with the deck wire. At one hundred twenty knots plus the jet covered the last few meters of the approach and then like a boa constrictor grabs its prey and squeezes the prey to death the wire grabbed hold of the offending Pterodactyl and captured its prey. Fully in control the instructor applied reverse thrust and within seconds of contact the aircraft came to rest. Ian's insides were thrust to his belly cavity and finally came to rest; incontinence could be a real problem he thought, but over the next few weeks he was able to control his bodily functions. He would however stick with the porridge for breakfast.

Each day they would complete sortie after sortie repetition making the training smooth and predictable.

Within ten days Ian was in control and the instructor took the back seat of the forty million dollar jet. During the third week, the training shifted to night landings. The night silhouette of the carrier combined with the deck lighting and the sparkling green wake at the stern of the carrier gave the ocean a certain degree of mystique. On several occasions Ian flew with other pilots who engaged in air combat (dog fights) with the other carriers pilots.

Ian was only allowed to sit in the rear but he took it all in and continued to admire these young pilots and their skills.

The entire experience was truly amazing and Ian performed as per usual very well. During this final phase of training Ian was permitted to pilot the Sea King helicopter and happily he put in over ten hours of flight time. It was like going back to the dark ages, jet vs a rotary driven flying machine.

During his off times Ian would rest and explore the carrier. By the completion of his tour he had been everywhere, including a tour earlier offered by the nuke boys. Ian had several more encounters with the

Wren, she had lost some fifteen pounds, solely due to sexual activity, no dieting was necessary. She was still very unattractive but the weight loss did help modestly. Of course she was madly in love, but Ian remained casually stoic and simply continued to use her for pleasure purposes only.

The love of his life remained Elspeth. The huge problem remained his career path, how could he possibly nurture a relationship given the course he had chosen? He quietly and sadly admitted to himself that he may not ever see the love of his life again.

Guantanamo

Ian departed from the carrier via Harrier jet. This was the fourth opportunity Ian had to experience the vertical take off jet, a British masterpiece of aviation design and technology. He was flown South West to Guantanamo Bay for one week orientation. The trip was less than half an hour with the jet cruising at just under Mach-1. Sir Billy had arranged this final leg of Ian's training, with the director of the CIA. The ground crews at Guantanamo, Delta Charlie, were extremely impressed when the Harrier which landed on the sixty-foot circular deck which normally catered to Helicopters only. The Harrier parked majestically on the pad and was re-fueled. The pilots stop was brief and within ninety minutes from start to finish the Harrier was back aboard the Sir Winston Churchill carrier.

Ian meanwhile was once again being entertained by the colonel in charge of the American base, now known the world over as the interrogation center for extremists and terrorist. With six years of history the Seals and Marines at the base had broken many men and women with their interrogation techniques.

The Americans had a passion for coffee and accepting the offer from the colonel Ian welcomed the change from tea.

The Colonel had recently received the British home office request to enhance the skill set of their trainee in the discipline of torture and interrogation techniques. Ian's stay would be the final topping of cream to an incredible fast pace training schedule that few people could excel; Ian had notably excelled in everything.

There was no need to mention the fact that the London Eleven (Black Watch Warriors) were at the camp, well at least six remained alive, the other five had suffered heart complications/failure post electric therapy. Although the losses were great the information gathered had saved hundreds of lives and brought the global conflict modestly closer to, perhaps, a conclusion.

Colonel Sangster was friendly and polite throughout their short visit, but he forewarned the civilian that his memories of Guantanamo would not all be good ones, but certainly memorable. Ian would know the true implications of this statement upon departure at the end of the week. Ian was shown to his quarters by an MP Sergeant, the rest of the day he was free to wander the camp, albeit he had to be escorted at all times with the assigned sergeant. He took in the camp and the detainees; they all looked alike in their orange fatigues. Almost all of them looked haggard and weak, no one was overweight and there were no smiles to be seen anywhere; the camp was a hell hole of misery. For the serviceman their only respite would be on a Wednesday when they were transported to Havana for R and R. The American Marines had been privileged by the Cuban authorities to enjoy the facilities of the island, a privilege that was authorized only when certain trade restrictions were lifted by the US government.

The following few days past by with Ian observing many varieties of interrogation techniques, some of them were worse than others but British history could only reveal similar tactics back in the mediaeval times. The Tower of London could enhance the Seals knowledge of torture techniques, but then again this was the twenty first century.

By the time Wednesday came along Ian was somewhat excited about an evening in Havana.

Twelve passengers climbed aboard the 212 Hughie helicopter, a relic of the Vietnam period but still very serviceable. Soon they were clipping the golden evening skies with the thud, thud, thud sound of the single rotor blade. They would fly thirty minutes or so west to the Havana airport. By the time they arrived the sun was a golden ball just slipping behind the western horizon, civil twilight had commenced. After two minutes the blades of the chopper stopped rotating and were braked. The crew disembarked. They were reminded of the departure time of 2:00 a.m.; no one ever missed the chopper as the penalty for doing so was three months pay. They clambered aboard the waiting mini bus and took off down the narrow streets towards the regular drinking holes. The evening would start downtown at the Poncho Via Bar. They all ordered Corona which was served within seconds of their arrival. The usual ladies of the night homed in on their evening prey and escorted a man each to the bar area. The night hawks obliged and doubled the order of cerveza. That was the beginning of the eight hour pub crawl which was enjoyed by all. Ian observed that the others were constantly asking questions of him, who he really was, who did he work for, what was his purpose at the base, who were his parents, where were they, the questions were relentless and for Ian the evening was tempered by their numerous personal questions. Ian was unaware that his R and R was just the beginning of the negative part of his week's attendance at Guantanamo. As the night went on the crew became more and more inebriated. In the fourth bar several Cuban locals decided to take on the drunks and foolishly initiated a fight. Almost immediately the veterans of the US forces sobered up and the fight became very ugly for the locals. Ian stayed clear of the fight and it was not appreciated by his companions. When questioned later the same evening Ian responded with, "I don't fight. I kill..."

That was good enough to keep the others at bay and somewhat confused, but they already knew that they would have their day, in fact it was coming up within the next twelve hours. Ian would be truly tested to see if he would break after intense brutality and twenty first century mediaeval torturing.

The night continued into the morning and the drinking and carousing never ceased. Had Ian known what was coming the next day he may well have switched from beer to spirits, but when it came time to leave he was sober yet his blood/alcohol content would be off the scale. Making their way back to Poncho Via they all adopted a sober stance, no one was foolish; the hookers had gone and the van awaited their arrival. Before the bewitching hour of 2:00 a.m. they were all strapped in their helicopter seats with the exception of Ian. He had been sucker punched and fell to the ground adjacent to the skid of the chopper. With the noise of the rotors swirling above his head Ian regained consciousness and immediately made himself fast to the strut/skid. With legs wrapped around the skid and his arms scissored around the brace he clung to the chopper framework. For the next thirty minutes he became sober by the second. With the warm tropical air flowing over his body he felt like a down hill ski jumper, this was flight with no effort. The chopper raced through the warm moist air at one hundred thirty-five knots and from the moment they reached one thousand feet. Ian could see the Eastern point of the island and the lights of the camp. Three more minutes or so passed and the chopper landed and Ian escaped the sight of the ground crew by slipping off the blind side of the heli-pad. He was in his quarters before the rotors stopped and the crew off loaded.

The ground crew had been informed that Ian failed to make curfew, a fact that had already reached the C/O. The following morning the crew would be surprised to see Ian at camp, but nonetheless they would still have the last laugh.

Ian was at breakfast with the rest of the crew, all of whom looked bewildered, wondering as to how Ian was back already. The C/O equally looked confused when he saw Ian at the table. Anyway that was one problem solved for the C/O, he dismissed the quandary; obviously there had been a miscount of personnel on the chopper.

What followed breakfast was the final training saga for Ian, and it was not good.

Minutes after breakfast, Ian was summoned to the courtyard which was immediately outside of his quarters. Ian was still in his fatigues and looked ready for anything. Upon existing his quarters he was immediately encircled by eight US Seals, all of these men had been with him the night before, they had shared many beers, but Ian knew that they were all sober and once again ready for play. None were under six feet tall and two were six-six. Each was armed with a night stick sort of baton, made of ebony.

The Seals stood there slapping the head of the baton into their open hands. They were all sporting a snigger and Ian knew exactly what was coming. The senior soldier opened up with the only sensible question which was related to Ian's trip back to base. He asked how did he get back and Ian simply replied, on the chopper. Satisfied with the answer, one way or the other, the soldier responded with the statement that Ian did not show his fighting skills the night before, so now he had the chance to test his skills, no holds barred; also Ian was told that he would answer all of the questions that were posed to him the night before, again no holds barred. Ian confirmed "no holds barred." With that the circle of men started to constrict.

Ian was in great shape and he prepared himself for the onslaught. Remarkably he did exceedingly well, at least for the first five to six minutes or so. He targeted the tallest men first and took them down with relative ease, but with two down the circle was quickly repaired with another two sadistic members of the Seals. The outcome was inevitable, but before receiving violent blows with the ebony sticks behind his knees, Ian had been able to eliminate two more Seals, one of which received a blow to the nose which fostered the most awful sound of cracking facial bone, he was down and out. The Seals performed pretty good also sporting a variety of Karate/Tae kwon Do moves, all of which were blocked and countered by Ian. It was the blows behind the knees that took Ian down and then as if in the streets of Gaza, the boots came in from all quarters. Ian felt his ribs crack; he felt his eyes closing with the swelling. Blood was everywhere, spewing from his nose, mouth and his hands, he was helpless. This time the blood was all his and not the Seals. They continued mercilessly the pummeling; even after unconsciousness they savored each and every kick and whack of the night stick. Wiping blood from his nose the senior soldier ordered the halt. Then two Seals grabbed Ian's ankles and dragged him some one hundred meters to the interrogation chamber. The chamber was a small room measuring fifteen feet by fifteen feet. The walls were adorned with a host of strange looking instruments, all of which were used solely for torture purposes. Ian thought that he may well have been in the dungeons of the Tower of London.

The Seals stripped Ian of his clothing and strung him up. He was spread Eagled, his body placed under tension from two nylon ropes attached to his wrists. His ankles were similarly restrained. Ian was oblivious to it all and was under the veil of unconsciousness at least that was the case until he was shocked awake by two full buckets of almost freezing water. The water flushed the spewing blood from Ian's face but only to be replaced with fresh red fluid. The senior soldier complimented Ian on his fine performance and then with a sadistic grin he exposed the "Rats Ass" as the Seals called it. It was merely an American version of a Cat of nine tails, an aged weapon used for centuries in Old England.

The same questions came as was presented the night before and Ian made every effort to answer with the corresponding responses as he had done the night before. The beating was merciless, it went on and on but Ian remained tight lipped, nothing was won by the Seals. Still spread Eagled with blood oozing from too many sources to describe Ian was once again shocked with two buckets of ice cold water. A cart was brought into the room and the lid opened to expose a bank of batteries complete with cables. A rotary device was hooked up and Ian, sick to his stomach understood the next trial. He would be the human recipient of an electrical generator, a Meggar guinea pig.

The Seals were enjoying every moment and really lost focus on the aim to retract information. Sadism took over for a while and Ian was exposed to horrific pain and suffering, in fact he was rendered very close to death.

The chamber was dark and dirty, no sunlight entered the room with the exception of a small hole on the west wall where a screw had been inadvertently missed during construction. Ian focused on this tiny source of light as if it were a comfort, a light from an angel. Sadly the light eventually became dark. The torture stopped, and given the loss of light Ian thought that the Seals had taken a break for supper, and of course this was the case. Ian was left alone suspended and leaking blood profusely.

The one hour break was savored and Ian's strength modestly grew, but it was one hour to the second when the Seals returned to engage in more play. They had not been successful in their efforts to extract information from this extraordinary British man. Before the evening session began the attending doctor paid a brief visit and was evidently sickened by the state of Ian. The doctor checked the vital signs and spent a few minutes stitching up the worse cuts over the eyes. The pool of blood beneath Ian's body was indicative of at least three pints having been lost. The doctor advised the senior soldier that there was to be no more blood loss. The soldier said nothing and escorted the doctor from the room.

The soldiers were somewhat more dedicated than ever to break this Brit, they had learned at dinner that one of their team had died after the morning barrage; Ian had killed Hank a seasoned hard nosed Seal of ten years service. He passed away at 1645, some eight hours after the engagement with Ian.

Ian's manhood had not gone un-noticed with him suspended from the ceiling. His naked body was black, blue and red with swollen tissue everywhere. His Penis lay limp between his legs some eight inches long and unscathed. The soldiers one by one used Ian as a punch-bag until the shortest of the group came in with a special treat for Ian. At six feet even the soldier carried a plastic bag which contained literally thousands of Red Ants / Fire flies. Ian's Penis was considered to be out of proportion to his balls and they had a remedy. Carefully they tied the plastic bag around his scrotum and the rest was history. The only way to stop the biting and the pain was to kill the insects. It would take only an hour before Ian's testicles were as large as a football, and slowly the pressure created by the swelling and the stretching of the plastic bag would kill off the invading insects. The pain was all Ian's, his screams echoed throughout the camp, the sound blasting through the speakers in the other holding cells of the detainees. Ian's throat became scratchy with the incessant wailing, but who cared? The soldiers brought Ian back to consciousness each time he passed out with buckets of ice cold water. Throughout this ordeal Ian divulged nothing, and he welcomed death for the first time in his life. The plastic bag around his balls was removed after two hours and Ian's testicles looked like a giant strawberry suspended between his legs. There were no live insects, but they had fought a magnificent fight with Ian. The proportion issue had been more than remedied.

Ignoring the doctors orders the interrogation crew engaged in more down to earth barbaric methods of torture. Methods included, lit matchsticks under the fingernails, drilling the patella with a regular Black and Decker drill and bit. Cigar burning, wet leather strapping around his skull, simple slicing of his skin with a carpet blade, yet nothing worked, Ian once again was passing the test. At midnight the doctor came into the room only to be horrified at the result of the Seals handy work of the day. Within minutes of his examination and return to the C/O s office Ian was ordered to be cut down and taken to the infirmary. The handy work of the interrogators was so bad that Ian would need to stay in the infirmary for a full two weeks to recover.......upon learning the facts Sir Billy was not amused and immediately left Downing Street to make his way to Guantanamo.

Ian lay inert on the examination trolley, the white sheets, now splattered with blood. He was given almost four pints of blood and a host of antibiotics. It was touch and go whether Ian would lose his testicles but after four days the swelling started to reduce and after ten days the proportion was once again out of whack.

Sir Billy arrived on the weekend, with other senior officials from Washington. In the presence of a three star general the camp C/O was disciplined as never before. When the Alpha Omega chief had finished the colonel was barraged again by the General. It was not good for the C/O, yet he survived, testicles remaining unaltered. Further advancement in his career would be stalled.

Ian welcomed the arrival of the only family that he had, or at least the closets thing to it. Sir Billy was sickened at the sight of Ian's body; the Seals had really gone overboard in what amounted to a sixteen-hour interrogation time frame. The stitching on his face would need the very best that plastic surgery could offer. Sir Billy made a mental note to arrange a Harley Street appointment.

Sir Billy stayed a full day and instructed his god son to make a speedy recovery and to return home. Ian was relieved that this final stage was over; he would welcome a trip back across the pond and London. Sir Billy left the camp and made the short flight to Washington where he dined with the Secretary of State. Sir Billy would use the improper handling of Ian to gain a favor for the future.

Alpha Omega

Ian left the camp with no one wishing him farewell. Exiting the base was somewhat less grand than his earlier arrival. On this occasion the relic Hughie took him to the Florida Keys where he would hire a vehicle and drive to Miami. Upon disembarking the chopper the pilot gave a short salute and was gone. That was the only positive gesture offered. The Florida Keys were absolutely charming and Ian made it a point to spend a couple of days there. No one was pressing for his return. Anyway he had a very important desire, he wanted a women; not so much for pleasure purposes but more for the purpose of functional assessment. He found and stayed at the very best of hotels and booked the largest room which happened to be the bridal suite. Being off season it was readily available and inexpensive.

The room was extra large and the king-sized bed was first class. He decided to dress down and wear his docker trousers and a white short sleeve shirt fitted with two breast pockets. He wore his favorite Hush Puppy loafers with light tan socks. Freshly shaven and a gargle of mint flavored mouthwash he made his way to the beachside bar.

He entered the bar and casually approached the wicker woven bar. He then ordered bourbon on the rocks and sat on one of the six bar stools. Ian's entrance had not gone unnoticed by the regular bar fly's. Ian was ordering his second drink when a young brunette pulled up alongside him. Ian was quite pleased with the attention; after all she was the more appealing looking one in the bar. They engaged in the normal banter of the day, her name was Lucille and she was a young widow, her husband was a navy seal and died a couple of weeks ago. Ian was curious and asked where her husband had served and the answer was as expected. Ian gulped at his drink, his Adams apple relishing the gold liquid and for a micro second thought about the situation before asking her to dinner that evening. She responded with a positive yes. Dinner was exquisite, they both stayed with a seafood medley and garden salad, chased with a white Californian wine. Ian felt pressured to take her to his room; it was as if both of them had certain issues to resolve. After a brief walk, they arrived at his hotel room; the night cap would be romance and passion. The next eight hours or so was indeed dedicated to resolving issues, whatever they may have been. The following morning Ian awoke with modest soreness in his groin, but given the nights work out he was well satisfied that the Seals had not compromised his sexual prowess....everything had worked just fine!!!!!, in fact he would rally the troops again before letting the widow vacate the magnificent king-sized bed fitted with now soiled silk sheets.

Throughout the next few days Lucille shared Ian's time while he was in the Keys, they both had a great deal of fun, and Ian assessed a lot, while Lucille had resolved all of her issues.

Finally it was time for Ian to leave. After several days of assessment Ian said his farewells and headed for the airport. The rental was a Blue colored Mustang convertible. The drive to Miami was pleasant, with the roof down Ian reminisced the past few days, concurrently soaking up the sunshine, his color darkening by the hour.

Ian was returning back to England with his testicles at normal size, although he had been kept at the infirmary for an extra two weeks instead of the planned one. It was learned that it was far easier to create swelling than to reduce it. None the less Ian had completed his training and was a fully fledged surgeon, an Alpha Omega operative, pending assignment. Ian dropped off the hired car at the drop off center and caught Virgin Air from Miami to London and enjoyed the Sleeper Seats offered in First Class. On the outside Ian looked like a male model yet his body beneath his dark blue Armani suit remained scarred and bruised. The bruising was now Ochre yellow, but Ian was ecstatic that he still had his vital parts; he had been so, so close to losing them; and more importantly everything now had been confirmed to be in good working order.

The flight took all of ten hours; the jet stream had accommodated an early arrival at Heathrow, saving more than forty minutes of flight time. Ian was met at the airport by Sir Billy's personal assistant. Together they were chauffeured to Mayfair, the back entrance of Michael Robinson's home. The recent identity of Ian would be mentally buried, hopefully for a very long time. The journey from Heathrow to Mayfair was the equivalent of six hundred nautical miles by the Virgin aircraft, but Michael enjoyed looking at the familiar sights, even though the west end was an architectural Picasso.

The Jaguar XJR provided a good deal of leg room in the back seats, leg room was increased substantially by the need of the chauffeur to sit close to the wheel, the chauffeur was a mere Five feet two inches tall, his legs could barely reach the pedals. Fortunately the chauffeur's hat made him visible as the driver; he was almost totally lost within the leather seat of this fine limousine. Sitting behind the driver Michael was prepped for the next weeks agenda which included day surgery to eliminate the scarring on his face....scars needed to be removed as global surveillance cameras were so precise these current times, scarring was easily detectable /traceable; clean surface skin was preferred. Michael was dropped off at the rear of his home; he had missed the place, and of course his parents.

He was welcomed by the home-keepers, (a new term for housekeepers), and yes the pot of tea was already underway. He ventured into the living room and took refuge in one of the armchairs so loved by his mother. The tea was delivered and poured; the home-keeper then politely left Michael to enjoy the tea and biscuits, in quiet. Michael enjoyed the tea and helped himself to a second cup which went down very easily. To Michaels surprise he felt an overwhelming need for sleep and for the very first time dozed off for forty minutes in the arms of this special chair. He awoke and took in all his surroundings, it felt grand to be back in this place full of so many good memories, he allowed himself this quiet time to reflect and remember the parents that he missed and loved so much.

Although a little somber Michael got up out of the chair and answered the telephone that continued to ring incessantly…it was Sir Billy.

The call was an invite to Claridges' for dinner, and of course Michael agreed. Subsequent to further chitchat the call ended with, "See you at 7:30 p.m."

Michael considered starting up the Bentley but thought better of it; he would hail a taxi after a half mile walk or so. Even with the time change Michael was ready to hit the town. Departing from the back door of is Mayfair home he started a brisk walk, his legs responded well to the exercise and he found himself hailing a taxi having walked well more than a mile.

The taxi weaved its way through the streets of London, although these taxis were black and ugly, they were magnificent for the narrow streets; in particular the turning circle was remarkable.

After ten minutes or so, the Claridges' was in view. Met by the doorman dressed in his top hat and mohair wine colored overcoat Michael made his way out of the back seat having already paid the cabby, having tipped generously. Upon entering the hotel it was clear the hotel was showing its age, the fine wallpaper was peeling at the meeting place of wall and ceiling, the carpets were thread bare in places, and the furniture had seen better days. This was however THE hotel for London. Many Arab princes liked to stay at the hotel, there being discretion on the part of the hoteliers with respect to certain ladies of the night. It was easy to identify the royalty, the Arab princes were like the London taxis, and the women of the night were simply garish. Michael made his way to the bar where he found Sir Billy chewing on a fine Havana cigar, and nurturing a gin and tonic. The greeting was genuinely a warm one, Sir Billy hugging Michael rather than shaking his hand. The bar man had already been advised as to Michaels choice of drink and immediately upon his arrival the crystal glass which cradled the fine bourbon and crushed ice was placed onto the bar top adjacent to the tall glass of gin and tonic of Sir Billy. The conversation naturally focused on Michael's health after the Guantanamo experience. Michael had matured beyond his years and held no grudges; he had assumed that everything was required to complete the training. Sir Billy did not totally agree but went with the flow of the dialogue. They talked about his visit to the plastic surgeon and jokingly Sir Billy advised him not to consider any reduction type surgery....the joke was in poor taste but Michael knew what he meant.

They distanced themselves from the bar and continued the talk in two worn wing chairs located at the entrance to the dining room. Michaels chair had a visible spring chewing its way through the seat of the chair making it totally uncomfortable, but he tolerated the nuisance, sitting still not to damage his suit trousers.

Sir Billy then advised the newly fledged Alpha Omega operative that he was now considered to be amongst the worse of the bunch of highly paid laundry specialists, mingling with the a variety of types of sadists, and perhaps social misfits recruited from Black Ops and Special Branch, or the SAS, they were all in his team, the Alpha Omega Group, but for the time being due to his PhD credentials he would be assigned to a field operation in Iran, followed by a similar program in Syria and Korea. A work visa was underway for him; he was to be employed as a nuclear physicist at the Nuclear power stations. His role was to detail as much as possible the strengths and weaknesses of the facilities and to establish whether the spent plutonium was being utilized for the production of nuclear warheads. He would be working on a six month term / location. Before leaving the country he would need to grow his beard and carefully tan, either in direct sunlight or at the tanning salons of London. Some what confused, Michael had thought he would be called to do other things; but he respectfully accepted the instructions and they moved on with their talk. The conversation was all business, and before leaving to seek a table for the dinner, Sir Billy slipped Michael a key. The key was to a safe which had been installed in the bedroom of the judge, it was located behind the safe of the judge, in fact the old safe would remain unlocked but access to the new safe was by physically removing the old safe.

There he would find a selection of weapons which had no traceable markings. He would also find a wad of notes, currency suitable for each country about to be visited. Additional passports would be made ready and new photographs would be required of him, complete with a beard. Michael was reminded of the importance of the assignment as action may be required at a later date to remove any threat posed by any or all of the named countries. It was imperative that he became intimate with the layout of each facility as he would for sure, be part of a team to return if a remedy was called for. Finally the conversation quickly changed to food.

They entered the dining room and feasted themselves on carrot soup, rack of lamb, crème brulee, followed by a selection of Danish cheese reminiscent of the Copenhagen days, which seemed to have been a life time away.

The cheese was savored with the very best of Port, Michael having nearly choked when he saw the cost per bottle, and they of course, had easily killed two bottles.

The evening was over and each of them made their way back to their homes, albeit Michael had no idea where Sir Billy lived...few did.

It was past midnight when Michael arrived at the rear entrance to his home, he was now feeling the time change and he was ready for what he hoped would be a five hour long sleep. After two days of beard growth Michael made the visit to Harley Street. Dr. Swan would be his makeover surgeon, and the first communication was, "Lose the beard." Even though the beard concealed smooth skin, the surgeon advised Michael that he wanted to perform the surgery with his team only; no other form of bugs would be permitted. "It does not matter how well groomed you are young man, that thing," pointing to his black beard, "is a club med for little beasts...cut it off by morning!"

The surgeon was very professional until he saw the markings of Guantanamo. With great compassion he exhausted a, "Holy shit," and advised Michael that he should prepare himself for ten days...pointing upstairs to the recovery rooms. The surgeon would perform his magic on the torso of Michael; and although he would end up not perfect, he would however be as good as Hollywood and medical science could allow.

The next morning Michael arrived clean shaven, empty of food and fluids ready for the surgeon's knife.

Michael was once again in the sterile environment of a medical facility, another period of his life would be lost to operations and recovery. The next ten days passed by very slowly but the results were quite amazing. The scarring above booth eyes had been transformed into facial aging lines. The swelling was gone within a few days of each slice and dice action. Dr. Swan had done a remarkable job. Other scar tissue on his torso was carefully transformed and or almost disappeared. Michaels body was fit for a swimsuit and almost ready to be tanned. Two molar teeth were removed and implants inserted. In addition to the implant one of the teeth housed a miniature transmitter; Michael could be tracked by the foreign office at all times. Another transmitter was implanted in his bicep; this was purely a deliberate measure to facilitate diversion if captured; the world of espionage, terrorism, would expect to find a homing device of some description on their special guests. Michael would be informed of the bicep implant, but this too was a diversionary measure as he had no idea of the electrical devices implanted into his jaw. On the eleventh day Michael was released with instruction not to engage in physical exertion for a two week period; walking was the order of the day. There would be no need for a follow up unless complications were evident. Michael healed quickly and spent most of his days walking the embankment and driving the Bentley.

Sir Billy had kept the vehicle up to scratch, in fact he had added a couple thousand of miles to the odometer while he had been training. The car remained an absolute pleasure to drive. Michael felt the presence of the judge and his mum when driving. He drove to the West Country visiting Plymouth, Exeter, Taunton, Bath, and Lynton and Lynmouth on the north coast of Devon. The recovery period came and went and then it was time to earn his keep.

In Between Years

Earning his keep would be dangerous yet exciting. For the next nine years Michael performed exceptionally well for the Alpha Omega team. His alias's had been many and his bank accounts globally grew proportionately, combined with his own inheritance which had yielded some twenty-two percent growth his net worth was close to one hundred million pounds. He had not been protected by Sir Billy by any means, he had survived many assignments, killed many more non desirables, been the recipient of five bullets and two stabbings; he had in fact outlived the normal life expectancy of an Alpha Omega operative. John was still alive and like Michael had battle scars to prove it. They had been involved in several operations and performed well together. Of the twenty-six agents, thirteen had been lost and replaced, there had been little if any bad press for Sir Billy. Of late the five largest oil companies had solicited the assistance of

the foreign office to remove certain obstacles that restricted fair practice; in fact the foreign office budget relied on the private sector for the additional funds required to front the global network of services discreetly offered by the Foreign Office. It was the same with the USA and Germany. Dirty Laundry seemed to be a growth industry and thriving nicely. Michael liked the oil companies as they were the most appreciative. Throughout the past nine years Michaels exploits were many but certain assignments had been of great interest, challenging and financial rewarding.

Michael had spent eight months in Iran, six months in Syria, six months in Saudi Arabia, almost a year in Korea and six months in Russia. He had performed his task assignments as a nuclear technician / informant without compromising his mission. Since that time Iran had suffered one nuclear melt down and in Korea a major fire had seriously delayed the operation of their newest facility. The Saudis had built a six hundred megawatt power plant which also provided 1,500 tonnes of fresh water per day. Egypt had commenced building their power plant mirroring the Saudi design, while Libya watched with bated breath. India was in full swing with short range nuclear missile development and Pakistan was neck and neck with them. The world was heading for a global melt down; it was not if but when?

Michael had been involved with the Iranian Melt down in a daring operation where Michael and John had been parachuted just off Kharg Island where they had to swim amongst deadly sea snakes and sharks to reach the shore.

Once ashore they had to make their way to the Khomeini plant, Michael knew the plant well, it was the plutonium source for weapons of mass destruction for the country. The Iranians had publicly declared that they would build short range nuclear missiles to defend their country, yet they also made it public that they would one day eliminate the illegal country of Israel. The weapons facility was adjacent to the plant hence a melt down at the plant would destroy both properties concurrently. Israel would be spared more time, and of course, they would contribute a very large sum of cash to the Alpha Omega operations as a token of appreciation.

Michael and John had successfully accessed the plant at night; the phase of the moon was new hence it had been as dark a night could be. They silenced only six security guards before completing their mission. The operation was extremely easy, the Iranians being lax in almost everything they did.

They were able to sabotage the water intake cooling feed with pretimed explosives. More importantly they had accessed the electrical panel of the Emergency Shut Down Control (ESD) and in essence reversed the operational functions. It was cleverly figured out by Michael when at the plant several years earlier. Apparently it only entailed cutting and splicing no more than six feed wires, and reconnecting them to terminals to achieve reversal. The plant operators would follow proper protocol only to make things ten times worse, there would be no time to source the problem to effect a fix. With the timed explosive devices on the intake feed water lines Michael and John were able to make it back to the safe haven of the south shore and rendezvous with the US Seals who were waiting in a small Zodiac inflatable dinghy, quietly they snuck out to the awaiting American frigate, one of many patrolling the shipping lanes of the Gulf. The following day the transit of the spy satellite confirmed the destruction of the plant. It would be one full week before the Iranian Government acknowledged an operational meltdown. No one had any idea in Iran what had actually taken place; the ensuing fire would have destroyed all evidence of the successful plot. Atmospheric air monitoring in India, Pakistan and Russia confirmed the radiation pollution within hours of the event.

On the global stock markets uranium mining companies stock prices remained on a tear away, price per pound of uranium had surpassed the $110 USD ceiling and forecasted to rise significantly more. Supply vs demand was out of whack with a 1:10 ratio. Nuclear Power stations totaled some four hundred fifty and supply of uranium was far too low. This was not a surprise to Michael as his thesis had forecasted the shortfall; in fact the thesis forecasting was becoming eerily factual. The Iranian melt down had little effect in the western world, and the Greenpeace movement and their concerns were barely noticed.

Given the news, Sir Billy arranged additional deposits in the accounts of the two operatives; this was the norm with confirmation of a successful strike.

The Israeli equivalent of the Foreign Office were so grateful they contributed a sizeable amount of funds to a UK charity, concurrently Michael and John received large deposits in their foreign bank accounts, the amounts being somewhat alarming to both operatives. All they needed to do now was to stay alive to enjoy the spoils. They both knew that they had been living on borrowed time. Both men had prepared their wills but that was of little consolation.

Michael was involved again with John in Somalia, certain guerillas were high priority for the US to eradicate. Both operatives succeeded but at a high cost. Both operatives were wounded and John almost bit the biscuit, but thanks to Michael they safely made it back to the UN base camp.

Michael returned to Africa on two more occasions with the mandate to terminate certain non desirables; both operations being clean and successful.

From one continent to another; Michael was assigned the assassin/ terminator role. Columbia, Venezuela, Chile and Brazil were all visited by Michael and numerous funerals were held post his departure.

Up until this juncture Michael had traveled extensively, most recently traversing the jungle terrain in Central America. There too his target was sourced and eliminated.

Hanging Around

Now in the northern jungles of Korea, under the guise of James J. Jeffries, on a hot and rainy June night, he was suspended from a tree, slightly swinging on a primitive yet effective wild Boar trap. Smiling to himself, he thought of his non de plume (James J. Jeffries) the hanging judge. Swinging from the snare, he mused over the thought of his father knowing his predicament, and the irony of his alias, the judge would have seen the humor too. Just hours before he had been with John, the mission was to destroy the Jong II Nuclear Power station recently commissioned by the North Korean authorities, once again the justification being the admission by the North Korean Government that they were advancing their weapons program. The success of the Iranian plot had a bearing on this mission in that the ultimate outcome would reveal an accident; this was preferable compared with Western sabotage. The Tumen river patrol had passed by and was down the trail when James performed a simple trunk curl and cut the rope snare. He allowed gravity to accelerate him to a soft landing, and quickly he took to the edge of the undergrowth and assessed his next move. There was no sign of John (this time John Bellamy) but then he had been on the other side of the river. Amidst the thunder James could hear the intense high pitched sound of the nuclear plant warning system. The sound did not last for too long as billions of gallons of water hurled down the river path towards the power plant. The target had been the upstream dam, the plant having been foolishly built alongside the lower river embankments. The dam was secured by eight regular soldiers, whereas the power plant may well have been secured by an army barracks. James had four soldiers on his south side while John had four on the north side. James had executed the soldiers with simple ease. Two suffered the fate of the graphite arrows and the one by his razor sharp blade. The fourth was taken from behind, and like many skinny regular soldiers, the neck could easily be broken with modest effort and technique. This was the case for James's final kill, which was just as well as the crack of the boney neck which followed was noisier than James had hoped for. John probably completed his work in a similar fashion. The plan was executed without a flaw. C2 explosives had to be placed at approximately one third height from the base of the dam. This would be the greatest pressure point exerted by the wall of water on the Western face. For good measure additional explosives were placed on the left and right of the initial location some fifty feet apart. If the first explosive did not breach the dam then the second and third detonation would surely do so. James and John gave themselves ten minutes to take large steps to the upstream side of the dam; they would hear the explosion and would know very soon by the irritant noise of the automatic siren which would alert the Power station, albeit the operators of the plant and soldiers would be rendered helpless. Upon hearing the sound James knew that hundreds if not thousands of people would drown, the power plant would be significantly destroyed and the manufacturing of war heads equally compromised. All that was left was to get clear of the area and make their retreat.

James decided to follow the edge of the river, a river that was noticeably getting narrower by the minute.

The Tumen River was far less patrolled at this particular location but he still needed to exercise caution. For years this twenty-mile section of the river had provided thousands of defecting North Korean refugee's safe access to China. Most refugees would traverse the shallow section of the river and merely walk across.

James however, would make his way up river a few more miles until one hour before dawn and then make his crossing. No doubt given the catastrophe still underway down stream the patrols will be either heavy or very light. As a precaution he would stop every forty-five minutes to climb a tree and view the area with his night vision Zeiss glasses. He would take nothing for granted.

Having climbed four trees and made some seven miles, he had discovered nothing untoward, the patrols appeared to be non existent. He found his crossing point and carefully observed the opposite bank and his own. Swimming with the snorkel only penetrating the shrinking river the crossing went without incident. With a swim of less than seventy-five meters, he found himself on new soil, China, Jilin province.

A few miles down river on the north side of the Tumen, was the heavily patrolled border with Russia. James knew that the Chinese side would be less patrolled and far easier to access.

The plan called for a twenty mile trek to a location referred to as Columbus Mountain, he had just six hours to do the trek. James completed the cross country journey with fifteen minutes to spare but to his surprise John was not there. The rendezvous chopper would be flying under three hundred feet elevation to ensure non detection by radar. The timing would be precise; the chopper would land on time as per the plan and would complete one touchdown only. No Alpha Omega operatives, then too bad.

James boarded the chopper from the port side, in full view of the pilot. Once inside the pilot asked about passenger number two, but James responded with…"I Don't Know!" With that, the pilot lifted the control lever and cleared the tree line before heading South East to the sea, and an awaiting Frigate. The chopper flew well clear of the nuclear power plant yet the plant was clearly visible given the failure of one of the reactors. The fire was huge even with the vast rise in the water level. Seeing the glowing sky James saw the results of his handiwork, a rare occasion but he found certain gratification all the same.

The chopper landed on the stern of the Frigate and James respectfully waited for the blades to be braked and then three of them, Pilot, Co-Pilot and James disembarked and proceeded to the briefing room. No one had heard from John and he was logged as MIA. There was little to address in the briefing room other than the confirmation that the assignment was complete. The Frigate would proceed to Singapore where James would take his leave and fly back to London via Singapore Airlines. Within the week James was back in London, and back to using his alias as Michael Robinson.

Nothing much had changed; the news reflected the usual scandals in politics, the growing concern of a nuclear threat and Al Qaeda being fully active in all western countries. Car bombings were the norm with suicide bombers self detonating their bundles of explosives everywhere. Frankfurt, Madrid, Rome, Manchester, Athens and Toronto had all experienced the horrendous bombings within the past five weeks; the world was going completely mad according to the Daily Times. The Iranian nuclear disaster had slipped to the third page. Global warming issues remained very much a focus the world over. All ready the USA had seen three hurricanes skirt the eastern seaboard and they were watching carefully the birth of a new system just west of the Cape Verde islands west of Africa. The Florida Hurricane center had already named the system *Diana.*

Michael had been given the luxury of a two day break before being summoned to the office of Sir Billy. Over the years the two of them had been very close. Sir Billy took charge of the many chores and needs necessary to maintain a Mayfair home with the owner absent for the most part of each year. Every Sunday without fail Sir Billy took the aging Bentley, now with forty five thousand miles showing, for a spin. Sir Billy usually drove to a Maidstone restaurant and bar that he had come to enjoy. It was either that or par take in the superb Sunday brunch at the Tower Thistle Hotel.

He always transited the Tower Bridge and without fail he pondered the fate of his good friend the judge. Michael did not know that the old diplomat, the old fart, had willed everything to Michael. After all of this time Michael did not know where Sir Billy lived, and certainly he had no knowledge that he had no relatives at all, excepting his God Father.

Michael walked to the gates of Downing Street and proceeded to the Foreign Office. Sir Billy's office had not changed over the years and it was in need of a little freshening up.

Years of Havana cigars had tainted much of the drapes and furniture; the ceiling had a yellowish sheen. Sir Billy himself was still very much the dignified diplomat but time had taken a toll on his god father. His eyes appeared to be milky and tired, lacking their prior lustre, however the aging eyes were in concert with his face which had now forged many deep lines. He now had a slight stoop and his hair had almost but disappeared. Supported by the tired frame however, was his head housing a keen brain, fully functional with a data base on par with any modern computer. Sir Billy had been the maestro of many plots; he had cleaned much laundry in his tenure. Michael now wondered what his next laundry assignment would involve.

Michael having closed the office door was directed by Sir Billy to take a seat. Sir Billy never mentioned the last assignment but instead, and as per usual, got straight to the point.

The CIA and MI6 have been experiencing a huge volume of chatter over their terrorist surveillance systems. Something is up and Al Qaeda continues to threat a dirty bomb, targeting most likely London, New York, or Washington. We need you to visit Washington and glean whatever you can from the Americans.

Terrorists' acts remain on the increase so we are taking the matter very seriously.

We have also confirmed that the transaction in diamonds transiting the diamond houses of Antwerp and New York have increased by more than thirty percent. This is very substantial!

Diamonds is now the currency commodity of choice for the terrorists and certain dealers are involved but we are having difficulties in breaking their network.

The transactions in the movement of diamonds in the last ten days have exceeded all other volumes ever recorded for the same period over the last twenty years. Something big is coming down and we must get to the bottom of it. Sir Billy did not ask for Michael's thoughts, but remained direct and continued with his line of thought. You will leave tomorrow with a new identity which you will have later today. You will meet with our counterparts in Washington late tomorrow afternoon. We shall assist the Americans where ever we can; Michael, this matter has been given the highest of priorities by the PMO.

Out of character, Sir Billy then concluded with, "Be extra careful on this one, Michael."

Michael was shown the door and he left the office of Sir Billy. Unlike Sir Billy, he had not offered him a cup of tea, yet the tea pot and tea set was clearly in sight. Michael now had the need for tea and went to the tea room for the liquid of champions.

Before leaving the tea room, Sir Billy's assistant sauntered up to Michael with a package. He was handed his new identity papers. This time he would adopt the name of James St Clair, business man, involved with the motor trade. Passport and relevant information comprised of forty pages of miscellaneous bumph, he would read the text and then dispose of it in the shredder. The new laundry assignment was about to take shape.

ETD New York 0800

The offshore anchor handling re-supply vessel Rigel-Kent sailed New York with two large, forty-foot-long containers, the contents of which according to the ships manifest and the bill of lading, were allegedly down-hole logging tools. Signs adhered to the container clearly identified radioactive components warning persons to be careful when handling. The 12,000-horsepower supply vessel had cleared customs without a hitch, indeed it had been an easy process. The containers had been offloaded within the last twenty four hours from the Korean registered vessel Pacific Shores. All containers were supposed to be screened with the x-ray scan trolley, a hazardous material detection system in place since 2004.

As a safe guard the North Korean manufacturers had installed a type of electro magnetic degaussing gear which set up a magnetic field throughout the container. This would shield the contents, however the port stevedores placed little emphasis on this pre requisite as the containers were destined to go offshore the next day, regardless they had received a pleasant envelope full of cash, they were simply to ignore the containers.

The containers were not screened. The supply vessel was on route to the dynamically positioned mobile offshore drilling unit named Deep Sea Explorer, albeit the drilling unit was unaware of the shipment, the Rigel-Kent was certainly not one of the three vessels assigned by charter to support the drilling program of the rig. The concern of something big being underway as stated by Sir Billy was indeed about to unfold, but it was far worse a plot than any normal person could possibly imagine. The vessel cleared the port with the pilot disembarking much earlier than he should have done, but then the navigation of the waters was quite simple given the draft of the vessel being only sixteen feet. The crew made ready their package, they would make the rig within twenty six hours sailing time. The stable platform of the rig was a critical component to ensure a safe launch. There was no time to waste as the supply vessel needed to be in the Gulf of Mexico before the arrival of Hurricane Diana which was slowly transiting the central Atlantic at a slow ten knots, growing in strength and size daily.

One of the containers would be made ready for a snatch lift. Although the container was large the weight of the contents and the men that would be inside armed with M-16 automatic weapons would be less than seven tonnes, an easy lift. Inside the container were four sixteen foot long missiles and a launching apparatus. A multitude of electrical ties completed the inventory. Everything would be set up once secured on the deck of the rig. The crew made ready the ten tonne safe working load slings, making sure that the safety lines were attached on each corner of the container. The tops of the containers were secured closed with butterfly screws; these screws would be re-greased and confirmed to be operational for ease of opening.

The missiles were marked with NY1, WDC1, and PHD1, the spare missile had no marking, and it was designed to detonate within fifteen minutes of the launching of the other three. The rig would be vaporized. Destination/targets were simply Manhattan, New York, Washington, D.C., and Philadelphia. The nuclear war heads would transit the two hundred miles or so at six hundred knots, hence impact would be in less than twenty minutes, giving the US commanders no time to make a judgment call. This was the major lesson learned by terrorist during the 911 world trade centre event; the confusion led to chaos and a total breakdown in the command chain; it was hoped that this plan produced the same result, in fact it was considered to be a forgone conclusion! Each warhead would produce a blast in the region of one kilotonne of TNT equivalent.

The destruction radius would be almost one mile and the fallout radius in the region of five miles. Property damage would be in the billions of dollars and the loss of life estimated at more than two million/missile. The missiles would hit their targets within seconds of each other; it was believed by the engineers of this vile plot that the USA would be brought down to their knees instantaneously. The majority of the decision makers would perish upon impact and like a ship without a rudder the USA would crumble. CNN would report the news globally and there would be utter disbelief. Finally the late report of a nuclear explosion offshore would follow.

Each crew member left on the rig would die for the Jihad (the holy war/the greater cause), all of them believing that seventy-two virgins awaited each of them upon their arrival at the gates of heaven. Concurrent to the sailing of the Rigel Kent from New York, James St. Clair departed Heathrow on a direct flight to Washington, D.C. The crossing was dull yet James took advantage of the time by reading up on the latest Missile designs; by pure fluke this opportunity to brush up his skill set/knowledge would benefit him greatly in the very near future.

James was met at the airport and whisked away, there was no need to follow the regular passengers, rather he was escorted via a short cut to an awaiting Black Lincoln SUV. He was in CIA quarters within thirty minutes of his arrival. Tensions were running high, there was reason for concern. On Aljaszeer and Al Alan television network a video was televised showing a senior Al Qaeda soldier announcing the pending strike on the West, the Jihad was accelerating. All of the Western countries went on a high level alert status, including London England.

The meeting included several high ranking agents and politicians including the secretary of defence.

The general consensus was that a dirty bomb would be used, most likely targeted at USA and or UK. Given that past threats always took place within two weeks of a warning statement, the President of the USA ordered that readiness within two days was a must. Plans were to be concluded and precautionary measures taken to ensure that the Devcon One personnel would be scattered through out the USA, avoiding the obvious targets, namely New York and Washington DC. The threat was taken seriously and the President was already heading to Denver to speak at a conference while the Vice president would stay at his Boston retreat, neither of them would see Washington until the alert was downgraded. Generals galore and two Admirals attended the meetings. It was confirmed that all of the air support would remain on readiness with ten F-18 permanently armed and in the skies, this applied to the East and West coasts. Almost fifty percent of the Norfolk Fleet would depart the port the next day and patrol the Eastern seaboard. Two aircraft carriers based in San Diego would sail within forty-eight hours to patrol the west coast. The prime minister of Canada offered two Frigates for both east and west coast pending there operational status. Goose Bay Labrador offered four F-18 aircraft to be based in Halifax Nova Scotia for additional air support. The National Guard had already been placed at ready alert status, and the head of the Navy Seals confirmed the availability of one thousand Seals who were standing by at various locations around the USA including Alaska. The list of "actions" was enormous, but would it be enough? Time would tell all.

The following morning the, Joint Chiefs of Staff, operational command team regrouped to discuss the latest chatter and updates from around the world. James listened and observed but contributed little.

Meanwhile the Rigel Kent blessed with perfect weather, with calm seas and a brilliant blue sky was coming alongside the Deep Sea Explorer claiming a crew injury in desperate need of medical treatment. The rig medic made the transfer by Billy Pugh net down to the deck of the Rigel-Kent, complete with his first aid bag of tricks. Immediately when inside the accommodation of the vessel the unknowing medic was silenced, two 9 millimeter rounds penetrated the back of his skull. There appeared to be no blood, the medic falling forward as if being pushed over from behind.

The plan for the Jihad Arab group was to have one of their team lay on a board stretcher with M-16 weapons concealed under the bright red blanket, along with plastic tie wraps. The leader of the group spreading the make belief victims face with Ketchup and then beckoned by radio the crane operator to standby to hoist them up. All together there would be four armed terrorist with the role to capture the rig. The crane operator had no idea what was about to happen but he obliged with the transfer

The stretcher was carefully landed on the heli-deck, and then the team went to work. Without claiming an M-16 one of the group headed for the crane, climbed the pedestal and entered the crane operators control cabin door. Armed with a 9 millimeter pistol fitted with an Italian silencer, the terrorist popped two slugs into the crane operators' forehead. He was peaceful as he slouched over the controls. The crane operator was a big man and the lightly built Arab struggled to remove him from the seat which was clearly visible from the deck below. No one had noticed a thing. Climbing down the little Arab ran to the heli-deck to claim the M-16. The operation was now fully underway. From the vantage point of the radio room the communications tech could see the event unfolding and simply considered this to be another drill organized by the OIM (Offshore Installation Manger), reality setting in only after one of the terrorist burst into the room and tie wrapped the two operators on duty. The radio room would be under constant guard from that point on. The remaining three entered the upper deck of the accommodation module and made their way to the rig office. Any party crossing their path would be silenced with their 9 millimeter pistols. Of the ninety crew on board, six persons lost their life in the takeover. Every crew member with the exception of the Geologist, Rig Manager and the Toolpusher were held hostage in the crew theater, all wrists and ankles were tied off with the plastic ties. It took less than thirty minutes to have the rig immobilized. The drill string which penetrated some 19,000 feet below was simply stalled. The next hour was dedicated to bringing four more Jihad warriors form the deck of the Rigel Kent. The little Arab departed to access the crane and initiate step two of the plan. Within two hours from the initial request for the medic the container had been off loaded and positioned on the west side of the box girder with the lid opened. A fish net tarp was placed over the top of the container for fear of inquiring satellites. The missiles could be launched within minutes, but first they had to wait for the instruction.

In the radio room the radio receiver was tuned to the same host frequency being monitored on the border of Pakistan and Afghanistan by upper echelons of the movement. The same frequency was being carefully monitored by the Rigel-Kent which was now headed for the Gulf of Mexico; a race was on between Hurricane Diana and the supply vessel. It was imperative that the supply vessel win this race, a lot was hinging on Diana. With calm seas the crew would alter the name of the Rigel Kent to the Offshore Supplier. The bow port and starboard soon sported the new name; the stern too was modified with the previously fabricated name plates. Port of registry being Panama. The spot welding took only a few hours and the vessels old identity was gone. For good measure the crew then painted the funnel from its white to black, another easy change.

Back on the rig fear was healthy and alive; the terrorist sadistically wounding several of the crew, the desired result was achieved. Food was not permitted but a large container of water was provided for the theatre room. One of the mess girls was given the task to assist each person with the water. She was a perfect choice as she continuously trembled with fear.

With the rig under the control of the terrorist special attention was necessary to ensure that the shore based management did not suspect anything. Each evening and morning the rig manager was required to telephone the shore, the Jihad Arab Geologist would witness the calls and ensure that the rig manager did not divulge their true status, it was a good try but this was the Achilles heal with their plot. The very first evening call, the rig manager made every effort to confuse the superintendent ashore. He succeeded in this in a variety of ways. Firstly he started to report the rate of penetration in meters per hour, when for the past two months they had been using imperial units, the USA still adopted the old method. Not only was it the footage, but the fact that the hole was reported as being 1,000 meters less than the day before. The superintendent was totally perplexed but he played out his role, totally confused but fortunately he did not counter his offshore representative. He had known this particular man for many years, and his gut told him that something was not right. Both of these seasoned oilmen had spent many hours in their respective homes playing charades, and games like cranium.

The shore based oilman decided to do his own fooling around and requested when they would be at the coring interval, to which he received a reply, in two days time, possibly three. This was the trigger that confirmed a problem as the core samples had been recently cut and sent ashore for analysis. The conversation continued with the shore based superintendent confirming a tight hole status and that the new MWD tools would be sent out after the weekend. This was confirmation that the shore management knew that something was terribly wrong, as the subject tools had been shipped and received the prior week. Brilliantly the superintendent stated that the test equipment was being sourced and he requested the availability of bunks aboard the rig and whether he would require additional cots. The banter was inspiring and the response went back with a request for eight more cots. After a little loose banter the conversation ended with, "Call me at 8:00 a.m. as per usual." With that, the call was terminated and it appeared that the observing Geologist was totally satisfied with the call. Meanwhile ashore the superintendent raised the alarm to his security department.

The operator was Exxon Mobil; the joint venture partners being Chevron and BP Amoco, Exxon were as up to date with terrorist threats as any company, if not possibly leading the pack in counter-terrorism protocol.

Alert Status

The oil companies' emergency response plan was triggered with a host of senior staff being notified including the Chairman. It was a short period of time when the Secretary of defence and the President officials heard of the situation. The top brass of the government had recently arrived at the bunker facility some sixty miles north of Washington, the operations room was some fifty feet underground. Representatives from Exxon were in attendance, the shore based superintendent enlightening his audience with the story. James was with them listening with interest what was coming down. James had assessed the facts and for the first time spoke out with valid questions and the beginnings of an action plan; the latter being well received as few people really had a grasp of what could be happening, and or what should be done. One thought expressed by a senior official suggested that the terrorists would compromise the rig and well, in fact the thought tendered was that the Arab group would pollute the Eastern seaboard and for that matter the western shores of Europe; then with a degree of authority James interrupted and addressed the people in the room.

It was Saturday at midnight when James expressed his thoughts on the unfolding subject matter. The people in the room listened, and they did not like what the Alpha Omega colleague had to offer.

James politely played down the idea of a pollution scenario; although very plausible it was not the style of Al Qaeda. The impact as indicated by the chatter and television media from the Middle East suggested something far more sinister, something far graver than 911 or the Wembley Stadium tragedies. James continued, he had advised the group that the recent capture of the New York terrorist involved a plot which entailed the use of stinger missiles. According to Guantanamo interrogation teams this was just an appetizer of what was to come. In assessing the situation given the facts in hand it must be assumed that the rig offshore the coast has been taken over by eight terrorists. For what purpose one can only guess, but fearing the worse one must assume that by some means the rig has been equipped with a nuclear missile and the target is either New York and or Washington. Given the short flight path of the missile it is doubtful that patriot missiles or whatever counter measures you may have (referring to the Americans) would actually intercept and destroy the incoming threat. Reality was sinking in; the gravity of the situation was visible on their faces. The generals and the air force commanders simply responded with a muted *mmmmmmmmmmm!*

James continued, gentlemen, time is of the essence, we need to know over the last seven days, rig supply movements within the Eastern seaports, manifests need to be screened, crew lists crossed referenced, anything that does not match normalcy and or causes a red flag to be raised we need to know. Upon hearing that statement an assistant left the room to secure the information requested. They would be in receipt of the relevant data within three hours or so.

James carried on, gentlemen there is another worse case scenario, the secretary of state intervened with, "What could be worse than this?"

James replied with the fact that, "There could be more than one nuclear warhead on the rig." Momentarily the room went silent, and then the secretary of defence, clearing his throat, simply asked, "What do you recommend?"

James had the floor and recommended that he and two seals take the rig back and then re-evaluate the situation. Without being asked to continue James suggested that three operatives would be transported to the rig site by coast guard air patrol and at five thousand-foot altitude, they would parachute under the cover of darkness to the rig. They would access the rig from the sea via the access ladders on both sides. Three against eight would be a simple challenge, and then we may know what we are dealing with.

James concluded that by midnight the next day they would have regained control of the rig. The Exxon officials looked elated, but their glee would be proven to have been premature.

The room was quiet with numerous eyes meeting others, but eventually an okay was heard, the secretary of defence sanctioned the plan. With that James wrote down a lengthy list of equipment required and handed it to a US seal official. Feeling the time change and the lateness of the hour James requested a bunk, he wanted his four, possibly five hours rest.

Behind the scenes the CIA continued checking a host of leads but little was bearing fruit. For the first time in USA/Canada there had been two car bombings on the same day, one in Port Arthur Texas and one in Edmonton Alberta. Both involved suicide bombers detonating their body packages amidst the jungle of refineries. It was most evident that the terrorists were accelerating their agenda. The resultant damage sent the price of Crude up almost two dollars on the world markets. It was forecasted that North Americas oil supply would be compromised for the next four months by fifteen percent; a sizeable blow to the economy.

The Tower Thistle

It was Sunday, the week had been the busiest that Sir William Myers could ever remember. He had been with the Foreign Secretary and most recently the Prime Minister for the past week. The heightened alert was telling on everyone. All of the senior staff, including the Prime Minister, Defence Minister, and Foreign Secretary had relocated to the "tomb" a short distance from Maidstone Kent; it was in fact a concrete bunker but aptly nicknamed the tomb. Sir William decided to take a break and returned to London. He was driving his old friends Bentley. The luxury automobile was one of the last vestiges of his great friend and colleague, a man that he missed like hell.

For many years now Sir Billy enjoyed the Sunday brunch at the Tower Thistle. It was simply a buffet of traditional English Sunday lunch. Millions of people would be scoffing down a similar meal, it was just that Sir Billy had no wife, no children and more so, his cooking sucked.

He went to the second floor where he was ushered to his usual seat, a table for two, but for him it was never the case for two. The hotel was very reasonable but they probably never made a penny of profit with Sir Billy, at least not with the food. Sir Billy still had a monstrous appetite and could eat a horse. Offsetting the non profit items the hotel made good on the Port. Sir Billy would easily drink one full bottle when chasing down his cheese. On this occasion however Sir Billy would not have a chance to complete his Sunday tradition. He enjoyed roast lamb with mint sauce, roast pork with a good helping of crackling with apple sauce, Brussel sprouts, sweet peas, cauliflower cheese, sweet corn and roasted potatoes. For good measure he had two helpings.

The main course was followed by apple crumble and ice cream; it was delicious. The bottle of port was half finished when he was about to savor the selection of cheese. At this juncture and in full view of a full restaurant two men dressed in black security garb stopped at his table. Sir Billy looked up with tired eyes only to view the silencer of their 9 millimeter pistols,

Sir Billy was armed but he had no opportunity to respond, after all he was an old man. He looked ready to accept the round, and with a small smile he took the bullets dead center of his forehead. With the noise of the restaurant the execution went almost unnoticed but Sir Billy, his Omega having arrived, fell into his plate of cheese with quite a thud, and then chaos followed. Several women started to scream hysterically; the terrorist to keep the public at bay, simply fired indiscriminately into the crowd. The two made off running down to the lobby entrance and exited in an awaiting London taxi. No one followed and the restaurant patrons froze in amazement. Sir Billy sat in a plate of Danish cheese and four other patrons lay in a pool of blood, all four would later die of their wounds.

Within minutes the police were on the scene but the London taxi drove off amongst hundreds more, all of them looking exactly the same, black and ugly.

In the tomb the Foreign Secretary was shocked when informed by the commissioner of Scotland Yard what had recently happened; it was then his job to inform the Prime Minister. The loss of Sir Billy was never considered by anyone; he was a monument of a man and was the cornerstone of Alpha Omega. Sir Billy's replacement was Kane Austin but he was on assignment…the same assignment, a problem of monumental proportion facing the western societies.

The Tower Thistle was cordoned off and the numerous bodies taken to the city morgue, the press were having a field day but the black cloud which blanketed London and Washington remained menacing. The Tower Thistle had lost the old fella, as he was referred to, a fine, fine gentleman.

It was 6:00 a.m. in the US equivalent of the tomb when James was awakened to hear of the news. James was sickened to his stomach a feeling that he had not endured for quite some time. Here he was now losing the only person that he could call family. He requested a moment alone and for the first time for many years he cried and then he prayed. With tearful eyes and a heavy heart, James continued to pray. Prayers continued for almost thirty minutes after which he took a shower and prepared himself for the day.

Before entering the operations room, James took several deep, very deep breaths; he needed to maintain composure and leadership. Everything that he had asked for was made available to him. Two Seals had been appointed and would arrive by air force jet within the next hour.

The vessel movement within the Eastern ports was ready for James to review, the list had been shortened to a mere ten supply vessels. James focused in on the Rigel Kent quite quickly as the crew count was thirty five, this was considered to be far too top heavy for such a vessel. Glancing at the manifest he looked up with frown. Gentleman this vessel had two containers on board, we are most likely looking at multiple targets. Continuing on, James questioned whether the satellite transits had identified anything on the deck f the rig.

Photographs had already been blown up on a four feet square format. James looked closely at the photograph. As usual there were many containers measuring eight feet-by-eight feet-by-eight feet, but he could see nothing larger. He requested that the port box girder be re-examined and blown up further. All of the vessel particulars were later confirmed to be false so with that they had the rogue vessel, what else was there and where was the vessel now?

With the clock closing in on 8 am it was time once again for the rig telephone call, the room fell silent and James listened in to these two veterans of charade continue. The shore based superintendent commenced the questions with why the video monitor was still showing the same well information as two days ago.

The response was fast by the on rig manager as he had most likely anticipated the obvious question. The response was that the rig technician had isolated a certain integrated circuit board which had burnt up. A replacement was on order. With that the shore superintendent commented that he would like the unit to be back tonight but he would wait until the Wednesday crew change chopper. As sharp as a tack the rig manager responded with, "I understand," and he did.......the charade had told the rig manager that something would happen that night. The conversation reverted to rig jargon and hole conditions, all relevant stuff yet all bullshit.

James was introduced to the two seals, but then he already new them. He had requested two of his Guantanamo colleagues to join in on this mission. One of the Seals quietly asked of James how his balls were, to which James responded, round, well and functional! There was no animosity between them, it was just that James wanted some comfort with respect to who was going with him, he needed to trust these soldiers.

James took the soldiers to a private room where he briefed them of the mission and the fact that they thought that they would confirm nuclear warheads on board the rig. They studied the rig layout, the general arrangement having been provided by Exxon. They each committed the layout to memory.

The seals were emotionless, yet the fact that the threat to their fellow citizens could be nuclear weapons was a concern; they knew only too well the consequences of failure. The truth of the matter is that they remained on a high, an adrenalin rush that only people with a license to kill understood.

The game plan was discussed and questions answered, they would depart from the bunker for 9:00 p.m., departure time 10:00 p.m. and a drop time of 10:38 p.m. James requested the Seals to inspect the weaponry and to confirm that everything was in order. James was now beginning to feel the effects of his own adrenalin rush, and he liked the feeling.

The Florida Keys

The offshore supplier sailing in calm beautiful turquoise waters was now rounding the Keys of Florida, the vessel was at least twenty four hours ahead of the arrival of Hurricane Diana, which was making a B-line for the Bahamas and already rated a category four hurricane; she was going to be ugly.

The vessel was now headed for the oil fields almost due south of New Orleans. The Florida Keys passed by as if unaware that they too may be clobbered by Diana within the next twenty four hours. Already the Governor of Florida had issued a mandatory evacuation alert. People took note, it was a grade four and that truly meant evacuate to the seasoned residents. None the less there would always be the hardy type that defied the authorities. Certain people learned their lesson after Andrew, Wilma and Katrina, but somehow time had a way to harden peoples resolve, so once again there could be a pending large loss of life. By the time James and his two seals took off for the aircraft and the parachute drop, the Governor of Mississippi, Louisiana, and Texas had issued the evacuation alert. Hurricane Diana would negotiate the waters between Cuba and Florida and most likely drift to the north to north east to strike Texas or Louisiana.

Masses of people from five southern states were driving bumper to bumper north to avert the hurricane; meanwhile offshore the rigs, and following normal hurricane procedures crews were being evacuated, the rigs would be people less by the time the Offshore Supplier arrived. The Offshore Supplier Captain new the importance of the Hurricane, timing was everything. The plan was being executed remarkably well; they arrived at an abandoned rig and launched the Zodiac. The sea state was choppy but still manageable. Back in the Bahamas Diana had continued her westerly track, having caused two billion dollars worth of property damage and killing twenty people. The Florida Keys had yet to report damage but it was huge. With the announcement that Diana was now a Category 5 hurricane and almost stalled in the Gulf of Mexico, the entire south coast was bracing for the worse.

The Offshore Suppliers crew had no time to waste. Boarding the rig in exactly the same manner as James and his team of two were about to do within the same hour, the terrorists ventured closer to the rig. They approached from the leeward side and boarded without incident. They then had to figure out the location of the emergency generator in order to power up the emergency circuits of the rig and hopefully the crane. It took them twenty minutes to locate the eight hundred kilowatt generator and a further twenty minutes to get the motor running. Once running one of the Arabs climbed the Liebher Crane access ladder and entered the cabin to test the operational controls. They were in luck, and gingerly the terrorist raised the boom of the crane plumbing the leeside of the rig.

They were on track, as indeed was Diana.

Almost stalled Diana was rebuilding her strength for the knockout blow that she would deliver somewhere on the south coast of the Gulf of Mexico. The barometric pressure was dropping like a stone, aircraft surveillance reporting 870 milli-bar pressures in the eye wall of Diana. The pressure at the rig was 978 mill-bars and falling off the chart, the sea state was deteriorating; the rain had started to poor, the terrorist needed to get the container aboard and quickly.

Another half hour passed and it was done. The container was stowed safely on board, the top was opened and the circuitry triggered. Hurricane Diana would make landfall in about twelve hours, so too would three nuclear warheads destined for Houston, New Orleans and Miami.

The Zodiac crew left the rig with the emergency generator running, getting off was a challenge with one of the team being momentarily squashed between the outboard engine and the rig column. Other than that incident the crew climbed the scramble net of the Offshore Supplier safely choosing to leave the Zodiac to Neptune the sea god. The job was done, the crew of the Offshore

Supplier battened down the hatches and doors and set course for the Yucatan and onwards to Lake Maracaibo where she would hide amongst other working vessels. Once there, the crew would make their planned escape to Columbia, Chile, Brazil and onwards to Africa and home.

Three Down

James St. Clair and his two support seal team members boarded the Coast Guard twin otter aircraft, and discussed the destination with the pilot. The coordinates were imputed into the flight computer and they were ready to head ease to the Deep Sea Driller rig. The aircraft stank of jet fuel, but then this was common to these old workhorses. At ten pm precisely they taxied down the runway and braked at the stop line, once given the final OK from the tower they were off speeding down the runway Speed V1 and moments later V2 and take off. The flight time was thirty-eight minutes; the sky was overcast and clear with westerly winds at fifteen knots. The three operatives were dressed in black neoprene suits with pockets on thighs, arms and body.

Weaponry was concealed in waterproof hold alls which were clipped to each person's body belt. They casually covered there faces with black goop making them more menacing than ever. These three large men were ready for the kill, the adrenalin running fast and furiously through their veins. James was comfortable with his knowledge of rigs and advised the team of where he expected immediate contact with the terrorist. First location to hit would be the engine room, and the radio room; they had to have at least one or two men guarding those key areas. The next place to hit would be the theatre room and or the mess room, that's where the bulk of the crew would be found, that's if logic prevailed. The final place would be the rig office. James cautioned his team to ensure that they keep at least two alive for R and R and interrogation. The team of three was as one, totally focused with the most important task of their lives ahead of them. The pilot gave his five minute warning call and each member synchronized their watches, then it was one minute and then Go, Go, Go! They dove out of the aircraft to blend in with the night sky. They had black nylon chutes, they were totally camouflaged. From their vantage point of less than five thousand feet they could see the rig lights below. They had agreed to make their landing on the south side of the rig, and let the warm Gulf Stream current propel them to the port and starboard side of the rig, both stairwells were easily accessible. James would take the starboard side and the others would take the port side. The sea state was moderate with modest sea caps occasionally breaking at the surface. This was not the case for the Gulf of Mexico the sea being prepped for turmoil by hurricane Diana. The operatives splashed into the water some 200 meters from the stern of the rig.

The water was a comfortable twenty degrees Celsius; swimming to the designated positions was an easy task for each of these men. Almost simultaneously they accessed the ladders. James noted that he rig was floating at a draft of seventy five feet, the air gap between the rig deck and the sea was probably some sixty feet. One by one they climbed the ladders which were protected to some degree by the sea by the large thirty feet diameter column legs.

From their position they could look up at the two stairwells leading onto the main deck of the rig. The lighting of the rig was fair which provided a positive plus for the team of three. Once at surface they would make ready their weapons. The plan called for James to take control of the radio room and for the other two to take the engine room. There would be no communication with the exception of an electronic vibrator, a small electronic device which was worn beneath the strap of their watches. The activation of this miniature transmitter receiver was a direct tap on the watch face. Two taps meant plan going A1, whereas multiple taps created a constant vibration which meant the plan was failing.

James was suitably impressed with his team mates. They had accessed the engine ballast control room, taking the two guards there by total surprise. They executed the guards with two rounds each to the head. For a brief second they looked at their handy work to compare entry points, they were of course almost identical, causing the two to grin modestly.

The two operatives spoke with the attending rig engineer and advised him to conceal the bodies and mop up the blood. He was to do nothing more, but wait for their call. It had been five minutes only before James felt the two impulses on his left wrist. He knew his team mates would be at his location very shortly.

He was outside the radio room looking in and he could see that the operator was supervised by only one of the eight terrorist. He also knew that the radio room doors would be heavy and noisy; hence he cautiously decided to wait for his colleagues to arrive. He did not have to wait long; they raced over the short deck to his location. One of the seals asked what the delay was but James dismissed it with a counter instruction. There are two doors giving access to the radio room, they will be heavy and noisy. He pointed to one of the doors and told them to access that one, James in turn would take the other. James waited for the guard to lower his weapon, placing him temporarily off guard. The signal was then given by James and in they went. The seals witnessed the guard spin around with a half hearted effort to raise his M-16, but James carefully with his "Cara Parry" pistol complete with his Italian silencer, extinguished the lights of number three of eight, the only noise being that of the customary *pop pop!*

They gave the same instruction to the radio operator, as they did the engineer below; he looked painfully pale, this was evidently not his cup of tea. From the radio room they confirmed their next targets.

James would take on the rig office on the upper deck, while one of the Seals take the theatre on the lower deck, the third seal would access the second deck and make his way to the messroom. As expected the crew was in the theatre with two guards. The terrorists made an attempt to shoot the menacing black figure that entered the room. The element of surprise was working to everyone's best interest. The terrorist were no match for the seals, and following instructions they simply immobilized their prey with a bullet in each knee cap. Both terrorists were incapable of response. James did not need to shoot his two; they simply raised their hands and placed them on their heads when James entered the rig office. Throwing down electrical ties he permitted the terrorist to tie themselves, wrists only. Once secured James sliced the restraints of the rig manager and the Geologist and then requested that they re do the restraints on the terrorists. The entire operation took less time than expected, but before calling to the shore James waited for the others to reach the rig office. The two wounded terrorists were stripped of clothing and placed in the vessels hospital, no medicinal aid was offered, in fact the two injured were strapped to the cots with electrical ties and left in the care of the steward. Both terrorists were screaming with pain but no one cared. The two survivors were escorted by the seals to the upper television room; the seals had the job to interrogate these men, the seals referring to them, not very politely, as "Sand Niggers."

The rig Manager was given the task to inform the shore that they had taken the rig. James would now inspect the deck container which he easily found on the west facing box girder, still covered with the net tarp.

James climbed the exterior of the container and lowered himself inside. Armed with a lithium battery powered flash light he shone the beam of light onto the angled short range nuclear missiles, he counted four. Without wasting anymore time he exited the container and raced back to the rig office. The rig manager was advised to call the base again and request a scrambled line to the secretary of defence. Within seconds the bunker folks were all ready for the news, good or bad. James did not hold back and delivered the bad news. We are sitting on four short range nuclear weapons, he needed more time to evaluate the status, but suffice to say the President should remain out west and await our further investigation. There was a muffled voice from the base saying, "Are you sure?"

James did not acknowledge, but told them of his next plan. We shall evacuate the rig as quickly as is possible, but first off the drill crew will need to shear the pipe and disconnect the lower marine riser package. The rig will then be skidded some 1,000 meters clear of the well head. This should not take any longer than one hour, and with that the rig manager took off, he knew the grave situation they were in and the one hundred million dollar well was minuscule to what was unfolding. James advised the base that he will attempt to disarm the missiles but he needed to rig up lights and assess the apparatus. The weapons appear to be targeting Philly, New York, and Washington, he estimated that the bombs were one to one-and-a-half kilotonne, large enough to cause significant concern; a deliberate understatement by James. He quickly advised the shore staff that they were currently interviewing the two terrorists that were kept alive for that very purpose, he would report back in one hour. Again there was an almost choking muffled okay and then silence.

James had the rig electrician rig up several lights, after that he had no problem seeing the deadly weapons, and more importantly the sophistication of electrical panel. He agreed to the assistance of the electrician who had offered assistance willingly. Together they pondered the circuitry. The units were rigged in parallel yet there were anomalies to the logic, evidently trip circuits were designed to prevent premature disarming. Together, with sweat pouring down their foreheads, James and the electrician pondered the situation and after an hour or more with careful consideration James had no choice but to seek additional help.

James dispatched the Lecky (Electrician) to obtain a video camera, they would install the camera inside the container and connect up to a wireless lap top and create a direct feed into the nerds ashore. The circuitry was very cleverly done, everything that they thought they could do had a trip circuit; even the antenna could not be removed. The lap top was set up and they resumed their course of action, or perhaps non action.

The rig had been moved off location and under the instruction of James the two aft lifeboats were launched with all crew and the four terrorists except the rig manager; the rig had just James, Lecky and the seasoned oilman aboard. The lifeboat crews boarded the attending support vessel and made their way to a position twelve miles upwind.

This distance was in keeping with the navy alert for the isolation of the area from merchant shipping. A naval exercise area had been declared with the caution that live ammunition would be used. The naval exercise area had been declared with the rigs position and, in fact a fifteen mile perimeter defined.

The seals had left their spare cell phone batteries for James and already he had exhausted two of them. They were in constant communication with the bunker and the very best of bomb disposal crews they had. After the passage of yet another hour the progress was zilch. James changed his cell battery, the last but one. It was clear that if the first three warheads were neutralized then the fourth would automatically trigger ignition.

It was a brain teaser yet the answer unfolded from the seasoned oilman with a simplistic approach.

He had listened to the conversation and he gleaned that the fourth missile would be triggered by the trip solenoid or by the receipt of the transmission signal. He asked the question whether they could attach a magnet to the solenoid switch to prevent operation leaving the fourth warhead live yet the other three would be neutralized. The plan was simple and immediately the nerds ashore confirmed that it should work, the problem being where do you get the magnet? James knew the answer, the rig manager already rushing off to the drill floor. He returned with rope and the largest magnet one could possibly find. It was a common device used by drillers to recover debris from parts of tools lost down hole. It was a heavy sucker and it was not an easy task to strap it on the side of the solenoid, but with rope and magical duct tape the job was done. The solenoid would never move. James offered the other two members whether they would like to take off in the man overboard jet launch. Both said no. The shore staff crossed their fingers and wished the three of them good luck. With that James disconnected the warheads one by one. With two down and one more to go James felt sick to his stomach, and he was close to being incontinent but his anus muscles managed to maintain control. On disarming the third warhead a weird noise was heard but came to an abrupt stop. The anus muscles barely maintained their function but here they were all three alive. The Lecky said, "Let's get the fuck away!" The remaining warhead remained active, but ignition could only be achieved by radio signal, the origin of which was yet to be determined.

Relief was apparent in the bunker and in the tomb in London England; they had all been linked by satellite to what was transpiring, minute by painful minute.

With dawn breaking James and his triumphant team pulled the release brake to permit the descent of the man overboard jet boat. In a few minutes they would be heading to the safety of the supply vessel. Traversing the Atlantic Ocean the craft was skimming the surface at twenty five knots, they made the twelve miles in less than half an hour. With the sun rising at their backs they clambered aboard the stand by vessel. James made it on deck first and then made a dash to the closest washroom where he threw up, he then relieved himself and spent five or so minutes sat on the john rethinking what they had just done; three down, what else was there?.

James freshened up at the sink and washed his face of the black goop. He then regained composure, no one had witnessed his bathroom releases but then again he did not really care, he was after all human.

James made his way to the bridge and introduced himself to the Captain, a slim fellow with a well groomed silver beard. They were all watching the Miami weather station, Diana capturing their focus. The speed of the Hurricane was now at twelve Knots and the track forecasted to make landfall at 4:00 p.m. Louisiana time, the most probable location being Pearl River LA. Wind speeds of one hundred eighty knots was already being reported which ranked the wind speeds right up there with Camille, a powerful sixties hurricane. Diana however had the same diameter as Katrina in 2005, and everyone knew that Katrina set the bar for damage and death toll.

The Captain commented that New Orleans was in for a "shit kicking." Back in Iran, Al Qaeda operatives confirmed the hurricane landfall time to their superiors, the signal would be given to launch simultaneously.

James downed a coffee before taking off to see the two wounded terrorist and the other non injured scum. James wondered how his fellow seals had performed.

American Airlines Flight 105

The flight left on time from London Heathrow, departure time 12:00 noon. Flight time, seven hours, forty-five minutes direct to New York. Four of the Black Watch Warriors boarded without incident. They took their aisle seats throughout the plane. Strapped to their bodies was plastic make belief explosives, the plan was simple; they would hijack the aircraft and threaten to blow up the plane. On the ground somewhere in the streets of London the chatter would reveal that there was a nuclear device in the cargo hold of AA flight 105.

This additional threat was purely a diversionary measure to aid the success of the other six nuclear warheads programmed to strike six major US cities. It was hoped that the US air force would destroy the aircraft before reaching the coast, an irony that would later be realized by the Americans when Aljazerra television reports that the aircraft had no explosives or warheads on board at all; it would be declared a hoax. The nuclear attack would hopefully render the USA to a third world country, an Iraq equivalent.

The terrorist had to make their move at the half way point, approximately three and half hours flight time across the Atlantic. They knew that they had an appointment with their maker that day, but then that's why they were there.

Getting through the security was no issue; the plastic dummy explosives had no metal components. They all had British passports, good credentials, clean driving licenses and no prior convictions. Taking over the plane would be equally as simple.

The flight departed on time, the Boeing 767 souring into the skies, challenging a head wind of forty knots. Two hours into the flight the Captain was informed of the bomb threat, an instruction initiated from the tomb in London. Both sides of the Atlantic were consumed by the gravity of what was happening, first the rig matter, the other container and now AA Flight 105. The Captain confirmed that everything was ok onboard but requested instructions of where to land. There was silence from the tomb the problem lay in the fact that the chatter had revealed that the ignition source was a device triggered by atmospheric pressure, the pressure equivalent of altitude 20,000 feet. The aircraft was at 35,000 feet, so they were doomed. No one could think of anything, as jettisoning cargo was not an option given the ceiling in question. Orders from the tomb recommended that they cruise at minimum speed so that they could buy more time, meanwhile altering course to Goose Bay Newfoundland/Labrador.

The pilot reduced speed to three hundred miles per hour ground speed and sat in disbelief of what was happening. With the reduction in speed the Captain made the grave error by advising the passengers that they had been diverted to Canada for mechanical reasons.

The message alerted the terrorists to advance their plan; they needed access to the cock pit. Since the event of 911 the aircraft cockpit doors had been reinforced and were to remain locked in flight. Accessing the cockpit would be a real challenge, at least that's what they thought.

With five hours remaining if on track for New York, the terrorists were flabbergasted at the opening of the cockpit door. The Captain had his family in business class and he felt compelled to see them, it could be for the last time. The terrorists seized the moment, all of them rushing to the front of the aircraft.

The captain made an effort to stop the group but he was a small man and was easily overwhelmed by the group. They now had access to the cock-pit, the leader instructing the co-pilot to resume course and speed to New York. Two of the terrorists stayed outside the aircraft cockpit door with their shirts tore apart, bearing the array of explosives neatly strapped to their chests. Fake or not, the devices looked very real. On shore flight control monitored the drastically altered flight path; the news quickly reached both bunkers. On board flight AA105 the co-pilot activated the hijacking toggle switch which merely confirmed to the bunker boys that the worse was yet to come.

Bitter Memories

James St. Clair made his way down to the television room where the four terrorist had been corralled by the seals. James entered the room and immediately there was a gaggle of chatter between the four. Little did they know that James understood everything they were saying, he was shocked at what he heard. One of the uninjured men referred to James as the son of the judge. James listened carefully and their loose talk revealed that Kane Austin was at the top of the Al Qaeda list of most wanted, and quoting George Bush, dead or alive. Memories flooded James' mind and the adrenalin flowed through his veins like a raging river. James instructed the seals to take out their knee caps pointing to the uninjured Arabs. With their pistols, the seals obliged. The whaling was immense but James was not deterred. He wanted answers, where was the other container bound to which he got a joint, "I do not know." James ordered the seals to take out all shoulder joints, pointing to all four Arabs. The 9 millimeter. Pops were followed by screams, the screams were absolutely horrific, yet they continued to say, "I don't know." Their cries and groans emanated throughout the accommodation of the supply vessel, but there was no aid coming.

Walking amidst the blood and splintered fragments of bone James sadistically instructed the seals to use the fire flies. The special pre-order, the request of James was made ready. The terrorist were drifting in and out of consciousness but then there was lots of sea water to freshen them up. The seals tore off their trousers and underwear to reveal the jewels of manhood. They repeated the torture that James had endured. The effect was instantaneous. With swelling testicles one by one capitulated and unsealed their lips. The pain of the fire ants was obviously far worse than the bullet wounds in their knees and shoulders. The voracious little beasts were removed from their genitals and James spoke to them in their mother tongue as fluent as anyone of them could be.

James asked who had killed his father, and two of the four pointed to the one named Mahar. With that James shot the culprit in the groin, he would surely die with loss of blood in a short while. James realized that he was now enjoying these barbaric acts far more than he should do, but after all, *it was the right thing to do.*

The interrogation went on and the blood continued to swamp the room. The terrorist revealed that their would be a nuclear device on an American Airlines flight that day bound for New York, but getting the other information was lost, they actually did not know the final plot, hence they endured far more torture than most could ever humanly take. One by one they met their maker.

With the last terrorist dead James went to the Bridge to call the bunker. He advised them of the AA flight and its deadly cargo; the bunker team acknowledged that they already had the play in progress.

James was exhausted and was hoping for a second wind when once again the skipper turned up the volume on the television which remained tuned to the weather channel. Hurricane Diana would make landfall in two hours.

Ashore in both underground havens the reality was sinking in, the politicians and Joint Chiefs of Staff concluding that they had little choice but to destroy flight AA105. Time was running out and the aircraft remained at five hundred sixty miles per hour ground speed and rapidly approaching Cape Cod and Long Island.

From the bridge of the supply vessel James witnessed the two F-18 accelerate off the deck of the USS Constellation Carrier some five miles distance away, he knew what their orders would be. James took another cup of disgusting stale coffee, yet it held certain magic. Something was not right with the scenario taking place, why would there be two nuclear devices targeting New York? It did not make sense, James needed to know more. He called in again to the bunker and requested the details of the aircraft bomb. The story was unveiled and he was told of the atmospheric triggering device. James pondered the situation and supped at the black gruel. The coffee magic stimulating his grey cells; and then he mumbled to himself, "Of course, what did they have to lose."

James followed with, "Get the air plane to reduce altitude to 18,000 feet. Get that message to the pilot. It's a hoax. Do not shoot the plane down, damn it, it's a hoax."

James now had the respect of the bunker boys and immediately the signal was sanctioned and discretely given to the pilot of flight 105.

Within five minutes the F-18s was on the tail of the AA aircraft in perfect position to eliminate and destroy.

At 20,000 feet altitude nothing happened, at 19,000 feet, 18,000 feet the same, the bunker crew came to realize that this was indeed a diversion. Realizing the situation the co pilot of flight 105, with the seat belt sign illuminated, started to do some aerobatics of his own. A severe roll to the left followed by a counter to the right, left, right and left again, the rocking and rolling succeeded in knocking the once standing terrorist to the roof and floor of the fuselage. After several minutes of violent maneuvers the terrorists were down having suffered broken arms and bruised skulls. The co pilot leveled the plane and instructed the passengers to restrain the four terrorists. Several of the men obliged and aggressively took their prey. Within minutes of being destroyed by their fellow country men, flight 105 was saved. The F-18 fighters were then instructed to escort the plane to a base near Portland Maine; they would later land in safety. The prize would be four more terrorists for Guantanamo. The flight passengers discovered the play like sticks of dynamite and informed the Captain who once again, sitting next to his co pilot took control of his aircraft, and relayed the message to Tower control Boston that the threat of a bomb aboard was a hoax. The bunker teams in both UK and USA was now very much aware that the day's events had not yet finished. The burning question remained, "The Diversion, what was the plot?" Time would tell and very soon.

Mushroom Cloud

Back on the supply vessel James remained stoic, enduring the foul tasting coffee. There had been sweet *dixie* from all of the brain trusts on both side of the Atlantic, a massive blow was about to be inflicted on the most powerful nation on earth. Even with terrorist threat matrix/models and the best of the best of nerd power no one had any ideas or answers. James racked his mind but he could not explain the puzzle.

In the background James could hear the weather channel confirming the landfall of hurricane Diana; she was right on track and on time. Like Hurricane Katrina years before she would deliver a knockout blow. The knockout blow this time however would be a two punch combination.

With the announcement of Diana's landfall, the early evening offshore the Eastern USA coast was illuminated with a flash of light with blinding intensity. The radio signal had been sent from the other side of the world triggering the circuits of the six nuclear warheads. Three had failed to launch from the rig, but the fourth had functioned as per the design. The deep sea driller was gone, vaporized, replaced with a mushroom cloud ascending some fifteen thousand feet upwards into the troposphere. The stem of the mushroom was a menacing gray color supporting above the unfolding umbrella of a dirty white mushroom cap, radioactive particles superheated providing a recipe of death to everything within the mushroom shadow. In the area where the drilling unit had been a ten foot wave emanated from the location, a small tsunami radiating a full 360 degrees. The ship's captain turned the bow into the direction of the wave, it would not be a problem for vessels at sea but for comfort and to avoid an unnecessary roll, bow to sea would be preferable.

James watched in awe and wondered what was happening elsewhere; moments later the sickening news started to filter in. CNN was now the news center for the world, the audience estimate at over eight hundred million.

Hurricane Diana having masked the incoming warheads was now taking a back stage to three nuclear strikes, the targets being Miami, Houston and New Orleans. The nuclear divide was about to be borne.

A significant portion of the city of Miami was raised to the ground. Estimated deaths even with the prior evacuation would total excess of one million. The fall out was mainly to the north and west, the nuclear pollution blanketing Tampa, Orlando, Melbourne, and many more towns and villages. The majority of the people were aged and unable to cope with the reality of what was taking place. People wandered the streets as if zombies. Tears flowed in every community; the event was unbelievable; this was a monstrous act of cowardice delivered by the radical few. The governor of Florida had declared a State of Emergency, yet FEMA and the National Guard could not cope with what was unfolding. Looting was already abundant and the streets of every locality was lawless...chaos ensued.

It was the same story in Houston and the surrounding areas. Grief was everywhere. The death toll was similar to the numbers in Miami, yet they were still finding bodies and partial bodies in vast numbers. The later death toll estimates due to radiation would match the initial blast victims. The burn victims that survived the explosion wished that they were dead, and of course with infection and limited medical assistance available meant that most would have their wish come true. The stench in the air was as dangerous as the nuclear fallout. Chemicals galore clouded the lower section of the state.

Those that survived could barely breathe; eyes were swollen and facial expressions were clearly ones of desperation and disbelief.

People would ponder, "How could this happen in the USA the land of the American Dream, the most powerful nation on the planet?"

Miami and Houston was horrific, unbelievable, tragic, grave, but New Orleans was all this and more. For years the city had been rebuilding from the devastation caused by Hurricane Katrina, but this was something else, in fact words could not describe the devastation suffered by this old and tired city.

Diana made landfall just a few miles to the east of the city, bringing with her a storm surge of thirty-five feet, causing the levies to fail prior to the nuclear blast. No one would know the chain of events that unfolded as those that knew perished with the arrival of the kilotonne warhead.

All of the early warning systems had failed to detect the incoming threat; this was bizarre and beyond comprehension considering the high alert status.

Under the veil of a massive storm system three short range nuclear warheads beet the finest of detection technology, all three made the short distance to their respective target. Had it not been for the Alpha Omega team the impact could have been worse, with three more cities down.

New Orleans was under water for the second time in their history, however this time the resolve of the people was nil, in fact drowned.

Post Katrina, New Orleans had regained almost seventy-five percent of their 450,000 population but now there was no one. Only those people that evacuated survived the blast, whether they survived the fall out only time would tell. The city outskirts were ablaze with refinery fires, manufacturing and chemical plants, there being no one to render any form of assistance. Lake Ponchartrain had increased its boundary by one hundred miles and the perimeter was still growing. The beautiful old city of New Orleans was literally drowning in the muddy waters that deluged the parishes of Saint Bernard and several others. The Mississippi river and Lake Ponchartrain and the Gulf of Mexico became one muddied body of water. Standing alone as if a pillar of strength the Hotel Le Pavillon stood tall, for some reason spared the effects of the blast, the majority of the other tall towers were leveled or partially so. The outskirts of the city was not spared, the destruction was eerily similar to the destruction caused by Hurricane Katrina several years before. To compound the problem Diana was still alive and well and tracked to the north east spawning over thirty tornadoes and inflicting more damage to a nation already on its knees. Economically the country was now teetering on bankruptcy; the recent blow to Houston and New Orleans had curtailed the Gulf of Mexico oil production to nothing. Combined with the terrorists events that took place in Canada, the USA crude imports and production would be down some thirty percent. Although little consolation the US policy to increase the strategic reserves by one hundred percent had just been completed, however it meant little now given the tragedy now strangling the nation. The additional industry losses as a result of three nuclear explosions were indeterminate yet obviously massive, without a doubt the victory was momentarily the terrorists.

It was not too long before the Black Watch Warriors and Al Qaeda claimed responsibility for the victorious event. This declaration had infuriated the shocked the senior staff still housed in their joint bunkers. The president of the United States was somewhere in the air over the USA, suppressing tears for his people and at a temporary loss for the solution. One thing was for certain there would be retribution; the people will want retaliation but first the entire country needed to breathe and think and morn.

Back on the supply vessel, James, like all of the others was engrossed in watching the television, even though the same scenes were being released time and time again. The CNN reporters had flown over the cities from all points of the compass. It was thought that the continual rain offered some degree of protection from the radioactive dust, perhaps they were right. Regardless they were the eyes and window for the world and the sights televised were staggeringly horrible. Already the Red Cross, Salvation Army, United Way and a host of other charities were rallying to the urgent need. Countries around the globe were donating millions and billions of dollars. The unity between countries was inspiring and immediate.

Hurricane Diana however appeared to fall off the radar, her property damage being of concern to the insurance markets only, albeit lawyers in the southern states were licking their chops like pigs to a trough, from Jacksonville, Atlanta, Destin, Jackson to Baton Rouge the regular legal parasites were figuring their next moves to create class action law suits wherever they could. It was after all the expected ethic of the lower state lawyers and not truly the American way.

CNN would concentrate on the worse of the worse events, and would reign supreme in the news world.

The incoming call was for James it was the Foreign Office, the minister himself calling from the Maidstone tomb. A solemn voice could be heard, and James answered, "Yes, I saw it on CNN."

James carried on a brief exchange with the minister, apparently they wanted him back within twelve hours, quite the task given his location, but then this was the gravest of times. James instructed the supply vessel Captain to head for the USS Eisenhower, the carrier just to the west of them. He would board the carrier and wait the arrival of a British Harrier jet which was already on route and expected to be arriving within the next hour and forty minutes.

James then turned to the Seals and requested that they promptly proceed ashore to Portland and take charge of the four surviving terrorists; they were to be taken to Guantanamo.

The seals had grown to respect the British Alpha Omega guy and smiled with his last statement, which was, "Make sure that you spare no mercy, and get everything out of those sand niggers before they give up the ghost; Oh! and don't forget to take the little Beasties with you."

With that James was about to leave, the opportunity to shower and get out of his neoprene garb was pressing. The Captain of the supply vessel offered the use of his shower facilities and acquired a blue set of extra large coveralls for his guest. Before James left for the shower the entire crew of the rig wanted to express their thanks. They were all apprised of the disaster that had manifested in the Deep South. Many of them having homes in New York and Philadelphia, but all were US citizens. One by one, they made their way through the confined space of the bridge, some were crying while some contained their emotions, all of them extended their hands and offered a simple thank you for everything.

It was a very touching moment for James as only then did he realize the scope and success of his assignment, he could not possibly have known the complete devious plot of the Al Qaeda and for the first time reality sunk in that he and two others had saved three key US cities and countless numbers of lives, perhaps millions.

After James freshened up, he headed once again to the bridge. The Captain was maneuvering alongside the giant ship lording above them. In position beneath the crane wire and Billy Pugh net James took his leave. With a farewell to the Captain, the oilman, Lecky and his Seals he made his way down to the deck of the supply vessel. Moments later he was hoisted aboard the USS Eisenhower and greeted aboard the Carrier, once again he was touched by his reception.

Climbing out of the Billy Pugh net he was greeted with applause, everyone without exception was clapping their hands. Escorted by a tall lieutenant, James was taken to the Admiral. The applause did not stop until he had met and shaken hands with the silver hair and silver bearded Admiral. The Admiral congratulated him on a job well done; it was as if they had momentarily forgotten about the disaster still unfolding on their southern shores. With full knowledge that Protocol was about to be breeched the Admiral had a bottle of Bourbon, a bowl full of ice awaiting his arrival, the Admiral and a few other privileged officers joined in with a toast of gratitude.

James savored the drink and for the first time felt drained; he had to take a grip of himself; all of this attention and admiration being totally foreign to him.

The conversation turned to the cities that were not saved, the tragedy being televised on the bridge of the carrier also.

The Admiral commented that the repercussion would be far worse and he hoped for a steady hand at the tiller of government. Everyone offered their opinions on what should take place and of course many were radical and far off the wall, yet totally understandable; all agreed that the president had one hell of a job to do.

The British Harrier arrived shortly after James had downed his third drink; he enjoyed every one of them equally. The pilot of the jet refueled and took the opportunity to visit the washroom and down a Starbucks coffee while James suited up. Within forty-five minutes of the jets arrival they were gone headed North East to the south shores of England.

James was once again in his element albeit he was merely a passenger in the back seat. It was a time for reflection and a time to think what the US response would be and when? It was a terrible time for the world and he knew that there would be many more deaths of innocent people before it was over.

In the back seat of the jet James tuned into the BBC radio where he learned the British perspective of recent events.

The blame was being placed fully on Al Qaeda and their sponsors of terrorism, namely North Korea, Syria and Iran. James wondered how much of the statements were supported with sound intelligence. No doubt he would learn more upon his arrival at the tomb.

London

Surprisingly, James was taken to the city airport and not Maidstone. Apparently, the threat of London being attacked was played down and the bunker folks had been informed to return to their London center. James thought that this was premature but he was out of the loop as it were. Landing was achieved as per a normal flight, there being no need to engage in a vertical approach. Once stopped and on the tarmac James climb out of the machine and was met by Military police. He was driven to Downing Street where he would have an audience with the Prime Minister, Defence Minister and the Foreign Secretary, and a host of other senior officials including certain members of the shadow cabinet. The drive to Downing Street was short, and thankfully the MP's took him across the road from Number 10 to the Foreign Office where Sir Billy's personal assistant had the initiative to prepare James's civilian attire. James climbed the familiar stairs to Sir Billy's office, except it was not Sir Billy's anymore but Kane Austin, a new brass plate adorning the office door. Sir Billy's personal assistant was now Kane's. Wow he thought, he had not had the chance to consider the appointment, but he knew all the same, that he would take it, especially after the past events in the USA.

Kane took a few minutes to strip and shave; he then clothed himself with fresh attire. Fully dressed and looking like a city gent he informed the MP's that he was ready to cross the road.

A short walk and they were knocking at the famous black painted door of Number 10 Downing Street with two six-foot-tall, heavily armed London Bobbies watching on.

The senior butler opened the door and Kane was escorted into the large conference chambers. Affirming his London presence he was offered tea and biscuits, he took the tea and stood standing waiting for someone to take charge of the meeting, and perhaps certain introductions. The Queen Ann china tea cup was empty when the prime minister entered the room and greeted everyone, "Good Evening. Thank you for coming at such a late hour."

The Foreign Secretary Kane's boss entered immediately behind the PM, he took his place at the mid point of the table. The group was requested to sit down and then the Prime Minister ordered one of the several butlers to bring out the port. The portions were generous and a dozen or so bottles soon adorned the rich mahogany side table, indicating that they would kill a few bottles that night. With the port glasses full the Prime Minister stood up to make a speech. "Gentlemen, I introduce you all to Mr. Kane Austin who is taking over from the late Sir William Myers. I need not remind everyone that the events of the last twenty four hours have been extraordinary and beyond normal comprehension, but the tragedy in the USA could have been far more grave, and believe me it is horrific and mind boggling as it is. We are in the presence of this man who successfully disarmed three nuclear warheads which were targeting New York, Philadelphia, and Washington. I have been given the authority by the president of the United States to bestow full American citizenship privileges upon him and to express the entire nation's gratitude for his service under dire straits and extremely stressful conditions. In keeping with the sincere thanks of the Americans, the Queen has ordered knighthood privileges. Please stand and toast with me, a sincere heartfelt gratitude to Sir Kane Austin."

They all stood up and gulped at their port prior to a round of loud applause. For the third time Kane was humbled, but this time amongst his fellow countrymen he was almost reduced to tears.

Life Continues

The celebrity status was soon subdued, the meeting continued on, the port glasses were never empty; the talk remained somewhat loose; Kane thought, a ship without a rudder. In the early am Kane was asked of his opinion to which he echoed the thoughts of the prior evening. "Gentlemen, it is unlikely that the Al Qaeda have another attack planned. Their mission was fifty percent successful so let them gloat for the time being. It is time to reflect and regain composure. We need to solicit the strongest of our allies to join forces to inflict a knock out blow to the terrorists and to the countries that finance them. It can be done but not now, I recommend patience and reflection, having said that take nothing for granted and stay on the very highest of Alerts."

The room was full of muted *mmms* and groans. Talk continued more loosely than ever and thankfully the Prime Minister called it a day, he said to everyone to reflect on the matter and think outside of the box.

Kane was so pleased that the meeting was done; he needed his own reflection with closed eyelids. The meeting adjourned and Downing Street at 2:00 a.m. became a flood of overweight suited gents, most of them tipsy with port smelling breath.

Kane retreated to his Mayfair home and as per usual made his entry via the back door. The home keepers were immediately awakened and met Kane in the hallway, the butler armed with an old 12-gauge side by side Purdy Model B rifle of his fathers.

Whether it was loaded or not was another matter; Kane even doubted that the gentleman knew how to use it.

They greeted each other, Kane with a slight grin; he then made a mental note to get the home keeper a sensible weapon and perhaps some police training at the Maidstone police shooting range.

Kane accepted the traditional welcome with a pot of tea, even at that hour it was a courtesy. The three of them supped at the hot tea and discussed the US tragedy and some world politics, little did they know of Kane's intimate knowledge of the event, and of course, they would never know. With the tea drained the three retired to bed. Kane had four good hours of solid sleep before the butler informed him that breakfast was ready, it was 8:00 a.m.

Kane showered, shaved and put on his Armani threads. He eat breakfast alone, but before doing so he had made a suggestion that they all eat together in the future unless there was reason not too. This was unheard of within the circles of those with and those without. The British snobbery was alive and well, many *wannabees* trying their best to be aristocratic.

Kane had a simple breakfast of porridge, toast and tea, and then he was off to Downing Street and his new office.

Life was anything but normal; upon arrival at his office he requested his assistant Pamela Grabham, Pammy, as Sir Billy called her, to show him the controls for the television which was stored behind a fake bookcase. The assistant like most PA's knew everything. Pammy was a solid employee with an IQ of 140.She was articulate and trustworthy. She usually wore a black jacket and skirt with a white blouse. Her jewelry was minimal with no wedding bands. Her neck sported a necklace of white pearls; Kane believed that she had no other jewelry. While waiting for the television to emerge from behind the false bookcase he thought that the fifty year old assistant must have been very attractive in her day but alas the flower had started to wilt. Working for the Alpha Omega group could do that to anyone he mused. Within moments the bookcase peeled off to one side exposing a sixty-inch-by-forty-eight-inch screen. She automatically tuned into the BBC, but Kane asked her to switch to CNN. The same scenes remained with only minor variances compared to the day before. Nothing could change the fact, the aftermath remained horrific, soul destroying for the nation and the rest of the world.

The President had landed somewhere close to Washington and an address to the nation was planned for noon Washington time. The volume was muted and Kane turned to Pammy enquiring of her knowledge with respect to the nuances of the office. Engaging in light conversation they started to cement a good assistant, supervisor relationship.

Kane asked Pammy where she lived; he had seen her for many years but never had more than a brief conversation when passing through the office. The answer came, Brighton sir. Kane asked many more questions and Pammy had all the answers, and as expected she knew an awful lot of the daily workings within the office, and Alpha Omega. Sir Billy's funeral would be the following morning and Kane requested that she attend the funeral. To his surprise she quickly responded that it was against the Alpha Omega policy, callous though it may seem we keep alive longer that way. Kane knew that she was absolutely right; Sir Billy would be buried with no attendees or family present. By the way sir you will need to see his personal notes that he has left for you, the information includes his will. You will need to view his day work journal which is in the safe, right side of your desk.

He always said that it was the Alpha Omega of operational knowledge. James thanked her and sourced the document, the key was in the safe but the combination was left for him to figure out. The tumble locking device was so old that the Clicks of the worn mechanism could be heard loud and clear, the safe was opened within seconds. Kane made a mental note to change the safe.

Kane opened the legal sized pad and started to read the last twelve months of entries.

It was fascinating reading; he gleaned so much on the business workings of the Alpha Omega Operations and also a little more insight into the mind of Sir Billy. The documents included cash flow projections as well as past income statements, the revenues being stellar.

The document was so painstakingly detailed; it was as if these were the handover notes of one operative to another. The Alpha

Omega Group was in fact a limited company self financed with huge revenues and reserves. The reserve funds totaled half a billion dollars, and revenues consistently exceeded one billion dollars per year. The funds were never audited outside of the foreign office after all the department never existed. The Head of Alpha Omega had complete control of the funds and answered to no one, not even the Prime Minister. The operations were vast and of course Kane recognized the ones that he gad been directly involved with.

The compensation packages too were amazing. Sir Billy had been the recipient of ten percent of all revenue funds; he had accumulated a small fortune in his thirty year tenure. Later Kane would also learn that vast sums of the fund ended up in legitimate charities, Sir Billy being a director of several. They included the salvation army, Red Cross and several orphanages around the globe.

The journal was indeed a valuable piece of information. Kane would re read this journal one more time before the week was out in addition to the other twenty-nine volumes that were stored in the basement of the foreign office.

Sir Billy had made reference to the Iranian advances with respect to their "Shahab" short range missiles. They could actually traverse 1,000 miles. Sir Billy had already received confirmation intelligence that the missiles were indeed ready to spearhead a nuclear device; a test was imminent, if indeed required. Suffice to say the Israeli government ministers were gravely concerned as Iran continued to threaten annihilation of Israel. Something would have to break and soon. The entry made comment that perhaps the Iranians should be allowed to strike Israel, this permitting the West to strike back at Iran, Middle East chaos would remain heightened but Israel would be out of the equation. Kane re read the entry and could not believe what he was reading, the content severely worried him.

Recent entries referenced the loss of four more operatives in Saudi Arabia, Syria, Iran and Pakistan. They were down to twenty-one. The entry referenced the North Korea dam and nuclear power plant event, highlighting the fact that John Bellamy had not checked back in, large question marks remained by his name. Kane too reflected again on the circumstance of John and what had happened; everything had gone so well. The most recent entries referred to the

CIA concern and MI6 with respect to another threat to the USA and London UK. The movement and volume of diamonds; was it time for a dirty bomb? Then there was the break in at the bio chemical storage depot in Wiltshire, certain products to be verified as lost, a notation next to the entry said, Urgent follow up!!

Kane called in Pammy and asked of the event, apparently the ministry of defence was sending over a document pertaining to the incident today. Kane advised her to chase it and to give the document the highest of priorities.

Kane then opened the beige envelope which read Last Will and Testament of William Myers.

Similar to the journal the will was very clear and precise. Kane was not surprised to see that he was the executor and the recipient of eighty percent of the estate. What was surprising was the value of the estate.

Four bank accounts were identified all with balances excess of two hundred and fifty million dollars. There were four properties, one in the south of France in the region of Sanary, one in Vancouver Canada, one in the Caymans and one in Berne Switzerland. Kane had no idea as to their value but he estimated it would be a large number. All four banks had a copy of the will and they would be expecting a call from Kane Austin and or Pamela Grabham upon Sir Billy's his death.

His loyal assistant (Pamela Grabham) was to receive ten percent of his estate, five percent was to go to the restoration fund of St Paul's Cathedral, and five percent to the policemen's widows' fund in London. It was simple and extremely generous for Kane, but then he was already well healed. He would later set up a fund for the victims of the recent atrocity inflicted on the USA. Kane would address the will the following week; this was not the time or place.

Kane had been so engrossed in the year's journal entries that he missed the Address to the Nation by the president but he new that he would catch up with later viewings. Pammy had heard the address on her radio linked ipod and told her new boss, that the message was one of restraint; anger was understandable and revenge acceptable yet the immediate concern was the needs of the southern people.

The address was given by a tearful president; he did not apologize for his demeanor as he too had lost relatives in the Houston area one of which was his elderly mother. Action was promised to follow.

Kane requested Pammy to make arrangements for a new safe and while she was at it organize a couple of day's firearm training for his butler at the Maidstone police range.

It was early evening when the ministry of defence document arrived, Kane was handed the envelope by his assistant who was leaving to catch the 8:00 p.m. train to Brighton.

Kane helped himself to a port and opened the tin of shortbread biscuits, he was hungry but food had to wait. He was anxious to do Sir Billy's urgent follow up.

Kane started to read the investigation report provided by military police, the facts were alarming. Three containers of Agent Orange were missing, four one litre containers of the Anthrax spores, total weight of the bio logical product was forty grams per container, a container of twelve vials of the Ebola virus and a powdered form of the bubonic plague virus, five pounds worth. Kane had no idea what this meant but he could guess only too well. Kane immediately called the deputy minister of defence to get to the facts, he must determine the risk. Kane knew it would be bad but the brief education revealed an alarming risk to the British public. The products were stolen by London based cells of Al Qaeda and it is believed that the target would be London.

When asked what was being done there was a sheepish response, it was unbelievable but true….Nothing, the nuclear attack on USA had created a temporary diversion. Kane was shocked and requested the deputy minister of defence along with, MI6, Special Branch, Scotland Yard Commissioner, the anti terrorist department and their Bio Chemist attend a meeting that same night. Kane would get hold of the Foreign Secretary and the minister of defence; he would also telephone the big guy across the street, and seek an immediate audience.

Given the Prime Minister was available Kane was granted an audience, hence he made his way some fifty meters to the familiar Number 10. Subsequent to the normal greetings and the readiness of a pot of tea, Kane informed the Prime Minister of the seriousness of what he had just uncovered.

The PM was visibly furious as he had no knowledge of this new/belated threat. After sharing some ugly language expressing his disgust at his fellow dignitaries; he carte blanche gave full authority to Kane to investigate the matter and to undertake whatever measures were necessary, he placed emphasis on the words whatever measures repeating the words twice more. He also requested a telephone update every day until something positive broke.

Kane left the conference room for the second time in less than eighteen hours and made his way across the street.

The night staff arranged for tea and coffee to be ready for the upcoming meeting which should be within the hour. It was painfully evident that the bulk of the attendees did not want to be there, Downing Street twice within the day, but Kane dismissed their reluctance and once all were in the room he verbally attacked them all. The CBRN (Chemical, Biological, Radiological and Nuclear) team was in attendance also and cowered as Kane looked in their direction.

His attack was not targeted at any particular person or ministry but he left nothing unsaid, they were told that he, with the PM's blessing would take control of this mess and that people had better perform. The room was quiet; the china tea cups remained untouched with the tea or coffee cooling, as was Kane. Kane requested the Bio Chemist to explain the imminent threat with respect to each of the substances that were stolen. The response was equal to or greater for loss of life numbers compared to the nuclear experience of the USA. The only plus was zero property damage; some compromise he thought. Turning to the police commissioner he requested their initial take on the theft and possible suspects. The commissioners' response was at least a token; they had suspects in five areas, namely Manchester, Bristol, Leeds, London and Birmingham.

There were approximately two hundred fifty suspects, with the largest cell being in London. Apparently they had lots of circumstantial evidence but not sufficient to substantiate arrests. Kane thought briefly and then simply said that this is not a perfect world gentlemen and this matter will never be handled through the hopeful means of diplomacy and dialogue with the countries that harbor and finance the terrorist, neither will the law be adhered to. We have no alternative but to think outside of the box. We will take immediate action and eliminate the threat where ever we believe the threat originates, certain innocent people will be harmed and that's unfortunate; tell the same story to the Americans.

The police commissioner responded that we may be breaking our own laws! Kane calmly said no, you won't be but others will. The commissioner did not like what he heard and Kane had to reassert his mandate and stressed to everyone that feelings, the law and moral issues would have to be placed to one side. Kane continued and for the first time mentioned a newly formed vigilante group, actually known as the Vigilante Corp. This radical group was formed immediately after the US nuclear strikes and their target was clearly that of al Qaeda. It was very apparent to Kane that the governments of the world could only deepen the rift with other countries sympathetic to the Al Qaeda cause if they were to directly retaliate.

No Western country would support or embrace a vigilante movement but at least the blame for their actions would be perceived as vigilante, in exactly the same manner as Al Qaeda. Like Al Qaeda the countries supporting the vigilante group would have no control, other than perhaps finances, a moot point until the perpetrators of the funds become equally as exhausted with the world chaos and fear that terrorism invokes. Kane pointed out that the Irish IRA movement died overnight after 911 when the source funds disappeared. The retaliation of the vigilante corp. will be so great that Al Qaeda themselves will be threatened by their source fund providers, their funds will shrivel up like a prune, they will slowly diminish in stature and eventually like a dog with no teeth they will be starved. Innocent people will die but there is little option given the length at which Al Qaeda has demonstrated they will go. For the moment gentlemen we shall permit the barbaric actions of the Vigilante corp. to do the work that governments can not afford to do, and or be perceived doing.

The question came back from the defence minister, where is this so called group and who is funding them? Kane responded that they had a war chest excess of five hundred million dollars and that they would make their first headlines in the British tabloids imminently but rest assured they are alive and well. Kane of course knew that his Alpha Omega team had just established a new dimension.

Kane requested the police commissioner to ensure that all relevant up to date information on the theft of the bio hazards and the suspects was handed over to MI6, and likewise for the MI6 director to be in his office by noon the next day. Although he had made requests of them it was clearly taken as a direct order by both parties.

The meeting was adjourned with no coffee or tea having passed any one's lips; Kane stayed behind while the others left for their beds. On that note Kane eyed the Chesterfield where he knew he would spend the night.

After they had disbursed Kane for the first time continued Sir Billy's work ethic, he opened the diary and entered certain facts gleaned from the meeting.

Kane knew a little about the plague, in fact everyone knew the area south of the river known as Black Heath, a burial place for so many infected by the bubonic plague.

London's rat population was now in a growth mode paralleling the infestation during the famous Black Plague period of London and Europe.

According to the bio chemist the infection is caused by the Yersinia Pestis organism. In the past Vermin like rats were infected and the disease transmitted by fleas. Transmission from an infected person can be airborne, this being the main trigger for an epidemic. Millions in the past died of the disease. People died of infected blood, lungs, lymph nodes and or a combination of all three.

The incubation period could be as long as two to ten days, but in severe cases a matter of hours.

British Bio chemists, on behalf of their governments for possible war time purposes had created a stockpile of the virus, stored of course in the countryside of Porton Down Wiltshire.

The volume of materials stolen had the killing factor of several millions.

The anthrax threat was equally as bad. Anthrax spores if inhaled usually results in death. Symptoms are similar to influenza; death is brought on by severe breathing problems.

The volume of product stolen, although by weight almost insignificant (160 grams), the CBRN (Chemical Biological, Radiological and Nuclear) teams confirmed that it was sufficient to kill millions of innocent people, if not entire populations, especially on a small island like the UK.

The Ebola virus was another airborne killing bug. To some degree Ebola resembled the plague. Flue like symptoms is common but in this case red eyes and skin rash is an early signature of the virus. Incubation period being between two to twenty-one days and death is the most likely result, albeit some people survive the killer bug. Product stolen sufficient to infect a city, if London then fifteen million people.

Kane wrote more on the Vigilante corp. and made a note for himself to call the PM the next day. He also required more operatives and his thoughts jumped the Atlantic to Guantanamo; he wondered how the Seals were doing with their interrogation of the AA 105 group of four. He would address all of the issues the following morning.

Making himself comfortable on the aging chesterfield, he stretched out for four hours sleep. Sleep came easily and the four hours passed by as if on a fighter jet traveling at Mach-2. Kane awoke and tuned into the US CNN television network. The aftermath was unfolding and chaos was everywhere, Martial law had been declared in nearly all large cities. Mosques and the Islamic people were being targeted, the people hunted like vermin, the national guard not truly attempting to curb the rebellion which was taking place in a host of cities around the country.

Canada provided hundreds of RCMP police officers and hundreds of the remaining soldiers that were not involved in the Afghanistan effort. Somewhat embarrassed at the low numbers the provincial governments across Canada rallied the support of reservist and public volunteers to assist the States with the policing effort. The number of people killed as a result of the three warheads was staggering and forecasted to be eventually in the five million mark. The nation had every right to be angry. The USA was a melting pot for so many immigrants and matters of hate and its consequences could spread as rapidly as any epidemic.

The president of the USA was back in Washington and congress was looking for his response. Even though it was a late hour in Washington Kane made the effort to contact the president. Unshaven and in need of a shower, Kane made himself coffee, using instant coffee and boiling a kettle of water he brewed the drink that buoyed him through many long hours at boarding school. With coffee in hand he placed a call to the switchboard and requested the President of the United States. The call was placed and the President on the line in less than five minutes. Of course the president was already aware of the pending Knighthood, and even with his country in turmoil he had the courtesy to congratulate Kane on the very prestigious award/ recognition.

They both discussed their past twenty four hours although Kane omitted the initiative of a Vigilante Corp. That could wait until the Prime Minister blessed the plan. The President of course eventually said what Kane wanted him to say namely, is there anything we can do to help your situation. Kane then volunteered that he hoped to have an initiative approved later that morning which he would then put to the President. This was welcomed news to the President as he and his advisers had wrestled continuously with non start ideas to retaliate. Kane asked for and received immediate verbal confirmation that he could access twenty of the US seals for covert operations. Kane could seek whomever he wanted. Prior to concluding the call they agreed for another call at the same time twenty-four hours hence. Kane liked the President and felt his pain; he thought that no one should be burdened with such a mammoth task.

Kane once again used the office facilities to freshen up, the old building had it all, but it was an old building with most of the conveniences having died some sixty years ago; nonetheless he performed his ablutions and returned to his office to call the PM. The Prime Minister was briefed on the Vigilante corp. and recognized the pros and cons of the countermeasure. He did not need much time to think about it and because of the non involvement of government, which he painstakingly verified to Kane, he thought that the concept was sound, he did however propose that the group be called the GVC, meaning Global Vigilante Corp; the latter would infer the world was responsible for the global retaliation and not restricted to just one nation. The fact that certain innocent parties would perish was after all collateral damage and for the greater good. Kane then advised the PM that he intended to recruit certain US seals for his campaign hence the US president would also be privy to the plan. The PM was in full agreement and the conversation was complete.

The phone call ended with a repeat request to keep the PM informed on progress. Kane responded with keep your eyes on CNN and perhaps the BBC.

Kane would call the President of the USA at breakfast Washington time.

It was now time to call his new friends at Guantanamo, it was very early, but Kane thought that the boys were getting close to getting up any way. He placed a call to Colonel Sangster who was already up and appeared quite alert, Kane not wasting any time immediately requested to speak to the two seals that was working to some degree on his behalf.

Kane was placed on hold and waited, listening to a Spanish radio station which was quite pleasant, he particularly liked the language; eventually they were both hooked into his line. Kane knew that these boys were sadistic, cruel men but extremely proficient in what they did; he shifted his groin position subconsciously while talking to them.

The interrogation was going well, in fact they had planned a call for him that day to give him what they knew so far. Two of the four could not cope with the treatment and died after the beastie treatment.

Apparently they died of toxic shock. Two left alive, at least barely so. They had revealed that there would be a bio chemical release in certain major cities, and that there never was a plan to nuke London, at least not yet.

The captured terrorist confirmed that the chemicals or bio hazards came from the British stockpile in southern England; they knew it was from Porton Down, Wiltshire. The processing of the chemicals/ bio hazards would be done in either Birmingham or Manchester and the attacks would take place at the beginning of the Jewish New Year Rosh Hashanah, which was just one month away. Targets included Tel Aviv, London, Paris and Frankfurt. Kane was not surprised at what he had heard, but the very confirmation confirmed his thoughts on a GVC movement. They would have to work quickly.

Kane then asked the two if they would like to continue their work with his team on a contract by contract basis. Of course they were interested but reminded Kane that they were already under contract with their own government.

Kane further explained that the President had given him the authority to do whatever it took to reduce the ongoing threat of terrorism. Kane expanded and advised them that bank accounts had already been set up in the Isle of Man and Luxembourg to accommodate the contribution they had already made with respect to the rig event.

The two seals had no idea where the Isle of Man was or Luxembourg for that matter, but they liked what they had heard, in particular they liked the quantum of each account at $1 million/bank account. Their joint answer was a candid yes.

Kane then requested of them to identify eighteen more men, and like them their exiting from the military would not be an issue. A signing bonus would apply of $250,000.00 per person. Kane emphasized the fact that they would not be hired under any formal contract and in fact, they would all be part of one team unless projects went sour. The work was always dangerous and life expectancy explained. Termination would be by mutual agreement but never in the midstream of an assignment. Completion bonus was discretionary and handled by Kane, but always generous. The first assignment was linked with the recent nuclear incident, and their availability would be immediate. The two seals confirmed that they could choose anyone that they knew, and with Kane's response of yes they answered with, "Give us four hours and we will have the team." Kane would phone back in four hours. It was now almost 8:00 a.m. and Pammy came into the office. She saw the blanket and pillows on the chesterfield and then beckoned with her white manicured finger for Kane to look at another wall. Taking a few strides to the north facing wall she grasped a small leather strap which was the pull down mechanism for a single wall bed. This was Sir Billy's greatest idea, he slept here quite often. Kane felt somewhat foolish but thanked her for the revelation. She then asked of him Tea sir? The entire UK drinks tea voraciously throughout the day, in the evenings it was beer or wine or both.

Kane responded with a thank you and then said when you return we have a lot to do.

The tea was good and the shortbread sweet but they both complimented each other. Kane asked Pammy if she took shorthand notes to which the response was "of course sir." Kane then advised her that she should make arrangements for five different down scale hotels within London to accommodate expectant visitors from the US. There would be four to a hotel and he would provide names later.

In fact they would need to arrange passports for each new operative, two each for the time being. We need to arrange for weapons, perhaps Tech 9s and M-16s; thinking out loud Kane said, perhaps give them the same suite of weapons that I have used in the past. We can sort out the "I likes" later!

We will need offshore bank accounts corresponding to the passports and you will need to wire transfer $100,000.00 into each of bank accounts. Also please arrange to have cash ready on hand for each person say $10,000.00, but in UK currency.

I expect to have these gentlemen here by tomorrow. Please arrange for photographs and book the large conference room for the next two days.

I also need to have an audience with the Israeli Ambassador and his senior security aid, ideally within the next hour. Pammy then took off to organize the days work. In the meantime Kane phoned his contacts in the named targeted cities, the consistent response being immense shock when the reality struck home.

Shortly after 9:00 a.m. the Israeli Ambassador and his security aid entered Kane's office. Neither had met before. The ambassador was another large man as was his security aid. Both sported large black moustaches. They were your typical looking Israelis, with permanent oily sun tans. Both wore the standard London pin striped Savile Row dark suit. If bowler hats were in they would have them too, but fortunately the Bowler was a thing of another era. They started the meeting with, yes, tea!!! Pammy did the honors, using the Queen Anne china. Kane explained the operations and the most recent results from the Guantanamo interrogation team. The threat was revealed and their response guarded, although the eyes of the Ambassador suddenly took on the appearance of large saucers. They inquired about the missing bio hazards from the west country but Kane revealed little, simply satisfying the two colleagues that the matter was under investigation and that it was a very high priority issue. As a courtesy the Ambassador offered assistance to Kane's team but Kane responded with a polite no, but qualified the statement with, "Perhaps later!"

The two Israelis supped at the tea and they discussed the status in the US, the status was deteriorating with almost civil strife in the streets. Kane once again emphasized the need for calm, cool heads.

The threat that now presented itself was equally as frightening as a nuclear attack, if not worse. The ambassador stated that they would return to their country later that day to inform the prime minister and the heads of their homeland security; the matter would be given the highest of priorities. With the tea pot empty the ambassador and his security aid quickly departed.

With the office quiet Kane decided to review the personnel files of his remaining team, all twenty of them. The files were in four inch ring binders; Sir Billy as usual had kept excellent notes. Kane knew a handful of these people but regretfully not too well. He saw his own binder which was quite fat and decided to look at his own at a later date. Most of the team were scattered about the world engaged in intelligence research, a nice way to say spying on other countries.

Of particular interest related to three operatives one working on the border of Pakistan, one other in Turkey, and one in Qatar. Their proximity could be of great interest. He placed the three binders on the side and decided to call the individuals in due course for their status update. He would also advise all of his operatives of the current threat that umbrellas the country, and Israel.

Kane asked the impossible of his assistant Pammy, but then she always outperformed every ones expectations. In addition to the pending phone calls to his twenty Alpha Omega operatives, he would request Pammy to prep him on all twenty and to provide a summary of their current individuals assignments, one page per operative would suffice. Like all good assistants Pammy had already done the task and entered the room within three minutes of the instruction.

Each agent had three pages of intriguing summary. Kane was astonished and his respect for the old bird grew a tiny bit more, but just a smidgen. He went immediately to the summary details of the three agents he mentally took note as being TPQ.

The Pakistan assignment was related to the border safe haven for the Taliban and Al Qaeda. Kane read with interest that the agent had gained access to the group of three hundred, many of whom were Pakistani patrol guards. Not only was the terrorism alive and well but the opium market was booming. Estimates of one tonne per day was being channeled through this open market, the US currency was one hundred dollar bills.

It appeared as though the shipments of Opium were stored locally until the latter part of each month when the cargo was shipped south to Karachi, Kandla and Khalifa where it would be shipped and transshipped to the West and Europe. The notes also indicated that prior to shipment there was the mass prayer followed by feast and a great deal of allegedly non alcoholic beverages. Kane's thoughts immediately took him back to Kuwait and Dubai where there too there were a lot of non alcoholic drinks, yet of course they all seemed to carry a heavy punch.

The Turkish operative was assigned to monitor the nuclear power station new build at Lake Van some one hundred miles west of the Iran border. Now almost completed, commissioning was under way; power was already contracted to Syria, Saudi, Iran, Kazakhstan, Jordan and Egypt. In Pakistan the commissioning of Pashawar nuclear power plant had already commenced.

All engineers knew that commissioning was the riskiest time of any operation, if there were screw ups it would manifest itself during the first few weeks of start up. Kane would see to it that these plants would be compromised and that the GVC would claim credit.

Kane was enjoying his review of these operatives having first hand knowledge of their respective roles and challenges. Before he knew it, the Guantanamo seals were on the telephone. Kane took the call and was pleased to be informed that his team had now grown by a factor times two.

There were twenty seals ready to be honorably discharged from the corp and to contract to a company that did not truly exist. They all knew the work was dangerous and that the pay was gravy and more, their motive was pure greed with a large element of revenge for the recent nukes. A personnel list would be sent to Kane after the call. The new crew could be available immediately the colonel released them. Kane advised them to get ready to leave and that he would arrange for them to be brought to the UK as quickly as he could. Kane thanked his colleague and terminated the call. The next call would be to the President of the USA, which would be followed up with the names of the Seals that needed his stamp of approval for immediate honorable discharge.

The next hour was consumed with one call or another but

afterwards the train as it were was well in motion. A commercial Boeing 757 executive jet located in Miami was charted to pick up the new hires from Guantanamo and transport them to Gatwick where Kane would personally greet them. The Colonel had never seen such a rapid deployment of men, evidently this Brit must be well connected he thought. Meanwhile the colonel struggled to get his own replacements for his loss of twenty men; the task would take a full two weeks or more. The twenty new hires would arrive in the UK within the next twelve hours; it would be another late night for Kane.

As planned, and just before noon the office was once again full of dignitaries, the Minister of Defence, the mayor of London, the police commissioner and the counter-terrorism department, the emergency response coordinator for the city of London and certain IT types who had been monitoring and attempting to decipher the global chatter. Pammy had also used her initiative to invite the security chief for the US embassy, a slight oversight on Kane's part. Given the size of the group Kane escorted the group to the conference room where, once again Pammy, using her initiative, had arranged for side tables displaying beverages and an assortment of Danish pastries. The meeting would be a long one and topics discussed included alert status, police exchange of information pertaining to Bristol, Birmingham, Leeds, Manchester and the London terrorists cells, Emergency response preparedness, evacuation plans for the inner city, transportation preparedness, Medical facilities, various Vaccines and global supplies, the availability of beds, the availability of body bags, burial arrangements, incineration arrangements, air support, the channel tunnel, troop deployment, police reinforcements, special hazards clothing, breathing apparatus availability and deployment, emergency food supplies, water reservoirs contamination, etc, the list was endless.

By 6:00 p.m. the group had taken pages of notes and the severity of the risks clearly explained. The GVC the Global Vigilante Corp was not discussed in the closed meeting but with the exit of the bulk of the attendees the counter-terrorist department and the minister of defence stayed behind and were informed of the next stage of the plan which would be fast tracked given the time frame which was governed by the Jewish New Year.

Kane advised them that the GVC would be set up in the West Country where they would work with the minimum of police to stage a strike on the five terrorist's cells simultaneously. The British public would consider the event as a cowardly act with horrific acts of murder having taken place, the press would be provided with the relevant facts for global distribution and the birth of the GVC will be heralded around the world.

Over the ensuing days and weeks the GVC will be made responsible for acts of vigilante terrorism around the globe. The economic cost will be so great that the Al Qaeda movement and other similar supporting groups will be constricted of their support funds, and hopefully the acts of terrorism throughout the world will be slowly choked to death. The meeting came ended and Kane took off in the old Bentley to Windsor for a late supper. He frequented the Swan Inn, allegedly the second oldest pub in the UK. He pondered, wondering which pub was the oldest. He sat in the bar area which was small with very low ceilings, ceilings that looked as if they suffered from acute arthritis or leprosy. His mind replayed the memories of Eslpeth and the pub in Scotland. He then realized that they had agreed to regroup there when the ten year anniversary was up, it would be the following week. Even after all these years of covert operations, several, no many encounters with beautiful women, he had never fallen out of love with her. Sat there looking around the confines of the aged pub he felt very much alone, he missed his parents, he missed the old fart Sir Billy and even more so he missed the love of his life. He wondered whether she would remember to go. Ten years is a long time. He ordered a steak with a baked potato and spinach. He continued to sup his brown ale and thought about the Scottish Highlands and his Elspeth, he knew that he would go to the pub near Balmoral and hope that she would be there.

The food was great and the beer was warm as was the case in the UK pubs. None the less he enjoyed every morsel in addition to his recollection of events that took place nearly ten years ago.

Gatwick

The old pub had a television and after the meal Kane watched the ten o'clock news. The aftermath in the USA remained front news. Death tolls changed by the hour and the chaos in the streets remained a major problem for the nation. Various countries around the world were second guessing the next terrorist attack, in addition to wondering what the USA would do in response. The news ended with the weather forecast which suggested fine and clear warm weather for the next five days. At eleven pm the bar closed and Kane drove to Gatwick to meet his crew, he was about twenty minutes from the airport.

The old Bentley remained a pleasure to drive, it was one tangible item of his father that he cherished, and he knew that he would keep the treasure for always.

Approaching Gatwick from the North West he took a right following the sign Flight Charter Hangers. A mile or so down the road he could see the lights of the hangers and the perimeter fencing. Driving slowly he approached the entrance which was manned with armed patrol guards. Stopping the vehicle he was approached and asked to go into the office. There he showed several pieces of ID and was frisked down with hands and the magic wand.

Kane had no weapons on him; the Bentley was searched but they found nothing. The weapons inside the door panels remained undetected. Kane was then accompanied by a guard to the hanger where the charter flight would taxi to. The Boeing 757 jet arrived within twenty minutes of his arrival as did the transportation coach/ bus, which parked momentarily adjacent to the awaiting Bentley. The jet turbines came to rest and the noise abated, with that the door opened. Ground crews were ready at hand to maneuver the portable steps into position and one by one the Seals vacated the aircraft. Of the twenty Seals three were Caucasian and the others Black Americans.

They were all six feet tall or more and built like Greek gods. With twenty of the men on the ground Kane approached the only two that he knew and they welcomed him with solid hand shakes. The lead Seal stated, "We are all here, sir."

Kane appreciated the respectful "sir", and requested that they all board the bus, with the exception of the two Seals that Kane knew from the rig event. They were asked to sit in the back of the Bentley. There were no customs and immigration formalities, everything had been pre-approved; and with the baggage loaded they were on their way to the M-4 headed west to Tintern a small village on the north side of the Bristol Channel in county of Monmouth shire South Wales. All previous hotel arrangements painstakingly arranged by Pammy were placed on hold, albeit they would be continually paid for.

The journey would take about two hours especially given the speed they would drive and the fact that he motorway would be barely used at 1:00 a.m. They cruised at ninety miles per hour and the old Bentley thrived on the outing. The two passengers were enamored by the luxury vehicle, a vehicle afforded by only the well to do crowd. The Severn Bridge being the conduit between England to Wales was hidden in a blanket of fog when they traversed the Bristol Channel. From the bridge to Tintern was only ten minutes. Throughout the journey Kane discussed with his team leader the outline of the GVC movement, the strategy and the hopeful result. The next few months would be intense, the damage and the death toll of Al Qaeda would be greater than ever before; there too would be unfortunate collateral damage. Kane's assistant had taken charge of a thirty two room hotel; all previous guests were transported to other hotels and paid five hundred pounds each for their inconvenience. The management of the hotel was temporarily dismissed with full pay until Sir Kane Austin was in no further need of the facility. Suffice to say the hotel owner operator was well compensated for the interruption of normal business, and had already left for Spain that same day. Pammy greeted Kane upon his arrival. Entering the hotel it was evident that the IT teams were still working on the various communication systems security, the lobby entrance of the hotel was a mess of cables and light machinery. The bus was unloaded of men and baggage, and departed retracing the drive back to London. Meanwhile the new staff of the hotel, who was in fact men and women of the Welsh Guards, escorted the host of black faces and the few white faces to their rooms. They would be required to congregate in the main breakfast room at 8:00 a.m. Kane too went to his room and settled for four hours of solid sleep.

The morning came quickly heralded by a cockerel close by and the bleating of sheep in the fields. Looking out of his window Kane could see the River Wye weaving its way down to the river estuary near Cheptsow. The salmon were jumping and feasting on the insects that populated the two feet of air immediately above the murky brown water, creating ripples which ringed their way to smooth calm. The water quality was supposed to be improving although it had not changed in appearance from some ten years ago when Kane and John Bellamy had driven by; Kane remembered that John particularly liked this area of Wales. There was a slight mist yet the morning sky was blue, it was going to be a fine day. The peaceful surroundings of the Ross valley was world renowned and Kane breathed deeply, taking it all in. Looking to the south he could see the ruins of Tintern Abbey, and he made a mental note to visit the ruins and read the history of the area. Kane showered and dressed in readiness to meet the crew, this time in daylight hours.

At seven am Kane went down to the breakfast room to find that everyone was already up and eating a traditional English breakfast. Nowhere else in the world can one find eggs with such a rich yoke, superb back bacon unlike the North American bacon slivers, mushrooms the size of small saucers, pan fried potatoes many of which were slightly burnt with crispy edges, and finally black pudding oozing with very un healthy bacon fat. The aroma was magnificent and spoke directly to ones gut. The Columbian coffee too had a pleasant fragrance that complemented the air. Regardless of the cholesterol consequences Kane would partake and eat his fill.

Kane sat next to his unofficial team leader Seal, and Pammy who had completed a bowl of cereal and was now well into a bowl of healthy fruit. They talked about the serenity of the location and the peace that blanketed the valley. Pammy stated that she would one day retire to such a place, and Kane thought that she could do whatever she liked given her financial stability; he also agreed that the area was outstanding and merited retirement consideration. With the meal concluded, by eight am they had a one hour jump on the day. They stayed at the breakfast room and Kane addressed the group, anxious to get things underway. In the cellar of the hotel the weapon stash was being unloaded from their crates and being checked, it was essential that all items had no traceable serial numbers.

Kane addressed the team, they all listened carefully, each of them anxious to know what their tasks would be. Kane went over issues that Sir William Myers had done so years before and to a point he was somewhat aware of Sir Billy's spiritual presence. Kane told his crew that the next few days would be the beginning of retaliation as a result of the nuclear attacks on the USA, on hearing the statement the team cheered collectively a loud Hooray. Given the gravity of the events that took place, the horrific act of terrorism; the results of which had rendered the world to be on a very unstable platform, global war would be inevitable if the USA did not respond in a responsible manner. To this end the USA will not respond and neither will the western worlds, at least not for the foreseeable future. Kane continued to explain.

We have created a movement called the Global Vigilante Corp. We are it. We shall be the western equivalent to an Al Qaeda movement and we shall, in due course inflict significant blows to those countries harboring terrorist cells. We are not approved by any Western Countries, in fact we are persona non gratis, in labor terms we are referred to as Scabs, yet we few, hope to change the course of history with respect to the threat of terrorism. Gentlemen we shall fight fear with fear. This assignment we hope will take several months and not several years, none of you can leave unless in a body bag. Our task is to rid the world of the cowards that fight without uniform.

We look after our own, we take no survivors; there will be huge collateral loss which is unfortunate but we are looking at the greater picture. The nuclear attack on the USA was a pre curser to yet another equally vile event. In recent weeks the UK cells have stolen several large volumes of biological hazardous chemicals, chemicals that were stored by the British Forces not too far from here. Our intelligence informs us that the targets where these lethal biological hazards will be used is London and Tel Aviv, Paris, Frankfurt and very soon. A list and quantities of the hazards will be provided to you during a briefing by the special task force group at ten this morning. At eleven the police counter-terrorism task force and MI6 will share the locations of five targets that we shall eliminate. Again, we stress for our own survival, we take no survivors. From now on you carry no means of identification with the exception of a small implant which we will implant in your arms today; we will have the means to track you. If captured then you must divulge nothing, in the event of death your families will be well cared for, they will of course receive your completion bonus which will be generous. Key to our success lies within our anonymity. Although the western nations will not openly condone our antics they will privately salute us all. We will have all of the assistance we could ever require by our usual police and armed forces, but only in the event that our plans are on track. When things go off the rail we are on our own. In addition to our own efforts, we shall be implementing global strikes with our primary team concurrent to your efforts here in the UK.

This hotel will be your base, your vehicles will be black Transit Vans and your plates when imputed into the police computers will identify joint task force. If stopped by the police, then kill them as they will be hostile. Your weapons are below us and your uniforms will be supplied to you today. If you require anything at all, clothing, medical, documents then you must let my assistant know this evening. Mrs. Grabham will be talking to you all later about passports and bank accounts and cash advances. You can make calls to the US from this facility only but no one can call in. If asked where you are right now then answer with military maneuvers in Norway. All of your families believe that you remain with the US Seals; we shall leave it that way, at least for one year. With that Kane, and taking no questions, he left the room to continue with other matters, but first he would drive up the valley to Ross on Wye to meet the SAS special commander who would be discussing tactics with the GVC later that night.

The drive up the valley was incredulous the beauty beyond belief. Some thirty miles of rich fertile soil, brilliant green pastures, trees with full green foliage providing shade to wooly sheep that appeared everywhere. The Bentley met the chorus of the bleating lambs with the purr of the high compression engine. The River Wye was in full flow providing melody and background noises which successfully broke the peacefulness of the morning. The traffic on the road was almost non existent, Kane had passed an old XK 150 S Jaguar roadster, which was guilty of polluting the morning air with exhaust fumes; the vehicle was in desperate need of a ring job. The only other vehicle was going south, a red welsh single decker bus with only a handful of passengers. The valley was indeed a treasure, quite the contrast to the carnage an ocean away in the southern states of the USA.

Kane was as per usual early so he thought he would park in the town center of Ross, he would find a tea shop and read the morning paper. The town center was charming and in keeping with the rest of the valley. He found a parking spot and then walked briskly following the scent of freshly baked pastries. Some seventy meters from his car he found the source of the aroma, a Maynard's tea house. The display cabinets were full of fresh delicacies, Kane settled for a Venetian slice, an apple turnover, and a pot of tea. He looked around for a seat and was shocked to see the black person sitting alone in one of the wooden booths. Both sets of eyes locked onto each other. Kane carrying his tray of delights smiled from ear to ear, and the reflection was similar. It was John Bellamy looking as well as ever. Putting the tray down Kane grabbed the arm of the now standing John and hugged him as if a brother. The hug too was reciprocated and what appeared to be for many minutes, yet seconds only they shared mutual affection. Kane opened up with, "I am so glad that you are alive."

John smiled and said, "Me, too."

Kane was sensitive to his colleague and discussed the Wye valley and reminisced about their trip there a decade ago. Eventually of course the subject surfaced with respect to the North Korean matter, and what had happened. John in responding, appeared somewhat emotional, possibly scarred psychologically, painted the picture for Kane. John had apparently killed all of his guards with the exception of one who had faked death, only to sneak up behind John to impale him through the neck with an old rusty bayonet which had been attached to an even older 1945 Remington rifle. John pointed to the still healing wound at the front of his neck and at the rear.

John finished the job and killed the guard with a solid neck twist, not only clockwise but for good measure in the opposite direction as well. John had made it back to the Russian border accompanied by three refugee women who carried him on a makeshift stretcher. Losing copious quantities of blood John had lost consciousness. He was told that they carried him for fifteen miles before reaching a small village.

Complete with the bayonet in tact as if connecting his neck to his body, the three women cared for him and with the aid of the villages self appointed doctor the bayonet was removed and certain herbal remedies applied to the wound. John regained consciousness a week later but he was fragile and for once in his life he felt drained of energy, his batteries were flat and almost unchargeable. Kane had wondered why they could not track him but the answer was simple, the transmitter implants some fifteen years ago were implanted in the neck and the steel fid like spike had forced the implant out through the rear exit wound. John declared that he thought that he was getting sloppy and that his time was overdue. Kane knew that his time was overdue but he also knew that his friend was not sloppy, shit happens. Tears welled up in John's eyes and it was clear that he had lost a degree of his self confidence.

Kane interrupted and made a brief call to the SAS fellow and delayed his meeting by one hour.

Kane asked John what he would do, namely the Alpha Omega team. John was hesitant but said that he would contact Sir Billy soon and resign his position. Kane then informed him that Sir Billy was dead, assassinated and that he had taken his place. John was visibly shaken by the news and asked for the details. John and Sir Billy had been very close; Sir Billy in fact had been a father figure to John.

The talk continued and the events that just took place in the States and the fact that Kane had been on assignment and had successfully neutralized three of the six nukes. John was overwhelmed by all of the insight. The topic then came to his reason for being in the Wye valley. Kane had already been told why John was there, even though the statement had been made a long time ago. Kane respected John and the café was as secure a place as any could be. Talking softly, he told John of the bio hazards and the upcoming threat to London, tel Aviv and the other targets. The horrific plans of Al Qaeda had the same effect on John as a blood transfusion to a patient with Kidney failure. John's stomach churned with the reality check and his resolve grew by the second. Kane briefed John on the GVC movement and the upcoming planned events, and then Kane slipped the question, "Are you still in, John?"

John answered with a definitive *yes* and stretched his hand across the table to firmly grasp Kane's. With the conversation complete Kane said that they should go to his next appointment. Kane and John left together and once again they were in the old Bentley, this time working towards the well-being of Millions of innocent people. An hour late the two of them arrived at the SAS military base where they were grilled at the gate by a young guardsman. John was not prepared for the meeting and hence Kane had to pull some weight, and of course he got them both inside. The meeting was really a courtesy call for Kane to come face to face with the British equivalent of the seals.

The commander was a young twenty seven year old, six feet tall with a willowy build. He had piercing blue eyes and a head of blonde hair, a definite Anglo Saxon. The meeting was brief and informative, the two left knowing that they would see him again that same evening. The drive down through the valley was almost a trip down memory lane, however there was a definite tension in the air between them, Kane was uncertain as to the reason, and put it down to possible depression on Johns part. They spoke of the future and Kane was hesitant, uncertain, where as John wanted to complete this last assignment and return to the Valley. John had advised his friend that he had fallen in love with one of the women that carried him through the jungle north of the Tumen River. In fact he asked if Kane could assist in getting her into the UK. Kane obliged and simply said, "It's the right thing to do."

John asked Kane about Elspeth and Kane responded that he still loved her but it had been such a long time. John responded with, "You have not read your file, have you?"

Kane said, "No, should I?"

John replied, "Yes, and soon!"

Kane would have questioned John more but they had arrived at the hotel. They went in and met Pammy who was reduced to joyful tears at the sight of John. Together they went into the all in one dining room /training room /conference room. The GVC were undergoing briefs from the various departments of MI6, special branch and the police counter-terrorism teams. Kane politely interrupted the group to introduce John. John was surprised to see so many black faces, all of these gentlemen were over six feet tall, their ancestry tracking back to Natal South Africa, the Zulu tribe…a heritage of fine but ruthless warriors. John immediately felt at ease and when Kane informed them all that John was his appointed designate, the acceptance was clearly visible in the eyes of everyone, John and Pammy to boot. It was a good morning for John as it was for Kane.

Kane left John to the meetings; he would know exactly what to do. It was time for Kane to motor off to London, he already knew in his heart that the up coming raids on the cell groups would be successful, John would see to that.

Driving back to London was fast, there was a speed limit on the motorway but no one adhered to it. The Bentley negotiated the drive to Earl's court in one hour twenty minutes…that was fast by any standard. The time taken to reach Downing Street however was painfully slow taking almost the same time.

By early evening Kane was at his desk reviewing the latest police efforts in tracking the Bio-hazardous materials. Informants had been numerous and reward amounts tendered by most of the informants. The most reliable source came from an old informant Malik Alfaisal, he had a highly successful track record with the British Police. The sum requested was ten million pounds; the quantum made the informants knowledge even more credible. Given that the funds would not transfer unless the capture of the bio hazards was successful the arrangement was confirmed to be risk free. The deal was going down and the Joint task force and the police were handling the matter. Kane would involve himself in a minor way in that he hoped that the recovery of Bio hazardous materials could be achieved in conjunction and concurrent with the cell group assassinations.

GVC

The British police had already squirmed to the whole plan but Kane's instructions came from the highest of levels, the plan was endorsed and a green light given. All of the raids would take place in two days time, in five cities, at 6:30 p.m., in each location there would a massive cull, no survivors taken, and the buildings would be raised to the ground. Kane discussed the operation to the relevant ministers and the prime minister, in addition to the US president.

Within forty-eight hours the GVC will be borne and Al Qaeda will have a western equivalent. Kane made contact with the Alpha Omega operatives in Turkey and Pakistan and gave them instructions to destroy the nuclear plants at Van Lake and Pashawar. The plants were to be "toasted" as Kane called it within the next ninety-six hours, and both operatives were to head back to London. Within ninety-six hours the Islamic countries harboring terrorists would be awakened from their somewhat insular cocoons and made fully aware of the realities of terrorism, there would be more to follow. Part of the deal with the US president would be exposure to the press with respect to the GVC. The GVC would be condemned in the press everywhere, yet there would be an underlying support by the general public, the same would be true in the UK press.

With everyone leaving for the evening Kane decided to call his Mayfair home and advised the homemakers that he would be there for supper. He would take his files home, including his own dossier.

Again he pulled into the rear of the home; he parked the car and entered the back door. Kane walked to the study, it was good to be back in his father's office. Everything about the Mayfair home portrayed his mum and dad. It was as if they remained in spirit watching over him; it was a comforting feeling to Kane.

Kane was hungry and could smell the roast lamb, the fragrance filling the lower quarters of the large home. Sat at his desk he picked up his dossier. He read and read more, it was like a novel. The beginning referred to his abandonment at St Paul's cathedral, the press clippings were still easily readable yet discolored yellow with age. His fathers fight with the social services/authorities for his adoption. He never knew, he never queried his lineage why should he? Tears filled his eyes, and his appetite was lost to history, his history, his reality, his evolution. The fact that he had been adopted was not a negative issue for him, in fact his love for his parents deepened.

He read on to uncover that Sir Billy had monitored his life growth which included all of his sport, his language skills his sexual liaisons, he knew it all. Elspeth was there too, he even knew about the ring and its cost. Kane remembered the conversation so long ago, the questions asked by Sir Billy, when the answers were already known to him. It was clear that Sir Billy had recruited Kane at a young age and fate did the rest. Sir Billy often used terms of endearment with respect to Kane, this was strange to Kane but he read on to find even greater revelations.

Elspeth had left the oil rigs some four months after meeting Kane. She had undertaken a drug screening test which had also included a pregnancy test. She was positive, pregnant and had to resign her offshore appointment. Elspeth had little financial capacity and when she was seven months term Sir Billy paid her a visit. Sir Billy knew the paternity of the child and asked of Elspeth her intentions for the future. Elspeth had resigned herself to raising her child on her own, as Kane's career was yet to unfold; she was determined not to pressure him into a path that was not of his own choosing. Sir Billy had stayed with Elspeth for almost one week, and he grew to love her as a father, Elspeth took his breath away as it had Kane. Sir Billy had explained that Kane's role was classified and that his compensation for his skill set was generous. Sir Billy would ensure that she was well cared for. This was manifested when Kane's daughter Mary Ann was born, Sir Billy providing her with an annual income equivalent to a

North Sea geologist as well as a fine old traditional Scottish cottage located at Grantham on Spey. Elspeth never wanted for anything. On her birthday Sir Billy generously provided her with gifts of money and cars which included a Range Rover and a Jaguar saloon. Sir Billy visited Scotland every anniversary of Mary Ann's birthday, and like Elspeth he spoiled her daughter. He had arranged a scholarship for her and encouraged activities such as skiing, he had even taken them both to real mountains in the Swiss Alps and once to Lake Louise in Canada. Throughout the last ten years Sir Billy had kept Elspeth well informed of Kane's status. Sir Billy had relayed to her that he truly felt that Kane had a true purpose in life and that the purpose had yet to be manifested. Kane put the dossier down and with a mind that was racing as if at Le Mans, he made his way to the dining room. He was hungry yet all he could do was pick at his food. His mind was elsewhere, in central France doing one hundred fifty miles per hour around the Le Mans racetrack, or something akin to that. Kane was so engrossed in matters of the mind that his Home keeper asked whether the food was satisfactory. Kane responded stating that it was excellent and told her the absolute truth that he had a lot on his mind. Shortly after that he asked for his meal to be left in the fridge and that he may microwave it later. Kane went to phone John in Tintern.

Kane called and shared his findings with John. John already knew about Elspeth and that she had had a daughter, he was pledged to Sir John to utmost discretion. John obliged but did not agree with Sir Billy on the matter. John tried to answer all of Kane's questions but he was at a loss to most of them, instead he suggested that he speak with Pammy, she knew all.

Kane slowly accepted the fact that he had a family; he was a dad in his own right. The whole world chaos suddenly took on a new perspective for him. Emotions were running crazily wild having been unknowingly latent for too many years. Adrenalin was pumping through his veins for entirely new reasons. Kane called Tintern again, this time for Pammy. As John had stated Pammy knew everything and she was not surprised to receive the call from Kane, it had to come sooner or later. She instinctively knew that he had read his own dossier. Kane repeated most of the questions to Pammy that he had asked of John. Pammy was understanding and provided all of the information and more.

Bombshell

If the night's discoveries were not enough then the final bombshell capped it all. Pammy lovingly said to Kane that Sir Billy was his biological father and that Kane's mother; Sir Billy's fiancé had passed away in Sir Billy's London apartment when giving birth. In panic Sir Billy left the child at the foot of St Paul's cathedral and then monitored the outcome. It was his life's deepest regret and Mary Ann was his greatest joy. Kane was rendered speechless and impolitely hung up the telephone. Kane's gut was now on the same racetrack as his mind, but this time he had little choice but race to the washroom. He stayed on the throne for half an hour and then washed his hands and face, and then made his way to his office. Kane called back to John and informed him of his findings; John too was somewhat emotional at hearing the news, albeit he had on occasion considered the possibility. Kane had not seen certain photographs of Sir Billy when he was twenty-five years old, they were as twins. Kane wanted to rush up to Scotland yet the current operational climate was too tense, too onerous to allow him to.

John then suggested that he wait until the conclusion of the operation, code named Striker, and then make his way to Aberdeen. Kane knew of his prior schedule to visit the pub on the ten year anniversary and as it happened that was in three days time, he would do just that. Kane thanked John for his candor and friendship and ended the conversation with, "Perhaps we shall retire together, after all it is the right thing to do."

Kane filled a tall glass of bourbon and then headed to the kitchen where he retrieved his unfinished meal from the fridge. Three minutes in the microwave and it was ready. The meal was magnificent and his gut started to settle, accepting the digestive process, his mind, too, was decelerating, but he knew that he would have very little sleep that night.

Kane refilled his bourbon, Woodford special reserve and sat on his father's leather wing back chair. He was comfortable and content to contemplate his future. He drank several more glasses of the gold brew and then with the thoughts of Elspeth and Mary Ann he fell into a deep serene sleep.

Kane awoke at five am and immediately went for a shower and shave. He looked somewhat disheveled but he was enormously happy, in fact excited. He would see to it that mission striker kicked off on time and confirm matters with MI6 and the police counter-terrorist tactical force to raid the warehouse where the Bio hazard products were allegedly stored, double check matters with his alpha boys in Turkey and Pakistan and then jet up to Aberdeen, hoping and praying that Elspeth would still want him as much as he yearned for her?

The daybreak sunlight filled the east facing rooms of the Mayfair home, London was stirred to new life, Kane wearing a dark wool suit, hiding Kevlar armor protection beneath a crisp white shirt with black pin stripes, a silver and gray striped tie, a Windsor knot perfectly tied; his shoulder holster discretely supporting his pistol, he set off just before 7:00 a.m. to walk in the morning sunshine, it was as if the sun was recharging his life batteries, the adrenalin continued to pump energy through his veins enabling him to walk more vigorously to Downing Street. God help anyone that got in his way as he had never been so alert and ready for anything in his life, he now had a real purpose, in fact a new lease on life.

Immediately upon his arrival at the Foreign office he was fielding calls from Tel Aviv, the Israeli Ambassador to London was requesting an update on the bio hazard threat. Kane had little to report but advised the now very concerned Ambassador that he would update him immediately if there was a break in the situation. Within five minutes of the Ambassadors call the Police Commissioner was on the line. The call referenced the fact that the

Bio hazards were going to be moved to a location close to Dover and that the police counter-terrorism wanted to intercept the transfer that day rather than wait for the Striker operation which was now thirty-four hours away.

Kane of course agreed and planned to stay out of the way of the London Police, at least providing things were running smoothly. The transfer of deadly chemical products would be on route to the Dover area by noon, the interception would take place close to the Folkestone turnoff on the M-2 motorway. The bio hazards were being moved by a five tonne Volvo truck, yellow in color making for an easily identifiable target. The police had over one hundred special task force personnel ready for the operation hence it should be a reasonably easy task. The London police had a good record when it came to the apprehending of terrorist, the failure in the system was in the courts, sentences had been getting lighter by the year.

Malik Alfaisal, the Judas of Islam, if accurate with his information would soon be basking in his new port of refuge somewhere in South America with a tidy sum of money to ease his conscience, that's if he had one.

Kane spoke with John who appeared to be quite upbeat. His opening statement to Kane was that he agreed to retire with him after this operation was over. Kane did not openly respond, his mind drifted to Elspeth and he wondered whether she was indeed ready for him. Kane not realizing it, changed the subject to the preparedness of the GVC.

John relayed the facts; the teams in Tintern were going over and over the plans for the joint raids. Five teams in all and all teams at 6:30 p.m. The next day, they would be in their respective locations, the cull of human life would be punctual. They would all depart for their respective locations at 8:00 a.m. the following morning, five teams of four, well trained mercenaries each in their own right millionaires, each one of them anxious to survive and enjoy the spoils.

Pammy had been preparing the statements for the news media; certain of their closest trustworthy reporters were given the heads up for a statement by 7:00 p.m. the next day.

The morning went by quickly and at 11:30 a.m. Kane was advised by the Police commissioner that the yellow truck carrying the ingredients to kill millions had been successfully intercepted some thirty minutes before, the operation went down without incident and that two East Indian gentlemen were apprehended. The Yellow truck had been stopped by a barrage of police cars and Hummer vehicles all fully occupied by sinister looking men in black battle fatigues, all of them armed to the gunnels with sinister looking weapons. The two drivers Jaber Badarvi and Abdul Hamed Ali were both known terrorists; in fact their capture was a profitable venture as the USA had a two million-dollar bounty on each of them. The funds would eventually boost the coffers of the Alpha Omega London bank account. Neither of the terrorists offered resistance yet it was discovered that the glove compartment on the passenger side contained two snub nosed .38 caliber handguns. The bomb squad detachment had provided for three units to check out the truck for fear of booby traps, yet the truck was clean.

Kane asked about the cargo and the response was, "Everything but the four one litre containers of Anthrax spores." The seizure of the biohazards would be kept classified; the British public had after all had not been informed of the theft. Kane requested that the two apprehended terrorists be brought to Tintern where he would arrange for them be interrogated by his colleagues from Guantanamo.

Next on Kane's agenda was a phone call to the Israeli Ambassador to London. While making the call Kane wondered where the snitch, Malik Alfaisal would go, most likely Rio De Janeiro, he thought after all it was a haven for many people in similar circumstances, hiding from the law or their past and or both. With that thought, the Israeli Ambassador to London picked up the telephone in Tel Aviv, and Kane immediately got to the facts and addressed the success of the Kent and London police in their morning interception of the bio hazards....everything but the small canisters of Anthrax, whereabouts still unknown.

The Ambassador then volunteered on behalf of his government, as was the custom for contracting the Alpha Omega group, to pay a contribution to world peace in the amount of $20,000,000 USD. This was one method of transaction which had occurred throughout Sir Billy's realm and this was Kane's firsthand initiation to the process. Kane handled the matter professionally and advised them that they would accept the contribution and banking details would follow shortly. This was the first deposit into the coffers for this global problem, more contributions would follow allowing the coffers to balloon. The conversation with the Israeli Ambassador was brief which was beneficial for Kane as he needed to call the Prime Minister and provide him with the news of operation striker and the recovery of most of the Bio hazardous material. The call to the PM was equally as short, no one really wanted to deal with this matter, and after all it was dirty laundry, very dirty laundry. Kane spent the rest of the day reviewing documents ranging from Emergency Response Procedures for the city of London, Manchester, Leeds, Bristol and Birmingham. To his surprise none were consistent, each plan was totally different from the other, a true recipe for disaster, and truly indicative of city managers and councilors doing their own thing. Kane would address these serious weaknesses in due course but now was not the time. Reading more he delved into the military preparedness which was far more detailed and credible than the city plans, however a great deal of action was based upon working with the City plans, the fuse for confusion. Again, Kane made a mental note to address these matters at the proper time. The airports emergency preparedness plan were intriguing as they were complicated, evidently a great deal of thought had gone into the matter, the same could be said for the Channel tunnel emergency plan but the authors of these plans and many others had lost the concept of KIS i.e. keep it simple. The reading of these documents only cemented the fact that a great deal of editing and streamlining of procedures was necessary, Kane recalled his time offshore and remembered the well defined plans that the oil industry had devised and implemented with copious numbers of hours in training their staff. Kane committed to himself that he would examine the different industries and put forward recommendations for change, perhaps a good job to wean him into retirement?

The office was not the same without the presence of Pammy, Kane called her several times through out the day; each time he appreciated just how important she was to Alpha Omega. The Israeli government had been given a Swiss bank account to make their contribution and Kane had made inquiries of contacts in China to have John's girlfriend officially immigrate to the UK.

By the days end Kane had provided Interpol with a status update and on the personal front everything was in motion to accommodate Johns request, a few dollars had to be transferred to secure the arrangements but the transaction costs were minimal, Johns girlfriend, his love would be in the UK within the next ten days. Kane knew that John would be most grateful. Kane took time out to drain a pot of Earl Grey tea and pondered thoughts concerning his life's love and his daughter of almost ten years. With the tea pot empty Kane left the stately offices of the foreign office and walked home. When approaching the rear of his property in Mayfair he tried to recall the last time that he had entered the front door, it had been many, many moons before.

Kane joined the homemakers for the evening meal and unlike the night before he was better prepared to eat his fill. The meal was Beef Wellington, complimented with cauliflower, brussel sprouts and peas, with fluffy whipped mashed potatoes, topped with Bisto gravy. The British cuisine lacked the flair of Europe but it was the staple diet of some sixty million people, well perhaps fifty percent or so thrived on curry and East Indian spices. Kane took pleasure in dining with the homemakers; they were in some way surrogate parents, having no authority.

After the meal the role reversed to what would be perceived as normal, with the home keepers cleaning up and retiring to their quarters.

Kane retired to the office and tuned into BBC radio. The next twenty four hours would hopefully be successful and the beginning of the end for the financial support of Al Qaeda.

Before retiring to his bedroom Kane made more calls to Tintern. John had everything under control, the Striker operation would commence on time, and hopefully by the same time the next evening the four Anthrax containers would be recovered safely and under lock and key at the Wiltshire military base. Similarly the cancer like terrorist cell groups seeking refuge in the UK will have been severely impacted for the first time by the culling crews of the GVC. John was ecstatic with the news of his women, for him ten days could not pass by quickly enough. Both John and Kane would sleep well on the eve of operation Striker, the common reason being their passion for genuine love. Kane enjoyed five hours of sleep and thereafter took to reading Tolstoy, he never enjoyed the book but in itself it was a tedious task, a challenge that few books had to offer. Even at the half way point he was tempted to give in but persistence prevailed he read on until the waft of breakfast filled his nostrils.

Some one hundred fifty miles to the west back in Tintern the boys had been up since 5:00 a.m.; and engaged in a five mile run, they would all be leaving by eight. Each of their vans were outfitted with GPS positioning, one of the harder tasks which had been an oversight was that no one had much experience driving on the left hand side of the road. They had no choice but to catch on quickly.

Just before 7:00 a.m. Kane called John and wished them well and ordered them all to stay alive.

Precisely at 8:00 a.m. Kane flagged down a taxi from two blocks down from his Mayfair home, destination Downing Street. For the GVC they were all departing, one to the Severn Bridge and Bristol and the others in the opposite direction heading north and north east to connect up with the M1 motorway. The team heading for Leeds departed thirty minutes ahead of the others. In their garb they all looked like security guards, big black and menacing, the three white guys accepted.

The Bristol Striker force had to make their way to an old warehouse close to "Temple Meads" railway station. The warehouse, chosen for its East West orientation, supposedly facing Mecca had been converted into a Mosque, and was apparently lavishly appointed. The mosque could hold two hundred followers, but tonight the numbers would be less than forty. The Bristol GVC would arrive in the general area within one hour drive from Tintern. Negotiating the motorway was an easy task for the new arrivals but the small inner city roads was another matter, on occasion certain of the black members were visibly white in their efforts to stay on the correct side of the road.

The Guantanamo boys had permission to do whatever they wished to do in order to achieve a successful outcome, and being US trained professionals they brought a different variety of skill sets to the table. They would utilize certain of these skills in order to stay alive.

Upon arrival in the city center of Bristol, the famous city of John Cabot and the famous engineer Brunell they adopted their own tactics. They drove into the car park adjacent to the old city

Hippodrome theatre and parked the Blue van. Together they exited and walked a hundred or so meters to the Hertz car rental. They hired two BMW 540 saloons and one Audi wagon. They drove back to the van, where they changed clothing from their black fatigues, and replaced them with regular dark clothing and outer jackets. The weapons were placed in the Audi and covered with the fatigues. From the car park they left in the Audi to survey the building. They had the benefit of time so they would use it well. The drive to the location from the city centre was less than five minutes.

The Audi was parked and they each took off to locations with different vantage points around the subject target. Besides being armed with pistols and razor sharp knives they each had the very best of Bushnell binoculars. They would survey the target for a two hour period and then regroup at the restaurant within the Temple Meads railway station.

The weather was accommodating albeit the morning sky was becoming overcast with ominous grey puffy clouds. Within the hour each had viewed the target and the surrounding buildings. The ominous grey clouds were a backdrop to something even more ominous. On two buildings tops with a higher elevation to the target building there were two armed men casually walking the building roof, their sniper rifles left in position already poised with the barrels facing down at the target building. All four team members witnessed the tardiness of the obvious ambush and walked quickly back to the railway station. They had been gone less than one hour when they sat down to discuss the status and to re engineer the plan.

Drinking the coffee was a pick me up, mainly because it was so putrid. The four described their findings and each had identified the group of four men of East Indian descent, one in fact was wearing a white turban. It was agreed that they would immediately notify the other team players that there must have been a leak of intelligence as their target was already staked out by snipers.

The other teams when at their destinations would be exchanging vehicles and changing attire in a similar manner as the GVC (Bristol Boys), but they would not have the benefit of time which was fortuitous for the Bristol team. The other four teams were duly notified of their findings and cautioned to be aware of the possibility of ambush.

The Bristol boys in the grungy confines of the railway restaurant made their plans to eliminate the snipers and then place the explosives on all four sides of the target building. They would monitor the building and confirm whether there would be any movement of people in or out. They would drive their vehicles to separate parking locations and leave one of them laden with explosives to detonate a full hour after the deadline of 6:00 p.m. The intent would be to capture terrorist onlookers after the fact. They would inform the police closer to the time to eliminate too much collateral damage.

Outside of the railway station the heavens opened up, a good omen to commence the sniper termination. The Bristol Boys made their way in the heavy rainfall to the parked Audi. The streets were almost barren of pedestrians, the weapon cache was quickly accessed and they moved off in two pairs with a building rooftop each to capture. Accessing the building tops was an easy feat, neither entry points were guarded. On the south building top the two East Indians were huddled under a single raincoat completely soaked, completely unprepared for the elements and completely unprepared for death. The GVC team permitted death to come silently and quickly. The pistol shots were muffled by the silencers. Unable to see their victims beneath the raincoat the huddled figures were shot with eight rounds. Upon inspection of the bodies the victims received a final bullet in the center of their foreheads. They were toast as Kane would say.

On the east facing building the other team had silently accessed the roof top only to find two of the snipers huddled under a roof top overhang sucking on a joint of Marijuana. The sniper sporting the white turban saw the two open the door to the roof top but his weapon laid on the ledge of the flat roof some five meters away. He half started to run to the weapon but was shot simultaneously with the other one. Both rounds had killed their victims but it was clean to pop the skull with another final bullet. It was only a matter of ten minutes when both team members poured into the muzzle of the sniper rifles quick setting epoxy gel. In the event that these weapons were fired without close inspection the handler of the weapon would be rendered equally as dead as the snipers. The two teams propped up the snipers so that their heads were marginally visible from the ground below. Even with this hick up the GVC were well on their way to a Bristol success. The rain continued to pour; no one in their right mind would be out in the down poor. With the rain providing a natural shield from on lookers the teams made their way down from the buildings to set the charges. The Audi was accessed again and driven to the north alleyway behind the building. The explosives would be set to create an implosion whereas the Audi with over two hundred pounds of Trinitrotoluene would be protected from the north wall until detonation. The set up only took fifteen minutes and they were done. The two teams made their way back to the parked BMW. It was twelve noon, six hours to go.

The rain eased off by two o'clock, both teams remained soaked through, they had taken it in turns to wander the area and to revisit the roof tops. Team A had encountered one more East Indian running down the access stairwell; they had met momentarily only to lock eyes on each other. With fearful eyes the East Indian watched as the bullet flashed from its origin only feet away and buried itself into his brain. The back of his skull had splattered against the stairwell wall. There was no need to expend another round but instead they searched his body for a cell phone, there was not one. Team A discarded of the body in the boiler room three floors down but they could not take the time to clean up the lengthy blood stains that straddled stair after stair.

There were no other interventions until the Go time of 6:00 p.m. At that time no one had entered the building and of course the team was not surprised, no one in or out all afternoon. Punctually at 6:00 p.m. the radio signal traveling at the speed of light triggered the TNT, the building was destroyed, all but the north wall.

The team stood by to watch the aftermath. Fire crews arrived within ten minutes and police within five.

Westward television came after twenty minutes and after thirty minutes or so dozens of East Indians and Arab countrymen came to witness the damage. At 6:45 p.m. the team leader made the call to the police contact and gave the instruction to evacuate the fireman, police, television crews and the press to a distance of 1,500 feet. The drama was unfolding before their very eyes. The police responded on key and the bulk of the people were at a safe distance from the north wall and the surprise that was in the cargo space of the Audi.

At seven pm the timely explosion was impressive. The north wall became a gattling gun spewing bricks rather than bullets. None of the East Indian and Arab onlookers would survive. Those that were scheduled to be culled on the inside of the building were toasted on the outside, at least that was the hope. The B plan worked very nicely, the team was pleased with their efforts and made their way back to the Hertz rental and then to their parked van.

The Audi had been fully insured and was reported as stolen, the team had no surprises. At 7:05 p.m. the television crews reported to the west of England that the newly formed Global Vigilante Corp had claimed responsibility for the bombings, moments later the news would precipitate south, the declaration being confirmed of similar events having taken place in Leeds, Birmingham, Manchester and London. The hard part now became the ride back to Tintern, driving on the wrong side of the road; the Bristol team took their time and arrived at 9:00 p.m., all of them famished and ready for a good feast.

Kane had witnessed the news on the Bristol event and then the Midland news cast and finally the breaking news from ITN and the BBC. The announcement of the GVC was perfection in itself. Pammy had provided scripts for certain of the most cooperative reporters, the message was very clear.

Kane departed from his office and instead of driving back to his Mayfair home he decided to boot it down to Tintern, he arrived at the same time as the Bristol team. The team had finished their meal when Kane and the Birmingham team arrived, one of the team had been wounded, but upon inspection it was clear that it was a flesh wound only and nothing of consequence. The Manchester crew arrived by midnight almost at the same time as the London crew. The last team to arrive back at the base was the Leeds team. All of the teams concurred that here had been a breech of security, but fortunately the Bristol Boys had tipped the scales of surprise. Each team had encountered a set up with snipers; no building had any occupants that evening. All of the buildings were duly destroyed and all of the fifteen snipers had been eliminated except two from the London Mosque, although it was confirmed that one of them was later captured by the Mets in the London Aldgate East tube station complete with a bullet wound in the leg. The largest cell destroyed was the Bristol cell, yet, that was really an assumption. The terrorist cull had not been a success but the destruction of the properties was one hundred percent. The birth of the GVC too was a great success. CNN in the USA was already doing their thing; the news was repeated almost verbatim as per the request of Pammy. Kane listened carefully to the reports from each location and was greatly concerned that the mission had been compromised by a leak. Of greater concern was the disappearance of John who was supposed to have been at Tintern and available for Kane's 10:00 p.m. planned phone call. Kane was deeply troubled by this and he recalled the earlier tension between them, tension that Kane had dismissed as signs of perhaps a nervous breakdown.

Kane shifted gears and asked whether the two drivers had been delivered from the Kent police, Pammy responded with, "Tomorrow morning."

Kane turned to his past interrogators and stated that first thing tomorrow they were to interrogate the two vigorously, and for the two not to survive the interview. Kane drifted off into a deep trance, his brain was racing once again around the Le Mans race track.

Pammy handed him a tall glass of Bourbon when he exclaimed, "Let's prepare to get out of here now; Call in the Welsh Guards immediately and secure the building."

Without informing the team Kane had reached the conclusion that the only source of the leak was John, he must have turned; they were in jeopardy and needed to relocate. The team instinctively saw the importance of their new boss's assumption and without question they took to arms. They were ready and alert within minutes. Surveillance teams were scouring the roadside and the access points from the fields with their night vision glasses. The instruction was substantiated within twenty minutes of Kane's statement. Wading across the River Wye was a team of terrorist, wading across with their arms raised, each holding an automatic weapon.

Kane was informed accordingly. Immediately Kane dispatched four of his crew to the outside South perimeter and four to the north. Two of the crew was sent to higher ground at the rear of the building. The rest of them, twelve in number including Pammy, armed with stylish ladies' .22 caliber pistol, stayed inside the building. Looking through night glasses Kane witnessed the terrorist traversing the Wye River. They had yet to traverse two fields to reach the hotel front.

Kane had his hotel crew open the windows from the upper levels. The upper levels remained in darkness, the lower room lights illuminating the road. Surprise was once again their savior. It appeared as if the number of terrorist crossing the river was upwards of forty. There was no movement from the north, south or rear of the hotel, evidently the terrorists were confident that the element of surprise was all that they had required. Kane instructed his team to open fire when the terrorist were at the fifty feet marker, across the road. The terrorist must be caught in the crossfire. To clarify the matter he confirmed the distance by referencing the barb wire fence. The next few seconds seemed like eternity and then the gates of hell opened wide for the terrorists. Up in the heavens vestal virgins were running wild, at least that's what Kane thought of when he started to kill indiscriminately the mass of human flesh some fifty feet away. The onslaught was horrific. The terrorists attempted to shoot back but with little success. The barrage of gunfire was all coming from one direction, namely the hotel front. Bullets rained over the terrorist and one by one they fell to the wet grass. Kane was shooting in an angry fashion and was totally pissed off that John had duped him. Amongst the gunfire Kane suddenly thought of Elspeth and his daughter. Leaving his vantage point he dropped the automatic weapon and grabbed the telephone. Amidst the gunfire he opened his wallet to extract Elpseth phone number. He dialed the number and to his relief she responded. He stumbled with his words, but then said to her, "This is Kane," to which she replied a simple, "Hello." Her voice was the same, the tone consistent. He told her that this was an urgent call to tell her that he loved her and that she must vacate the property immediately, rendezvous point at the ten year anniversary location. Say nothing, and speak to no one and to not trust anyone. The gunfire and the shattering of glass was like an orchestra playing Tchychovskis 1912 overture. Elspeth questioned Kane as to his safety but Kane urgently left her with a repeat of the message, namely get out of her home right then and await his contact. She ended the conversation with, "Okay, I will be there."

The gunfire slowly ebbed to leave the silence of a peaceful night. Across the road lay dozens of dead and wounded terrorists.

The Welsh Guards arrived as if in a western Cavalry movie, somewhat too late, but they were given the task to check the bodies and to safeguard any that were still breathing for later questioning. Those that lived would regret the next twelve hours, and then for sure they would meet the awaiting virgins, that is, if there were any left. When asked if John was face down in the grass opposite, the answer came back as No.

Kane mustered his team and confirmed only three injuries, the worse injury was sustained by the same guy who had a flesh wound before except this time he had been the recipient of a bullet in his right lung. Thanks to his Kevlar jacket he would survive and was sent to French Hay Hospital for emergency surgery, somewhere close to Bristol. The other two were flesh wounds only and both men would be patched up with field dressings after minor stitching.

With the Welsh Guards fortifying the hotel there was no need to leave, but Kane still chose to embrace the quarters of the Welsh Guards up in Ross. The whole group would all be there within the hour.

They arrived at the barracks, somewhat less grand than the private setting of the hotel but it was clean. Everyone retired to their bunks upon arrival, Pammy was the only one who had a private room complete with a modern bathroom.

Pammy unperturbed by the recent killing spree, was already frame working the press release with respect to the massacre that had just occurred. The GVC would claim responsibility accordingly and the news media would make a feast of it all.

The night was a night of death everywhere. London was no exception and by early next morning, 2:00 a.m., Kane was awakened with the news from the Police commissioner that his home had been raided and that the house keepers were dead, two bullets to the head each. If that was not enough the house was set alight and was a total loss. Kane was lost for words as liters of adrenalin ran through his veins. Kane was angry at himself and John, he had trusted him completely, but the nagging question of why continued to irk him. Apparently Al Qaeda quickly claimed responsibility for the action in Mayfair and expanded the fact that they wanted the home owner next. Kane was clearly their priority target. This was further confirmed by the fact that the illusive Iranian assassin Hanif Kassam, well known to the CIA, MI6, and Alpha Omega had been seen in the city, caught on video surveillance, apprehension of this little ferret of a man was however unsuccessful; this had been the case for years, just like a rodent he had eluded capture on dozens of occasions, quite often by minutes only. Kane had already seen the file on this fellow, he now wondered if the Mayfair killings were the work of Kassam?

The morning came quickly, Kane made the brief arrangements with Pammy with respect to the need to interrogate the captured terrorists. He would be going to Scotland. Pammy had everything well organized, the Guantanamo boys would be doing their best work by late morning. Kane took off to the BAC aircraft hangers just north east of Bristol. A phone call from Kane to the ministry of defence had provided him with the use of an experimental vertical take off Harrier. The Harrier was capable of super sonic flight but Kane had agreed to stay below Mach-1 speed. He would be in Aberdeen within forty minutes of take off. He was at the hanger by ten am and was duly impressed at the lines of the Harrier. It was painted a dull matt black, and looked like a streamlined menacing killing machine. It had a long range fuel tank enabling the aircraft to travel excess of two thousand miles in one sortie, at less than Mach-1 the range increased by another eight hundred miles. The plane had no markings; it was akin to a black sheep in aircraft terms. Kane loved the thought of flying the beast to Scotland, and after a prep talk with the test pilot he suited up and commenced a normal take off stance from the Number 3 runway. The flight was everything and more. The power was simply awesome and the maneuverability just incredulous. By noon he was landing at the Aberdeen airport where he was met by one of his old colleagues form Goose Bay Canada. The aircraft was to be taken to the RAF hanger and stowed out of sight. Kane was at the Hertz car rental counter obtaining his hired vehicle when he observed three olive colored skin men staring in his direction. He would watch them carefully.

He hired a Ford Taurus and drove to the A road which would take him West to Balmoral. After fifteen minutes or so he confirmed that he was being tailed by a red Lexus, quite the conspicuous of vehicles he thought. Kane was outfitted as usual with his proper attire which included his weaponry and Kevlar jacket. He confirmed the tailgating vehicle was truly following him by turning to the side of the road close to a parked police vehicle, Kane asked the policeman for directions. The Lexus drove by and turned into a lay-by a mile up the road. Kane passed the parked red vehicle and observed the callousness of amateurs taking their positions far too close to his vehicle.

Opening up the distance by using his leaded foot Kane sped off in the distance and slowed down only to negotiate the entrance of the Glen Eagles hotel. He drove to the car park and then vacated the vehicle to enter the fine old establishment, a true treasure of Scotland.

Kane saw the red Lexus park close to his vehicle, the three men then approached the hotel. Propped up to the bar with only a few guests in the room Kane ordered his bourbon, his weapon was already drawn but hidden under the local gazette, the only newspaper Kane could find in such a short time. The men too approached the bar and ordered drinks; they were speaking Arabic quite loudly and made the foolish assumption that Kane did not understand them. He heard perfectly clearly that they were planning to take him out as soon as he left the bar, they would kill him in the car park. To Kane this experience was like a gong show. Total incompetence and ignorance would ensure that another group of vestal virgins would be losing their cherries in due course. Kane swallowed his drink and casually walked towards the door. Having barely touched their drinks, the three looked on only to witness another black killing mechanism stare them down. Pop, Pop, Pop.

The pistol beneath the Gazette performed as usual perfectly well. Each terrorist fell over to meet their brides. It was a full thirty seconds later before Kane could hear the screams from the old biddies that were indulging in an early afternoon tipple. Kane exited the hotel, popped one of the Lexus tires with one round rendering the vehicle modestly undriveable, just for good measure and sped off in his Ford Taurus. It was his turn to meet his bride. On route to the pub, the ten year meeting point Kane received the best news of the week. Pammy called and stated that John, had been found in the Ross hospital, the isolation ward for tropical diseases.

Prior to the completion of operation Striker John had suffered a Malaria relapse, he had gone to the hospital to request the drug Maluprin, but on arrival he was already bordering on collapse. Throughout the Striker operation he had been rendered incapacitated suffering from high temperature and violent shaking. The hospital had isolated him and he remained in their care. Of greater importance Pammy had arranged for a full body MRI. The results identified a small electronic device which had been inserted into his neck in the area of his neck wound. The radio device had been determined to be a low frequency receiver, someone somewhere could hear all of his conversations, the device however had its limitations, the range of the receiver was less than fifteen feet. Upon hearing the news Kane felt somewhat guilty jumping to his conclusions, but then he had good reason. He would discuss this matter with John when he was free of his tremors, it would be another week. He closed the telephone conversation with the request to inform the Scottish police commissioner that three Al Qaeda terrorists had just been terminated in the Glen Eagles Hotel by, what they believe to be the GVC, he instructed Pammy to ensure the world press knew of the event.

Kane in good spirits drove into the car park of the INN it looked exactly the same as it had done so ten years ago. To his surprise he noticed certain of the locals, it was as if in a time warp, they looked slightly older yet the clothing looked the same, still tatty and dirty. Kane asked for Elspeth and was shocked to hear a negative response; the Inn had at that time no guests. Kane felt his stomach roll, but then he questioned the location. Perhaps it was the Swan and Finch? He took off in a hurried fashion and drove further west.

As with the first Inn the Swan and Finch too had slipped into the same time warp with the exception of a beautiful young lady sat in the hearth of the fireplace. Elspeth had sat in the same place for hours, as she had done so the day before.

Kane gently leaned over and kissed her sweet lips. It was a wonderful moment for both of them. Elspeth had the return of the phantom and tried desperately to keep her legs tightly crossed. She only hoped that her eyes remained in position and not popping out of her sockets. Kane admitted that he did not recall which Inn it was that they should meet; Elspeth said nothing, as she too had forgotten which location they had agreed to, her memory of ten years prior was blurred by the honeymoon that was real but not sanctioned by the big fellow in the heavens. Elspeth simply locked her eyes onto his; she was glued to her seat feeling somewhat uncomfortable. Kane saw the diamond ring on her left finger, and he felt a tear in his eye. Elspeth was understanding and cupped his hands into hers. Kane was stumbling for words and the remedy was another soft kiss. Kane soaked up the emotional attention the initiative being all Elspeth's.

The mood was slightly disrupted when the barman came to the fireplace with large Bourbon. "Welcome back," he said in Gaelic.

Kane did not understand at all but the drink was welcomed. Kane swallowed the drink down, the spirit invoking some Dutch courage. The words started to flow out of his mouth and he talked and talked and talked more, while Elspeth listened and tolerated her wet thighs. It was more than an hour when Eslpeth responded, and it was Kane's turn to be aroused.

Her beautiful voice mesmerized him, and as if in a trance she told him about Sir Billy and his constant support and care. She possibly knew too much about Kane's work but she needed to in order to comprehend the isolation and the lack of correspondence. She had been totally devoted yet imprisoned to Scotland and perhaps a dream; the dream was now happening. The topic eventually turned to their daughter and Kane's tears flowed freely down his face. What with the talk of Sir Billy's death, the news that he was in fact Kane's biological father and the joyful talk of their daughter, they were both bleary eyed with tears. The remaining folk in the bar could see that a reunion of great love was underway and they removed themselves to the opposite side of the bar, they were in fact a little embarrassed with the scene, but they chose to accommodate the young lovers.

The couple eventual had to move from the hearth, besides being emotional wrecks they were roasting. Together they retraced the rickety old floors and stairs to Elspeth's room, the same one as ten years before. There they quickly explored each others bodies and eat each others lips with aggressive energy and passion. Kane was as before with the exception of an additional ten pounds of body fat. He was a hunk of a man in his full prime. Elspeth had aged slightly with her hair peppered with thin lines of grey. She too was a magnificent female in her prime. They made passionate love and Elspeth's dreams came and came and came.

With the world in chaos Kane remained hidden, in the safe haven of this Scottish pub, reunited with the women of his dreams, he would allow this time out and permitted his life's batteries to be opened up and thoroughly inspected and recharged. He knew that he would never let this women go and that his life had to change.

They stayed in their room until the early morning and then Kane had to refocus his mind to matters of the world. Elspeth watched his every move; he showered and shaved, later dressing complete with his Kevlar undergarments. Elspeth watched with interest yet concern. Although she knew a great deal of Kane's work the reality was somewhat of a shock to her, especially the evil looking pistol. Blinded by immense love she accepted the fact and dressed accordingly for breakfast. They both enjoyed the refueling and then made steps to depart the Swan and Finch. Kane told her to make her way to the airport and to park the range rover in the long term parking area; he would follow with about a half mile between them. Mary Ann was still at boarding school and would be escorted by the Scottish police to the hanger, in fact the excited young daughter was already at the hanger awaiting the arrival of her mother; she had no idea that she would be meeting her father that day for the first time.

Kane and Elspeth drove without incident to the airport, meeting at the Hertz rental counter where Kane handed back his keys and contract. Kane had checked in with Pammy at Ross on Wye. She had little to report other than commenting on the cruelty with respect to the manner in which the GVC were interrogating the captured terrorist. She made particular comment to the inhuman use of certain ants! Kane knew the score and allowed her whining but the results were already favorable. The anthrax containers had been shipped by road to Tel Aviv and should arrive within two days. The actual identification of the vehicle and drivers had not been gleaned; in fact one by one they would perish due to attempts by the GVC to extract the information. Kane made a call to the Israeli Ambassador who accepted the information with a fearful comment of, "OH SHIT."

The Harrier

Kane and Elspeth made their way to the RAF hanger where Mary Ann was sitting in the flight office. The Harrier was ready for flight, fully fueled and available to Kane. Kane had said nothing to Elspeth where he would take her; it was his place to keep these two precious women alive and free from harm.

Kane and Eslpeth crossed the tarmac to the flight office entrance and for once in his life Kane was apprehensive of meeting someone. They opened the door and Elspeth led the way to the awaiting arms and hug from Mary Ann. She was tall for her age, slim and stunningly beautiful. Her skin was smooth as silk and shone as if porcelain. In her school uniform she looked smart, fully alert and with a perfect posture: in fact she was drop dead gorgeous. Elspeth introduced Kane as a very special friend; she would tell her the whole story at another more appropriate time. When Mary Ann asked where they were going Kane replied with a short flight south, you should enjoy it. Mary Ann said that she had flown before and that flying was somewhat boring. Kane said that he would change that viewpoint for her.

The new harrier was fitted with three seats all in the longitudinal direction, the third seat was the most uncomfortable of the three but then it was there to accommodate two trainees when required, it was a cost savings of fifty percent for the Ministry. Kane suited up and proper attire was made available to the two ladies. Mary Ann was in awe when she realized that they would be boarding the black aircraft which was visible through the office window. Elspeth too was somewhat surprised to realize that Kane had yet another skill that she had not been told about; her man was quite the man!

Kane taxied from the hanger to a position three hundred feet or so beyond the hanger.

He cleared his take off with the tower and as if flying a helicopter engaged full power and became airborne, the vertical take off was impressive and the forward movement to 100 miles per hour with fifty thousand pounds of thrust pushing them through the air immediately changed the mind set of Mary Ann, flight was suddenly quite something. Kane flew down the East coast prior to obtaining clearance to accommodate airspace at forty thousand feet on route to Berne Switzerland. At almost Mach-1 they would be landing in just under two hours.

The weather was perfect for the transit and of course Kane permitted his daughter to take the controls. She was confident and keen to learn, but the lesson was kept very simple, yet by the time they landed in Berne Kane had already decided that he would soon teach his new found women to fly.

Berne was under a blanket of cloud when they landed conventionally at the international airport. Kane then taxied the aircraft to the military hanger. The ground crew looked perplexed when they saw three people disembark this new prototype craft. They were even more confused to see one man accompanied by two women. Kane requested that the crew fuel the aircraft for a morning departure, and then proceeded to clear customs. Clearing customs was a mere formality and within thirty minutes of arrival they were traveling the clean roads of Berne to one of Kane's newly inherited homes, in an elegant rented Mercedes saloon. The housekeepers had been duly informed of their arrival and after ninety minutes of sightseeing for the two passengers Kane drove into the driveway of his Swiss residence. The skies were now a canopy of fluffy white clouds with the sun peering through the gaps of what looked like white candy floss. The house was as elegant as the automobile now parked outside. A six-bedroom home with a huge living room, graced with a Sandstone fireplace which was taller than Kane. To the left of the hallway there was a large dining room with a suite of furniture that could accommodate a seating of twenty people.

The hard wood floors had been imported from Canada and inlaid with mother of pearl designs, the floor by itself was a masterpiece. The large heavy wooden doors too were quite remarkable. The home had been built with large windows which provided every room with brilliant sunlight and warmth. The inside of the home was complimented by the grounds, it was somewhat similar to large stately homes of the rich and famous as seen on television, but then Kane was rich, just not famous, and for good reason.

A meal had been prepared and the three of them enjoyed veal scallipene, and truly it was a delight. The main meal was followed by a Greek Baklava which too teased the palate. The meal concluded with a variety of cheeses and was washed down with a twenty year old port. Mary Ann commented on the cheese and port saying that her Uncle Billy had the same passion; Mary Ann did not know of Sir Billy's fate, which was another chapter to discuss with her, again, at a more appropriate time.

After lunch the three of them went to walk the grounds of the Swiss retreat. Kane was getting along fabulously with Mary Ann. Mary Ann's laughter was infectious and they were all enjoying the frivolity. The grounds hosted a kidney shaped swimming pool, the natural invitation of blue water and brilliant yet patchy sunshine was too irresistible to turn down. They raced to their rooms to change into swim suits. Elspeth was in a full body suit while Mary Ann was in a light blue bikini. They were obviously mother and daughter and they were both flowers akin to birds of paradise. Mary Ann observed the passion in Kane's eyes for her mother; it was mirrored by her mother's eyes. Instinctively she knew that there was a lot more to this story but with an almost schoolgirl crush on Kane her approval was automatic, her mother was deserving of such a man.

Kane was in his swimming trunks which were white in color; he had a tremendous physique yet one that was totally natural. His body was peppered with scars some of them circular in shape while others were elongated. Elspeth had already told her daughter not to ask questions of a personal nature but to wait the right time for all of her questions. The arrangement was fine with Mary Ann, she had already agreed with Kane to learn to fly and he had promised her that he would have her flying in no time, as a consequence Kane was already very high on the pedestal of life, and he could do no wrong in her eyes.

All that afternoon they played at swimming, a little tennis and croquet on the lawn. All of the activities were performed in their swim suits and by early evening the results of the sun was telling.

They were inside the house by 6:00 p.m., showering and enjoying the oversized bathroom; a quirk of Kane's, he loved the generous space that Sir Billy had allotted to the bathroom. The shower facilities were just wonderful. They dressed and made their way to the living room where Kane was waiting dressed in dark slacks and a white clean cut cotton t shirt. The atmosphere with the two women was just electric. Elspeth was sophistication and totally charming where as Mary Ann was vivacious, naughty and child like, she was intoxicating to Kane and he loved her presence. He supped on newly poured Bourbon and handed a Château du Pape red wine to Elspeth, while Mary Ann had a coke cola. Mary Ann was just bubbling with laughter and chatter; it was as if she had partaken in her own alcoholic beverage……mmm thought Kane may be she had her own stash of moonshine? The laughter was enjoyed by everyone, even the house keepers were taken by the exuberance of the young lady.

Dinner was served at 7:30 p.m. and was absolutely exquisite, Elspeth later commenting on the meal as if a divine gift from the God of fine dining. The remaining hours of the evening passed by extraordinarily quickly, a mark of having a humorous joyous exchange. They eventually retired to their rooms. Respectfully Kane defeated the urge to enter Elspeth's room but he thought it wise to wait for the approval of Mary Ann. Although frustrating he had waited for so long anyway this would be but a temporary situation.

Elspeth too had the same urges yet too decided that to secretly enter Kane's room would be inappropriate given the circumstances. Elspeth was kept occupied for yet another two hours with their daughter, she was totally taken by the pilot, the hunk and encouraged her mother to deepen her relationship with Kane; Mary Ann openly stated that she would love him as a father. Elspeth could not wait to communicate the exchange. Sleep would not come easily for either Elspeth or Kane but eventual they found a silent peace, albeit in separate bedrooms.

Kane woke as usual at a very early hour and decided to make his way downstairs to turn on the television. He tuned into CNN and was pleasantly surprised to see that there had been a nuclear explosion at the Pashawar nuclear power plant and that the GVC were claiming responsibility. The notoriety of the GVC was growing daily. Any event that could be claimed by the GVC was claimed regardless whether they were involved or not; providing it was to the detriment of Al Qaeda Kane did not care. Apparently there had been an explosion in Frankfurt, a Mosque was destroyed and a terrorist cell group (six in number) was confirmed to be amongst the dead. A similar event took place in Italy, Spain, and in the USA, the windy city of Chicago. The GVC had been extremely busy.

Busy Pammy

Pammy had been doing overtime with the publicity but Kane was indeed very pleased with her work. Later that day a televised interview with a senior GVC member was planned, on CNN the GVC would tell the world that they would stop only when Al Qaeda stopped their terror actions around the globe. The western sentiment towards the GVC was growing in leaps and bounds. Although Kane had not been notified of the fact, but the countries that had used Alpha Omega over the years had made contributions to the various bank accounts around the globe. For some reason they had concluded that Alpha Omega was involved at arms length with the GVC. The deposits had already surpassed two hundred fifty million dollars. Financing the GVC would certainly not be an issue.

Kane went to his room and showered and shaved ready for his flight back to the UK. The aroma of breakfast was filling the hallway and his room, European bacon at its best. The girls too stirred at the fragrance of yet another feast, Kane could hear the two of them engaged in morning banter and infectious laughter; the karma of happiness permeated the home confirming the fact that he had a new purpose to live, and soon he would make certain major changes in his chosen path of ten years.

The breakfast was a mixture of wholesome cooking and the exchanges of warm smiles, both with the mouth and eyes. Both of the ladies would enjoy the safe haven of the residence, schooling for Mary Ann would be addressed before the next semester, meanwhile

Switzerland would remain their summer home. Elspeth was gleaming she was more so in love than anyone could imagine.

Kane delayed his departure until mid morning but then he had to leave the two ladies to do more laundry for his government. He said his farewells and departed by taxi to the awaiting Harrier jet. By noon he was back in the air traveling at six hundred knots towards his destination, London's city airport. It was a quick flight with light headwinds. He circled over special branches city video monitoring location in West Central London, and wondered whether their cameras focused upwards at the sky, was his arrival already known to them? He hoped so but then these were strange times. By mid afternoon the Harrier was parked at the city airport as if it were a regular auto, assigned solely for Kane's usage.

Kane was back in Downing Street by 3:00 p.m. He called Pammy who was still in Ross on Wye and requested an update. Little had changed other than the GVC were planning with Special Branch to hit other known areas where there was a significant concern with regard to links with Al Qaeda. Special Branch wanted to dispatch teams to Paris, Rome, Madrid, Frankfurt and London to engage in laundry clean up operations. Kane reviewed the material already on his desk and later the same day provided the approval.

The next week was an onslaught for the terrorist, a total of two hundred twenty-nine terrorists known or suspected were washed and spun dry prior to their post-death meeting with some sixteen thousand-five hundred awaiting virgins in the departure lounge of life.

Every news cast contained more and more about the GVC. The success of the Van Lake nuclear plant incident/destruction did not surface on the news until three days post the event, but the effect none the less was extremely beneficial to the GVC's reputation. Al Qaeda were not sluggish with their retaliation but they had had their alleged victory with the three nuclear strikes. The US resolve was deepening and for the moment the GVC activities had relieved the pressure from the US President but the citizens of the USA wanted to inflict a knock out punch, the question remained how and when?

Temporary Residence

John recovered from his Malaria outbreak and returned to London to assist with the Alpha Omega operations. Kane had discussed the security leak with him and they had both considered the Korean girlfriend to be linked with the North Korean government, her assistance to relocate and to join John was halted at the very last moment; John, once again and greatly disappointed, assumed the role as a bachelor in good standing.

With Kane's Mayfair home destroyed he had taken up temporary residence in the Savoy hotel, John too was a guest being Kane's immediate neighbor. The rooms were adjoining and each day they shared their thoughts on life and the future. Both were committed to leave the laundry business as soon as was practicable. The GMC team were doing remarkably well while the rest of the Alpha Omega teams played their part. The operatives that had completed the remodeling of the Peshawar and Van Lake power plants had already been assigned work back in their familiar areas, but this time it was for them to work together and place missile homing devices in six key areas of the Middle East, Afghanistan and Pakistan. Kane's next plan was the very worse of Alpha Omegas black operations but he had figured that the knock out blow had to be just that.

Kane was now worth thirty million dollars on the Al Qaeda most wanted list, a factor that concerned the British authorities far more so than it did Kane. The money was a significant driving force and of course the very best of assassins was seeking the bounty.

Hanif Kassam had been seen on several occasions by means of the London system of security cameras, yet he was still able to avoid capture. The rodent was out there and Kane was the source of his expected windfall.The Iranian supporters of Al Qaeda wanted Kane dead before the Jewish celebrations which was imminent. Kassam was being pressured to accommodate their wishes and quickly.

Disguised as a Savoy hotel waiter he was able to access the hotel employee entrance on the East side of the building. The Savoy was a rabbit warren of hallways, elevators, stairwells etc, it was easy to lose oneself in the architectural maze. The British intelligence men assigned to perform the surveillance of the hotel and certain teams from special branch did not notice the little man; Kassam's short stature and his olive skin allowed him to blend in well with a host of Maltese waiters. Early on a Friday morning some two hours before the breakfast serving Kassam had quietly and successfully accessed the floor where Kane was on using the service elevator. Using a staff access card obtained from the maid now lying in a laundry room closet with her throat cut cleanly through to her jugular artery, he entered the room of John.

John was dripping wet and stark naked having just turned off the shower. He grasped at a bath robe. Unknowingly to John darkness came uninvitingly and peacefully. With the ease of a true professional the rodent implanted two rounds into the back of the skull of John. John was to meet his maker and for the rodent he was to meet Kane.

Kane too had just showered and was in his shorts shaving his stubborn growth. With the bathroom door ajar Kassam came face to face with Kane, Kane's face being a mass of soapy shaving cream.

Instead of performing a couple *POP POPs* with his silencer equipped pistol, Kassam gestured that Kane remove the foam with the hand towel and to enter the bedroom. Kane was not in a position to retaliate; his weapon was on the other side of the room, so he followed the rodent's instructions. When in the main bedroom/living room Kane peered toward the opened adjoining door. Kassam with a smirk on his face satisfied his query with a simple, "He's dead."

Kane wondered why he had not been shot immediately but instinctively knew that the assassin was making a terrible mistake, after all his reward was guaranteed with him dead, did Kassam have another agenda he thought?

The little man did indeed have another agenda and placed his gun on the far wall mantel, removed his shoes and beckoned Kane to stand his guard. The little rodent was actually challenging Kane to a contest! Kane was shocked; this little rodent of a fellow was a foot shorter than he was and was for certain outclassed weight for weight. Then with lightening speed the rodent flew at Kane with a barrage of martial art kicks and blows. Kane was taken totally by surprise and shocked at the ensuing pain that followed each blow. The little man carved his way through the air like a Cirque de Solaire gymnast. He was extremely fast and thankfully for Kane extremely confident. The rodent continued with very little response from Kane. Kane blocked certain of the blows but chose to accept the beating from the rodent and lure him into his web. Kane knew that he could snap the neck of the little man with ease; he just had to catch the annoying wasp like fellow. Kane's forehead and face began to swell, blood oozed from his nose, lips and brow. The little shit was damn good.

It was apparent that the rodent/wasp was enjoying the game, Kane having only hit the weasel modestly on several occasions. The kick to his groin caused a referred pain to his right side; at 145 pounds body weight the jerk had an uncanny ability to land a heavy blow. Kane was learning just where the Iranian shits confidence came from. With the passing of twelve minutes Kane had taken enough blows from the little man, it was time to demonstrate his own strength and deliver a blow of his own to the face or snout of this menacing rodent. The weasel came in fast with another kick which stung the already split skin above Kane's right eye. The rodents follow up punch however never made its target. The block from Kane suddenly came much faster than the weasel had expected and then came the blow to the face. Full on target the right fist of Kane landed on the Weasels nose. The little man flew backwards several feet to land on his back, his body lay twitching with Kane looking on. It was a repeat of years before with the driller, yet this time the body that lay on the floor was half the size. There was no need to break his neck.

The frontal lobes of the brain were now midsection of the brain deep inside the cranial vault. The autopsy would later reveal that the supraorbital process, glabella, nasal bone and nasal concha, the Zygomatic, the Maxilla and Lacrimal bones on both sides of the rodents face had been totally shattered. Kane's fist print forensically was clearly evident in the new face of the rodent.

Kane had transformed the little character into a cabbage patch doll look alike. With the Weasel dead Kane went in to see his friend John, he was indeed dead, naked with the hall mark of a kill by an assassin. Kane leaned over to close the eyelids, hiding the staring dark eyes of John. Kane could not hold back the pain of his colleague's death and tears flooded his eyes, the salty content stinging his wounds a little more. The same fate should have been his to share but the ego of the Iranian was Kane's saving grace, instead of Kane accompanying John to the departure lounge of life, it was Kassam who was his traveling cohort. Kane placed a robe over John and squeezed his right hand, a gesture of farewell.

The Special Branch team somewhat embarrassed on hearing the news was called to the room to remove the two bodies, John was taken away to the morgue but the Weasels body was sent to the GVC London group location. At the request of Kane they would later that day suspend the body from the rafters of the largest known mosque in the UK frequented by terrorist. The early evening news would address yet another victory for the GVC; CNN, too, would be on the story to inform the rest of the world. Al Jazeera and Al Alan networks would inform the viewers in the Middle East.

Kane cleaned up, dressed and left the hotel having lost his earlier appetite for breakfast. He made his way to Downing Street in the back of a BMW special branch vehicle. On arrival at his office Kane was surprised to realize that his wounds needed attention. He requested the services of the medical doctor in the Foreign Office who obliged with the stitching and commented on the depth of the wounds. Kane countered with an explanation referring to the depth of the wound that he had inflicted on the little mans face. The doctor replied that he had already been made aware of the event. Bad news still traveled very fast Kane thought. Kane sat in his office for the rest of the day in a very somber mood. He achieved very little with the exception of two calls from the Israeli Ambassador, he of course wanted to hear some pleasing news but there was little or none to have.

The Ambassador relayed the fact that they had searched container after container at various ports, and literally thousands of trucks had their cargo inspected. It was the same story provided by Interpol. The results yielded nothing. The Israeli government was gravely concerned as the Jewish festivities were almost upon them. The fireworks were about to happen.

Fireworks

The anthrax containers reached the destination in the heart of Tel Aviv. The transit from Porton Down to the Mediterranean country was uneventful. Transit van to the channel tunnel and rail to Paris. Transshipped to a separate vehicle and driven to Marseilles. From the south of France to Malta by way of packaged goods destined for a hotelier chain. Packaged and transshipped again via a cargo vessel destined for Beirut. Finally the killing cargo was shipped from Beirut by truck to Tel Aviv. The precious killing dust reached its destination on time, executed exactly as per the plan. The four containers were easy to conceal and had finally reached the destination in a coffin, accompanied by a decaying women of some 87 years of age. When the cargo was recovered at the memorial center, the stench was noxious. The final destination for the containers was a fireworks factory which was within walking distance from the memorial center. The factory was one of many that would provide the fireworks for the annual celebration. The terrorist particularly liked their fiendish plan given that the Jews would lite the fuse of each rocket that would explode in the sky with an abundance of light and glitter yet the fallout of Anthrax spores would descend and the process to kill thousands would commence; the irony was sick but unfortunately the plan became reality. The celebrations began on time with the country on a High Red Alert status. Sadly the joyous onlookers would be looking skyward in awe at the display, smiling not knowing what was being rained upon them. The plan was executed again right on time, flawlessly, the south west wind enhancing the kill radius and spread of the disease. The world once again was about to witness the anguish of so many Jews needlessly slaughtered. The disease manifested itself only days after the celebrations. The Israeli forensic teams already knew moments after the fireworks display that the Anthrax spores had been deployed, it was airborne and hundreds of air monitoring systems raised the alarm, but it was too late. Millions of spores had been inhaled by the crowds, millions more would be made airborne by the coughing and choking of the victims. The incident took on a gruesome parallel similar to the Kurdish attacks performed by Chemical Ali in the Iraq regime of Saddam Hussein.

The terrorist group Al Qaeda claimed yet another victory but they must have been aware that their time was running out, a global response was about to take place which would shock even Al Qaeda. The global response of the atrocity around the globe was in itself frightening. There was a call to arm state supported vigilante groups if the governments did not find a solution and or immediately send in the troops. The response of course was reactionary without thought, without discussion and without merit strategically. Just as the USA handled the nuclear attack and remained coping with the aftermath, the order of the day remained composure, reflection and cooperation with joint forces all of whom had the mandate to rid the world of the terrorist, it was time once and for all that the axis of evil was severed.

North of Sixty

The US president had called for an international meeting of all G8 countries and other world leaders. The meeting would take place in Canada, "the under belly of the USA", in a remote location north of sixty degrees latitude.

The Israeli Ambassador to London, one of few diplomats left, had been saved from the threat of contracting the disease having been in London on the day of the event; however, he had lost thirteen of his family members. The Ambassador continued to work at his role as Ambassador to London, today he reported the Israeli death toll at 350,678; however, over 100,000 of these victims were Palestinian; the wind factor had been grossly misjudged by Al Qaeda. There was little else for the Ambassador to talk about; emotionally he was a basket case.

The GVC were doing well across Europe, but the latest Anthrax event overshadowed everything due to the enormity of the kill. Given the recent history of events, Kane was compelled to forward his ghastly plan to the Western leaders, it was time.

The historical meeting took place in Yellowknife Canada, a city located in the North West Territories, where precious metals, gold, diamonds, uranium, natural gas was plentiful, so too was the snowfall. Already outside the ground was a blanket of fluffy snow, few of the dignitaries had worn the appropriate footwear and clothing for the inclement climate, but they coped with the minor nuisance.

The meeting took place with over two hundred attendees, the head of the United Nations, Ministers, Prime ministers, presidents and certain of the remaining monarchies that peppered the globe.

The meeting took over four days with so many people continually in disagreement to what amounted to a nuclear strike. Naturally so the subject was frightening yet the reality was so overwhelmingly conclusive, they had to deliver a knock out blow, they had to put Al Qaeda onto the mat, Al Qaeda had to be defeated or at least submit.

The US President sanctioned Kane's plan with others, namely approving the use of five 1 kilotonne missiles and one ten kilotonne warhead. Kane's plan was approved by the US president, the chancellor of Germany, the President of France, the Prime Minister of the UK, the president of Russia, and dignitaries of fourteen other countries, the balance of countries respectfully abstained or refused to support the plan.

The plan itself was not discussed but only the general concept forwarded to the attendees. Kane had requested that the planning would take upwards of a year to implement, yet the truth was contrary, a week was all that was required. The Alpha Omega teams had done their preparatory work and all that was needed was approval from the now nicknamed North of Sixty Group. Approval was given.

The exodus of people from the North West Territories was brisk; aircraft took off to all points of the globe, the snow remaining pure white behind them. Meanwhile the rest of the world remained numb after the event in Tel Aviv, the people of the USA wanted revenge at any cost. Peaceful countries reverted to prayer while the most powerful countries prepared for the possibility of all out war. The world would soon witness the evil of nuclear warheads for the third time in one hundred years.

Swiss Chocolate

Mary Ann had already commenced school in a private girl's school in the heart of Berne. She had discovered a flare for languages and was already conversing very well in German and French, but she had one language already mastered that Kane had not attempted, at least until now. Elspeth had spoken to her daughter throughout the ten years in her mother tongue Gaelic. They both talked the mysterious magical language when together. The two females would challenge Kane to prepare himself for perhaps his final academic test, i.e. to speak Gaelic.

Kane returned to Berne to enjoy a few days with his two ladies. He arrived at the International airport to be greeted by Elspeth and Mary Ann. Mary Ann gave Kane a huge hug and a kiss on his right and left cheek. The smile was warm and affectionate, cradled in her hands she held a huge box of assorted Swiss chocolates, she lovingly handed the gift to him on the understanding that they could share the spoils. Of course he agreed. Elspeth hugged him equally hard and in the presence of Mary Ann pressed her tender lips to his and kissed momentarily. Besides the greeting and affection Elspeth had decided to show her daughter that this was her man; Mary Ann was in awe at what she witnessed, but she had already figured quite a lot of the jigsaw.

Together they sped off in the Mercedes to the safe haven of his Swiss home. At the request of Kane all of the Alpha Omega team and the GVC boys had been recalled to London. Six of the GVC squad had been assigned to the Swiss home in addition to four Alpha Omega operatives. They would stay on assignment for Kane. All of the other operatives had been in receipt of their rewards, and as promised the quantum was beyond their wildest dreams. Given the bounty of funds Kane had authorized three million dollars each for their recent efforts. The team's motivation was running high yet when requested to take advantage of a five day time out they graciously accepted the offer and took to the skies to see their families. The atmosphere was refreshing and the scenery as always unbelievable, beauty in the car and outside, Kane was very pleased to be home, he needed this boost to charge his soul for the ghastly deed he was about to do to his fellow man. Kane decided that he would eat the chocolates and share his love with his new found family and attempt to console his woman on matters of mass destruction.

Mary Ann was anxious to have the chocolates opened, Kane of course loved chocolates, as much as anyone, he visibly showed his excitement and appreciation for the edible gift. Having devoured three or four they decided to make use of the pool. The sun was still up and there was still a degree of heat in the rays. The short wave radiation penetrating the atmosphere pricked Kane's conscious, reminding him of nuclear radiation, its cause and effect. His mind remained troubled and it was difficult for him to be one hundred percent aware of his immediate family. Elspeth watched with modest concern, whatever was troubling him she would help resolve. They went again like penguins to water, they dove together to swim in the pool. The water temperature had been increased to eighty-four degrees; hence it was similar to swimming in the shallow waters off the Caribbean. Kane had once rented a small townhouse located at Grand Cayman; it was on the east side of the island where the reef protected the land from continuous wave action. The pool and the sky mirrored the Caymans and he made a statement to Elspeth that they should go on vacation at the Christmas break.

Kane observed his ten year old beauty; Mary Ann had appeared to grow since his departure to Canada. Her bikini top appeared to be fuller than before. Kane looked at Elspeth and motioned at her breasts, Elspeth placed her finger over her lips indicating that she would explain later. Kane later learned that two of his embroidered handkerchiefs had been on loan to his daughter, they had been stitched into her swim suit top; evidently the ten year old was not satisfied with her development. Kane was also told that many girls advance their growth in similar fashion. With a PhD in physics, Kane was bewildered to learn of such feminine traits of a 10-year-old, and wondered what other tricks these ladies would get up to at that age?

They went swimming again and again, they thoroughly enjoyed the heat of the pool and the fun that the pool offered. The two women were swimming like mermaids; Elspeth was swimming the breast stroke with real breasts popping over the top of her full length swim suit, it was as if her breasts were buoyancy chambers. Elspeth's were real enough he thought and he knew their authenticity intimately. They stayed in the water until their skin started to wrinkle, then it was time for a shower and freshen up. Later that night they would be going to the theatre, albeit Kane had not told either of them.

Dinner was served as requested by Kane; it was a light seafood salad with freshly baked French rolls. At the dinner Kane told them of the outing, his reward was by way of smiles, two faces stretched from ear to ear by two beautiful look a like ladies.

Before 7:30 p.m. they were exiting the Swiss home to partake in another form of fun. Kane was beginning to unwind, but it was a slow process.

In the rear of the Mercedes he sat arm in arm with the two ladies, his mind searching his faith and seeking heavenly approval for his mission; the approval never came but none the less he kept searching.

The support team of four drove in a black ford some two hundred meters behind the Mercedes; the operatives had split the shifts to cover Kane 24/7

The theatre was a marvel; it was a humorous satire of George Orwell's, Animal Farm except the characters were Mississippi lawyers, another breed of animal, or perhaps parasite.

The lawyers dedicated their time to filling their jeans with millions of dollars on the backs of thousands of misfortunate policy holders who suffered weather calamities and property losses after each storm season. The performance was hilarious, Kane had laughed so much that his jaw ached. Kane only hoped that the basis of the plot was grossly exaggerated and that lawyers in the southern US states were not as bold as portrayed on stage. Mary Ann too enjoyed the show, almost as much as she did her chocolates that she snuck into the theatre.

Elspeth was enamored with the evening show and the fact that she was with her man, later that night she would sneak into his room and express her love. She was ready for him as soon as she saw him threaded out in his evening suit.

The show ended with two standing ovations, the crowd too obviously enjoyed the performance.

The drive home was fast; the two cars sped through the mountain passes with grace and elegance. Mary Ann was already asleep when they returned to the house. Kane carried her effortlessly in his arms to her bedroom where he gently placed her on her bed. With a duck down quilt to cover her she remained somewhere in Peter pans never land. Leaning over he affectionately kissed his daughter and turned to leave. Standing at the door Elspeth had watched her man adopt the role of a dad, and like everything he had excelled. Together they went to the lounge, Elspeth to enjoy an Australian sherry and Kane a belated after dinner port. They sat opposite each other in two high backed wing chairs; they were like King and Queen of their castle. They talked about the show, Mary Ann and how Mary Ann had accepted Kane. According to Elspeth she/they would have no problems with their daughter. The decision to tell Mary Ann that Kane was indeed her Dad could wait; there was no rush at this juncture.

Elspeth asked of Kane what had been troubling him, to which he honestly replied, "Government matters, grave government matters that remain strictly confidential, he could not divulge a word to her but admitted that he would really like to."

Elspeth knew not to pry into his work; she knew from her endless conversations with Sir Billy that the work was highly irregular, highly necessary and highly confidential. Kane had still not mentioned the loss of Sir Billy, he would tell all after the imminent Middle East raid. Kane was like Sir Billy, alone with his thoughts and his decisions. As exciting though his life may have appeared it was scarily beyond the normal parameters of a homo-sapien. Elspeth would comfort him all knowing that love would calm his mind and prepare him for the next day, whatever it may unveil. They eventually left the living room and the comfort of the wing chairs, making their way upstairs to Kane's bedroom. There they comforted each other with their playfulness, their bodies and their minds. All thoughts were temporarily short circuited with the moment. As before they made love with immense passion, time and time again. By 4:00 a.m. Elspeth was drained of energy having no calories left to burn, sleep deprived she embraced him with a gentle kiss to bid him farewell, and then she crawled over her man to exit the bedroom. Kane fell into a deep sleep and awoke at 8:00 a.m. on the button to a room full of golden sun rays; it would be another pleasant day. Unshaven and naked in his bed he heard a little tap on his door. He thought it was Elspeth and he answered the tap with, "The door is unlocked come on in."

To his pleasant surprise it was Mary Ann, sheepishly she approached his bed and then pressed her lips to his furry face and kissed his cheek. Within moments she was alive and beaming. Her little face was quite a joy to see, her dark hair was accentuated with the back drop of golden sunlight which filled the room. The next fifteen minutes or so she just motored away with dialogue, Kane's place was to listen and answer with a short reply Yes or No. Breakfast aroma was permeating the air and Kane somehow needed to get up and shower. Thankfully Mary Ann popped the question that she would like to go to the caves nearby and perhaps, weather permitting they could swim later on. Kane agreed to everything and then the final question came completely out of the blue. Like only children can she asked of him whether he would be her daddy. Kane was choked and found it difficult to stop the flow of tears from his eyes. He took her up in his arms and replied, Thank you I would love to be your daddy. Mary Ann's eyes were wide and staring, a huge smile exposed her pearl like teeth. Kane kissed her brow and then said that he needed to get up and get ready for breakfast. Mary Ann knowing that her new found dad had few clothes on, respectfully ran from the room making a B line for her mothers' bedroom, the good news would be told before Kane showered.

Thirty minutes passed and Kane was ready downstairs awaiting the arrival of his women. Breakfast was ready, each food item being placed midsection of the table in warmers. It was the same as any small hotel buffet. In the meantime he would drink his mild Columbian coffee, black with one sugar.

The two ladies eventually made it down to the dining room. The ladies helped themselves to scrambled eggs, bacon and mushrooms. Mary Ann too took a liking to American style waffles with cream and Canadian Maple syrup. Playfully she referred to her father as "pops." Kane looked into Elspeth's eyes and they shared a smile. The transition was taking place superbly.

Kane helped himself to a good helping of the same and they sat down to enjoy the kicker meal of the day. Orange juice and grapefruit complimented the breakfast. The girls did not share Kane's passion for coffee; they left Kane to enjoy his fourth cup.

The Alpha Omega and the GVC crews had already eaten and maintained surveillance of the grounds. One of the attic rooms had been outfitted with CC monitoring screens of the grounds and the approach road as far as five miles east. Sir Billy had done a very good job. The telephone lines were original as well as an Inmarsat link line (satellite). Combined with cell coverage, the original and the new telephone systems communication was sound. The crews were doing a fine job, albeit it was rather simple given the remote location and the fact that few, if any, people ever frequented the home site.

Kane was already content with the location and thought seriously of making the Berne residence his main home; he would discuss the matter with his future bride.

Kane finished his meal advance of the girls; they were laughing and joking, the topic being the prior evening theatre performance. He watched them carefully and could not help but share in their laughter; both of them were a breath of fresh air, their smiles illuminating the already bright room.

Eventually they too finished their breakfast and left the room to clean their already perfectly white teeth.

There was a race to the stairs Mary Ann beating her mother, who of course permitted her. Kane followed but at a respectable pace. By 9:30 a.m., and with clean sparkling teeth they were ready to hit the road, and as promised Kane would take them and his shadows to the Caves of Hannes.

The morning was still and the sunshine pleasantly warm. The shadows driving in the car behind had sunglasses on making them all look rather sinister. Kane drove the Mercedes and quite liked the vehicle; it was somewhat less opulent than his old Bentley.

Later in the day Kane would permit Mary Ann to sit on his lap and steer the car; it was a great thrill to her but she still wanted desperately to take the flying lessons as promised.

The caves were interesting yet the visit took them into the darkness of the caves leaving behind the final days of summer. The caves housed a multitude of murals depicting life thousands of years before.

Kane only hoped that his future actions did not set the course for the rest of the world to return to such times. The caves were impressive and Mary Ann lapped up the history and the artwork. She was obviously very bright, no doubt having the jeans of her mother. Elspeth of course with her knowledge of Geology was also impressed by the teachings offered by the caves. Two hours slipped by and Mary Ann, desperate to pee suggested that they leave the dampness of the cave and go outside to the awaiting sunshine. Outside of the cave the sun seemed naturally warmer than before.

Mary Ann came running out of the washroom, only to rush directly to the kiosk to purchase a coke cola.

It was noon and Kane recommended that they find a restaurant with a patio, and enjoy some European cheeses. The idea was adopted and they took off again to search for a suitable café. Driving for the first time Mary Ann sitting erect on her Pops lap did well. Immediately she was addicted to the automobile, but Kane had to stress the issue that the roads had to be extremely quiet for him to prop her on his lap, after all, it was illegal.

The café was safely sourced albeit the selection of cheeses was that suited for Pizza only. Mary Ann had won over pops as a promoter of fine foods. It did not make any difference as they and the shadows enjoyed every morsel. After their snack they returned to the home and the waiting warm waters of the Caribbean, well the pool!

The two ladies donned their swim suits while Kane made some calls to Pammy. The Harrier was being made ready for Kane's use the following week. As usual Pammy had everything well organized and there was little for Kane to do other than check in with certain Special Branch and the other members of the anti terrorist squad.

Kane noted the list of calls to do and one by one went through the list. The list included the President of the USA and the Prime Minister and the Alpha Omega operative in Qatar.

As far as Kane knew the US President and the British Prime Minister were the only two people who knew the time frame referred to as operation Cumberland, Kane making reference to the butcher of Culloden.

Kane took ownership of the phrase, but was not proud of the work to be done.

The calls were completed after two hours; Kane having instructed the Qatar operative to make his way promptly to the port of Bandar Mashur oil terminal in Iran and to plant a series of radio activated explosives ready for later use. He was then to proceed to Kharg Island to do the same there. The call was short and sweet the operative answering with a, "Yes, sir."

Kane spoke with the British Prime Minister and then the US president, the President of the USA basically repeating what the Prime Minister had said moments earlier. It was evident by the latest intelligence that the Arab world was divided on the action recently taken by Al Qaeda, the Palestinian death toll was not at all planned and the status was worsening by the day. Each evening the sea breeze came in from the high pressure (sea) air mass, moving eastward toward the low air pressure mass over the Palestinian lands, blowing what remained of the Anthrax pores even deeper into Palestinian territory. The scary reality was that the eventual death toll of Palestinians may exceed the targeted Jews. The irony was not a comfort, as many innocent Palestinians too would die a painful death. The chatter being collected inferred that the Al Qaeda needed another victory and soon. Kane's mission was even more important than before and as requested the mission would be advanced, in fact, to commence within the next forty-eight hours. Kane went to the drinks cabinet and poured himself large bourbon; he was sick to his stomach and wrestled once again with his thoughts. He felt compelled to pray and decided that he would find a church and have a quiet time alone with his maker. Kane summoned one of his shadows and instructed him to get the car. He then went to the pool and informed Elspeth that he needed to go into town and that he would be back within a few hours. Elspeth chose not to question him, as it was evident that he was deeply troubled, she knew that he had just spoken to very powerful political men. Prior to leaving the peace of the residence Kane once again called Pammy to orchestrate the arrival of the Harrier in Berne within thirty-six hours.

Kane was driven with three of his shadows to a church some twenty miles down the road. It was a catholic church but it made no difference to Kane. He entered the fine old building and made his way to the front pew. There were a couple of women in the front rows fervently in prayer; the caretaker was working sweeping the rear vestibule. It had been a very long time since Kane had been to any church, but he knew in his heart that there was a greater being, he accepted that and now he humbled himself before the alter. He crouched down to his knees resting them on a small red velvet pillow. He leaned forward and requested of his maker to listen. Kane had a one way conversation with God, he poured out his heart and God as always listened. For more than two hours Kane barely adjusted his posture and finally he stood up. He looked up at the cross and felt comfort in the sight of Jesus nailed to a cross, accepting judgment/penalty for the sins of the world; *it was the right thing to do*. Kane was not certain who was talking to his heart, it was either God, his parental dad the judge, his mother and or his real dad Sir Billy, their voices were the same, but nonetheless he listened. He gazed at the cross for a good ten minutes, and then he turned and made his way out of the now empty church. The shadows uttered not a word, their respect for this man was of biblical proportions as it was, but they knew in their own hearts and minds that something big was coming down, something very big, it was a given fact.

On the way home Kane kept hearing in his mind, *It was the right thing to do*. He wondered was this answer from God?

On the side of the road a billboard came into view. It was an advertisement for sunscreen. The slogan stated, *That it was the right thing to do.*

Kane on viewing the sign cracked a smile and then closed his eyes for the remaining journey. After twenty five minutes drive, the Mercedes glided into the driveway of the home. The shadows were not sure whether Kane had been sleeping or praying, Kane had been silent for the full twenty miles.

The truth of the matter was that Kane was planning his next visit to church, but God willing that would be to marry Elspeth and for him to assert rightful ownership to his Mary Ann.

Mary Ann came rushing to the car and greeted pops with a kiss and directed him to the pool. His swimmer and Elspeth were waiting.

Swimming was a delight and Kane took great pleasure playing with his daughter. She was a fine swimmer and she loved to splash and throw the beach ball. Together they had attempted water polo, piggy in the middle and water ballet. Kane abstained from the water ballet but he could see that his little girl was a talented young performer. The afternoon ended far better than Kane could have dreamt, he felt good, as well as famished. Together they changed for supper and Kane, light of heart took his bride to be, to watch the sunset. On the patio, without a ring, he got down on his left knee, asking her softly, "Elspeth, would you honor me and marry me, tomorrow?"

To his surprise she acknowledge with a yes, but the surprise was not in the answer yes, but with the endorsement of, "It's the right thing to do."

Kane was ecstatic and immediately contacted the authorities. The task at hand was enormous and to most normal newlyweds it be would be impossible, but in this case the almighty dollar substituted the white knight in shining armor. Throughout the evening Kane fielded a host of calls and by the end of the evening it was done. Arrangements had been made for an afternoon wedding at the same church where Kane had just met his maker hours before. The time was 2:00 p.m. and Mary Ann had already insisted on being a bride's maid, she also insisted on a new dress for the auspicious occasion. The next day would be hectic. John asked the Seal who had almost destroyed his manhood with fire ants to be his best man. The response was that it would be an honor…sir.

Mary Ann went to bed bubbly, she could barely contain herself, but within moments of her head laying on the pillow and a kiss good night from Pops, she drifted off.

Kane and Elspeth retired to the living room for the final night cap. Kane requested a snack from the kitchen; he had barely had time to eat the prime rib that was served for dinner. With a ham sandwich and a port Kane watched over his bride to be. She was glowing; little did he know that tomorrow she would give him the news that she was pregnant.

The evening raced on and eventually eclipsed midnight. Elspeth went to her own bedroom and Kane to his. The wedding day would be memorable not only because of the special nature of the events but because of the craziness of time, or the lack thereof. Kane had kissed his bride good night and retired to his room only to read, he was wide awake and needed some work out for his brain. He read a novel extract downloaded from the internet. His book of choice was "The sin of Marriage" the title had caught his eye. He read some one hundred and fifty pages before his eyelids became weighted and started to shut out the light from his side table lamp. He allowed himself to sleep. The house was quiet with only the night crew monitoring the grounds and the home, one person taking station in the attic surveillance room; all was well, rounds complete. Morning would come soon enough and marriage a few hours afterward.

Paris

Farshad Estackhri and a team of Iranian terrorists checked into three separate hotels in Paris. The team totaled ten in all and their assignment, which was driven by a thirty million dollar bounty, was Sir Kane Austin, dead. The leader Farshad Estackhri alleged killer of three Israeli Ministers and one foreign diplomat of Canada. He had come very close to assassinating the US President but was disturb by the CIA /FBI agents that came dangerously close to his sniper position; he had to leave quickly leaving the rifle and tripod in place. Farshad had been wanted for the past ten years, but continued to elude capture by hiding in the tribal villages of Libya and Egypt. He was very good, very expensive and was climbing the most wanted list daily; he was now number eleven from the top. At six feet tall and weighing in at 200 pounds, he was a fit man and in his prime at thirty six years of age. His other nine colleagues were seasoned terrorists, seven of them having been trained in Afghanistan and with two of them part of the cell group based in London, UK, these two being of Libyan descent and having been trained near Tripoli at one of the main underground training camps. They had linked up with the French sleeper cells and the London Black Watch Warriors to source the whereabouts of Kane Austin. The Savoy, Claridges, Hilton, Dorchester, and the Grosvenor Hotel staff had reported that they had not seen him for several days. He was at presently off the map. Farshad had his IT hackers vigorously engaged in chasing credit card usage for a Kane Austin, passport data and immigration records for all European countries. They had a host of aliases previously used by

Kane but little was working. Something would break; they just had to be patient. They would work on relentlessly.

Interpol and Special Branch were aware of the presence of the terrorist in France, they had been tipped off that certain known terrorists were headed for Paris. They had tracked most of the group arriving into the International airport via five different cities. The police wanted the group to clear the multitude of civilians at the airport and apprehend them on route to the city. The plan failed when following them to their three separate locations. The mix up on all three vehicles being tailed was at the Arc de Triumph when suddenly a fleet of vehicles of the same color and make joined in at the Place de le Toile. This was a deliberate decoy well planned and well executed by the sleeper cell teams. The police had failed and once again the terrorist remained at large. The terrorist were in town but that's all they knew. The hotels had been booked and paid for more than three weeks prior to their arrival, hence the suretee would have no luck in finding new registrants; the terrorists were safe for the time being. Needless to say the French government was embarrassed; the other international authorities would be informed immediately of the status.

Paris has everything a man or women could ever need. Theatre, fine dining, clubs and bars, gambling, recreation facilities etc the list is endless. The terrorists however were confined to their quarters; they could only order food into their room and await instructions. Their weapons would be thoroughly cleaned and cleaned again. A deck of cards kept them preoccupied between meals; cards sleep and cleaning their weapons was their preoccupation. They were in for the long haul, all they had to do was to put their minds in neutral and coast until the order arrived to get up and go. The only question remained was Where?

The Wedding

The following morning the complete household was up early, breakfast was prepared thirty minutes early and was eaten faster than normal. The women wanted to be in the city upon opening time of the stores. Kane wanted for nothing, he took out a dark blue Armani suit and a pair of size twelve black shoes that were hand made in London two years before. He had worn them only once before and planned to keep them for the official ceremony of his knighthood which was planned to be the following month. His wedding took precedence so he buffed them with a soft rag; they were really good looking shoes, and polished up well. He then prepared a new shirt from his bank of many. White and with a neck size of eighteen, he draped the fresh new shirt across his mahogany wooden valet stand. Finally he found an appropriate silk tie and matching breast pocket handkerchief and he was as ready as anyone could be. Like most grooms he had to organize the carnations which he simply dedicated to his home keeper, who was enthralled to be included in the joyous event. Kane too would do some shopping of his own, wedding bands, engagement ring and a ring for the bridesmaid.

The women were on route to the store accompanied by two operatives by ten and Kane with two of his crew went direct to the most notable jewelry store in Berne. Kane had given Elspeth a sizeable wad of cash, his instruction was that no credit cards were to be used, he emphasized the importance of the request and Elspeth got the message, loud and clear.

Kane with a briefcase absolutely stuffed to the gunwales with one hundred dollar US bills was going to enjoy his splurge. Certain sales staff too would be overwhelmed at the generosity of Kane on his wedding day.

The morning was fresh with a cool crisp air mass enveloping the valley. The sun was beginning to burn through the moisture; it was going to be just perfect for a wedding.

Elspeth found a store that specialized in wedding gowns. For the next two hours she and her daughter dressed and undressed until they found the dresses of choice. They were stunning white satin gowns with an assortment of stitched in Zirconia's and pearls. Shortly after noon the store manager received payment in cash and marveled at his good fortune for the day, Elspeth also tipped the Manager and staff generously for their attention to detail and their whims. From the store they went to the Marriot where they had booked a room for the sole purpose of getting their hair groomed and to dress for the occasion. They would be picked up at 1:45 p.m. and transported to the church a short distance away.

Kane meanwhile was in the jewelry store and had chosen the ring for his bride and the same design for his daughter, albeit the daughters ring boasted a 0.33-carat solitaire whereas Elspeth's was six times larger. The wedding bands were simple bands of 22-karat white gold, with no design. Kane had already confirmed the ring sizing and waited for the jeweler to make the adjustments.

Again to the surprise and shock of the jeweler Kane purchased ten Rolex Oyster President Watches for his team, and a similar matching set for his homekeepers. With the packages complete the store manager politely asked for the method of payment. Kane responded that they should go to the rear of the store to the managers' office. If the surprise of the orders had not shocked the retailer then the sight of a brief case laden with hard cash would certainly do the trick. Although the brief case was full of cash the store manager did a very good job at reducing its content. More than seventy-five percent of the cash had been rung into the store register, most likely one of the larger transactions for the year. By 11:30 a.m., Kane and his crew were on their way back to the house to make their final preparations. On route to the residence Kane received a call from Pammy, she informed him of Farshad and his cell group now confirmed to be in

Paris France. Kane listened carefully and took everything aboard, including the arrival later that day of the Harrier in Berne. The Harrier would be fueled up and ready to depart for Kane's flight to the Arabian Sea, the very next day.

Kane arrived at the residence and handed out the wedding gifts, the smiles and tears of the female housekeeper was heartfelt. Kane was feeling really good and enjoyed Bourbon on the rocks before he went to his bathroom to freshen up. He would shave at the very last moment. By 1:25 p.m. he was done, not only did he look great he felt like a billion dollars. His one regret was that his parents were not there but he knew that they would approve of his choice, and that of course they would be there in spirit.

They departed for the church arriving with only ten minutes to spare. The church was of course almost empty. Kane had paid triple the price to have the choir there at short notice; he only hoped and trusted that the reverend actually paid them the extra funds.

Standing in front of the alter with his best man; they patiently awaited the arrival of Elspeth. In due course at 2:03 p.m. the organ erupted playing the appropriate music. The church echoed the notes and the whole building vibrated to the music. Kane stood facing forward but his best man turned to see the bride and bridesmaid walking down the Isle. On her right hand was one of the tall operatives looking as civilian as anyone could be. There were no weapons in the church, no Kevlar under protection. The black skin operative looked like a movie star. The pressed starched white shirt, a white silk bow tie, his polished bald head and a set of brilliant white teeth; dressed in his first ever Armani suit he could have been walking the row to collect an Oscar in Hollywood. This was the operative's first wedding and he took the request to stand in for Elspeth's father as a great honor and a privilege; he was truly enjoying the festivities. Elspeth was stunning, her outfit was breathtaking, her train clutched in the hands of Mary Ann who looked a miniature Elspeth, equally as beautiful. Elspeth was glowing as most pregnant mothers do, but in this case she looked like a Cinderella, a Princess Leah from Star wars, a sleeping Beauty from Walt Disney, she was quite unbelievably ravishing.

Finally Elspeth reached her man and Kane trained his eyes on her. He gasped at her presence; she was a two hundred out of ten. He was so pleased that he did not have to speak right then as his facial muscles were temporarily frozen, his heart was pumping liters of adrenalin and for once he felt week at the knees. Elspeth gave him a smile and a naughty little wink which stimulated Kane's facial muscles back to life, in addition stimulating a rush of blood to his lower loins, one thing that was inappropriate at the time and quite possibly a risk of imminent embarrassment. Kane attempted to look at the architecture in front of him but his eyes always returned to this goddess next to him, at that moment he longed for a bourbon and ice, or perhaps just ice.

The wedding service was done in less than thirty minutes, they each said their *I do's*, on queue without faltering. The newly weds exited the church as man and wife and ecstatically happy. At the request of Kane, and for security reasons they had not signed the register. They were married in Gods eyes and paper work was to Kane irrelevant and far too dangerous.

They drove back to the house chauffeured by the best man. Mary Ann sat in the front of the car and the bride and groom sat in the back seat. Arriving back at the residence they were greeted by the caterers who had provided a magnificent spread. The buffet meal was arranged on two thirty foot long tables; there was not a square inch that was not covered by decorative arrangements of food. The array of food reminded Kane of the Cruise ships which guarantee ten pounds additional weight for every week of sailing. Fish, Poultry, Beef, a whole pig, racks of lamb, duck, pheasant. Grouse, Ptarmigan, salads, and potatoes that looked like pieces of modern art. In the middle of the table the wedding cake stood tall, a five tier cake full of marzipan and fruit. The color was awesome and warranted a photograph before the festivities truly got underway. The wedding guests made short order of the banquet. The wine flowed, and flowed, but the entire group maintained decorum. The afternoon carried on into the evening. The pool became a temporary haven for those who wanted to refrain from the feast albeit just for a short period of time. Mary Ann had eaten her fill and volunteered to go to bed at 9:00 p.m., she was exhausted but extremely happy for her mum and Pops. Downstairs the party rallied on into the wee hours of the morning. Elspeth was careful to drink only orange juice, and by 2:00 a.m. she was ready for her wedding night. Kane had indulged somewhat with the Bourbon and a good portion of the Champagne yet he was very much in control of his senses, he too was now ready to meet his newly married wife.

They left the party downstairs to the household staff and the crew. Elspeth went to the bedroom first and freshened up in the bathroom, Kane lagged her arrival by ten minutes, he had gone to the lower guest room to shave and brush his teeth. By the time he reached the bedroom Elspeth was waiting for her husband wearing a silky white embroidered teddy suit. Her long legs seemed even longer, her dark hair and eyes penetrated his own, Kane undressed at the foot of the bed and Elspeth looked on with passion in her eyes. Her lips were moist and pouted somewhat giving her the appearance of a saucy cat, purring, waiting to be stroked. Before he grew in size Eslpeth had a revisit from the Phantom, she tried to hide the fact but after seconds of gushing pleasure she offered a moan and closed her eyes. She permitted her man to lay by her side and he gently kissed her ears and neck, Elspeth merely moaned with great pleasure. Kane wanted to make this night very special, there was no rush, he fixed his mind on Elspeth's pleasure alone and not his, well at least for the first two hours of fore play. Elspeth did not mind at all, her loins was saturated, she was in effect sleeping with two magicians, namely Kane and the Phantom. The teddy suit had been sensually removed by Kane and discarded to the floor, revealing the lustful soft body of his bride. Subsequent to the passage of two hours Elspeth had been there and back so many times that she thought that she had nothing left, but then Kane with some significant force penetrated her very soul and brought her to ecstasy, not once but three times. By four am they were spent, Kane finally removed his firm body, untangling her legs from his back and waist.

If there was a train nearby it would be entering a tunnel at great speed with whistle blowing, leaving the two exhausted newlyweds to drift off quickly into a deep and serene sleep.

Kane awoke at ten am and looked at his wife for the first morning of their marriage. She lay there, slightly stirring and then her eyes opened. To Kane's surprise she pulled him back onto her, her appetite yet to be satisfied. Kane obliged her desire and she said good morning once again to the two magicians.

By noon they had showered and made themselves ready for lunch.

Mary Ann had been outside for the best part of the morning playing with a stray cat, she was mature enough even at ten to permit her mum and pops privacy on their wedding morning. Nonetheless she was beaming to see them both dressed and downstairs. Kane grabbed her in his arms and gently squeezed her; Mary Ann loved the attention and kissed her pops on the forehead. Kane without giving Mary Ann any warning, grabbed her arm and a leg, and propelled her through three sixty degrees spinning her around and around. She was flying, laughing and loving the feeling of flight. Eventually Kane placed her down on Terra Firma and Mary Ann, a little giddy from her flight ran off to find the cat. She of course found the furry little cat and brought it into the house cradled in her arms as if a baby. The cat had no name tag, and seemed content to stay. Kane permitted the cat to be a part of the family unless claimed by the rightful owner. Mary Ann was delighted; she now had a new friend. When asked what to name her/him, Mary Ann suggested "Mystery", as they did not know where she/him had come from, and it was fitting. So it was, a new family addition on the first day of their wedding life together. Elspeth approved but said little, she just observed her husband taking the reign as a father.

Lunch was being served in the dining room; Kane and Elspeth were in desperate need of refueling, thousands of calories having been dispensed within the past twelve hours.

Lunch was an assortment of Quiches with a variety of salads; many of the items were a carry over from the masses of food the day before. It was delicious and nourishing, Kane could feel the strength returning to every molecule of his being. Elspeth discretely tucked into her food, probably devouring twice her normal intake; after all she had satisfied beyond belief at least one man in her bedroom and quite possibly two. Kane had requested tea in addition to the coffee. He was evidently dehydrated after his mammoth performance that most men can only achieve on the honeymoon night. He drank a pot of coffee and then switched to tea. Elspeth understood as she too had lost a great deal of fluids in their romantic endeavors. Elspeth stayed with tea, lots of it.

An hour past at the dining room table when the peace was disturbed as the telephone rang, of course it was for Kane. The Harrier was refueled and ready to go, but Kane was not so eager to leave, he delayed his departure until first light in the morning. Today he would enjoy his family, Elspeth, Mary Ann and Mystery.

The delay in Kane's operation schedule of twenty-four hours did not sit well with the Western governments, but little was said. It was well-appreciated what the task entailed. It was a massive responsibility to impose on any human being. Kane had wrestled with his thoughts and likened his task to that of the Duke of Cumberland and Culloden, but on a far greater scale. It was the right thing to do, he was almost certain of that.

The afternoon and evening appeared to be like a movie on fast forward, the sun setting modestly earlier than the day before. As each minute slipped away the character of the Duke of Cumberland became more and more of a reality to Kane. By 9:00 p.m. Kane was mentally fatigued purely with the knowledge of the daunting task that he had stated that he would manage him and him alone. He was aggravated by the nagging little man in his head questioning the right or wrong of the situation.

It was bedtime for Mary Ann and unlike the night before she took the cat to bed with her. The cat was well fed on herring and sardines from the banquet venue and was stuffed, ready for a prolonged nap.

Kane was instructed by Mary Ann to kiss the cat goodnight also, and of course he did so. He told Mary Ann that he was very pleased to be her Pops and that he loved her very much. Mary Ann soaked up the attention and returned the affection with I love you pops.

Kane and Elspeth spent the last minutes of the evening discussing the future when Kane returned. Kane had committed to resigning his post before Christmas and they would seek a place in the sun and perhaps create a boy child. Elspeth had not told him of her surprise and left the news for the morning, she knew that the news would boost his morale.

They retired to a second honeymoon night, yet the passion was somewhat less intense, Kane clearly had other things on his mind. Kane tried to dismiss his morning schedule but it haunted him throughout the passage of the night. The love making was just that, nothing like the night before, the endurance too faltered, not so much physically but due to Kane's preoccupation with the Duke of Cumberland. Finally sleep ensued and morning placed on fast forward. Kane lay inert in his bed with Elspeth by his side. Quietly at

5:00 a.m. he rolled over and placed his feet on the carpeted floor. He would shower and shave drink coffee and make his exit.

Kane had finished his coffee and returned to the bedroom of Mary Ann and Mystery. Both were fast asleep although Mystery stirred only to open and close his/her eyes. Kane kissed his daughter on the brow and left her room. Returning to his own bedroom he leaned over to kiss his bride and once again the bride awoke as if sleeping beauty, her lips pressed on Kane's and she in turn said to him that she loved him deeply and for him to return safely, we need you home all four of us. Kane was momentarily perplexed and to relieve his mind of mental gymnastics she stated that they were pregnant. Kane suddenly felt the news as if his mission was endorsed again and that this was indeed the right thing to do. He was elated with the news and hugged his bride so tightly that she had to ask him to ease the squeeze. "I will be back and we will have a beautiful life together, I love you so very much."

With that, Kane left for the awaiting Harrier. On route to the airport he glanced back at the billboard sign, it was still there, "It was the right thing to do." Kane felt good, really good, yet he knew that he would join the same league as the Duke of Cumberland, inheriting the alias of "The Butcher."

USS Reagan

Kane departed at first light, leaving his loved ones in the safe haven of Berne Switzerland. He flew the jet at a modest speed of five hundred knots south east to the Mediterranean; he would fly to the Red Sea where he would rendezvous and overnight on the USS Reagan, one of several nuclear powered aircraft carriers in the Pacific and Indian Ocean theater. Once over the sea he would level out the jet at three hundred feet altitude accepting the safety offered by the blind sector of radar.

Kane was enjoying the flight; the thought of his women already pregnant was exciting, he was truly blessed. When flying on auto pilot he quietly prayed for his family and for his mission, thankfully the little nagging man had left the confines of his mind. The flight to the aircraft carrier was pleasant; after sighting the monstrous steel structure, Kane finally approached the ship flying somewhat like a hummingbird, he descended to the deck of the mobile airport, the journey ending with a slight thump on the steel deck. He then taxied the Harrier to the parking lot and disembarked the jet. The crews had their instructions and immediately went to task at refueling the jet and outfitting the missile housing with nuclear tipped missiles. Kane left the aircraft to join the Vice Admiral in the confines of his cabin.

The Vice Admiral was a good looking senior gentleman with white short cropped navy looking beard. He greeted Kane with a solid handshake and the offer of Bourbon. Kane was ready for that and accepted accordingly. The Vice Admiral was aware of the use of weapons but few knew the targets. Kane kept that information closely guarded. No questions were asked by the seafarer but he did offer comforting advice and stated that action was called for. Apparently the Palestinian death toll due to anthrax had now surpassed the Israeli count and the support for Al Qaeda was for the moment diminishing. The timing was appropriate.

In the USA matters were desperate, the people wanted to see some action and the President had committed to a retaliatory strike imminently, but first they had to regain control in several key cities where civil strife was crippling. The Vice Admiral took a liking to Kane and appreciated the burden placed on such young shoulders. He offered him to accompany him and the Chaplin later in the ships chapel. Kane was not embarrassed at all and cordially accepted the invitation.

As usual the monstrous vessel became polluted with the smells of the galley. Lunch was being served and Kane stripped out of his garb and made his way with the Vice Admiral to dine at the head table.

The meal was quite different to the past couple of days; it was very noticeable to Kane. The meal of the day was Tom Turkey with all of the dressings. It was good and filling, desert followed with a type of spotty dick and caramel sauce. The head chef came to the table to greet the visitor; Kane complimented the chef on the delightful meal. The chef smiled and stated that he could do so much better if he was in New York with a restaurant of his own. Kane casually agreed with the chef and wished him well with his dreams. The afternoon was left for Kane to wander the ship; the Vice Admiral would take in his usual afternoon nap. Kane was given an AB seaman to escort him to wherever he wanted to go. Kane took full advantage and requested a visit to the engine room. The two of them stayed in the city of pipes, steam and noises for over two hours. Kane finally needed air and the tour continued above decks. He watched the Harrier receiving its last warhead, it looked innocuous and lame yet the missiles could destroy and kill so many. The AB commented that the missiles were nuclear warheads, to which Kane responded, "I Know." Gratefully, the little nag of a man was still absent from his mind.

The tour ventured up to the tower. Kane was welcomed on the bridge and immediately offered a fresh coffee. Coffee is the substance of war machines; Kane made a note to obtain a flask of coffee in the morning to accompany him on operation Cumberland. They spent another two hours on the bridge supping the coffee, four cups in all. While on the bridge they watched CNN television and observed the chaos unfolding in Atlanta, Jacksonville, Dallas, Las Angeles and St Louis. The nuclear strike on the USA was callous and cowardly, the next twenty four hours, he hoped would change everything.

Eventually they had had their fill of coffee and dialogue from the officers of the watch. The two of them made their way down to the quarters where Kane had been given a cabin with an adjoining door to another cabin. He was truly honored as space on these mammoth vessels was at a premium; wow he thought I have been given almost two hundred square feet! Even more of a surprise the other cabin had its own shower and toilet. Kane sniggered when looking at the shower as there was no way he could fit into it; he would shower down the corridor in the men's communal showers. Kane thanked the AB for chaperoning him throughout the vessel and then excused him. He would freshen up and get ready for the evening meal.

Life aboard the carrier was much the same as he had seen before; the only difference was the name. Kane eat once again at the head table, this time dinner was either steak or Basa fish. Kane chose the Basa. The meal was just fine, washed down with plenty of ship made water, the purest water one could find, almost all of the minerals having been extracted by the onboard water making process. Kane skipped the desert and took his leave. He needed to visit the gym before paying a 7:00 p.m. visit to the chapel.

Kane stripped down to sweats only he made his entrance into the ships gym. He settled for the running machine. He jog for a full thirty minutes, onlookers would say a very fast pace. After thirty minutes he was dripping with sweat, but the benefit to Kane was exactly what he needed. He felt totally ready physically for his morning endeavor; gratefully, the little nagging man was still not present in his head.

Shortly after 7:00 p.m. Kane met up with the Vice Admiral and the Chaplin. Together they went alone to the four hundred-square-foot area designated as the prayer room. They stayed in the room talking about the mission, talking about the death of the USA nuclear attacks and the most recent biological attack. The death toll was still climbing. Kane advised them that his strike would be far worse than those already witnessed by the world. Kane talked for a little while on Culloden and the Duke of Cumberland. With the talking done the

Chaplin lead the prayer. His conversation with Kane, the Vice Admiral and God was incredulous. His message and request of spiritual strength and guidance was awesome. The Chaplin was a flying angel in his own right and his prayers were more powerful to the soul than any nuclear warhead could be on the ground; he was simply magnificent and or perhaps it was the great almighty talking through him? Continually a voice echoed in Kane's mind that *it was the right thing to do* and with that they said Amen. They left the chapel after Kane received a heart felt hug from the Chaplin. It was obvious to the Chaplin and the Vice Admiral that the task at hand for the young knight was simply immense. Along with the hug came a genuine "God Bless You." Kane once again felt the peace that he had discovered at the church in Berne, the place of God and the place of his marriage to Elspeth.

From the chapel Kane was taken to the bridge for light banter with the deck officers and to catch up on world affairs; they watched CNN news cast only to confirm that chaos remained the norm in the USA, and particularly the lower states.

They drank more coffee, and enjoyed a variety of US cheeses; the platter was an excellent replacement for the forfeited desert. Kane longed for a glass of port but alas, it was not going to happen.

The large warship ploughed through the plankton rich Red Sea with grace and dignity. At twenty four knots they steered South East towards Yemen and the port of Little Aden. The bow wave churned up the sea and the result was a magnificent glow, the bioluminescence literally making the sea come alive with a green light. Porpoise performed wonderful feats of their own, diving in and out of the water alongside the vessel as if demonstrating that they too could swim at twenty four knots. The observation of nature in the brilliant starlit night and the sea below acted as a tonic to Kane. He was at peace, he was in a place that he could stay and absorb. Staying on the bridge wing until the watch change at midnight, he then had to leave the sanctuary of this creation and go below; tomorrow he would leave peace behind to become the modern day butcher of Culloden.

Sourced

In the hotel room of Farshad, the terrorist cell group leader had gathered the team of assassins. They kept the other two hotel rooms but chose to use Farshad's hotel and make use of the adjoining suite. Together they continued to play poker, and drink beer. The room stank of stale curry, pizza, cigarettes, beer and stale farts in addition to unwashed humans. Even with the two rooms the stench of the atmosphere was overwhelming. The second room was hired due to the internet connection availability, the other hotels were so non descript that they had not entered into the twenty first century, albeit they had nineteenth or twentieth century bed bugs. As the butcher was waking on the aircraft carrier the IT nerd of the terrorist cell within the confines of the Paris shit hole of a hotel shouted out loud in Arabic several times, "Allah be praised. Allah be praised. Allah be praised."

He was so jubilant anyone would have thought that he had won the lottery. Farshad rallied to his call and queried the jubilation. He had been searching for the past thirty six hours, screening credit card usage and airport travelers and anything that would search out a Kane Austin. He had dismissed a handful of maybes but this one really did fit the bill and in his mind warranted the adulation and praise to Allah. He had tapped into the registry of marriages and he had sourced the marriage of a Sir Kane Austin and Elspeth McTavish, location Berne Switzerland. The instruction clearly given to the Reverend performing the wedding had been breached. Kane would later learn that the breech was an honest mistake by the intern Reverend who had made the assumption that the aging reverend had forgotten to make the entries. He was simply covering the tail of his superior. The consequences of his act were just horrible, a simple mistake having grave dire results. Farshad examined the information and produced a wicked sadistic smile; he then cupped the head of his computer nerd tightly in his hands and kissed his IT nerd three times on his cheeks. They then all joined in with "Allah be praised."

It was early morning in Paris with the sun yet to rise. Farshad ordered his men to wash and shave and make ready for the relatively short journey to Berne Switzerland, it was time for Sir Kane Austin to meet his maker and for Mrs. Austin to be widowed.

Farshad made contact with his Paris cohorts and requested vehicles and safe access to Switzerland. Safe access was guaranteed if they drove to the border crossing at Basal. The border immigration control point had three of their sleeper cell group employed as immigration officers. It was the terrorists main access point to Swiss bank accounts, accounts where deposits were made regularly by Saudi, Syrian and Iranian supporters. Basal was north of the Berne, they could do the drive in ten hours if they applied lead to the accelerator. The contact person ensured that they would be attended by one of their people; they only needed to know the approximate time of arrival. They would supply stolen vehicles with safe plates. They were told to stop at a position two kilometers before the border crossing and telephone the contact person again. They would ensure that there would be no delays at the crossing.

Farshad's team was ready to go within the hour, when they were called by cell phone. The contact had three vehicles ready to go; they had been parked side by side only two minutes walk from their hotel. The cars were found with ease, one Citroen, one Peugeot and one Mercedes. Farshad took the Citroen,

the Gear was stowed in the three trunks and they were off. Farshad chose the Citroen due to the GPS mapping system, he entered his destination and then listened as the machine spoke to him with directions in addition to illuminating a map centered in the front console. By day break they were on their way to Switzerland, all of them smelling of Camay soap and Gillette shaving cream, topped with a splash of cheap hotel cologne.

Poppy Day

The departure from the Carrier was defined by two thousand men who had been ordered to the deck in full uniform to salute the pilot. The crew had an inkling what the pilot had to do, but their thoughts were speculation only, they would have to wait for the return of the Harrier, less the cargo and of course CNN. Everyone was there on deck, including a small band. The Chaplin said a prayer and the order was given for the crew to vacate the deck. Five minutes later Kane was airborne on route to Afghanistan.

Kane departed the deck of the USS Reagan at civil twilight. His aircraft roared down the deck of the 1,100-foot-long carrier and with full thrust applied the aircraft propelled Kane, his flask of coffee and his deadly cargo into the morning skies. He would fly at two hundred seventy-five feet, at six hundred fifty knots to avoid detection and to conserve fuel. Within three hours and undetected he was flying over the target area Number 1. The province of Pakita was well known for Taliban strongholds, as well as being a significant producer of opium. Seventy percent of world supply of opium came from Afghanistan, some four thousand tonnes of it. The target drop point was set for the township of Orgun. In the immediate area almost half of the countries opium came from the soil of Pakita Province, and it was speculated by the CIA and M16, that more than half of the terrorists around the globe were financed by the proceeds. The computer released the ten-kilotonne warhead which was designed to explode two minutes after contact with the ground. At six hundred fifty knots Kane would be almost thirty miles clear when the nuclear detonation would take place. Kane was allowing the computer to fly the aircraft, the mountain tops were dangerously close and at this speed the human brain could not cope with the necessary control adjustments. It was like being in an arcade video game but this time it was for real. Kane heard nothing astern and, in fact, saw nothing as he was concentrating on the next target. After the passage of two minutes seven seconds the detonation took place astern of the harrier. The town of Orgun complete with a possible 60,000 population was vaporized. The ten-kilotonne bomb would render the opium producing soils to a sterile dust incapable of supporting vegetation for another twenty thousand years. In one foul swoop the Al Qaeda money tree/plants had been eradicated. The poppy crop would no longer support the terrorists, and the Afghanistan people would now have a new Poppy Day to remember, and no doubt on November 11 each year the western world would by mere poppy association remember the first nuclear attack performed by the GVC. Next stop for Kane was Islamabad. A beautiful city with a myriad of Greek architecture and population of just over one million people, the Islamic capital of Pakistan and home to many of the worlds known terrorists. Kane was flying over the Potohar Plateau and the Margalla hills. The computer was fully operable and after Kane had made his ten mile bank and turn to the north of the city when the computer started to retrace his flight path back south west to the Arabian Sea. Again the computer signal set in motion the triggering mechanism which released one of five one kilotonne warheads. Two minutes, seven seconds passed by and Islamabad, a relatively newly constructed city, was now on par with Houston, New Orleans and Miami.

Concurrent to Kane's target Number 2 release, CNN had launched their own media weapon, stating that the nuclear attack on Orgun had been claimed as the responsibility of the GVC. A retaliatory measure as a result of the US nuclear attacks and the Biological attacks on Israel. It appeared as if the news media lagged nuclear detonation by the passage of one hour, for Kane that was six hundred fifty nautical miles of flight. Kane had seen and did not hear anything of the explosions, for which he was extremely grateful. He flew over target one avoiding the clouds of dust, yet at his flight speed he had no time for sight seeing. He extracted his steel straw from his coffee flask and supped at the perfectly brewed coffee. Next stop CSS Halifax, some one hundred miles offshore Mumbai.

Back in the States, CNN were having a field day reporting the devastating morning that had targeted Al Qaeda strongholds. Already there was a weird respite from civil strife as millions of US citizens watched fervently televisions around the country all of which tuned into CNN.

Western leaders were quickly denouncing the action as improper and without the sanction of the United Nations, it was, of course, propaganda, a big white lie, but given the GVC movement it was a fabulous diversion for any government leader. The President of the United States made the statement that the US did not approve of the measure yet forewarned the Islamic fundamentalist world that Vigilante groups were hard to control and that the recent world events had pushed the human envelope in the West to unprecedented heights and that the retaliation was in fact, one way or the other, an inevitability. Ironically enough similar statements were echoed by the European community and of course the Prime Minister of the UK. The only immediate voice of shock and horror came from the Vatican but then that was because the Vatican needed a diversion of their own to offset allegations of fraud, racketeering, embezzlement, child abuse, and matters pertaining to homosexuality. Al Qaeda, at the time, had remained silent.

Kane made it safely to the Arabian Sea and rendezvoused on time with the Canadian Frigate Halifax. Unlike the USS Reagan, the frigate had no runway but merely a forty-five-foot-square helipad. Nonetheless, it was perfect to accommodate the refueling needs of the Harrier. Kane made his approach to vertically descend onto the deck of the awaiting Frigate. The sea state was good with force three winds from the south west. Kane enjoyed the flight yet he was keenly aware of the death and destruction that he must have caused. Al Jazeera television had exaggerated the death toll by stating that over three million civilians were killed. The true number was more likely one million. Kane took advantage of his rest period; he showered and shaved for the second time that day. By two pm he would take to the skies again to hit targets numbers 3, 4, 5, and 6.

When completed his shower and ablutions Kane was invited to the bridge to observe CNN newscast, but Kane thought better of it and declined the invitation. He was anxious to get back in the cockpit and get the ugly ordeal behind him. He wanted like hell to get back to the two women in his life and prepare for what he had hope would be a normal life. The Canadians were very hospitable and praised the pilot for his courage and conviction, but Kane did not want to hear praise, he just needed to be in the air. With a fresh feeling of clean Kane boarded his aircraft and performed a perfect vertical take off, with full thrust he was airborne and then adjusting course and speed to target Number 3 he flew off to the entrance of Ras Al Had, or, as seafarers would call it "The Quoins." By mid afternoon with the sun beaming directly ahead in through the tempered glass, Kane entered the Persian Gulf. The cockpit was hot and he was sweating far more than he had done so earlier that day. His Zeiss sun glasses protected his eyes yet the beads of sweat would sting on occasion. Kane persevered knowing that it would not be too long now and his task will have been accomplished and he could make his way back to the USS Reagan and then home.

He flew at the same altitude and the same speed as before. Like the mountains on the moon, the mountains of Iran stood majestically to his right and slipped astern of him quickly while the turquoise sea passed by equally as fast below. He was anxious to get the job done, for some unknown reason Elspeth and Mary Ann had replaced the once nagging little man in his mind. He supped this time on Ice Tea his thoughts continually turning to Elspeth.

The Drive

The assassin squad drove at speeds well in excess of 100 miles per hour, a speed which was acceptable on the French motorways. After two hours of travel their speed lessened as they listened to the French FM station 96.9, which broke the news of the nuclear attack on Afghanistan and Pakistan by the GVC. All of the occupants in the Citroen could understand French, their shock was apparent and Arabic blasphemy inside the car was loose and abundant. Farshad's resolve deepened further for their mission, as did their hate for the infidels of the west. The beautiful countryside of France roared by the group, their focus being centered on the stainless steel radio immediately below the GPS mapping system, and not the panoramic views afforded by the French countryside. The news release continued unabated, death tolls estimated and comparisons drawn to the US cities that were still crippled. Comments on the after math for the US economy which now was mirrored to the doom for Afghanistan whose GDP depended upon the opium production. Simply stated the Afghanistan country was that day placed one hundred years back in their already slow development. By 1:00 p.m., the mountains were clearly in view, they would be at the Basel border crossing very soon. As pre-agreed they stopped when two miles back from the border, the mapping system annoyingly keeping them informed too frequently of their progress and location. The telephone call was made and the contacts made at the immigration point. Moments later they were contacted again by cell phone and instructed to let the lead car through and there after the others would follow at fifteen minute intervals. The terrorist cell group had their system working very well, within the hour they all congregated ten miles east on the Swiss side of the border. They had lost the FM news station hence they concentrated on the drive to Liestal, Solothurn and Berne. If they continued like this they would be in Berne within two hours.

Eating was brief for the group; they stopped at a Greek fast food place in Liestal and ordered a take out, the food was scoffed down while driving at speed to Berne. With indigestion they arrived at Berne at 4:00 p.m., the mapping system gave them directions visually and audibly to the church where Kane had talked to God and where he had God bless his marriage to Elspeth.

Farshad had no time for catholic priests and his disdain was evident. The church was empty but for the reverend. He met the group as they entered the church. Farshad had his men pistol whipped and beat the reverend. Sadly the fate of the reverend was already sealed as he had no knowledge of where Kane Austin lived. Fifteen minutes or so passed and finally the silenced pistol produced the *pop pop* sound indicating that there were two rounds embedded deep into the skull of the reverend. They drag his body to the confessional box and took off.

Within a few blocks of the church Farshad stopped at a pay phone and wrenched a phone book from its anchor point. Flipping through the pages he leafed through the section for wedding receptions/ caterers. After only seven phone calls he had sourced the caterer of record and secured the location of the property; the mystery was solved easily and it was still daylight. Farshad and his band of thugs drove the twenty miles and passed the location at slow speed. They could see the home was secured by black guys, they assumed probably FBI or CIA agents. Further up the road they turned again and retraced their route back, once again slowing down as they passed the safe haven home of Kane Austin. By six pm they were back in Berne at one of the local taverns. They were duly instructed by Farshad on their next move.

Having downed a jug of lager they departed to a quiet car park where they would ready their gear. With weapons checked again by the terrorist group, they drove west in three cars to the three dedicated stop points. Farshad would take the front of the house and the other teams would flank the east and west side. They would monitor the house for one hour with thermographic binoculars before the attack took place.

Kane Austin in the meantime was returning to the Red Sea having deployed the remainder of his cargo.

It appeared as if CNN had a direct link with Kane Austin and his flying Harrier, but it was not the case. US Satellite imagery clearly indicated every move that Kane had made and within minutes of each strike the popularity of the GVC grew. Early in the afternoon that same day when off the oil terminal known as Kharg Island, Kane altered course and headed north towards Tehran. Kane wondered whether the terminal below had been rigged with explosives as requested.

The three hundred sixty nautical miles would be traversed in approximately thirty-two minutes. It was a temporary relief to have the sun on his left side instead of right ahead. Again Kane allowed the computer to fly his aircraft. He was in dangerous territory as the Iranians had a fleet of fighter aircraft and a team of very experienced pilots, yet he was safe there were no bogies to be seen on his radar. Kane supped once more on the iced tea prior to souring over the city of Tehran. He saw the warhead leave his right wing just before he banked to his left to head for target Number 4. Two minutes seven seconds, and then detonation, boom. Once again Kane focused on the aircraft with all of his attention given to the one hundred eighty degrees of vision afforded in front of him. He had no idea how many people were down below, he knew that he province of Tehran had some thirteen million people but the city itself he was unsure, more so he did not really want to know. He now had almost ninety minutes of Flight time at six hundred fifty knots, his mission was now half over.

With miles slipping by the Harrier, Tehran at his rear was pulverized. Emergency systems had failed miserably, and as was 911, the Wembley Stadium incident, the nuclear attack on the USA and the bio chemical release in Israel, surprise was the key element in every case.

Kane Austin had no other aircraft threaten him and now with the chaos below there would not be a chance of an interception by enemy aircraft. Kane's black Harrier, void of any markings was propelled with sixty thousand pounds of thrust towards Ramallah his next target. Wearing sun glasses and again taking refreshment from his iced tea flask Kane sat in his now very hot seat anxious to get to the next release point. Kane had time to reflect while he sped through the air. He would be in effect raining fire on the city of Ramallah, rather like the ancient city of years past Sodom and Gomorrah. Kane wondered whether the Almighty approved of his actions which were proportional to or worse than biblical events, or whether he indeed was the infidel of the west as described by Al Qaeda. Ramallah was chosen due to the rise of insurgents, a safe haven for terrorism and the fact that the government, who continued to not accept Israel as a country was predominantly located there. The time came soon enough and the computer right on time activated the release of the port side missile. Kane banked again to his left and headed towards target Number 5. Kane offered a, "God Help Them."

At almost thirty miles east of Ramallah the Harrier raced towards Buraydah, in Saudi Arabia. The sun was now astern of Kane and he removed his glasses to wipe the sweat from his brow. Astern of him the one kilotonne bomb replaced the sun with a flash of light and a monstrous mushroom cloud. The death toll for the day was closing in on the US numbers for Houston, New Orleans and Miami combined.

An estimated one billion people were watching CNN around the globe as each event unfolded, each time the GVC stressed the fact that they would stop their retaliatory action if Al Qaeda would openly declare that they would cease any more terrorist action throughout the world, but so far there was nothing, Al Qaeda were shocked and for the time being silent.

Kane approached Buraydah from the west; the fifth missile was deployed as per the plan. Below certain of the wealthy construction companies, chemical and manufacturing companies that supported Al Qaeda were about to reap their rewards from the GVC. Just over two minutes and like clockwork the nuclear device detonated, another menacing mushroom cloud grew tall into the sky behind him.

With the fifth explosion the news media were suggesting that the GVC had gone too far, yet in the states blood was what was called for by the majority of the public. The rioting in all of the US states had totally ceased, simultaneously the CNN viewers increased by the minute.

Still on his easterly course Kane headed for Riyadh, the most controversial target of all. It was a known fact that the monarchy was extremely fragile below, it was also a known fact that the terrorist were being financed by the same members of the Royal Family, both the Sauds and the Fauds that catered to the western world, the very same people that promoted and provided business and finances to the construction companies that favored Al Qaeda. It was a land of traitors, traitors amongst traitors with no solutions to turn the tide. The Alpha Omega team referred to these weak cowardly people negatively as "sand niggers", a term that Kane did not approve of.

Sat in his multi million dollar killing machine Kane seriously thought that this target would be cancelled by the people in the highest of public office, but the instruction never came. From the setting sun to the west Kane hurtled through the air and finally launched his last nuclear warhead. The wealthy below would become either dead or poor; they had better hope to be dead. The last nuclear device for that day killed many millions of people, the bulk of them totally innocent yet acceptable as collateral damage. With the butchering completed Kane banked to his starboard side and flying at Mach-2 he raced across the Rub Al Khali desert to the Red Sea and the USS Reagan, his safe haven for the night.

Within the hour Kane reduced speed, the aircraft carrier would be in sight within the thirty minutes. He had not had any hostile engagement and quite honestly he had not expected to. With the evening meal completed and at the approach of astronomical twilight Kane landed once again onto the deck of the USS Reagan; suffice to say it was a great relief.

The Vice Admiral was there to meet this extraordinary man, and he hugged him rather than shook his hand. He followed up with, "I truly hope and pray the Bastards now refrain from any more foolishness." Responding Kane nodded, but said nothing. Kane looked at the underside of the wings of the Harrier, confirming that the cargo was indeed gone, he felt momentarily ill, but he knew that it would pass.

Kane left the company of the Vice Admiral to clean up. He was totally saturated and was in desperate need of a shower plus the trimmings.

Having cleaned up and given his palatial quarters Kane was met by Lilly one of the female stewards. She had been assigned the duty to deliver Kane with a dish of carrot soup and a main course meal of roast leg of lamb. Although Kane was not too bothered to eat, he did so and to his surprise he thoroughly enjoyed the meal. He was grateful that his earlier queasiness had passed. Lillian returned an hour later to remove the tray and passed on the request from the Vice Admiral to meet with him on the bridge deck. Lilly, a very attractive slim Asian woman had obviously eaten her fill of something laced in garlic as her breath was quite offensive. Her lips were glossy red and her teeth most likely porcelain veneers, one of the teeth had a small diamond which caught the light when she smiled. Her smile and her general demeanor was quite appealing. Being forever the gentleman Kane followed Lilly until he got to the elevator and then he smiled at her as he entered the tiny capsule that performed the function of a two man capacity lift. He pressed the appropriate button up, and momentarily regretted that he had not climbed the eighty feet of stairs to the bridge, as he desperately needed to stretch his legs having been cramped up for so long in the Harrier. The elevator accessed the bridge having moaned and groaned all the way up. The Vice Admiral had ready a pot of tea which was well received by Kane. Together they walked the bridge wing and talked at length about the current response in the US on the days events. Kane was told that the US president would be calling the ship later that night. Kane was ok, a little drained and of course battling with a few nagging friends or foes in his mind. He was still struggling with thoughts of Elspeth but felt hopeless about his whereabouts. He would make his way home the next day, departing at 10:30 a.m. and on arrival the honeymoon would start. With the fresh evening air and the glow from the wake of the aircraft carrier Kane started to replenish his mental batteries. The stars were shining brightly, he could see the constellations of Orion, the center star Alnilam. Alnilam having zero declination was a key star to operatives as it rose due east and set due west day in day out. Combined with Polaris, the pole star, the celestial compass was freely available, visibility permitting. A little later he may well see the Southern Cross, and the stars Acrux and Gatrux.

The Vice Admiral enjoyed his tea as much as Kane; they easily drained three large pots of morning breakfast. The peace of the bridge wing was disturbed by the call from the US President. He had simply wanted to talk to Kane and to relay the gratitude of all Americans on his day's accomplishments. Kane was grateful for the call but really did not want to hear too much about his historical and awful days work. He had fought and struggled enough with the voices in his head prior to engaging the task; he now simply wanted to put the matter deep into the vault of his own mind; his priority task now was to pray that the dreadful dead paid dividends by way of peace. The call was almost immediately followed by a link call with the Prime Minister who casually stated "An awful job well done." Kane sniggered at the oxymoron statement but it was after all very true.

Kane stayed on the bridge until the watch change at midnight, and then he returned to his two hundred square feet of luxury cabin and bunk where he would attempt to sleep. Sleep did not come easily yet Kane wanted desperately to close his eyes and pretend that the prior day never really took place, rather it was a dream. Stretched out on his six foot by two foot six inch. bed he tossed and turned in an effort to be comfortable. The vibration of the ships propellers emanating through the longitudinal steel members and the transverse web frames provided a degree of hypnotic noise/drone and sleep eventually came but it was troublesome sleep; he dreamt of Elspeth, she was in trouble but he could not reach her, something was terribly wrong, what was it, he kept asking himself the same thing, what was it?

Widower

Although they knew of the first two nuclear detonations the terrorist group crouched outside of Kane's home had no idea that Kane had single handedly killed millions of their country men, friends and family. Similarly at the same moment in time Kane was safe on board the USS Reagan with an ETD the next day at ten thirty am, destination Berne.

The terrorist cell headed by Farshad had been surveying the grounds of the home where Kane should have been. They had identified between ten and thirteen people within the confines of the house and garden wall. Up in the attic the operatives had also determined that the house had unwanted visitors. They had been detected very early on and were being monitored by infra red binoculars and thermographic video surveillance equipment. Elspeth had been assigned two operatives; they took refuge in the cellar for safety. Elspeth and Mary Ann, Mystery and the housekeepers, the two operatives armed with AK-49 automatic weapons waited amidst thousands of bottles and several barrels of fine Italian and French wines, for the others to eliminate the hostile unknowns. The household members had no idea what had happened that day on the world stage as the television was rarely used. The peace of the evening was about to deteriorate rapidly as two of the hostiles were picked off by two of the operatives. Farshad was totally pissed off when he lost two of his men; they had not even stepped onto the grounds of the home. Farshad responded with two shoulder launching rockets which transited the hundred meters to the home in less time than it took to breath. Within minutes there was gunfire galore, it was impossible to ascertain from which directions the rounds were coming from. From the attic which was still in tact the operative reported the location of the two unknowns with rockets; it was his last message as the rocket blew the top of the house into the swimming pool below. Four rockets penetrated the stately home and four of the operatives lay dead with limbs scattered about, whose was whose was irrelevant.

The fight went on for the best part of twenty minutes. Farshad lost another two men but only one had been shot armed with the rocket launcher. Two more rockets into the house rendered the second floor to ashes. The house was ablaze yet the cellar remained cool and ventilated. The two operatives with Elspeth looked gravely concerned and searched for another way out, but there was none, no magical escape door or tunnel. Mary Ann accompanied by Mystery was placed inside an empty barrel and told at all costs to be silent. Elspeth gently kissed her daughter and told her to be brave. Elspeth was amazed at the calmness of her little girl, but in fact Mary Ann with eyes wide, was terrified, she could not speak even if she had the desire to do so. The final rocket launched by the unknowns killed all but one of the operatives still above ground. Kane's team leader was the next to perish. Farshad had armed the awkward shoulder unit and as if shooting on the moors of Scotland he aimed and fired at the shape some twenty feet ahead of him. The black American operative was reduced to nothing more than pieces of flesh indistinguishable amongst the fallen leaves on the blood soaked lawn; his head had sailed through the air as if a soccer ball. Farshad with his remaining crew of five carefully examined the grounds. The only noise was the burning rafters of the house which crackled as if it were November 5th and Guy Fawkes Night. In the cellar the two operatives left made the choice to venture out. They armed Elspeth with a Glock handgun, the safety mechanism checked to be off.

The door to the hall way was blocked by the fallen debris and when the operatives put their shoulders to the task, the unknowns' were alerted to their position. They crouched down on one knee and monitored their progress. After several minutes they broke free, the debris skidding to the left of the door. The two operatives accessed the doorway only to be greeted with a flurry of automatic fire. They died quickly but for good measure Farshad walked to the two men and lorded over them. He shot them twice more in the head. Farshad leading the pack ventured down into the cellar. It was still cool and the air fresh. Not more than ten feet away Elspeth stood the guard with her arms outstretched holding the Glock. Her hands were trembling; she was terrified for herself and her daughter. Involuntary she urinated, incredulously, she took her attention from the unknown intruder to look at the floor; with that Farshad pulled the light trigger of his pistol, bang, bang, bang three bullets to the face of Elspeth. Elspeth and her baby were dead. The house keepers too looked as if they were about to be incontinent, but they did not have to wait too long. The bullets left the sanctuary of their chamber to rendezvous with the housekeeper's forehead and into their brain. As if in a German concentration camp in the last century they were mercilessly terminated. Mary Ann as instructed stayed deadly quiet inside the barrel. Mystery appeared to know that something was dangerously wrong too and like Mary Ann never broke the silence.

Farshad surveyed the cellar and seeing nothing untoward returned to the ground floor. He checked the bodies, all of the operatives were black, Farshad knew that he would not collect all of the bounty but at the same time he was confident that Kane Austin was now a widower, and he was correct. They sensed the urgency to leave and vacated the property. On route they passed a fleet of fire trucks and police not more than five miles down the road. Farshad accelerated making their way throughout the night and morning back to Paris. On route they had learned of the other nuclear attacks that had taken place hours before. Of his own team remaining, all had suffered family losses, they just did not know to what extent.

The police having already been to the church to investigate the shooting of the priest arrived at Kane's home to witness the aftermath of the carnage. The house was no more than a partial slab; the cellar however remained basically unscathed, even the wine bottles were salvageable. Up top was another matter. The mess of bodies littered the crimson lawn; body bags had to be dispatched from the city morgue. The Swiss department of Interpol was duly notified and they in turn informed the proper authorities in the UK. Special Branch in London joined the CIA to catch a flight to Berne. Pammy was informed and she in turn recalled the operatives that remained in the

US on field break. There was no need to bring in the fire forensic teams; the evidence was crystal clear what had taken place. German Shepherd dogs scoured the area sniffing intently with their noses close to the ground. Once in the cellar they easily identified the barrel where Mary Ann and Mystery had stayed silent. Upon opening the barrel, Mary Ann was found to be in a catatonic state and could say nothing. She looked at her mother dead on the cellar floor, her beautiful face now disfigured by the small holes that resulted from the high velocity rounds, two in the forehead and one below her left eye. Her beautiful, wonderful and loving mother was no more. Alongside her the very people that she had come to be so friendly with in such a short space of time, kept her company having met with the same fate. EMS paramedics assessed the girl as physically ok, but it was painfully obvious that she was in severe shock. Her eyes were wide open as if she had seen an alien. She could not speak and she could not walk, hence they carried her and Mystery to the ambulance. Mary Ann Clutching Mystery tightly they were whisked away to the main city hospital.

On scene police collected the array of firearms which included hand guns AK-49 automatic weapons, Rocket Launchers and hand grenades. The entire area was taped off with yellow crime scene four inch width tape. With the fire losing its hold on the once beautiful home, the fire teams fought on and continued their efforts to douse the fire hot spots. In the meantime the on scene commander requested flood lights to be sent to the location. The morning no doubt would reveal the true terror of the night before.

The police commenced their enquiries with neighboring property owners, the problem being that the closest neighbors were four miles down the road and three miles up the road; of course no one saw anything or heard anything untoward. By early morning the ghoulish scene at the property confirmed the terror of the night before. By 9:00 a.m. all parties would be at the site, everyone being sick to their stomachs at what they saw. Photographs were taken, hundreds of them, the evidence of the event would never die. Video tapes were taken and commentary made. The bodies were tagged and bagged as if carcasses of dead animals. Parts of bodies filled garbage bags and tagged accordingly. One severed head was placed in a bin liner bag, again tagged. The scene was so horrific that the very forensic teams would need counseling immediately after the event. With investigators from everywhere roaming the grounds the gray clouds in the sky parted permitting morning sunlight to penetrate the cloak of death which enveloped the property. To the East with no knowledge of the massacre Kane flew at Mach-1 towards the Berne airspace.

The Loss

Kane had eventually fallen to sleep but as always he awoke early. He tried to remain horizontal but gave up and went to the shower room. After a shower he felt much better and decided to join the morning crew with exercise above deck. The Carrier was longer than a regulation size soccer field and each morning hundreds of the crew would run the perimeter. Each lap was more than ½ mile so they targeted ten laps. Before breakfast came around Kane had done twenty and he had enjoyed every stride.

Showering for the second time Kane readied himself for the feast of champions, porridge. Joining the Vice Admiral Kane eat his way through two bowls. More coffee and he would follow the Vice Admiral to the bridge. They were now as it were patrolling the waters in the area of the horn of Africa. The US were still heavily involved with Somalia, the troublesome region had required the presence of one carrier for the past eight years. The morning was warm with a haze that rarely disappeared until late afternoon, and sometimes never. Kane asked of the Vice Admiral how things were going as a result of the prior days work. The response was for him to tune in to CNN and see for himself; Kane, however, thought better of it. He needed a little more time out.

The Harrier was ready to go; in fact it had been refueled and inspected the night before. Kane on time and having said his farewells to the bridge officers of the watch and of course the Vice Admiral, made his way to the suit up room and prepared to board his jet. The giant carrier was turned head into the wind and Kane with a clear runway accelerated at full thrust to the deck edge some 1,100 feet ahead of him. The jet climbed into the skies effortlessly. Kane loved the plane and felt excited to be on his way home. He banked the aircraft to the west and set course for the Mediterranean Sea via the Red Sea. Again he would fly at the low altitude of two hundred seventy-five feet and at six hundred fifty knots, just shy of Mach-1. He would arrive in Berne just before 12:00 noon local time. With the sun behind him he flew without his Zeiss sunglasses. He mulled over the difference twenty-four hours could make, today was a relief for him, little did he know the chapter in his life that unfolded only hours before, his greatest loss was about to be realized. The red sea was blue beneath him and it disappeared into a stream at the head near Aquabah. Almost following the Suez Canal Kane's aircraft eventually roared into the airspace above the Eastern Mediterranean Sea. A slight adjustment in course and Kane with the sun creeping in view to his left donned his eyewear. He was a lot cooler than the day before yet he had filled his flask once again with iced tea. His excitement grew by the moment, his heart coping with bursts of adrenalin as he thought more and more about her, he edged up his speed to six hundred twenty knots.

Kane eventually left the denser air mass at three hundred and twenty-seven feet and increased altitude when encroaching Italian airspace. When flying over Rome he was at twenty five thousand feet, he would arrive in Berne at 11:40 a.m. local time. Pammy was already there waiting for him to arrive.

Kane landed conventionally at the Berne International and taxied to the hanger checkpoint, his heart was pumping furiously with the anticipation of reuniting with Elspeth, only Elspeth could make him feel this way. The ground crew met him and escorted him to the hanger office where Pammy stoically stood with tears in her eyes.

Kane immediately knew that something was amiss for her to be there and he approached her thinking that something operationally was awry.

Pammy sat down with him and Kane placed his arm around her shoulder, ironically consoling her, and told her to let it all out. Pammy summoned up the energy to deliver the crushing news. Kane was not prepared for the information that he had encouraged her to release, his face drained of blood immediately on hearing that his bride was gone. He became deathly pale. His arm fell from Pam's shoulder and she in turn reciprocated the prior embrace and cradled his slouching body with both her arms. Kane for once in his life was breathless and speechless; he was mulch, and his brain temporally stopped functioning. It seemed forever but then he remembered Mary Ann. What of Mary Ann he said, and Pammy's response kicked started his failing heart. On hearing the news his eyes welled up with even more tears, but at least his heart was pumping solidly. Kane was unable to stand, his legs were as if jello, his muscles had lost their strength, his life was crumbling yet he had his Mary Ann. He then asked about the event. On hearing the details, much of which was left out Kane's stomach churned and churned. He questioned his actions and momentarily wondered if this was the price that he had to pay for the actions that he had invoked on the Arab world just hours before? Had he left the Carrier on his arrival the day before perhaps the outcome would be different? The questions would nag him but the outcome would not change, he had lost the most precious person in his life's journey. Gasping for more air Kane quietly listened to Pammy. He was well aware of killing and the pain but he had never had to endure such pain in his heart, his head and his entire body all at the same moment. Pammy carefully, respectfully painted the picture although she had got the information second hand from the special branch boys who were still at the location.

Kane did not need to know any more of the details; he wanted to see Elspeth and then Mary Ann.

Kane was so weak at the knees he asked Pammy to enter the changing room with him and assist with his change of clothing. By the time he was dressed and after a shot of cognac provided by British Airways, a miniature that Pammy obtained on the plane hours before, life was stirring in his limbs. Taking in large volumes of air Kane regained his composure, more air more composure it worked well.

Pammy took Kane in her hired vehicle to the city morgue. They went inside and after formalities complete Kane was inside the cool sterile freezer room with twenty or so, human steel boxes inserted into the south facing wall. The box containing the love of his life was pulled clear of the wall and onto the steel trolley. Kane looking at his wife, now cold and stiff with three holes in her head where the life of such a wonderful person had been extinguished. The honeymoon had not even started. Kane, with Pammy looking on, took her hand in his and sob his heart out. The pain in Kane's heart was profound, overwhelming, and for the second time his legs gave out. Pammy had foreseen the pain and dragged a stool to the steel trolley to permit her superior and friend to sit. Kane stayed for half an hour before he took to the deep breathing. He drew in monstrous breath of cool air and slowly his legs were capable of supporting his frame. Kissing his bride for the last time fully on her purple lips he said his farewell.

Kane left the morgue with Pammy to find a bar. He needed some Dutch courage to continue on, another cognac would be fitting, or perhaps several.

They left for the downtown core and looked for a quiet bar. Kane was alive but his feelings were numb, he remained in a fog. He remembered Sir Billy; his fiancée, his mother passing at such a young age, now it was his turn to lose the precious gift of true love.

They stopped at the foot of a charming hotel; the valet accepted the keys and parked the rental vehicle, while the two of them made their way into the lounge. The lounge was tastefully decorated; the armchairs were leather with gold leaf inlays within the cleverly crafted carvings of the arms. A 1907 Steinway piano glistened in the corner, but thankfully no one was playing, Kane was not ready to be catered to with musical master pieces form Mozart or Brahms. He was ready however for that large cognac and within seconds of their sitting down the hostess/sever took their order. Pammy had a gin and tonic and matched Kane's consumption. They revisited who was responsible for the event and Kane asked what progress was being made if any. The partial answer confirmed the assassin Farshad Estakhri, and as expected, his whereabouts unknown.

Kane and Pammy were alone in the lounge sipping on their beverages, with the piano silent Kane requested that the LCD television to be put on, he requested CNN news. The news as expected covered live telecast from the Middle East, six locations where the GVC had inflicted their return volley to Al Qaeda. The television scenes showed the horrific aftermath of the nuclear attack and comparisons drawn to the US attacks and the two earlier events in Hiroshima and Nagasaki. Kane watched the screen with little if any emotion; he was ambivalent, he had lost any inward compassion.

He never thought that he could be so indifferent and frigid cold but here he was the author of the mass murders, yet now without a consciousness. For the moment he did not like himself, he was a monster of monsters, the butcher of the world. For many minutes he was riveted to television broadcast. Disgustingly the reality of what took place almost stimulated his body and soul with a renewed strength and purpose. Shit he thought, he had done a millenniums worth of laundry for his country and for the western world. Pammy advised Kane that the GVC had announced that they would make another attack on the Al Qaeda at the commencement of Ramadan unless they break their silence and commit to a unilateral cease-fire. Kane listened only but privately, in his mind he said that he would pilot the Harrier accordingly.

The pianist entered the room to play Gershwin, and at the commencement of the key notes Kane and Pammy exited the Lounge. It was time to see his sweetheart Mary Ann.

Pammy summoned the valet who appreciated the generous tip; the rental was at the front door promptly.

They found their way to the Hospital where his little girl remained silent and still in shock. She had been placed in a private room with a special branch person assigned to the room and two others assigned to the corridors. Breaking the hospital rules the staff had permitted Mystery to stay clutched in her little arms. Kane entered the room to see his little child blank with emotion. Her eyes were wide open yet they saw nothing. Kane took her hand from the cat and kissed her knuckles, leaning over he kissed her on the cheek. With tears flooding down his face he struggled for the words, "Pops is here, I am so sorry, I love you so much."

With no response from Mary Ann, he laid his head on her tummy and wept.

Kane wept for quite sometime and then he sat up and told her that he would return shortly, again no response. Kane, with Pammy left the Hospital to visit the home, or what was left of it.

The drive was exactly twenty one miles and on entering the grounds Kane's eyes surveyed the scene, what was once a beautiful unique property was now a scene from Vimy ridge.

Even to a seasoned operative Kane was horrified at the scene. The police were everywhere as was Special Branch. Respectfully those people that knew Kane approached and expressed their deepest regrets. Kane took on the leadership role and stood solid, but inside he was crumbling. Pammy on several occasions patted him solidly on his back confirming to him that he was not alone. Words at this juncture were few. Kane longed for his Elspeth but she was gone forever; Kane struggled to maintain composure but he knew that he had to succeed. They surveyed the grounds for over an hour and then Kane had had enough. He would make his way back to town and book into a hotel and gather his thoughts. On route to the hotel where they had enjoyed cognac and a silenced Steinway piano Kane noticed the bill board sign which had inspired him was being changed to advertise Coca Cola and the slogan, *Things go better with coke.* Kane was not amused. Kane then instructed Pammy to organize the GVC operatives remaining to make their way to Berne.

Kane was going to break protocol and attend his wife's funeral which would be in three days.

They booked into the hotel and Pammy immediately went to action, she started organizing a host of tasks. Kane on the other hand called the Foreign office and the Minister to check in. He would also call his operative in Qatar to confirm the status of the assignment with respect to the oil terminals at Kharg Island and Bandur Mashur.

The phone call to the Minister was as expected, a great deal of condolences and reassurance that he would cope with everything. The call to the operative in Qatar was purely business and very short. The answer was, "Everything is in order, sir."

Kane appreciated the direct and short response, and he too appreciated the efficiency of his Alpha Omega operatives. All that he wanted was the right response; there was no need to know how he had achieved the goal. The two key oil terminals in Iran were ready to destroy, and destroy them he would, when was the only question.

Kane and Pammy returned to the hospital tailed by the Special Branch organized by Pammy.

Kane spent hours just sitting with his little girl. He was able to continue to talk to her albeit there was no visible sign of response from Mary Ann. Kane cried a great deal, his eyes became swollen and red with the tears and his constant rubbing. Mystery was content to stay forever in the warm room, it was as if she was a guard dog, but of course she was not.

Still with no response from Mary Ann, Kane left the hospital for the night. They both drove to the hotel and chose to listen to the classic Steinway. While in the lounge Pammy provided the daily update, confirming three locations where the funeral ceremony would take place. The actual decision which location would be chosen would be made within one hour of the pick up of the coffin by the hearse and crew. Kane took it all in and then made the surprise decision that he would like the property on the hill cleared of debris, he would donate the land to the city to be used as a cemetery. Elspeth would be buried on the knoll of the hill having the mountains and sky to view. Pammy had her work cut out but of course she would succeed in her task, after all it was merely a function of money.

Kane asked about the status on Farshad, but there was nothing to report; Kane was provided with the most recent photographs of the man and his most likely accomplices but that was it, nothing else. Kane, thinking very evil thoughts, wondered where the assassin was.

They stayed in the hotel lounge and enjoyed several drinks before each took their leave to their rooms.

Kane entered his room only to sit down on the bed and grabbing the remote control tuned in once again to the world news. The nuclear war on terror was a sad sight. The US cities were a mess and the recent Middle East strikes were indeed the work of a Butcher. Palestine had been crippled not only by the Anthrax release but by the Ramallah strike; for that matter it was clear that the Arab world was on its knees. Thousands of people were now housed in tents, an irony of their past lifestyle. The world was in complete turmoil, and yet there was still no submission by the Al Qaeda. Kane truly believed that the pressure would yield results; he just hoped that it would be sooner rather than later.

Kane watched the news over and over, the content changed only marginally with each passing hour.

With sleep not happening Kane decided to go back to the hospital. Accompanied by Special Branch they made their way through the quiet streets to the hospital entrance. Kane made his way to Mary Ann's bedside and watched her carefully. He was not certain whether she was awake or not as her eyes remained wide open. The doctors stated that she would at some point just snap out of her trance, the problem being when. Kane had bought her chocolates, the same type/box as she had given him not too long before. He talked to her continuously; he talked about a vacation and her desire to fly. He would do just that as soon as she was well, in addition he talked about sailing, hiking and winter skiing. They would do it all and more together. With his head on her tummy and Mystery comfortable on his neck he fell asleep, Mary Ann held her Pops head in her hands but it was uncertain whether it was mentally inspired or just mechanical. Kane sitting by her side fell into a deep sleep for a full four hours, only to awake and find no change with his little girl. He talked to her again until 8:00 a.m. before deciding to leave for the hotel and to freshen up. Kane kissed his little girl and left the room. Kane arrived back at the hotel having negotiated the morning rush hour traffic. The journey took twenty minutes, having listened to hundreds of car horns tooting as frustrated workers weaved their way through the morning gridlock. The hotel was perfectly peaceful with the aroma of morning breakfast wafting through the small lobby. Kane went to his room, quickly shaved and showered and made his way down to the buffet. The coffee was perfect and the scrambled eggs providing an ok start to his day. Not that he knew it but the ten GVC crew would be arriving within a couple of hours.

Pammy not knowing that her supervisor had been absent of the hotel joined him for breakfast although Kane had just about finished when she sauntered into the breakfast bar. At breakfast she advised him that the GVC boys would be arriving at 10:15 a.m. With Kane's permission/approval they would be staying at the same hotel. Kane approved and requested the conference room to be booked for 11:00 a.m. He would address them all at that time.

Pammy asked if he would be going to the hospital after breakfast and was surprised to hear him say no. Kane did not elaborate on his earlier visit, he just said that he had work to do, things to arrange and phone calls to make. Interpreting the mood totally wrong Pammy decided to say little, it was safer.

Kane returned to his room and made his calls. His list was extensive and each call related to Farshad and his possible capture. Interpol within the last three hours had once again caught the image of Farshad on the security cameras leading to the Paris Metro, but in each case the police were just too slow to respond and capture the terrorist. None the less Paris was Farshad's temporary residence. Kane would dispatch his men there that same day, or at least seven of them.

Pammy was sent to the airport to greet the team; upon arrival they looked like a team of NFL players, large men with excellent posture, their black faces smiling, showing off an array of beautiful white teeth. After the Tintern episode Pammy had grown to really appreciate and like these Americans, and they in turn thought highly of the "iron lady" as they referred her by. Pammy had forewarned her group that the cheese was not in the best of moods, so to be wary.

The team were escorted in three separate taxis to the hotel where they were greeted by Sir Kane Austin, given the circumstances Kane was the perfect host and Pam's warning had no merit. They were all respectful of his loss but they too knew that Kane was like them, he had to detach himself from the emotion, it was difficult yet fundamental to survival, after all Kane was now twice removed from his life expectancy curve, something that Kane knew only too well. The team went into the conference room, filled their cups with black coffee and sat down to listen to the AO/GVC head.

For the second time that day Kane welcomed his crew to Berne. The address was brief, and focused on the recent event that took the lives of half the GVC team, a realization that shit really does happen albeit regrettably so. Kane advised the team that circumstances like these tap the very heart of your being and one can be easily overwhelmed and consumed with hate and desire for revenge. He continued to say that revenge would be achieved but he stressed that he did not want to be the bearer of more sad news to GVC family members that their team member had been killed. "Globally, we have inflicted a massive blow to Al Qaeda and we must not permit the momentum to wane, but quite the opposite, we need to keep up the pressure. To this end there will be another strike in Iran within the next two weeks or so." Kane did not mention his own loss, but advised the team that he would be heading out to a remote location with his daughter, yet he will be available at any time for AO/GVC matters. Pammy would have the contact details and all communication should go via that source. With that Pammy handed out a photograph of Farshad Estakhri. Kane went on, referring to the photograph, and instructed them that this was their new assignment.

"Seven of you will be dispatched to Paris today; three will accompany me to a safer location."

Kane expanded on the known history of Farshad, the talk culminating in the fact that this terrorist was the cell leader that had succeeded in causing ten American ladies to become widows and one party a widower. "Before leaving Berne, you will all proceed to what remains of the property where our worse loss in our short history took place. This should cement a picture in your mind as to how ruthless the incident was and that I Kane Austin wants the culprit caught, interrogated and killed, ideally in that sequence of events."

Kane emphasized the danger and cautioned his team to be articulate, precise and to stick to their training protocol. Take no survivors except one, but in the event that that request can not be achieved then eliminate Farshad as well. When in Paris they were told to start their search with the most inexpensive hotels in the poorer section of Paris, dress down and always be aware that their minimal use of French speaking skills, matched with their obvious American drawl was a great disadvantage. Kane emphasized that he wanted everyone to return safely to London where he would integrate certain members of the AO team with the GVC.

Kane then handed over the meeting to Pammy who addressed the ten lost GVC crew. Her message was about the financial contribution that had already been wired to the families of the lost ten. Each household would receive a $2 million payment followed by $200,000.00 per year for life. The funds would not be traceable and discretion was again emphasized. The ex Seals took in a deep breath almost collectively, each of them well aware that in death their families were well cared for.......some consolation. The meeting came to an end and the group headed west to the war zone or what certain Special Branch members had already nicknamed ground zero.

When on route Kane chose the seven, he hoped they were his lucky magnificent seven. The leader of the Paris operation would be the shortest of the group, a black American weighing in at 220 pounds and barely six feet tall. He held the rank of Lieutenant in the past and was a Harvard graduate. At 37, he was the eldest of the group and was known to be a "fair" mean son of a bitch. He was the only one that spoke a smidgen of French, albeit with a Cajun drawl.

When at the property Kane consoled all of them for the loss of their fallen friends, it was to the others just an amazing anomaly that their boss, who had lost his bride, took time out to console the guys.

Their respect grew exponentially for this Brit, but they too knew that the head of Alpha Omega and the GVC was an emotional wreck inside.

The ruins at the property had indeed painted the picture indelibly into the minds of his crew. At the site Kane selected the seven and gave them their marching orders, Pammy would assist them with everything, and of course just about everything was ready to go. A Grumman jet was awaiting the team; they would fly to Marsden in Kent UK. From there they would separate making their way across to France, three by Hovercraft from Ramsgate and two by train via the channel tunnel, the team leader and one other would continue their flight into Orly international airport and commence to set up their Parisian operations.

Kane knew that the capture of Farshad was a tall order but then Kane's team was always working, as did the terrorist outside of the law. He hoped that they would pull it off.

Looking around for the last time Kane saw the remnants of his daughter's bikini. His handkerchief was still partially sewn into the bra cup. He smiled and thought of his incorrigible daughter, full of life and beans, and now she was in effect a zombie. He then decided to drive from the property to the hospital. Before departing he shook everyone's hand and smiling, ordered them to stay alive. Pammy left with the seven, operation "Romeo" was about to get underway. Romeo symbolically meaning R for Revenge. Kane with his three musketeers left the property and drove direct to the hospital.

Kane had requested Pammy to prepare for a charter flight to take him and the team to the Caribbean where they would vacation, recuperate in addition to running the day today operations of Alpha Omega/GVC. Kane had a property in the Cayman Islands but he had not seen it as yet. It was another inheritance property courtesy of Sir Billy. He hoped that the property would stay intact longer than the Berne property. They would leave after the funeral ceremony. At the hospital Mary Ann's condition was unaltered. Kane sat by her bedside and stroked Mystery as well as the forearm of his daughter. He talked to her constantly about their upcoming trip and of course good times shared with her mother. The doctors had encouraged him to discuss certain of the most memorable joyous occasions, and of course to Kane every hour shared with Elspeth and Mary Ann had been just that. He refrained from crying although at one time tears trickled down his cheek, only to be absorbed by the clean bed sheets; his musketeers seeing it all, but respectfully kept their eyes focused at the crease of the wall and ceiling. After another two hours Kane and his team left the hospital for the hotel. They would arrive within a few minutes; Kane was hungry and needed to exercise, possibly swim before taking on the fine cuisine of the hotel. The other seven should be well on their way on route to their Parisian challenge.

Hotel Angleterre

Although the routes taken by the seven were circuitous it was none the less necessary given the sophisticated extent of the surveillance network established by the terrorist cell groups. Money could buy the very best of equipment and the Al Qaeda did not lack funds. The seven all arrived in the Paris area within hours of each other; they checked in by way of cell phones and then made their way to their designated neighborhood. Armed with their photograph of Farshad their task was to search the neighborhoods individually in an attempt to identify their target. A huge task but then they were accustomed to perform minor miracles and working alone was their style.

Paris being segregated into twenty neighborhoods and conveniently numbered 1-20 the group of seven had chosen the east quadrant of the city, concentrating on neighborhoods 10, 19, 11, 20. They had decided to spend ten days in each area before adopting a new search area in neighborhoods 12, 4, 3, 2. They would each, as instructed find a low end hotel to establish a base and then perform a grid search independent of each other. They would communicate once a day by cell but they would not inform each other of their whereabouts, all they wanted to achieve was to make visual contact with Farshad. The Hotel Dubois served as a base in neighborhood Number 10. Being close to the Gare Du Nord railway station it was noisy as it was dirty. The US daily rate was a low $49.00 per day. The area was very much multi-cultural with a bohemian element. It would suffice very well as a base for one of the seven. After checking in and confirming his laptop wireless connection the Mississippi GVC member dressed down in clothes that would shock any homeless person with zero funds. The clothes came complete with a disgusting smell, a smell on par with a hog farm with poor drainage. Within the hour he had obtained a shopping cart and commenced his personal bottle drive. Hidden in the cart was an AK-49 automatic weapon with three spare clips. His armory included a Bowie knife fit for skinning deer or Al Qaeda terrorist and a 9 millimeter pistol with silencer attachment. In addition to the expected fire power he also carried C4 explosives and igniter cartridges sufficient to blow the "Bourse" (Paris stock market). He would walk a route that would take him to hotels on par with his own and in one case far worse. Neighborhood Number 19 was a lot larger in area compared to Number 10, hence the district was split into north and south and the GVC members two and three took their territory. Number 2 GVC, obtained a one star-rated hotel and was out on the streets of Chaumont within forty-five minutes of checking in. Wearing dark glasses and carrying a white stick he became a young equivalent of Ray Charles. A black crew neck vest covered his Kevlar vest, a black tattered leather jacket provided ample space for his pistol and two spare clips, a switch blade, and faded blue jeans with slits at the knees covered his black legs which housed an ankle browning 9 millimeter hand gun. If that was not enough his two side pockets provided a dry environment for two hand grenades, hence he was comfortable that he was adequately prepared. He walked the streets slowly taking in the sights of Paris from behind his dark glasses. Walking with a slight stoop and occasionally spitting in the street, he looked the part and played his character with convincing style.

Neighborhoods 11 and 20 were also larger than area 10, hence those neighborhoods or "arrondissements" as the locals would say, were patrolled by two of the GVC team each, this time however the Bastille area was divided into east and west as was Belleville the yuppie district of neighborhood 20.

Each operative was well armed with weaponry as well as a minimum of three cell phones. No conversation would last longer than forty-five seconds for fear of a possible triangulation fix. All cell phones would be carried on their person and placed on vibrate to alert them of an incoming call. The search was underway and methodically each GVC member in their various disguises walked or shuffled along their routes taking in everything. They would focus on specialty food stores that carried Middle Eastern foods, restaurants that catered to the diet of terrorist, outlets that carried Arabic newspapers, specialty tobacconists stores that carried the weed of choice for Arabs, low end hotels as instructed and parks where running would be or could be performed by their prey, the hunt was on and the hunters were exceedingly patient and as ordered, not allowed to die. The fall colors created a typical artistic scene copied for centuries by artists both new and old. Yellows, red, gold and faded greens were abundant and the city itself became a natural portrait. In a similar manner the GVC would be undertaking their own Masterpiece except their art form would not hang from the walls of the Louvre but rather the gallows of the Bastille. The days went by with the canvas remaining blank that was until day nine when at the Parc des Buttes in neighborhood 19 one of the GVC while walking the paths came face to face with the jogging Farshad. Contact was finally made, and with tremendous caution the operative looped his walk with ever increasing pace, monitored the jogging prey. Farshad ran a full mile back to his laird. On the cobblestone street, on the north side stood the Hotel Angleterre, a hotel that the GVC member had passed at least a dozen times before. Taking a secluded position across form the hotel he monitored the entrance, concurrently checking in with the team leader with the news. He used three cell phones before the leader had the location and details. The rest of the team would be summoned by the leader and the plan verified. Within minutes the six of seven were elated at their efforts and of course luck. The team leader notified Pammy who in turn quickly notified of the news to Kane. Kane had been embracing the Cayman Islands and making every effort to reach the inner depths of his daughters mind. Kane too, was elated and wished his team members well, and once again reminded them, with a great deal of sincerity that they were not allowed die.

The group of seven was in effect reunited albeit two operatives were positioned at the rear of the hotel. On the opposite side of the street there was the Café du Monde where the group of four met. One GVC crew relieved the successful operative at the far end of cobble stoned street so that he could attend the Café Du Monde to absorb the plan, and perhaps partake in very sweet Beignet and strong coffee similar to that found in the French quarter of New Orleans. The coffee was magnificent and the pastries a sheer delight. The four commandeered the corner table at the rear of the café, having full view of all patrons coming and going. The hour was 4:00 p.m., yet the café was ninety percent full. The aroma of all of the coffee beans filled the café combining with the mix of bakery smells. They all thought that this little place was a gold mine, and indeed it was. The popularity of the café had not gone unnoticed by Farshad and his team; in fact they visited the café each evening at about 5:30 p.m., immediately after Farshad had showered after his daily run. Today was no different and the leader of the GVC having received the call from the team member on the front side of the hotel advised them that there were five of them heading down the street on the same side as the café. The team leader immediately told two of his group to leave and position themselves on the opposite side of the road and to follow them to their destination. The two left and crossed the street. To the leaders surprise the group of five entered the coffee house and jostled with the crowd in order to find a table. With that the GVC leader gave up his table and the prey made a B line to the very spot vacated. After nine days of searching they were now in very close quarters, in fact far too close. The terrorist noticed nothing untoward with the exception of the stale smell that enveloped the table that they had just acquired. The smell was only momentary as the proprietor was busy grinding five pounds of Columbian coffee beans, the smells displacing all other fragrances. Fresh Beignets were being deep fried in canola oil permitting a new mix of smells to fill the café. The seven were now safely outside of the café in their various observation points. The leader took up position with the others immediately across the street. It was too obvious that the Café was too full of patrons to perform what would amount to be a repeat of the Valentines Day massacre of the Chicago 1930s. They would keep their positions and monitor the situation.

Cayman Islands

Kane, his daughter and three GVC members had left the mountains of Berne immediately after the funeral of Elspeth. At great cost and persuasion the home site that was destroyed had been scraped clean of debris and all evidence of the killings. Trees and flowers had been planted and Elspeth was buried beneath the tallest Oak tree amidst what would be in four to five months time a bed of daffodils and tulips and a host of other flowers that would compliment Elspeth's beauty. Security was tight but nothing untoward took place. Mary Ann did not attend; there had been no progress with her mental state. The mayor of the city attended, a courtesy, having been the recipient of a designated ten acres or so of very valuable land to be used as a cemetery. Kane stood alone with his team, Pammy and a few special branch associates. Kane did not stop the tears; he soaked two handkerchiefs and wished that he had three. He would forever miss his loves life and knew in his heart that he would be joining her one day. They left the day after the funeral and flew to the UK leaving Pammy to hold the fort. From London they went to, Ireland and onto Miami. At Miami a US air force plane took them to Guantanamo, Kane and the crew talked to the commanding officer for a couple of hours before continuing their journey. They flew by helicopter to Grand Cayman.

Back in Paris, Farshad had been advised by his network of informants of the funeral and was made fully aware that Kane Austin was alive and well. His expected thirty million dollars was not paid in full, but rather a partial payment made only. Farshad's Al Qaeda superior insisted that Kane be executed beheaded in order for the terrorist to secure certain favor from their already waning financial supporters. Farshad stayed clear of the funeral, it was almost as if by respect but it was not, he merely needed time out to fortify his crew, he needed another five cell group members; volunteers and recruitments had ceased since the nuclear attacks performed by the GVC, hence it would take some time to complete the task. Farshad had the knife ready for the decapitation; he would keep it readily available for the right time.

Kane meanwhile had spent the last week driving his daughter around the island in a convertible Ford Mustang. The island was not very large and one could drive to the east and north coast within two hours. Mary Ann was still not talking but Kane felt progress when he put her in the pool. He would hold her up as if teaching her to swim, but he knew that she was a fine swimmer and he longed for her to shake her body and swim the pool as if a wakened mermaid. The house was painted yellow with a wall completely surrounding the three sides the property, the sea front side was open. Security in the grounds and inside the house was beyond belief. Not only were the grounds monitored but also several banks in Georgetown and the arrival and departure lounge at the main airport. How Sir Billy had achieved all of this was beyond comprehension. Given that the island was a British protectorate and a center of banking and insurance commerce must have played a key role in permitting the surveillance. The fact that a great deal of laundered money filtered its way through the Cayman banks may also have had a bearing.

The house was a showpiece, and only completed five years before. The grounds were magnificent with an abundance of flowers and flowering trees. The pool, with its water lilies, was over forty feet long and the width thirty feet. In the middle of the pool a fountain spewed water high into the Caribbean sky. The pool hosted hundreds of colorful fish and large chunks of coral reef. Snorkeling in the pool and the surrounding beach area was a must, the Caymans rated at the top of all of the Caribbean islands for underwater adventure. Kane would teach Mary Ann to snorkel in due course and then they would explore the riches of the shallow waters which surrounded the crescent shaped island paradise.

The house staff were all locals, some quite dark skinned while some were swirls. All of them were keen to show their smiles and share their laughter which was contagious. This was a perfect place for his daughter as she was like kind, just a lighter shade of pale. In the living room a portrait of his mother and father adorned the hearth. Sir Billy's portrait as a young man was one of two paintings on the south wall. The like ness of Kane and his father (Sir Billy) was uncanny, they could have been twins. Kane saw himself for the first time sporting a moustache, something he had never chosen to sport. Behind this painting was a safe the combination of which the staff did not know. With the aid of a champagne glass pressed against the safe immediately below the locking mechanism, Kane listened intently. It was a tease yet Kane had it opened after thirty minutes. Inside the safe were bundles of cash, both US and GBP currency. In addition there were two folders which upon inspection identified bank accounts in the Caymans, Iceland and Switzerland. Kane observed that the balances of each bank account was very large. The other folder was clearly dormant accounts where laundered money still remained, the balances growing by the day. The file also included certain names of island citizens that were suspected of criminal Matters. Kane would review the files in detail later, but for the time being his focus was unaltered, Mary Ann was his immediate priority.

Kane truly fell in love with property and prayed in his heart for his daughter to be reignited with life and joy. On the day of the news of Farshad, Kane had been on the north side of the island swimming amongst the tourist spoilt stingrays. The area was known as "sting ray city." The stingrays tolerated the daily cruise ship visitors and their constant touching and lifting in exchange for easy food. Standing in the shallow water on a white sandy shoal, the turquoise waters of the Caribbean sparkled. The clarity of the water matched the purity of the skies, with no clouds to be seen from horizon to horizon. The various colorful fish danced gracefully amongst the sea rays, they appeared like semi precious stones representing the oceans jewelry. From crystal waters of "stingray city" they made their way to shore for lunch. Beneath the palm trees, they had eaten hamburgers and fries at Rum Point, enjoyed a celebration coca cola and beer. Kane and his team of three GVC were elated and took comfort in the thought that their fellow team players now had the upper hand. Kane was reassured by his team that the seven would not fail; they also expressed their view for the very first time that Mary Ann would celebrate in due course also, a fact that pleased Kane immensely. Mary Ann remained abstract indifferent, silent as if lost in a fog. Kane was not sure if anything was registering at all, but he would not give up as this was his greatest challenge in life and he was not accustomed to failure. From Rum Point they returned to the cheerful residence, where they would once again make use of the pool, Kane would hold his little girl again in his arms and hope that the mermaid would spring into life. While in the pool his thoughts too were with his crew in Paris.

Steps

The group of seven decided quickly that they would never have such a convenient opportunity to take down the five. The Café Du Monde was not the place to dispatch the terrorist to their awaiting gates of heaven or hell, the risk to patrons was too great. They agreed that they would take down the group on the return of the five to the Hotel Angleterre. They positioned themselves; two at both ends of the street, two across the road from the hotel entrance while the leader would be inside the doorway entrance of the hotel. They would attempt to keep Farshad alive. The decision was made and the wait was on. The evening suddenly cooled as a slight drizzle glazed the cobblestone streets. The group of five spent their last few moments on earth walking from the café to the hotel with their heads bent down, cowering from the rain. Their arrogance and overconfidence permitted them a first class passage to the departure lounge of life. It was easy; the group of five crossed the road to pass in front of the two GVC members sauntering towards the hotel entrance. The other two GVC strolled with their heads down but their eyes up. The two across the street stayed in position, four were more than enough. Two Renault cars passed by splashing the group of five who responded with certain Arabic blasphemous words, it would be their last spoken words. With pistols ready and silencers mated to the muzzle the air was filled with the familiar suffocated noise *Pop Pop Pop, Pop Pop Pop, Pop Pop Pop,* and all five men fell in total shock to the ground, their blood being washed away by the rainwater's into the gutters of the ancient street. Each terrorist looked with eyes like plums into the barrels of the 9 millimeter pistols. It took seconds for four of the group to catch the train to a higher/lower place, their ticket to ride being two small holes in their foreheads. Farshad expected the same but was picked off the ground, quickly frisked and dragged off across the street. Surprisingly the only weapon on the terrorist was a large knife, shaped like a half moon. With Farshad bleeding profusely from his leg wound one of the group waved down a taxi and took off to a drop point pre-agreed in Belleview. The remaining four walked casually towards the metro where they would make their way to the meeting point. On route they could hear the *Bee-Dah Bee-Dah* of the police sirens, but chose not to look back. They distanced themselves from the four men left in a crumbled saturated heap, they were not going anywhere soon, at least not in this life.

In the taxi, Farshad's leg was tied off with the bandana that one of the GVC team wore. A makeshift Tournekey, yet it would prevent the jerk from bleeding out. They did not care about the lower limb gangrene could set in for all they cared. There job was to keep the Arab pig alive, his pain obviously evident was just the beginning. They arrived at the meeting point only to hold the taxi driver and his vehicle hostage, the pistol in the back of the taxi drivers head was all that was necessary to gain full compliance. Patiently they waited in the warm dry taxi until the four emerged from the metro to rejoin the team at the rendezvous point. Pammy had been called and a citation jet dispatched from the Kent County Marsden Airport. The plane would make the short journey in less than forty minutes. Another taxi was hailed and the taxis ordered to make their way to the Montrouge airstrip somewhere south of the River Seine. The citation would land at the airstrip before they arrived in their vehicles. The GVC crew saw the awaiting jet and politely explained to the taxi drivers that they would come to no harm. Both taxi drivers were placed in one cab and tied together with plastic tie wraps. Apologies were given along with a Thousand dollars each or so for their trouble. The seven plus one took to the air and within the hour landed in London's city airport to be greeted by Special Branch and Pammy. Special Branch police took the plane back to Orly airport where they would land and make their way to the various hotels used by the GVC in order to remove evidence of the GVC. The taxi drivers would be released by the Paris division of Interpol. The investigation by Special Branch would be completed quickly, they hoped to be back in London by midnight.

Pammy commented on the smell of the GVC men and recommended that they get cleaned up. Reservations had been made at the London Hilton by Hyde Park; three rooms with two queen size beds, clothing would follow. There were no complaints with respect to their lodgings, although some sixty years old the hotel was still one of the better hotels in London, and besides it was in the heart of the Kensington night life. Pammy called Kane just as he was finished in the pool with Mary Ann. He took the call and reveled in the news. He asked if there were any injuries to his crew but the answer came back favorable, namely none. This too was news that he could revel in. After the call Kane asked his smiling housemaids to open the Champagne. The three GVC crew with him gave out a resounding "Yeh Man" when hearing the news. Smiles were abundant with the exception of Mary Ann.

The crew in the Caymans asked of Kane what next? and responding with a sadistic grin he replied "Fire Ants" Guantanamo. The sadistic grin of Kane was contagious, all three GVC members offering a duplicate expression of delight.

Kane never had chance to drink the Champagne as the phone rang off the hook. The Foreign office and the Prime Minister made their calls. Congratulations came from everywhere, including the US President. According to the CIA, MI6 and FBI the chatter on the world frequencies had dropped off dramatically, in fact by a factor of ninety percent. Suicide bombings had ceased and retaliatory attacks around the world were astonishingly low. Finally the Islamic world of terrorist had no more appetite for further loss of life, at least their own. It was a belief by the heads of states that the outcome required was imminent but they emphasized to Kane the fact that Al Qaeda had yet to make a truce but it was still not forthcoming. Kane ensured the politicians to hold the faith, and that they were right and to remain patient.

After his phone calls Kane made contact with his field operative in Qatar and instructed the Alpha Omega agent to detonate the explosives at the Iranian, Bandar Mashur oil terminal. The request was followed within fifteen minutes of the order. The radio transmission signal initiated the detonation instantaneously. The forty thousand tonne dead weight oil tanker alongside the dock loading sweet light Iranian crude complete with a thousand feet of jetty was blown to pieces, each piece left being no larger than a motor car. The vessel "Louise" that suffered a similar fate some sixty years before now had additional wreckage to keep her company. This time however the terminal jetty and destroyed tankage joined the debris pile. Approximately forty people perished in the fire and explosion. The debris of the terminal and the ship wreckage would ensure repair and replacement would not be achieved for a very long time. The oil exports from Iran would be instantly, seriously compromised. The news of the explosion flooded the Arab world and once again the GVC claimed responsibility and once again the request made for Al Qaeda to step up to the plate to declare a mutual cease fire.

Al Qaeda was desperate to strike back and to proffer news to their supporters. Nothing was happening in their favor, and support was diminishing rapidly. The death toll in Palestine was still rising; the ratio of Jews to Arabs dead was now 1:3, which represented a catastrophe, a huge blunder on the part of Al Qaeda.

The plan of Sir Kane Austin was working yet resolution was latent and yet to surface. Al Qaeda was banking on the head of Sir Kane Austin but at the time of the explosion in Bandar Mashur they had not heard of the Paris slaughter and or the capture of Farshad; and alas, the head of Sir Kane remained solidly on his neck.

Kane with bourbon in hand and with Mary Ann tucked in bed joined his crew. With the cool evening sea breeze and a starlight night sky they drank to excess but no one lost control; they merely soaked in the day's success of their fellow team, now enjoying the fruits of Kensington. In the morning Kane would fly to Guantanamo to visit the new detainee Farshad Estakhri. The peace of the Caymans permitted everyone to enjoy sound sleep; Kane would as usual sleep for four hours and then awake to enjoy a morning swim and a run along the beach. On this occasion he would be accompanied by two of the GVC team, one being left at the house to safeguard Mary Ann. The run was invigorating and all three kept pace with each other, the pace being blistering. By the time breakfast was served the three males had run more than eight miles, and likely sweated over a gallon of alcohol rich fluid. Returning to the property they showered outside by the pool. Oblivious of the fact that the maids could see them from the kitchen window, stark naked they washed their bodies. Inside the house the maids could not fail to notice the genitals of these three fine men, however they commented on the small size of the colored folk. Instantly the ladies had more respect for their boss.

At the breakfast table there was a great deal of chuckling going on by the maids but Kane could not appreciate the reason why, they were always jubilant and incorrigible, and regardless he preferred it that way. All at the table eat a good breakfast, Mary Ann picked at her fruit; this act in itself was a huge improvement. When one of the team asked what time Kane would be leaving Kane replied at Noon. He would be on the island of Cuba by 1:00 p.m., by which time the remaining team from London should have arrived with their sewer rat Farshad. Concurrent to the response the eyes of Mary Ann widened and she stood up and moved to her fathers arm. The little girl gripped Kane's forearm, her little nails scratching the surface of his skin. Kane was shocked and yet pleased with the response. It was obvious that she had been attentive and her response was one of disapproval. She obviously did not want to be left alone. Kane was in tune with his little girl and told her with a gentle soft voice that she will be having her first flying lesson that day. The remark was filtered in her brain and Kane sensed the pressure of her nails reducing on the surface of his arm. Mary Ann still remained silent, but a small smile was clearly visible. This was a tremendous leap forward for her and a magnificent boost for Kane. Immediately after breakfast Kane would charter a Lear jet, ETD 1300 ETA Guantanamo 1400, and crew number five.

The jet was ready and the party of five boarded the plane. Mary Ann sat up front on the starboard side of the Pilot, namely her Pops. At exactly 1300 local time they propelled themselves down the hot runway at the Cayman airport, reaching velocity V1 then V2 the jet climbed steeply up into the vast expanse of clear blue sky. Kane talked through every action and he could see that Mary Ann was absorbing the information like a sponge, still not talking though, but Kane was patient and already so happy with the day's progress, communication would come later. The flight to Guantanamo was short and sweet. Kane approached the airport at Havana from the east and talked once again through every action relevant to landing the aircraft. Mary Ann, in silence watched attentively. The commander of the base had the Military Police waiting for their arrival. The MPs recognized all of the crew with the exception of Mary Ann who once again gripped her fathers arm tightly. The drive from the airport was pleasant and brought fond memories back to three of the group; Kane however could still sense the pain of those fiery ants between his thighs, he had no fond memories of this place other than the flight out. The MP's, confirmed the arrival of an earlier flight with one new detainee. The guest was already undergoing interrogation.

Driving through the gates the MPs drove the visitors to the commanding officers Delta 1 base office. The formalities were adhered to and then leaving Mary Ann with the C/O's administrator, a female lieutenant who welcomed the opportunity to show off the better side of Delta 1 facilities, Kane left the group to monitor the progress in Interrogation room Number 3. The magnificent seven were already making headway with Farshad. It would appear that his threshold for pain was less than a girl guide. He had already divulged a vast amount of information which was being checked for accuracy by the minute. Kane requested that the interrogation stop for a brief period so that he could talk with his GVC seven, he would hug each of them and solidly shake their hand. He commended each of them for following orders, and in particular staying alive. The salutations lasted a mere five minutes but the seven ate up the praise, and then it was interrogation time. Kane was introduced to the detainee who succeeded in spitting accurately onto Kane's face. The spit was followed by several statements of profanity at which time Kane interrupted his guest speaking in fluent Arabic, he continued in dialogue with his guest. Unshaven, the disheveled looking Farshad had been seated in a metal chair, he was naked and his body was shiny with sweat, and dotted with a multitude of cigar burns. Three finger tips lay on the floor, the pruning scissors commonly used to prune the roses which encircled the base camp office lay on the floor still dripping with the blood of Farshad. The same device had been used on his scrotum was bleeding profusely. His legs were pulled to the sides of the chair and separation maintained with a two-foot piece of two-by-four wood slat. Electrician tie wraps secured his ankles, and his wrists were tightly tied to the arm supports. The seven had been busy, no mercy having been spared. Kane continuing to speak in Farshad's mother tongue discussed the decapitation order and the names of his superior who had issued the order. Farshad had not given up everything to his captors but the hungry little fire ants would shortly focus on the cuts in his scrotum. The pain threshold of this Girl Guide would be broken. Kane expanded on the miserable failure of his guests' cell group. Foolishly the Arab responded admitting to personally killing the pretty white women in Berne and commented that she was now in hell with the other infidels. It struck a chord with Kane who lashed out with a mediaeval looking cat of nine tails. The ferociousness of the lashing surprised the seven who looked on, none of them however had understood a word of the language, it was just gibberish talk to them. The pain inflicted was horrific, the screams screeching, but no one in the room had feelings for the guest, after all this is what they do and well. Farshad's situation was dire; the seven were inspired by the fact that this was the man that killed their joint family in Berne. The room fell silent when the door opened and a package was carefully handed over to the team leader by the MP. The bag contained thousands of half inch long hungry red fire ants. The plastic pouch had a pull string around its neck, a perfect design to tie efficiently around the scrotum of Farshad. Kane stood back and ordered the mike be turned on so that the other detainees in blocks 4, 5, 7, 9 could benefit from the screams that would bellow through the speakers momentarily. Seconds later, screams bellowed throughout the camp, the six foot terrorist had the lungs of a bull and he whaled like a pig to slaughter, which of course he was. The little beasts were chewing on the open wound devouring flesh with miniature bites. Ants that could not get near to the flesh wound, simply tucked into any flesh available. After five minutes of ear piercing screams Kane requested the gag to be inserted into the mouth of Farshad. The red ants continued nibbling away at the meal hanging between the thighs of the sewer rat. Shortly the swelling started, the swelling testicles filled the plastic pouch causing the red ants to be crushed. With survival instincts kicking in the red ants chewed more furiously at their meal but to no avail. Thirty minutes or so passed, the fire ants ferociously attacking Farshad's scrotum, before Kane suggested to his seven to remove the pouch. They would take a coffee break and leave the sewer rat to a moment of reflection, on their return they would go one step further and place a plastic one inch diameter test tube inside the rectum of their guest. Naturally the content of the tube would be the fiery little ants. Kane and his crew took a break, but before leaving the room they left the plastic tube in full sight of Farshad, without explanation Farshad knew what was coming next.

Outside in the warm tropical air the GVC team and Kane chatted casually about the Paris take down, Kane was pleased that there was no collateral damage and confirmed that Interpol had identified all of the dead terrorists all of whom had a price on their head. Total income for the Alpha Omega group in the last few days was forty million dollars. As a business, the government's laundry service was doing well.

Kane advised his crew to spend another hour with Farshad and then he would do the final act. Kane asked for a video camera to be set up in front of the seated villain and to place a white sheet behind the chair. Kane would decapitate his guest but he would not give the sewer rat the benefit of a sharp knife but rather a Hack saw. The death would be graphic, totally disgusting and cruel. The team of seven went inside the room and commenced the application of inserting the plastic container into Farshad's anus, but before they had inserted the tube one inch and before the ants had a chance to nibble, Farshad screamed for his captors to stop and that he would tell them whatever they needed to know. The man was broken and started to spew volumes of information to the seven. The verbal diarrhea continued for a full three hours at which time the seven determined that hey had sufficient information. It was that time again that the departure lounge of life received one more guest. Kane was accordingly summoned.

With the camera ready and with Kane dressed in GVC attire and a black ski mask, he entered the room. Two other GVC members donned their masks as Kane approached the terrorist, the murderer of his life's love. In his hand he held the familiar curved razor sharp knife owned by his victim. Kane placed the knife on the lump of Farshad's throat. He slowly drew blood and inwardly marveled at the edge that the knife had. Farshad screamed an agonizing scream. His eyes were wide as he saw Kane step backwards to place down the knife and to replace it with the Hack saw. Several of the team thought the same, specifically, *Don't piss off the boss*. They watched as Kane placed the Hacksaw in position and rock the saw backwards and forwards slowly and methodically the blade grating into the flesh. The seven looked on, surprised at the act that they were witnessing. They had done so many cruel and indecent acts in their time but this was pretty gross. They too were relieved that they did not have to perform the act themselves, but they also knew that they would do so if requested. The beheading took fifteen minutes; the cut was anything but clean. With the head removed it was held for a full minute in the grasp of Kane's right hand. No words were exchanged but later the verbal message was inserted requesting the Al Qaeda to declare a truce. With the execution completed Kane was anxious to return to the Grand Cayman Island, mentally he had already buried the gruesome act that he had just performed.

The entire group took less than one hour to clean up and to climb aboard the base bus. Mary Ann oblivious of the actions of her father and squad joined them, having thoroughly enjoyed the company of the lady lieutenant. Mary Ann took possession of her fathers hand, it was almost as if she were comforting him rather than vice-versa. Kane too held on tightly. They journeyed to the airport where Kane took the controls of the aircraft and whisked them away to the sanctuary of the island. Georgetown came into view, seven cruise ships lying close by offshore at anchor. Like red ants the tourist swarmed the jewelry stores in the center, a smile creased Kane's face. Kane landed the plane and then took his daughter and crew to the Ritz Carlton for a fine meal. Everyone was in fine spirits and the Ritz Carlton located on the famous seven mile beach was as expected, lavish and exceedingly good. They had jerk chicken and lobster complimented with fresh garden salad. Kane thanked his team once again for a job well done. With the sun setting towards Cancun, the group returned to the yellow house. The evening would be somewhat somber and a fair amount of wine would be consumed. The only person having truly enjoyed the day was Mary Ann. Mary Ann went to her room and actually returned the kiss that her father had given her when saying good night; the kiss was the only good part of Kane's day, other than that he just wanted to forget Guantanamo. The next day would be better.

The yellow household came alive at 5:00 a.m. when a clap of thunder sent pressure waves throughout the skies above the home. Rain poured from the heavens, soaking the landscape. Lasting no more than ten minutes the rain and thunder stopped as quickly as it had arrived. The purity of the air had improved and at six am the sun rise came breathing new life into the Caribbean islands. The sky was peppered with fluffy pillow like clouds. Like the day before Kane and seven of his increased team of ten took to the sands. The run was a tonic for everyone, the ugly task that was undertaken the day before was now history and this was a beginning of a new day. The run was completed faster than the day before and once more the men showered outside oblivious of the fact that he kitchen staff had full view from their vantage point. With eight men with soapy bodies and glistening skin, Kane won the day for the women who continued to chuckle throughout the day. Breakfast was served to the crew which included Mary Ann who appeared to be enjoying the attention of so many men. She was still very close to her fathers arm, but smiles were becoming common place. Kane had suggested that four of the group take advantage of the lull in operations and return to their families. The suggestion was well received and later in the day the yellow house would be home for only six of the GVC team. Meanwhile for Mary Ann and her Pops they would go sailing.

The sun was brilliant yet not too hot. As promised, Kane took Mary Ann and three of his GVC team to the beach located at the east end. The Royal Reef hotel had catamarans for hire so they rented three. About a mile offshore the reef protected the beech and created calm seas within the inner reef area. The water was mainly shallow with perhaps four to five feet depths. The temperature of the water was in the region of 83 degrees Fahrenheit making it very desirable and comfortable for swimming. The waters were crystal clear with an abundance of fish. With the wind at Beaufort scale three conditions were delightful for the purpose at hand. Kane taught Mary Ann to sail. As expected she was enamored by the speed and the ease of handling. Her smiling face said it all. They stayed sailing for a full three hours, their bodies slowly tanning with the sea air and the sun rays. The ex seals outperformed Kane but then he was not there for the challenge of racing, his little girl would challenge them all in good time. Returning to the white sandy beach they returned their sailboats and headed to the Royal Reef lounge for a late lunch. The entire experience was magnificent; it was a great shame that Elspeth was not there to enjoy the island, as she would have loved the peace and beauty that the island had to offer. Perhaps in the whispering palms she was there in spirit, Kane felt her presence and spoke to her silently in his mind. After lunch Kane and Mary Ann walked the jetty which extended some three hundred feet into the blue seas. The fish waited beneath for daily feeding of bread and certain fish eggs. Mary Ann armed with two slices of bread fed the fish. The speed of the fish as they accelerated to each morsel of food was hypnotic. The bread was gone within minutes and the fish dove to the sandy sea floor to search for other sources of food. Together they joined the fish and pretended to be one of them. His little girl was transforming into a mermaid, swimming for hours on end. The afternoon slipped into early evening announcing the onset of nightfall, it was time to leave the reef and head home. Kane and the others had enjoyed a remarkable day. Driving to the yellow house they noticed blue iguanas dangerously crossing the narrow roads. On several occasions they had to take evasive action not to squish one of the endangered species. Mary Ann was exhausted and decided to go straight to bed upon arrival at the home. Kane tucked her in again and shared a kiss. His little girl was coming back to life yet still no words, at least not from her lips, her eyes however said volumes.

With Mary Ann safely in bed Kane, knowing the late hour called Pammy in her Brighton home. Pammy answered on the second ring, the conversation lasting twenty minutes. She gave Kane a thorough update and informed him that a great deal of the information received the day before from Guantanamo had resulted in more than four hundred arrests in England, France, Germany, Bali, Rome, Madrid and the USA. The coffers of the Alpha Omega Group had swollen by four hundred million dollars. When asked if Al Qaeda had declared a truce the answer was no. Expecting that answer, Kane agreed to check in the next day and emphasized to Pammy that it may be a late night call or perhaps early morning. Ending the call with Pammy he immediately called his Qatar operative and instructed him to detonate the Iranian Kharg Island explosives. By early morning the next day CNN reported the news that Iran's oil exports were crippled. Pammy had again prepared a statement from the GVC attesting claim to the recent event. The announcement triggered crude oil prices to eclipse for the first time in history $100/bbl. Al Qaeda were starving for funds, and political pressure from the Middle East region as well as the Saudi monarchy was intense. Terrorism by Al Qaeda throughout the world had dropped off to nothing, public support for the cell groups shifting to contempt and disdain. Kane knew in his heart that the end was close, and now he had little left in his arsenal, what else could he conjure up? Even with a truce with Al Qaeda the world would still require some form of policing. The world would be identified by those countries with nuclear power and those without, the nuclear divide would be a headache to manage but Kane knew that he was one of few that could take on the task. He longed for resolution. Two days past by after the Kharg Island terminal was destroyed. The Gulf region was a sess pool of oil pollution; oil production had dropped off to almost nothing. With oil production crippled the addictive world demand for crude oil remained insatiably high. The tar sands of Canada boosted production to assist the USA hence Canada and the USA barely noticed the world shortage. Japan on the other hand and their economy was rapidly grinding to a halt, Europe too was severely impacted. Kane and company remained on the island, he watched CNN each evening after Mary Ann had retired to bed. The world remained in chaos but there did seem to be light at the end of the tunnel. In addition to his efforts around the globe Kane continued his relationship with the commander and chief of the heavens. He would pray for resolution on earth, and an end to terrorism, in addition for a healing for his little girl; the prayer content rarely changing as the days slipped by from one sunset to a new sunrise. Days drifted into weeks and still the Al Qaeda stood fast in their resolve. Finally Kane launched his own shock and awe campaign, a psychological attack. Pammy was instructed to provide Al Jazeer with a copy of the beheading of Farshad Estakhri. The gruesome act was shown the next day. The Arab world abhorred the action by the GVC yet the loss to Al Qaeda of their only hope was the final straw. Again the GVC requested a truce to terrorism and patiently the world waited for Al Qaeda to respond. The GVC had demonstrated a defiance to match that of Al Qaeda. The morning of the news was just another day in paradise for Kane and his Mary Ann. They had just returned from an early morning swim and sail. Kane and his team now had their own Catamarans, and Mary Ann was proficient to sail single handedly. As forecasted they would challenge each other daily. Mary Ann had also taken to flying a light fixed wing Cessna with her Pops. She was coming along just fine, yet communication remained unchanged. Kane was beside the pool when the unexpected happened. Kane had his head in his hands; he was actually shielding his eyes from the morning sun. Mary Ann must have taken the posture as a state of depression for her pops. An answer to prayer came when out of the blue Mary Ann wrapped her arms around the neck of her dad and softly reassured her dad with the spoken words "Its Ok Pops, I love you and I will look after you." Kane was overwhelmed by the statement and permitted a flood of tears to flow. Unable to talk himself he wrapped his arms around her little frame and continued to cry. The moment was captured by the kitchen staff who watched from the window, they too could not control their tears. Instead of chuckles from the housemaids their smiles were soaked by tears of joy, tears which flooded their faces warranting them to hug each other and to move away from the vantage point of the window. Kane's cell phone rang interrupting the moment, and taking in a deep breath Kane answered. It was Pammy. She told him to turn on the television and CNN. Kane scooped up his little girl not to let her go and carried her into the lounge where the LCD television hung like a picture on the west wall. Picking up the controls he turned on the power. The channel was always fixed on CNN. He watched with interest, a moment in history occurring there in his living room. Al Qaeda had agreed to cease any further acts of violence on the understanding that the GVC did the same. It was that simple. The world airwaves became alive with the news and an avalanche of phone calls would be placed to the small island of the Grand Caymans. The moment was tumultuous and Kane lovingly hugged his Mary Ann, almost too hard when she said, all knowingly, "You did it, pops. We love you."

Kane, somewhat in shock, asked her, "Whose the 'we?'"

The response from his little women was profound and Kane's knees were weak on hearing her crystal clear reply, "Pops the 'we' is me, Mummy and Jesus, you always do the right thing."

With that, Kane felt an inner strength well up inside him, but he too questioned the fact that the recent horrific game of global chess with Al Qaeda was only a stall. The burning question remained, had the GVC Alpha Omega Group really achieved checkmate with Al Qaeda or merely placed them in check?

The End, or is it the beginning?